"You do want me," said Lorna June.

"I'll always *want* you," Ferrell said. He no longer cared about anything else; he had to have her. He had never wanted her so terribly.

She stood submissively while he undressed her. "Will you believe something?" she said. "I never wanted anybody but you—I never liked it with anybody but you. I wish to God with all my heart, Ferrell, that I'd never had anybody but you."

They were so engrossed in each other they did not hear the rustling in the underbrush. Then suddenly they saw Gil Talmadge and the others standing just inside the small clearing.

"Get out of here," Ferrell said to her. "Get in that buggy and get to hell out of here. Dress on the road. Anything. Get to hell out of here."

On her feet, Lorna June was paralyzed with fear. Gil lunged forward and fell on top of her, forcing her to the ground.

"You little whore," Gil said. "Too damned good for Gil Talmadge, huh? Told you I'd get you— and by God, we got you now. We all got you. . . ."

———————————

Master of Blackoaks

Ashley Carter

A FAWCETT GOLD MEDAL BOOK

Fawcett Publications, Inc., Greenwich, Connecticut

The material for this book has been prepared for publication by Ashley Carter through special and exclusive arrangement with the Kenric L. Horner Trust.

MASTER OF BLACKOAKS

10   9   8   7   6   5   4

Master of Blackoaks

CHAPTER 1

HE PULLED UP hard on the lines to halt his sweated horses, hames, reins, and wagon-boards creaking. He flicked a coiled blacksnake whip threateningly, quieting the four bloodhounds secured loosely to the flatbed tailgate. Pushing his sweat-stained, wide-brimmed, planter's panama hat back on his forehead, he scowled up at the plantation manor house reared against a clabbery sky on a commanding and flowered promontory, awed despite himself. Heavy-shouldered, barrel-chested, in his middle thirties, he was handsome in a hard-disciplined way. Dust-streaked and exhausted, he sat straight, booted legs placed solidly apart. His belly was as flat as that of a man fifteen years younger, and he looked as if he'd been born self-reliant; square-jawed, with tilted left brow, unyielding brown eyes, strongly hewn features, and wide down-turned mouth. His dark hair was brushed back across his high forehead and trimmed along his collar. His body was tempered by rough work and long hours in the saddle.

He whistled faintly between his teeth and with a soiled handkerchief mopped sweat from his forehead and the inner band of his hat. "Jesus. You reckon we got her this time? You reckon she's really in there, Gree?"

The black boy on the seat beside him made helpless noises in his throat but did not reply intelligibly because his tongue had been cut out. The hacked stub wallowed, crusted, behind yellowing teeth. Except that he no longer had a tongue, Gree was not bad looking, clean and intelligent, though forever spoiled by disfigurement for any slave auction vendue. About fourteen, he had tight, kinky hair, a high, receding forehead, ridged brows, smoky brown irises and glittering pupils. His nose was flat across its bridge and wide nostriled, his lips thick and black lined, his jaw outthrust with a slight occlusion, his body muscular. Though Gree could barely communicate with the plantation blacks and humans who knew him best, it was as if there were mysterious bonds between the other dumb beasts and the mute black boy—the hounds and horses understood and trusted him. At a cost of seventeen dollars a year for food and found, Gree was worth his weight in gold. No, he'd never sell old Gree. Sometimes a man needed a poor disfigured grotesque like Gree around to humble him and help him keep his head on straight.

Gree nodded anxiously and pointed to the hounds milling and whining restlessly around the rear wheels.

"Them dogs tell you she's around here, huh? That's good enough for me, boy." Bax Simon scrubbed the kinky head hard and affectionately.

He hesitated, studying the house looming above the lane of pecan trees. His first appraisal told him sheer magnificence, but he squinted, taking a second, colder scrutiny. Hell, street sluts could fool a man when they plastered on enough powder, rouge, and cheap perfume, or if the man wasn't on guard. His profession as slave breeder had taught him early never to believe or accept anything at face value. Two subjects he knew thoroughly: slavery and slave holders. He had to know. He spent his life dealing with them and he grabbed every advantage. While his own plantation was financially secure, free of mortgages and unthreatened, this was not true of most of these big estates from the Virginia tidewater down through the Louisiana bayous. People talked savagely about the abolitionist movement up North and in England and of the coming bloody war that would destroy slavery in the South if those fanatical bastards up there weren't stopped. Hell, no sense spilling blood or killing anybody. The banks could wipe out Southern agriculture and with it the so-called gracious, landed gently in one day simply by calling in all overdue mortgages. Ninety-five percent of these old plantations would wilt like day lilies because they were mortgaged to the least slave, the last stick of

8

furniture, the farthest section of eroded, worn-out land.

Simon's undeceived eyes narrowed as if he were dealing with a slave trader who was trying to palm off a *bozal* as a prime. Instinctively, he felt that faint odor of duplicity in all this magnificence. Lands, home, and outbuildings were in good shape, far from decay, years removed from that blight of disrepair he'd detected in scores of spacious estates as he'd come east from Carthage. But like a flower with knots slowly strangling its roots so its top leaves are tinged with the faint stria of despair, this place revealed a deep inner sickness to the knowing eye.

Cotton plantings stretched almost as far as the eye could see, but they were stunted even for spring growth, leaves less than richly green. The big manor house didn't gleam in the hazy morning sunlight. Painting had been delayed this year while the money covered more pressing demands. He smiled tautly. No doubt this house would be scraped and painted—sometime this summer. Slave cabins would be whitewashed—later in the year. And next year? He shook his head. The first signs of decay were betrayed, as if the ornate border of a strangling first mortgage were visible from the road to eyes that knew what to look for. He pulled full left on the lines and turned the horses in through the massive entrance.

On each side of the iron gates, tall fieldstone posts were terminals for the low-slung fieldstone walls that tumbled, crawled, climbed, and wormed their way along the property line two miles in either direction. Wrought-iron bars were ten feet tall with "Black" in metal scroll in one gate wing and "Oaks" set in the other. The right wing was open and secured, wide enough for the horses and flatbed wagon.

Simon slapped the reins over the rumps of the horses and the wagon rattled up the rocky lane under susurrous pecan trees. A sleepy somnolence enveloped the vast estate in mid morning. The cry of a yellowhammer and the sharp bite of an axe ruptured the stillness, and he was aware of the distant bawling of a calf in the heavy quiet. He saw activity down in the slave quarters where artisan and craftsman slaves labored. In the cleared fields a white overseer rode on horseback through the lines of slaves

9

chopping cotton. The Negroes moved unhurriedly; they never varied their pace no matter what the overseer did, and Simon watched him curse impotently.

The wagon lumbered out of the crosshatching of shadows under the pecan trees, and Simon stared up at the mansion of fieldstone and brick, the likes of which he'd seldom encountered before. There appeared to be only two floors; probably the third was an attic suite of unceiled criblike rooms where the house slaves bedded—chilled in winter and sweltering through the summer. Six lean columns supported the tile-roofed overhang above a fieldstone veranda that had been chipped, leveled, and smoothed by slave labor. Two fieldstone steps at least twenty-five feet long by five feet deep led out to the cobbled driveway. A massive natural-wood front door of native magnolia dominated the front façade, oiled and polished until it gleamed dully in the sunlight. Six inches thick and twelve feet high, it was not a door kids ran in and out of all day long. In fact, it resembled the protective portals of feudal castles and there was something forbidding about it. Yet, in bright and easy contrast, to the left of the thick door, three equally tall French doors stood thrown open, flimsy curtains billowing in morning breezes like sails catching at the wind. To the right of the door three matching windows that reached upward to the second level were closed, but their shades were open to permit daylight in through flimsy draperies. Small courtesy balconies opened off two oversized upstairs windows on each side of a larger gallery with a slightly less imposing magnolia-wood door to match the huge downstairs entry. The house appeared self-contained—the kitchen and pantry quarters were under a common roof. Outbuildings were well constructed, with nothing extraordinary about them except for the small fieldstone cottage set apart on a knoll and topped with a silver cross—a private chapel or memorial of some sort.

"Hi, down there!"

Simon's head jerked up and he stared. His eyes widened, and he stared again. The incredibly lovely blond girl bending out over the upstairs center-gallery balustrade looked to be nineteen and she had the startling beauty of fresh and fragile lilies.

Beside him, Gree made animallike mewling sounds in his throat, unable to control desires that sprang pounding into his mind, uncontrolled by artificial restraints or restrictions imposed in civilized society. In the jungle to need was to take and Gree's pulses throbbed with ancient savagery. From the corner of his mouth, Simon spoke warningly, "Watch yo'self, boy," and went on staring up at that gentle vision.

He doffed his wide-brimmed hat in exaggerated courtliness and she laughed, an easy and artless sound. He detected none of the guile he'd learned to anticipate in all Southern white gentlewomen. She was as natural in her warm smiling as the breeze that bobbed a pale-gold ringlet against her finely structured forehead. She had yet either to encounter evil or to be touched by it. She reached out, unafraid, unaware of strangers. Her world had always been a warm and protected place and she loved it and welcomed you in. "What brings you way out here to Blackoaks, sir?"

He grinned back up at her—a reflex action despite the sordid business that obsessed him. "On—a huntin' trip, you might say, ma'am. . . ."

Dozens of brightly clad pickaninnies came running from all directions like ants converging upon a picnic. Visitors always roused excitement at Blackoaks. Two older boys, bare except for onasburg-remnant pants chopped off at the knees, fought to tend Simon's horses. The startled animals tossed their heads, eyes wild and wide. The hounds cringed under the wagon, growling. Simon gave all this mundane activity barely a glance. He had eyes only for the golden girl on that gallery. He had never even fantasized anything more fragilely, blondly lovely and so radiantly bright and friendly with a lack of affectation that was unusual south of the Mason-Dixon line. She was as outgoing as she was delicately beautiful with the sun highlighting her hair and rimlighting her body, and for the moment, she drove his bitter mission to the back of his mind. "Go 'way, you kids," he said from the corner of his mouth. "Don't need nobody to take care of the horses

11

. . . may not be staying." He didn't take his gaze off the girl above him.

"Are you from around here?" she asked.

"No, ma'am, I live out Mississippi way—"

"You *are* a long way from home."

He recognized that she was merely being friendly to a guest and nothing more, yet he responded to her as he had to no other woman. Truthfully, anything lighter of skin than a submissive mustee rendered him ill at ease. But he felt the impact of her beauty exploding through him violently until he quivered in every muscle of his body and he felt himself growing rigid against the tight-fitting linen of his trouser front. His face flushed hotly under his tan as blood surged upward in his head. Gree squirmed, wildly aroused, on the seat beside him. Simon struck him roughly with his elbow. "You want I should sell you to the cane fields?" he raged from the side of his mouth. "That there is not only a white woman, you black bastard —that there's a real white lady. . . ."

Gree understood only his instincts, and they came through the ages from the deepest bush country where a man stayed alive by slaying the enemies and crawling his women—where he found them. He moaned in guttural anguish. Watching them from the balcony, the girl laughed. "What's your name, boy?" she called to Gree.

"He don't rightly talk, ma'am," Simon said. "No more than he often see a white lady—and never one so lovely as you. His name's Gree. He's one of my niggers. Got a slew of them on my place—"

"Oh? Where is that?"

"Willow Oaks, ma'am. Raise slaves for the market, I do. Maybe you heard of it—Willow Oaks?"

"No. Afraid I never have."

"Out near Carthage, ma'am."

She laughed down at him again. "Afraid I don't know Carthage either. I don't travel much, and even when I do, I'm dumb about places. Don't know a Carthage at all."

"Carthage would dearly admire to know you, ma'am." Simon nodded vigorously. "Reckon Carthage, Mississippi, would just about go out'n its cotton-picking gourd were you ever to grace it with your lovely presence."

She threw up her hands in delight. "Well, aren't you just gal—lant!"

"No, ma'am. But I'm truthful. Terrible truthful."

They laughed together. "Who are you?" he asked. "You don't live out here, do you? Who are you, really?"

"Just me," she said.

"Just you? Ma'am, haven't you looked lately into a mirror? Hasn't anybody told you how gyascutus lovely you are?"

She laughed. "Not real recently."

"If it's been more'n fifteen minutes," he told her, "this state has growed some mighty backward men."

"If all the men in Mississippi are as gallant as you, I might just jump in that wagon and go home with you."

He pretended to look stricken. "Why, I can't even joke about a matter as heart stopping as that, ma'am."

Her head went up and laughter showered around the wagon. "Maybe you should speak to my father," she said.

"Where could I find that distinguished gentleman?"

She pointed. He turned and saw four people, a heavyset white man, a stout white youth, a Negro boy, and a cotton-haired black man, on a grassy knoll some distance from the house. The heavyset man held a large owllike bird out on his right arm and was making motions that puzzled Simon. "I do pray I'll have the pleasure of seeing you again, ma'am," he said, turning back.

The girl was no longer alone and no longer smiling. A tall, overly handsome young man had come through the door and stood close beside her on the balcony. Slender, dark-haired, and arrogantly aloof, he did not smile. His fine-hewn face remained chilled. His hand closed on the girl's arm so tightly that she winced. Her face was desolate, all laughter gone, as if she'd never laughed. Simon's face went cold and he replaced his hat. It was as if a shadow had passed between the gentle girl's golden face and the bright sun.

CHAPTER 2

SIMON GAZED once more up at the beautiful girl above him on the gallery, but she no longer smiled and the warmth was gone from the morning; the sun seemed abruptly chilled. His hard brown eyes struck against the cold gaze of the pretty man beside the girl; their gazes clashed and did not waver. In the slender youth's aloof and imperious eyes, Simon simply did not exist. Perversely, Simon bowed again broadly toward the girl. She gave him a tiny, defiant little curtsy and winked.

When he brought his gaze down, he found dozens of black children crowding around his wagon, grinning, talking excitedly, and reaching out toward the quivering, snarling bloodhounds that crouched together under the wagon, tails between their legs. Downhill, slaves stood motionless on the perimeter of their quarters and stared up toward the big house. White and dark faces decorated all the windows and doorways downstairs. Some of the white faces receded when his gaze touched at them, but the black faces peered, fascinated by a stranger inside the broad gates.

A black butler in an age-rusted broadcloth suit and shoes that glittered with polish tried ineffectually to chase the children away from the wagon. They ran away a few feet like frightened birds and then crowded in again. "Them dogs gonna bite you . . . they ain't pet dogs . . . they bloodhounds. Now git away from this yere wagon and behaves yourselfs 'fore masta sell everyone of you down the river."

He limped down the wide steps; his feet hurt; he winced with every step.

"Name's Baxter Simon of Willow Oaks," Simon said.

"That's near Carthage," the girl's teasing laughter caressed them from the gallery. "Carthage is near Mississippi, Thyestes."

"Yes'm, Miz Kathy. I'll remembers that," Thyestes promised. He indicated the grassy knoll. "Masta Baynard. Masta of Blackoaks. Yondah. Yas, suh."

The aging butler made one more swipe with his long arm at the swarm of children, brushing at them as if they were gnats around the horses. "You'uns best git away from heah. I gonna tell Jahndark on you all—every blasted one of you." He looked up and smiled at Simon through the grimace that warped his chocolate face with every step he took. "Them chillun's a caution, suh. A real caution. . . . Might I have our boys tend your horses? . . . Mayhap you like me to run up that li'l ole hill and fetch the masta?"

Simon grinned. He would liked to have seen old Thyestes run up that hill. He saw the butler recognize his smile and match it. "Thank you kindly, Thyestes." Simon tugged on the reins, turning the horses and walking them through the coveys of children in bright cotton shifts. "I'll just drive up and visit with him."

"Thank you, masta. And welcome to Blackoaks, suh," Thyestes called after him. And then, "Git back, you chillun. Them horses goin' walk right over the last blessed one of you. You chillun wants I should call Jahndark right now? Call Jahndark—feelin bad way she is, and busy and expectin' like she is right now? You know what's goin' to happen then? . . ."

The heavyset man on the crest of the knoll looked up and watched the flatbed wagon rattle along the incline toward him. Baynard was forty-nine, lacked an inch of being six feet tall, though vanity made him lie about that. His heavy-structured body carried its 230 pounds well, though he admitted he was at least 50 pounds overweight. A breeze touched at his black wavy hair, salted with gray, worn chopped close over his ears and curling upward at the collar of his linen coat. His hair grew deeply indented at his forehead and a bald spot the size of a silver dollar showed through at the crown. His eyes were a firm, unwavering blue. His short, straight nose and the fat in his cheeks gave him an odd look of gentleness and almost boyish innocence. But he was an imposing man, mouth unsmiling, chin jutting, and thickening jowls retaining traces of youthfully squared lines. He had the rugged look inherited from his border-Scot ancestry. "Welcome, sir," he said. "I am Ferrell Alexander Baynard."

"Name's Baxter Simon, suh. Yoah servant. From out near Carthage, Mississippi. Willow Oaks Plantation. Might be you've heard of it?"

Baynard's head tilted and he studied the man in the wagon. Here was a plantation owner; Baynard recognized the name Willow Oaks. He also knew what it stood for. Whether Simon belonged to the gentry was something else again. The rude wagon, the blacksnake whip coiled beside him, the brace of bloodhounds jerking at their leashes, said he did not. His face was charred by the sun and his calloused hands were too rough for those of a genteel gentleman planter. On the other hand, he was smartly, even foppishly dressed for such an errand as he pursued with bloodhounds and Negro attendant—expensive but weather-stained, rumpled linen suit and elegant but sweat-soured white shirt with string tie pulled awry. His appearance bespoke wealth if not polish and declared him a self-indulgent man with expensive tastes, who could afford to gratify every whim—even to the diamond glittering vulgarly on that finger ring. He also looked to be a man of unquestioned inner strength, a man of authority, accustomed by habit to being obeyed when he spoke. "I do know Willow Oaks," Baynard said.

"That's kind of you," Simon said. "It's a long piece between here and Carthage, Mississippi."

"I heard of you in New Orleans," Baynard said. "Often. In many places."

Simon grinned, more at ease. "Not surprised, suh. I git around to *many* places when I'm in New Orleans. . . . Mighty odd-looking bird you got on your arm there."

"This is a peregrine falcon," Baynard said. "A hobby

of mine, falconry. This bird sees the least movement, Mr. Simon, the least—the flick of an eye."

"Looks like he could git your eye mighty easy from that perch. Looks like everytime you blink, he'd just naturally git you."

Baynard smiled. "I suppose he could. I never heard of anyone's losing an eye to a falcon, but I suppose he could. These birds hate you. You can't believe how they hate you. But this peregrine hunts for me—catches a bird on the wing and brings it to me. Unwillingly, but it will bring it."

The teenaged boy laughed. "Sometimes this ole falcon will take off too. Fly away like crazy. No matter how well papa's got it trained. It flies away. Don't it, Soapy?" He glanced at his grinning body slave for confirmation. "You ought to see papa running around then."

Baynard laughed and placed his free arm about the boy's shoulders, bringing him close against his thick chest. "A falcon is an expensive hunting weapon by the time you get it well trained, Mr. Simon. It breaks your heart to lose one."

Simon glanced around impatiently. He had been many days and many sleepless nights on this mission and he was anxious to bring it to a close. Yet protocol demanded that he accept this planter's hospitality and let his host set the pace for any transaction between them. God only knew how these *gentlemen* farmers ever accomplished anything. "Don't know much about falconry," Simon said. "Afraid I concentrate on business twenty-four hours a day. Don't have time for falconry—much as I might purely enjoy it—once I learned."

Baynard spoke stiffly, recognizing the implied rebuff. "It's an art, a very ancient art."

Simon forced a smile. "Fine-looking boy you got there." He nodded toward the stout teenager. The boy was almost as tall and heavy as his father, and though Baynard's boots were size elevens at least, his feet were even bigger. "Growing him up to take over this place someday, I reckon?"

Baynard laughed and put his arm about the boy again, drawing him against him with an open display of affection.

17

"Afraid not. Morgan's my youngest. He is only fifteen—going to be sixteen in July—if I let him! Morgan's not bright enough to take over Blackoaks, Mr. Simon. . . . No, this boy is sweeter than yam pie, but he's not real bright. You can put his hat on his head and face him toward the front door—and you still won't be sure he'll make it. Isn't that right, Morgan?"

Morgan's smile was beautiful and simple and open. "If you say so, papa." He spoke without a trace of malice.

"If you say so, papa." Baynard mocked his son's tone good-naturedly. "What kind of answer is that? If I'm wrong, my boy, say I'm wrong." He rumpled Morgan's brown curls and clapped him on the shoulder. The hawk fluttered nervously. The thirteen-year-old body slave grinned at the exchange, teeth glittering whitely. The old Negro cuffed the black boy at the back of his skull.

"Are you wrong, papa?" Morgan asked.

"Am I wrong? Of course I'm not wrong. Why, you can't fart and pee at the same time . . . can you, boy?"

Morgan laughed, considering it. "I don't know, papa."

"You don't know, papa. Why don't you know?"

Morgan shook his head. "I've never tried, papa. But I'll try. If you want me to."

Baynard's border-Scot blue eyes glistened and he pulled the boy harder against his side. "You're a good boy, Morgan. A good, dear boy . . . and you do try . . . and we love you."

"And I love you, papa."

"See. That proves you're not smart." Baynard laughed and kissed the boy lightly on the cheek.

Simon stirred, ill at ease, unaccustomed to display of affection between males, even father and son, when the boy was in his teens. It was unheard of, queer and unnatural, like those rich homosexuals down in New Orleans who bought freak slaves to bed down with, and the freakier the better. Jesus. . . .

"What brings a man like you so far from Carthage, Mississippi, in a flatbed wagon, Mr. Simon?" Baynard asked.

"I'm chasing me down a runaway nigger."

Baynard frowned. "Must be some valuable animal, you

18

taking on the job yourself, and driving like this . . . just you and this boy and these dogs in an open wagon?"

"Tis valuable property. But whether it was or not, they's the principle. You don't keep slaves obedient and docile by lettin' runners git away from you."

"But . . . hundreds of miles! Days. Nights. This wet spring weather. Couldn't you have turned this matter over to the patrollers?"

Simon shrugged. "Slave patrollers. If they happens to meet a slave on a hard road, they surely stops him. But a runner that's smart—patrollers get him only by luck."

"I admire your tenacity, at least."

"Don't know about tenacity, suh. Gree and me and the dogs jes' started out—me full of rage, I reckon. Never meant to spend this much time, or to come so far . . . but she seemed always just up ahead a mite more . . . we never have been very far behind her. Ain't now."

Baynard glanced toward the cresting sun. "It's almost noon," he said. It was on the tip of his tongue to invite Baxter Simon into the big house for lunch as hospitality required for almost any guest who presented himself at Blackoaks, but then he stopped.

Simon caught the plantation owner's hesitancy and knew Baynard had decided against inviting him into the big house for dinner—for the moment at least. The hell with him. He glanced around and assured himself that he could buy Baynard out lock, stock, and barrel, and scarcely feel the pinch. Son of a bitch, pretending he was Baxter Simon's better. He could buy the land out from under this arrogant bastard, except that he wouldn't accept this white elephant of an estate as a gift. His smile matched Baynard's in quality of falsity. "Looking your place over as I rode in, Mister Baynard. Nice little spread you got here. . . . Yore cotton is lookin' a mite peaked, though, for this time of year, ain't it?"

Baynard's head jerked up. "You a cotton expert, Mr. Simon?"

Simon's smile widened and he shook his head. "I know a healthy crop if I see one, suh."

"Yes. Well, we're trying Tennessee Brown this year." Baynard's smile tautened. What he wasn't saying, Simon thought, was that last year's yield had earned a second- or maybe even third-grade rating down in the warehouses at Mobile. Like a kind of dying to get a check for third grade when your economy is built on expectations of being paid prices for first quality and choice grades. Death was playing with Blackoaks, all right. "Tennessee Brown. Do you know that strain, Mr. Simon?"

"Seed or strain ain't real important when it's the land that's played out—"

"This land? Played out? My God. Maybe you know breeding Negroes, but—"

"You ever thought of saving your nigger shit and dryin' it along with the cow manure for fertilizer?"

"My God no."

"I reckoned not."

"Maybe you'd like to stay for dinner, Mr. Simon? Afterward we might discuss this. Sounds like a very interesting new idea."

Simon peered down at him. Sure. Interesting new idea, only you don't believe in new ideas, do you? He said aloud, "Thank you kindly, suh, for that generous invitation. I recognize how generous it is . . . but if I could just buy a bit of corn pone and clabber for my boy—"

"Buy? Why, we've got clabber to waste, and corn pone, and good side meat, if your boy favors it. He's welcome to as much as he can hold."

"That's most generous and puts me deeper in your debt, suh. But as for me, I don't mean to stop just yet. We're too close on to her. We know that."

"Are you suggesting, Mr. Simon, that your runaway slave is here—at Blackoaks—on my property?"

"My dogs think so. My boy Gree thinks so—and he's even smarter than them bloodhounds. That's good enough for me."

"I can assure you, sir, your slave is not here."

"I have no wish to argue that, Mr. Baynard. I do pray for your permission to search."

Baynard sucked in a deep breath and held it. He stared up at the man in the wagon. For the moment each forgot to smile. An almost tangible tension crackled between them. Baynard clearly understood the contempt with

20

which the slave breeder regarded him and his administration of this immense farm.

Simon shifted his soiled jacket on his wide shoulders. Planters like Baynard despised the lowest of the slave-dealing trade—those sorry itinerant peddlers of black flesh who traveled from place to place at the head of an ugly, straggling coffle of human culls. And the slave breeder was only slightly elevated in this rigid caste system. In this agrarian economy, however, no matter how base and vile, the slave trader and the slave breeder were necessary evils. The traveling trader bought the trouble-makers, the mavericks, the runners, the dangerous. He toted away the mad, the sick, the psychopath—there was a miserable place for each of them in the hell-markets in which he bargained. Rarely, the trader had a black the farmer could use—at a price they could haggle over. But the slave trader was beneath the planters' contempt. They never permitted him nearer the manor house than the quarters or the barn.

Slave breeders—like Simon—were only recently acceptable in respectable circles. With that Southern syndrome for providing chivalric quality to gloss over ugliness, when that ugliness became indispensable, they now equated slave breeders with horse breeders. Slave studs became stallions, female blacks were dams or mares. Bloodlines became as important as pedigrees of other animals. Improving the breed became a topic of polite conversation. They even permitted a curt bow to men like Baxter Simon when they passed him on the street. Or, after thinking it over, they invited him in to dinner.

It was all shit. The truth was you raised the best look-ing, healthiest slaves you could whelp, as you'd produce the finest quality of any other commodity—because it sold better; it fetched better prices, and respect for your product; it was the difference between offering prime and ordinary. But, what the hell? To men like Baynard slave breeding was a filthy business and it always would be—mating blacks as mares are put to stallions, delivering screaming suckers dropped at all hours of the night, in every kind of nasty weather, and denial of the last human instincts in these blacks. No slave breeder, no matter how affluent, would ever be Baynard's equal in his own unalterable mind.

"With your permission, suh." Simon no longer bothered to smile. "I'd appreciate being permitted to search for my slave. I've wasted one hell of a lot of time already—suh."

CHAPTER 3

THE SUN BLAZED brazen and brassy crossing the faded roof of heaven and siphoning off the last drop of spring moisture from the red earth. Simon glanced around. Before August this land would be parched; it would take all the water in the Coosa and Chattahoochie rivers to revive it. It was totally unlike the bottom land of the delta country, where the big river deposited that shit-rich silt that grew cotton whether you wanted it or not. He inhaled deeply and watched the planter. He wanted only one thing, permission to search, to get on with it, to find that bitch and return home to Mississippi.

He saw two young men in their earliest twenties stride up the incline to the grass-carpeted knoll. Both were exceptionally handsome, well put together, erect and muscular, though pampered and faddishly slender. The taller resembled Baynard, with that wavy raven-wing hair growing indented at the temples, the pleasant-smiling warmth that emanated from an inner security, vigorous physical well-being, and an almost insolent awareness of family and impregnable position.

He was mildly shocked at the arrival of the haughty young man who had earlier wiped away the pleasure and gracious laughter from the face of the golden girl on that balcony simply by coming near her. His presence proved that curiosity occasioned by visitors to Blackoaks overcame even innate aloofness.

The chill of insolence and dislike vibrated between them; it struck against Simon and was reflected in kind. Recently in the bar of the St. Louis Hotel in New Orleans

23

he'd heard a new theory about the impact of vibrations between people. Someone declared that this Frenchman— he couldn't remember the name—preached the effects of animal magnetism and of vibrations between human beings —hostile, loving, fearful, domineering, passionate, or cold. Simon felt something of these vibrations throbbing here—instant hatred—between this insufferable young aristocrat and himself.

"My sons," Baynard said, voice pride charged. "Ferrell-Junior is eighteen, and this is my son-in-law Styles Kenric. Styles is a Kenric of the Kenrics of Winter Hill Plantation. Perhaps you recognize that fine old name, Mr. Simon?"

"Afraid not." Simon was pleased to be able to deny it. In its way it was a small victory.

"Mr. Simon is looking for a runaway slave," Baynard told his sons. "He and his boy have followed these dogs all the way from Carthage, Mississippi."

"Jesus," Ferrell-Junior said. "I admire you, Mr. Simon. But I sure as hell don't envy you."

"You can't let a slave run on you," Simon declared. "Hard enough to keep slaves in line without they see a runner make it up North or somewhere."

Baynard smiled as he explained that Simon bred slaves, yet only the retarded teenage boy may have missed the subtle disdain in his tone. "Fine animals are Mr. Simon's specialty. Willow Oaks Plantation. A great reputation. Mr. Simon is most well known and highly regarded—in New Orleans."

Baynard's words were impeccably friendly, his tone charming, and yet the total effect was hard, unyielding scorn. Simon matched his tone. "That's kind of you, suh. Never have any seconds when my animals go up on vendue. No, suh. No seconds. No thirds. No culls. A man comes to an auction of Willow Oaks blacks, he knows in advance he's going to be offered only prime animals. Or fancy . . . the quality a man might wish in the cotton he markets."

Baynard flinched almost imperceptibly and Simon saw with satisfaction that his parry had nicked blood.

"Do you actually mate Negroes to get better bloodlines, better body stock?" Styles Kenric asked, peering up at Simon.

"Certainly do. Nothing more important than breeding. You breed the best stallion you got to the best mare—and you get a healthy sucker dropped in season . . . Next most important, is never making the mistake of letting these blacks live together in families and git attached to each other—like humans do."

Styles nodded. "That's most interesting, Mr. Simon. I'd certainly like to discuss it further with you. . . . God knows, we have nothing but nigger 'families' here with pickaninnies the women won't let go of."

"They let go of them," Simon said, "when you take the sucker soon as they've nursed a week or so—like about the time they get their eyes open you break up the litter. She carries on some, but she gets over it. You get her a strong buck to ride her—and she forgets all about that sucker you took from her."

"That's most interesting," Styles said.

"It sure hell is," Ferrell-Junior agreed. "You line up the bucks to pleasure the wenches, huh?"

"That's right. I put the best buck and the comeliest wench together. Let 'em have all the carryin' on they want, long as they turn me out the kind of healthy sucker I'm looking for."

Ferrell-Junior laughed and shook his head. Simon winced because the sound of the youth's laughter forcibly recalled that golden girl on the gallery. A man looked at her and got a hard-on. It had been a long desperate search east from Carthage. A long time without a woman. He stirred restlessly, glancing again at Baynard. That bastard moved at the same pace as his slaves chopping cotton in the sun. Ferrell-Junior said, "You ever stand there and watch 'em flog it?"

"If I want to. Covers them wenches myself if I take the notion or if I has to. I can cover them wenches good as airy black. That talk about how blacks are hung heavier than a white man is just a lot of shit. A man's pecker is a muscle—so maybe they do exercise their muscles more. But you cover a wench so she gets it socked

25

up there where her good feelin's are, and she'll moan for you—black or white."

Styles stepped nearer the wagon. "And you sell those offspring of your own?"

"Suckers I gets dropped from covering them wenches myself? You better believe I sell them. Sometimes they're the primest quality I got to offer in a coffle. Light-skinned. Built good. Intelligent. Little human blood don't hurt 'em. Makes 'em prime, matter of fact. Clearer eyes. Most niggers got cloudy eyes, you ever noticed? Little human blood and it clears right up. Better minds too. I'll tell you one bloodline I discovered by accident but intend to develop more. Could make myself a million on that one bloodline. That's the sucker you get dropped covering an Indian wench with a good, strong, smart black buck! I tell you, you got some valuable merchandise then! I've found that purentee Indian blood is worthless. You ever try to get a shiftless Indian moving off his ass? You got yourself an all-day job. But you cross an Indian with a black—and if it's a good black, you got a prize foal. Smart. Ambitious even, sometime. Hard working. Work all day. Sometimes they's mean—Indian and black crossed. Meaner'n a sick jackass. But I always reckon the smarts is what caused the meanness—the smartest stallion you git is likely to be the orneriest. Now, ain't that the truth?"

"We got us a part Indian and part nigger," Morgan boasted. "Did you know that, Mr. Simon, suh? We have. Haven't we, papa? Jahndark is part Indian. She's lighter skinned than you are, Mr. Simon."

"That's mighty interesting," Simon said. "Might be interested in buying her—if the price was right."

Ferrell-Junior burst out laughing. "Sure. You buy Jeanne d'Arc. . . . But, mister, who's going to tell her she's been sold? You talk about grabbing the tail of a tiger!" He laughed again, putting his head back. Morgan laughed with him, matching his laughter note for note, and then moved closer to his older brother.

"Jahndark is not for sale," Baynard stated in a tone of cold finality. "Not at any price."

Styles had not bothered to smile and he brushed aside all this as inconsequential. "Have you found that a red

26

and black produce a superior bloodstrain, Mr. Simon?"

"Every time. A red-black buck will work all day in the sun and still be prancing and ready for stud service come sundown. A red-black wench can be trained to do the fanciest stitching, sewing, housework—the most intricate stuff. . . . Best price I ever got in New Orleans was on a pair of red and black. You won't believe this, but I swear on my pappy's grave, I got me $5000 apiece for them. Been meaning to go in on a bigger scale ever since."

Baynard laughed but without mirth. "I regret, sir, but you can't do it. You can't enslave Indians."

"Hell, Mr. Baynard, suh, there's ways around any laws, if you look a little. If they's certified Indians, then you run afoul of the law, unless you can prove their blood is tainted—making them more black than red. Then you got niggers. Then you got slaves. But you don't have to enslave the reds, and the blacks are already slaves. . . . If I see a red wench I want for breeding, so I can't enslave her. I *can* hire her. I get a few red dams on my place, and let nature take its course." He slapped his leg, pleased with himself. "That's how it happened the first time. By accident. So next time, I pairs them up and it won't be no accident."

"I wish you well." Baynard's tone was chilled.

Simon ignored the affront. "You best believe I'll do well." He glanced meaningfully toward the cottonfields. "I see a strain dyin' out—I see a way that don't work no more, I ain't stubborn or foolhardy. I'm ready to change."

Baynard flushed, struck hard by the sarcasm of that smiling bastard. He didn't like it. Simon didn't act as if he were an equal; he actually looked down along his nose at everything Blackoaks stood for. He wanted Simon off the place. "You have my word, Mr. Simon. Your runaway slave is not at Blackoaks."

"I got your word she ain't, Mr. Baynard, suh. But begging your pardon, suh, I got the word of my dogs and my boy Gree that Vinnie is here—somewhere."

"He ain't—got no tongue." Morgan's voice shook, his face contorted and he pressed close against Ferrell-Junior's

27

arm. The retarded boy pointed at Gree, shaking his head, pale and trembling.

Ferrell-Junior stared up at Gree and winced. "Jesus. What in God's name happened to that poor devil?"

"I cut his tongue out," Simon said.

He watched the revulsion and disbelief flare across the faces of the four white men and warp the chocolate brown features of the aged slave. Only Soapy, Morgan's body slave, thought it was pretty elegant to have one's tongue hacked out. He stared at Gree, fascinated.

"Why in God's name would you do a thing like that?" Baynard demanded.

"Didn't favor doing it none, suh. Hated it. Something I had to do."

Ferrell-Junior shook his head. "Nobody *has* to do anything like that."

Simon gazed down at him in contempt for the protected existence that had shielded him from the seamy facts of dealing with blacks. "When you tell a nigger you're gonna do something—you got to do it, no matter how bad you hate to. This boy lied. All the time. Couldn't stop him. Knew he'd grow up to be a bad nigger. But that's the way it is."

"There must have been some more humane punishment than this," Baynard said.

"No, suh. Not if you hope to make your living breeding niggers, there ain't. You ain't firm and fair with your niggers, you ain't nothing. Firm but fair. You tell 'em once you're gonna do something, you best keep your word— no matter what it is. You warn him twice, now you got no choice. . . ." Simon exhaled heavily. He was not defending himself; he felt no need for that; he was telling it the way he saw it. "You cain't no way equivocate, or shilly-shally. You let a nigger once know you don't mean what you say, and they're like a horse or a dog; they get sneaky on you. They push you to see how far they can go. They get mean. So you carry out your threat—you tole him you was going to cut his tongue out, you cut his tongue out."

"Name of God."

"But you do it calm. You cain't be fractious, either.

Yet, you got to strike while it's clear in his head what he's being punished for. Like airy other animal, they forgits fast. You cain't just lash out for no good reason, no more than you can discipline while you're raging mad. . . . You got to be calm. You got to let them see you're fair. You tried warning. You tried reason. You call all your slaves in. You let 'em see what you're doing. You let 'em know why you got to do it. You cut the tongue out'n one, you don't never have to cut the tongue out'n airy othern. Not for years . . . I hope never. God knows, I hope never. I throwed up after I done it. But I knowed I had to do it, and I did it."

"You've ruined this boy—for life."

"That's right . . . plumb ruined a good, salable slave for the auction vendue. Slave trader might take him— to work and die early in the cane fields. But a liar—you got to deal with him. This boy was a congenital liar— Doc Mayfield hisself told me that's what he was. He'd lie white was black. He'd make up wild stories that couldn't no way be true. He was sneakier'n airy egg-sucking dog. I tole him and tole him if'n he didn't stop lyin' to me, I'd cut out his tongue. He know now. Bax Simon means what he say. Just as I tole him. But like you say, he's no good to sell—except as a freak in New Orleans. Might turn a handsome profit selling him privately to some Louisiana Creole that has a hankering for freaks. Them crazy bastards got strange tastes. But I keeps him. We—both pay for what I had to do to him. And I'll tell you this. Gree's a good boy now. He cain't talk with folks, but he can handle dogs—and horses— like no man I ever knowed."

"You're a cruel man," Morgan burst out. "I liked you . . . but you're cruel . . . I don't like you." He wept bitterly, pressed against Ferrell-Junior.

"No. I ain't cruel, sonny. No crueler than I have to be. I deals with a kind of life I hope you never even have to see. . . . But you ask Gree if he thinks I'm cruel."

Ferrell-Junior laughed coldly. "*He* ain't going to say anything . . . you sure hell guaranteed that."

"No. Gree won't say nothing. Nothing you'll understand. But he can shake his head. He can smile. You'll know what he means. Just ask him. He knows. I done only what I had to do. Gree will tell you that."

Ferrell-Junior's mouth twisted. "What would you do to him now if he didn't agree? Cut off his ears?"

Baxter Simon laughed. "No. Gree knows I'm never going to harm him no more. He's my boy now. Took a hard lesson. But he knows. And," he moved his gaze to Baynard who stood rigid and set against him in the blaze of sunlight, "Gree also knows Vinnie is around here, suh. I plead that you allow us to search."

Ferrell-Junior said, "You shouldn't be allowed to search, even if your runaway slave is here. I can see why she ran, all right."

"No. You're wrong." Baxter Simon shook his head and his face paled under his deep tan. "Slaves don't run from Willow Oaks. You ask Gree. Never have no trouble like that. And I never had me no wench that runned before. All the years my daddy and me been breeding slaves. No wench ever run from Willow Oaks. But when it happens, I mean to get her back. Mean to make a 'zample of her."

"This slave seems mighty important to you," Styles Kenric said. "Is there something unusual about her?"

Simon sighed. "Her name's Vinnie. Bad wench. One of the best I ever had. She covered pleasant. Made a man's bed comfortin' at night, no matter what his day had been. Whatever you told her to do in that bed, she done it for you—no matter what it was—"

"I'll help you look for her," Ferrell-Junior said.

"It's true as I say. Vinnie enjoyed pestering. Liked to pleasure a man. . . . And I treated her well. She was some lazy—and I used to allow her to lay abed until seven of a morning when all the rest of us was up. Never had no trouble with her. All at once, she went bad. . . ." He shook his head, deeply troubled. "Niggers'll do that sometime."

"Why do you think she's here on our place?" Styles asked.

Simon's smile was cold. "Don't think it. Know it. Trust my hounds. Trust Gree. He and them dogs trailed her here."

Baynard remained standing with his legs apart, shoulders set. "I don't think so, Mr. Simon. A strange young woman, a runaway black. Any stranger. If she came on this place, we'd know it, right away."

Simon drew the back of his hand across his mouth. He'd come such a hell of a long way to be delayed by this bullheaded gentleman of leisure. "Maybe, suh. Maybe not. Niggers is funny—about other niggers. They'll do things for them they wouldn't do for white people . . . no matter how good you treat 'em. A runner—pretty like Vinnie—some of your people might try to hide her."

Baynard shook his head, unyielding. "My people wouldn't. But if one of them did try it, word of it would come to me."

Simon exhaled explosively through his lips. "Still, I hope you won't protest if I look around."

"I don't like my people upset, Mr. Simon."

"Won't upset nobody. My boy Gree can handle them dogs. They won't make no sound—less'n they do find Vinnie. They find her, they might set up a yalping. But —if like you say—Vinnie ain't here, you got no worry."

Baynard hesitated. He didn't want the man prowling around. Yet, the poor bastard had come a long way. He was so exhausted he looked half out of his mind, or else that slave meant more to him than he admitted aloud. And too, there might come a time when he'd have to hunt down a runaway slave. He glanced first at his older son and then at Styles Kenric. Both of the younger men nodded and Simon dared breathe a little easier. Finally, Baynard nodded. "All right, Mr. Simon. I'm so certain your slave is not on my property, I'll agree to your search. I must insist, however, that you keep your search as inconspicuous as possible and that you get it over with as quickly as possible."

Simon smiled. "I got no wish to discommode you in any way, suh. If you like, you might just show me around the place. A tour of the quarters. If Vinnie is there, Gree'll find her. Gree and the dogs. If she ain't, your slaves won't ever know we was searching for a runner."

"What will you do when you catch her?" Styles asked. "Will you brand her to mark her as a runner?"

"No, suh. Not her. In no way. She's a prime brand.

A fancy, really. She's a Fulah—or Fulani. Last one I got. They're more like the Moors that conquered Spain than bush niggers. You don't ever brand or lay a whip mark on a Fulani. They're perfect human beings, even if they are Hamitic. And you don't never mar perfection in any way. They ain't worth a tinker's damn if they're marked or blemished. But perfect—they're fancies—like no other niggers. Bring you an easy 5000 in New Orleans as the market is today. No. You don't never lay a scar on a Fulani."

Baynard transferred the peregrine falcon, leather arm band, and line to the cotton-haired black man. Simon and Gree swung down from the wagon. The seven of them moved down the incline, going away from the manor house toward the quarters. Gree led the horses, his hand lightly on a harness sidecheck. He mumbled softly to the animals as they plodded. Morgan and his body slave tagged along close beside Gree, watching him, fascinated and repelled at the same time. The anxious hounds trotted silently in the wake of the wagon. Baynard, his older son, his son-in-law, and Simon followed at a pace that infuriated Simon. He was sweating with anxiety to press the search but Baynard moved leisurely, breathing tightly as if he were climbing instead of descending the slight slope. As Baynard's guest, Simon was forced to accommodate his stride to his host's unhurried gait. Simon swore under his breath, wondering what in God's earth it would take to get these gracious elitists excited and off their cotton-picking asses?

CHAPTER 4

IMPATIENTLY, GROWING tauter by the moment, Simon permitted himself to be escorted exhaustively across the work area of Blackoaks Plantation. At a nod, Gree released the dogs from the wagon. They lunged against their leashes, pulling Gree at a half-run along the winding path into the slave quarters. Convinced by the frenzied bloodhounds that Vinnie was hidden somewhere near, Simon was able to give only cursory attention to the marvels Baynard displayed until finally they walked around the rear of the huge barn where six blacks were castrating hogs.

As they came down the incline from the knoll, Baynard swung his arm toward a pine hammock where blue mists still netted sunlight like fragile webs strung between the pines. "Beyond that new stand of pines yonder is my whiskey distillery." Pride buoyed Baynard's voice and lightened his soft-jowled face, made those blue eyes look younger in that aging man's face. "Got twenty-five people working up there around the clock—keep the distillery removed from the house because of that sick-sour smell of the mash. I find it beguiling, but my ladies dislike it."

"Papa's whiskey is his real pride and joy," Ferrell-Junior said. "Tell him his farm is beautiful, his children exemplary, his crops prime, and he'll thank you kindly. But praise his whiskey and you're his friend for life."

"Making whiskey's an art—prime whiskey," Simon allowed.

"It is an art. And more than an art," Baynard agreed.

"Everything in the manufacture of prime whiskey is important—the oak barrels for aging. Distilling. Handling. My whiskey is so smooth and unique, I'm forced by demand to sell it commercially, Mr. Simon. It affords me a prime profit. This should elevate your estimation of me and my methods."

"I have the highest regard for you, suh."

But Baynard wasn't listening anyway. He was deep in thoughts about his distillery. "I think what truly sets my whiskey apart is the water."

"Water?"

"Aye. Many years ago, I hit an underground stream. Well over a hundred feet deep. Water is clear, pure, icy cold. Taste of the clean earth itself. . . . No way for me to test, but I'd wager my last dollar there's no purer water anywhere."

"And papa uses it only for his whiskey," Ferrell-Junior needled his father.

"No sense wasting water," Baynard said and laughed. "Though I do come up and take a shower when I want to feel purely clean."

Simon saw that Baynard's entire estate, like the field-stone mansion on its high plateau, was self-contained. There was no make-work such as Simon had to invent to keep his slaves occupied at Willow Oaks. Instead, there was discipline and order everywhere. Each black man in every stall, shack, shed, booth, stand, and crib had his trade or craft. Each man had his work quota and the helpers and apprentices he needed to insure the vast estate had solvency and self-sufficiency.

Men sweated in the smitty. A black cabinetmaker worked carefully with spokeshave and near him carpenters labored in a high-roofed open shed. At the barn the animal tenders, the grain and fertilizer handlers each had his assignment. A half-dozen men cut, trimmed, measured in the tailoring hut and a dozen wenches sat gossiping as their fingers flew, sewing. Men worked in rows at the cobbler shop. In a cool barnlike structure, stores were shelved and from it the farm people drew their tow linens, onasburg cloth, bedding, cast-off and rebuilt furnishings from the mansion, work shoes, or boots, salt, flour, and staples.

As Simon walked out of the commissary with the Baynards, a woman's scream stopped them in their tracks. The thought flashed through Simon's mind as the woman screamed again, *they've run Vinnie down.*

Farrell-Junior was already running toward the slave shacks that lined both sides of a worn, grassless thoroughfare. Simon followed, his bullwhip slapping against his leg. The son-in-law was nearest him. Behind them, Morgan ran awkwardly, stumbling as he checked over his shoulder watching his father who was breathless after a few yards of trotting.

By the time Simon reached the whitewashed shack, slaves were gathered outside its stoop from all over the compound. Simon pushed through them and went up the pine-slab steps. He heard Ferrell-Junior laughing inside. The other white men followed Simon into the rudely furnished cabin. A wood-burning stove, a pinewood table, a sagging rocker, along with odds and ends of delapidated furniture, clothing hanging from spikes driven into exposed studdings, comprised the furnishings.

On the bed in the dimly lit corner a light-skinned woman lay exhausted. As the men entered the room a new-born baby emitted a lusty scream.

The elder Baynard went directly to the bed and knelt beside it. "My God, Jahndark. I had no idea it was your time. You hardly showed it. I would have been here."

The beautiful half-Indian, half-Negro, her raven-black hair severely parted in the middle and spread sweated across her pillow, managed to smile. She gripped Baynard's hand, her knuckles graying. "My baby," she whispered. "Is—it—all right? All its toes?"

"It's a little girl, Jeanne d'Arc," Ferrell-Junior said, laughing. He took the infant, loosely wrapped in a ragged cloth, from the midwife. "She's truly beautiful, Jeanne d'Arc. Truly beautiful . . . all her toes, and eyes, and ears—and the prettiest little rosebud between her legs you ever saw."

"You a bad boy, Ferrell-Junior," Jeanne d'Arc whispered from her sweated pillow. She managed to brush her lank black hair from her cheek with trembling fingers. "You always has been—a real caution."

Simon laughed. "Kinda white little sucker, even for a half-breed's drop. Don't see a lot of nigger in this one." He laid a golden eagle on the mother's palm. "Buy her something real nice," he said. "Looks like this little hussy is the makings of a real scandal for persnickety plantation swells like you Baynards."

Ferrell-Junior laughed. "Scandal. That's what we'll call her, Jeanne d'Arc! Scandal. Jeanne d'Arc's own little Scandal." He grinned down at the squalling infant cupped in his hands. "That's what she is, all right. Six pounds of regular little Scandal."

Jeanne d'Arc rolled her head back and forth on the pillow, protesting. "No. Want a pretty name," she whispered weakly. "Real pretty—and dainty name—for a dainty little girl." Then her lips pulled back in a tired grimace of a smile, revealing perfect white teeth. "But—she a scandal, all right . . . taking me away from my work right in the middle of the day—"

"It's all right, Jahndark," Baynard said.

"She couldn't arrive in the middle of the night like a respectable lady should. . . . And, oh my, what she done to me a-comin' out . . . that's a scandal too, all right. . . ."

"Way she got into you might make something of a scandal too, on a purentee genteel plantation like Blackoaks." Simon's voice was thick with sarcasm. He raked his gaze across the Baynard men, convinced that one of these aloof, holier-than-thou sons of bitches had bedded this wench down—though looking at her, even sweated, anguished, drawn with fatigue as she was, he didn't blame him, whomever he turned out to be. But the Baynards collectively waived his insinuations. Baxter Simon, slave breeder, hadn't the social status to bring blood with his prodding, no matter how pointed. And Simon saw this too. His face flushed and he spoke with some chill. "At Willow Oaks we proud of white blood in a new sucker. Brings up a real salable nigger when it's got some human blood in it."

But nobody heard him. The three Baynards and even the insolent and withdrawn Styles Kenric crowded around the woman on the bed. Hell, you'd have thought she was the Virgin Mary, at least, and this an immaculate birth, instead of living proof that the same miscegenation went on in these fancy-dan plantations as at his stud farm. Only they lied about it in this rarified atmosphere, as they lied about almost everything. He listened to their laughing and talking with the half-breed woman for a moment, then he turned on his heel and strode out on the stoop.

The sun was westering. Silence thickened across the slave quarters. Many blacks waited in silent semicircles outside the shack, staring at the open doorway. They'd go in and pay their respects to the woman and her sucker when the master and his sons left.

Simon squinted, searching the length of the quarters for some sign of Gree and the dogs. They were not in sight. He saw that the black boys had brought his wagon to the animal barn and fed, watered, and rubbed down his horses. He glanced about restlessly, troubled. Vinnie was around here. He felt it in his bones.

Finally, the Baynards came laughing out of the slave's shack. They wasted more precious moments laughing and chatting with the slaves crowded outside Jeanne d'Arc's front door. Then, at last, they strode around the animal barn to the hog pens . . . and Simon's heart seemed to stop for one full beat as he stared incredulously at the magnificent primitive who was slinging 600-pound wild boars as if they were shoats.

There was nothing elevating about nutting boars. Simon had performed the operation and seen it done innumerable times, but never as smoothly as it was handled here, thanks to the amazingly efficient performance of one man. It was this slave that caught Simon's eye, thrust Vinnie roughly from his consciousness, started his mind rattling like an abacus—calculating in the thousands and the hundreds of thousands in profits—stirred his avarice and gorged up his most obsessive greed.

This was the slave he had to own. Never in his greediest wish-fulfillment dreams had his imagination conjured up a more perfect specimen, a stallion neither black nor white but the coppery tan of ancient Moorish monarchs. His heart raced at the thought of the top-quality suckers this stud could sire through a fancy-grade dam. Good God! They'd have to bring the bank to his money! He had to have this boy. He wanted to finger him for possible blemishes, but he didn't need to touch him to know this slave was a pureblood Fulani.

He stared, gape-mouthed, as the boy worked proficiently, snagging the savage boars and stringing them up by their hind legs before the vicious beasts knew what had hit them. This boy was more than an ordinary Fulah. Hell, he looked like a direct descendent of those Moors and Fulahs who'd sustained a powerful Moslem empire that endured from the tenth to the sixteenth century east of Senegal. What the slave really looked like was stacks of gold eagles in the bank. With this stallion studding for him, he could offer a quality line of nothing less than prime and fancy.

Sweat broke out around his lips at the thought of opposition, of anyone's trying to keep him from getting this prize. He drew the back of his hand across his mouth, watching the Fulani. . . .

The white men stood in the narrow shade of the barn overhang and watched the blacks castrate the Berkshire swine. Hog nutting, the way this team of slaves working with the Fulani accomplished it, was fascinating to watch. Where possible, they castrated young pigs under three months of age because at this stage the piglets handled and healed easily. However, hogs ran wild on the 900 square miles of Blackoaks property, much of which was timber, pasture, thick hammock, or swamp. The swine grew wild, existing on nuts, berries, rattlesnakes, and salvage. Some were 800-pounders with foul boar odor that could be removed only by castration.

The bloated boars were snarling, slashing, squealing, struggling—and deadly. But watching the young Fulani handle them, one could almost forget that a swine tusk could slash like a machette and poison like a cottonmouth. The Fulani made handling hogs look easy. Moving with the natural grace of a dancer, he first snagged the swine with a loop about its upper jaw while the beast was still in the chute. This had to be done swiftly and expertly with

38

the noose caught and tautened around that upper jaw and behind those tusks—and the handler had one chance to make it.

"You've got to castrate them," Baynard was saying, "or the meat's not fit to eat—because of the smell. We've found it also improves the quality of the meat to nut them."

Simon didn't take his gaze from the young Fulani. The youth snared the beasts and tied off the free end of the line to a post in one fluid movement of extraordinary grace. By now the hog was squealing frenziedly and lunging backward from that noose on its tusks and snout. The Fulani caught the wailing boar by its rear hoofs and hoisted its hind legs above its head. Muscles and tendons strained against the boy's flesh, sinews blue and rigid, and yet he scarcely breathed hard. A helper tied the hind legs and the screeching hog was winched by chain, block, and tackle upward, and spread wide for castration.

"Castration also controls the quality of the breeding," Baynard pointed out. "You should be interested in that, Mr. Simon. Much like your own profession."

"I don't castrate. Men nor dogs." Simon spoke without taking his gaze from the sweated youth. The other helpers kept the struggling swine in position with ropes snugged taut about stanchions. With a razor-sharp knife, the Fulani ripped an incision in the middle of the animal's scrotum, between its testicles. The cut was uniformly made —as deep as one nut and twice as long and extending beyond the edge of the scrotum. Then the boy expertly squeezed the first gonad out through the incision and pulled the testicle to stretch the cord so he could snip it off at the edge of the incision. A smaller cut, made inside the first, exposed the second testicle which he removed with a sharp slice through the surrounding tissue.

"There you are, masta!" the Fulani laughed. He held up the hog nuts with coverings intact. Blood seeped along his sweated arm. "Real fine fresh mountain oysters, masta."

"Have them for your supper, Blade," Baynard said, laughing. "You're welcome to them."

"You can have my share too, Blade," Morgan said.

"I'll come over and watch you eat 'em, Blade," Ferrell-Junior decided.

"Mountain oysters makes your love juice richer, masta!" the boy laughed. "Puts powder in your horn too!"

"Yes. Well, I'm afraid I'll just have to limp along as I am," Baynard answered.

Simon sweated, studying that Fulani. He could only think that if he developed the bargaining cleverly, he might walk away from here with a prize that would make him undisputed king of the flesh breeders. The secret was to play it calm. Despite his pretensions, Baynard desperately needed cash. It required a fortune every day of the year to maintain a place like this and keep it solvent. Most of these old estates didn't make any kind of economic sense. This one at least was well managed. It might have made a profit if anybody could produce on tired land that was overpopulated and under-irrigated. Baynard was proud of his Negroes and their bloodlines and their high quality, but every man had his price. The way to play him was to start bidding low and keep raising the ante. He didn't give a damn how high he had to bid, he was going to own this magnificent stallion.

His gaze raked across Blade's laughing, sweated face. This slave looked contented here, subservient and devoted to his master. Well, he could handle the Fulani too, make him want to go to Willow Oaks. Convince him with promises—a different wench every day, the loveliest bed partners Willow Oaks money could buy to pleasure him any way he liked. And he'd keep those promises, as long as this godlike savage delivered for him.

Simon's breath felt tight in his chest. Blade made the castration pens look small. Not because he was huge; he was not, but he moved with the grace and poise of a ballet dancer. He needed vast spaces as he made one motion count for two. Blade held himself with the splendid, inborn, and unconscious arrogance of a purebred desert stallion, head erect, eyes alert. There was regal bearing in his bloodline that was truly noble. He was over six feet tall but not thickly or heavily structured in any way. His slender figure, bared to the waist, was corded with ropelike muscles.

What struck the slave breeder with most forcible impact was the metallic reddish tan of his skin. There was a sheen to it. Sweat beaded on his sinewy thews and gave his flesh a coppery gloss. His head was not large but well shaped, with a high straight forehead, crisp black hair, and close-set ears. His regular features might have modeled Grecian sculpture on a heroic scale. His nose was delicately hewn, a straight, classic line from his forehead. His nostrils flared slightly; his lips were full but not thick. His lower jaw completed these classic lines: sharply chiseled, squared, but neither jutting nor in any sense weak.

He stood with muscular legs braced apart, and one envisioned an ancient Moor commander on some embattled parapet, savage, barbaric, but confident and unflinching against the most insurmountable odds—the odds of slavery and the hot brutal work of hog nutting.

Despite all his caution in programming himself for a low initial bid, despite twenty years of buying and selling black flesh and the sure knowledge that because Baynard was hopelessly mortgaged and imprisoned by mounting interest, he had the planter where the hairs were short in this matter of acquiring the purentee Fulani. Simon heard himself muttering in a strange, hoarse voice he hardly recognized, "I've got to own that slave, Baynard. You name your price. Whatever it is, I'll meet it. We don't haggle—I'm buying him."

Baynard was whiskey-water cool. Baynard had read his mind and was laughing at him inwardly and this, as much as anything else, fanned his inner rages. "Blade is not for sale, Mr. Simon."

"I told you, man," moaned the odd, hoarse voice, "name your price."

"There is no price, sir. . . . Blade is not for sale."

"Could we shuck him down? I want to inspect him—"

"I told you, sir—"

"Four thousand?" Simon looked up, sweated. "You take him to the finest vendue in New Orleans, he won't bring half that on today's open market."

Baynard winced. Likely, the planter was toting up in his mind the temporary financial security 4000 in gold dollars

41

would buy for Blackoaks, his family, and for the slaves dependent on him and the creditors carrying him. Baynard shook his head. "I'm sorry."

Simon spread his hands in a phony gesture of surrender. "All right, Mr. Baynard. We won't haggle. I want this boy for breeding. He lives like a cosset at Willow Oaks —a pet right in my house—if them's your terms. I bring him the comeliest wenches money can buy. I treat him like a baby. . . . I'll pay you 5000—in gold."

Baynard looked as if he were trapped deep underwater and fighting to reach for breath. "As I said, sir. This boy is not for sale. We both know, Mr. Simon, your offer appears generous. But Blade's offspring would be worth many hundreds of thousands on the slave market over the years—"

"I'll make it 10,000. Cash. Delivered right here to your door—or to the bank of your choice."

Baynard retreated a step as if he were being struck about the head and shoulders and couldn't defend himself. His voice was less firm but he spoke louder to compensate. "I too intend to breed Blade, Mr. Simon. You're not the only man interested in perfect bloodlines—"

"That's shit, suh—if you'll pardon me. I'm interested in top-grade black animals. The way you get them is to buy a stud like you got here. That's what I'm offering you a fortune for—10,000 cash."

Baynard's voice rose. "I will breed perfect specimens—"

"Hog nuts, Mr. Baynard, suh. You got another purentee Fulani on this place?"

"Yes—"

"I'll buy them both. Sight unseen. You name your price—"

"—another Fulah-tribe boy. He's about fifteen— Moab—"

"You can't mate them, Mr. Baynard. Not Moab and Blade. Not less'n you know something I ain't learned yet."

"I'll find us a Fulah woman. I assure you. I shall."

"With what?" Simon's voice shook. "How many purentee Fulanis you reckon there are in this whole country? How you going to get any from Africa with the laws

42

barring slave importing? How do you expect to bid— against men like me—for prime Fulah wenches?"

Baynard swung his arm in an almost desperate way, as if physically defending himself. He spoke in a cold, final tone. "This slave is not for sale, sir."

Simon was incapable of retreating, or compromising, or accepting defeat. But he recognized that Baynard was as immovable as a boulder. It would take time. He would have to get around him; he wished he weren't so damned tired, his mind fatigued. He was so beat he was close to tears because he could not buy this black. He had to be smarter than this; he had to get around Baynard. He shrugged. "All right, Mr. Baynard. I accept your decision. But you must admit this here is one of the most perfect blacks around. I'd be most beholden to you if you'd shuck him down and let me inspect him."

Baynard's head tilted. It was on his tongue to refuse, but something in Simon's abject tone changed his mind. Here was a man whose lifetime habit was buying and inspecting slaves. He knew little else, but this was his driving passion. He was proud of Blade; it couldn't hurt to show the boy off. He nodded unwillingly. He motioned Blade into the shade of the overhang and told him to drop his trousers. "This man wants to finger you, Blade— unless you won't have it. You don't have to."

Blade stared at Simon for a long beat; ancient violences and rages, tamped deep inside his mind, swirled in his shadowed black eyes. Then, lip curled faintly, he shrugged. "Got nothin' to hide, masta."

He loosened the buttons and let his bloodied pants fall about his ankles. He stepped out of them. Morgan moved close, mouth parted, staring in fascination at the naked brown body. Soapy, Morgan's body slave, grinned.

"Kneel down, boy," Simon said.

Blade knelt on the rough-hewn flooring before the breeder. Ferrell-Junior said, "Just as well I'm not black. I'd be dead. First time some white man said to me, 'kneel down, boy,' he'd have to kill me."

Simon gazed at the naked body before him, entranced, but he spoke almost casually over his shoulder. "No. You wouldn't. A slave has got a different view of life than us

43

whites. He obeys because he's trained to obey. He don't know nothing else. If he's smart, he don't want nothing else. He feels better knowing he's got somebody to give him orders and look after him."

"Lot of them have told you that, huh?" Ferrell-Junior persisted.

"Don't have to. After generations, obedience is bred into them. The master—the master's orders."

"What's he doing to Blade?" Morgan said. "You beat me an Soapy for doing that, papa."

"Shut up, Morgan," Styles said. His voice had an odd ring to it. He watched, empty bellied, as Simon's experienced hands passed over Blade's head, cupping and flexing the boy's ears, pulling down his eyelids and then running his fingers around inside his mouth. Then the breeder struck the Fulani's chest a few times, pinched his paps lightly, felt him under the armpits, and stroked the depth of his chest.

"Stand up," Simon ordered, and Blade got to his feet. He gazed past the white men, across the castration pens, the quarters, to the pasture land—and beyond.

Styles took two involuntary steps closer as Simon ran his hands down over Blade's flat belly, splaying his fingers through the fine, black silk of pubic hairs. Styles caught his breath, his throat parched and aching, as Simon hefted Blade's pendulous penis and testicles in his hand. "He's built better'n airy bull," Simon said. "I could do great things with this stud. . . . I can tell you, Mr. Baynard, suh, mating a Fulani like this with inferior animals, you don't git Fulani stock, you get inferior animals."

"I'm most interested in strengthening the bloodlines, sir."

Simon worked Blade's foreskin back and forth several times. Blade's head tilted and he sank a tooth into his lower lip, holding his breath. His rod stiffened, blood pulsing into it so it stood thick and rigid in the breeder's fist.

Styles moved closer as if mesmerized, his face flushed. He drew his tongue across his parched lips. "I'd—like to learn—to inspect a slave like that," he said. He stared unblinkingly at the stiffening tool in Simon's browned

44

hand. "What are you looking for?"

"For his reaction. And it's great. Ought to test his fluid, but I won't. . . . Consistency of the fluid—that's mighty important. I wouldn't want to finalize a deal to buy him without making that test."

"Could—could I? Would you tell me what inspection you make?"

Simon stepped back and Styles reached out, his hand shaking slightly, hesitant, and took Blade's high-standing cock and gonads in his hand. Styles closed his eyes tightly, mouth parted, breath ragged, and stood for a long moment, working the tool in his hand.

Simon's derisive and savage burst of laughter wrenched Styles back to reality. He jerked his hand away and leaped back from Blade, feeling the slime of Simon's contemptuous laughter like spittle in his face. "Look at this fellow Kenric," Simon roared. "Great big hard-on. You ain't supposed to git a hard-on when you test a nigger, Mister Kenric, suh. Not when it's a *male* nigger!"

Styles straightened, looking around wildly, taut and white-lipped. "I don't know what you're talking about, sir."

"You know what I'm talking about." Simon's laughter flayed him. And for whatever slights and affronts Kenric had visited on him, any insolence displayed toward him, Simon was repaid in full. Simon had shown Styles for one raw fearful instant what he was.

Styles trembled, jerking his head around. "You can't say things like that about me, sir. You're a low, unspeakable son of a bitch."

"Sure I am, sonny," Simon said. "But I don't git a hard-on fingering a male nigger."

Baynard stepped between them and caught Kenric's lapels roughly. "That's enough, Styles. For the moment, Mr. Simon is our guest. I'll have to ask you to remember that. Consider that Mr. Simon was making a rough joke."

Styles glared at Simon across his father-in-law's shoulder. His raging voice quavered, but it was low, almost a whisper, fighting its way up through his taut throat. "Nobody makes jokes about a man's virility. It's all a man's got."

"I was making a poor joke, suh," Simon said, bowing. "An' I apologize—for what I believed I saw." His tone was correct but the words and the contempt in his face aggravated the situation. Styles's eyes filled with tears of rage and he struggled to get past Baynard. He may have lashed out at Simon, but the abrupt and excited yelping of the slave breeder's hounds brought them all up sharp, stopped everything for the space of a missed heartbeat.

"He's found her," Simon whispered. "By God! He's found her."

He heeled around and ran toward the yelping dogs. He strode, half running, half-walking, clasping his bullwhip, his knuckles gray, along the slight incline. As he came near the whitewashed shack before which Gree stood restraining the yelping hounds, Vinnie crawled slowly out on her hands and knees from under the front stoop.

"My God, Vinnie," Simon said.

She stared at him, her eyes cold and defiant, bleak. She was gray with dirt and streaked with cobwebs. Her full-breasted, shapely body, glowingly tawny, strained at the torn cotton dress that was blood-smeared and caked with mud. Her crisp black hair was awry about her head. Her arms and legs were laced with abrasions and briar gashes. She was barefooted. But she stood erect, rebellious, her long, well-turned legs apart, her slender supple form rigid. With a strange sense of loss and sadness, Simon recalled the first time he'd seen her naked. He'd gone out of his gourd. He'd never seen such high-standing full tits on such a slender girl. Vinnie got inside your mind. She heated up your blood and drove everything else out of your thoughts.

He heard the Baynards, Kenric, and the slave Blade stride up the path and stand beside him gazing at the runaway girl. Simon ignored them. He did not take his eyes off Vinnie. Behind him, the slave boys brought the wagon rattling up the stony incline, and he thought, *we'll be in it soon, on the way home*.

He heard Gree moaning anguishedly, deep in his throat, but didn't turn to look at him. Gree tied the hounds to the wagon tailgate, sobs boiling up from his chest, unintelligible, painful, stricken. Suddenly, Gree whirled and ran past where the white men stood. He ran to Vinnie and fell onto his knees before her. He clutched his trembling arms about her, pressing his face against her. He sobbed, trying agonizingly to speak, to beg her forgiveness.

Vinnie did not look down at him. She kept her head erect, but she pressed her hands gently into his hair, whispering to him soothingly. "I know, Gree . . . Vinnie knows how sorry you are . . . you didn't want to do it . . . you had to. . . . Don't cry, Gree . . . please don't cry no more, Gree. It's all right . . . it's all right."

But the anguished boy could not stop sobbing. Tears coursed down his cheeks.

Simon said, "Why, Vinnie? Why did you do it? Why did you go and run away from me?"

She stared straight at him. Her face remained taut in her terrible calm and resignation. "Toth," she said.

His shoulders sagged. The world seemed to wheel about his head and for a moment he was afraid he was going to fall. He bit back vomitus. "Toth? The slave?"

"Was trying to get to Toth," she said.

Simon's voice shook. "Sold Toth, Vinnie. Told you that."

"Toth is my man . . . my only man."

"Goddamn it, Vinnie. I been good to you. You got no man, Vinnie. No. You belong to *me*. You covered when I say you covered."

Baynard stepped forward. He felt a sense of outrage. He saw now what he had intuitively suspected all along. There was more here than the recovery of a fugitive slave. This man had started out, obsessed, days and hundreds of miles west, unable to think anything else, unaware of heat or cold or night or hunger. He talked so nobly of making an example of her, but this was an intimate affair, charged with jealousy, revenge, and betrayal. It sickened him. "Why did you come here, girl?" he asked. "What did you want on this place?"

"Was looking for Toth, masta," she said. "I knew only the name of the plantation where Toth'd been sold. Name of The Briars."

"Why, The Briars—that's only a few more miles east,"

Morgan blurted out. "You was almost there. Wasn't she, papa?"

"Oh, God," the girl whispered. "Oh, my God."

An aging Negro came hesitantly from within the shack. He walked down the steps, trembling visibly. He stood beside Vinnie and the kneeling Gree.

"What do you know about this, Obadiah?" Baynard asked. "Did you hide this girl?"

The slave wept, suddenly and helplessly, scrubbing at his running nose with the back of his palsied hand. "She was so tired, masta," he sobbed. "So scairt. Like a li'l girl, scairt. She jes' craved to res' a little while."

"I'll whup you," Simon said. "You black bastard. I'll lay your bones bare."

"We don't whip our Negroes, Mr. Simon," Baynard warned.

"Well, seems by God you better start. Seems you'd rather whup him yourself than have me turn him over to the sheriff."

Obadiah sobbed. "Oh, Masta Baynard, suh. Please. No."

"Be quiet, Obadiah," Baynard said. "Now, Mr. Simon, you have your wench back. Why would you want to turn this old man over to the sheriff?"

"He broke a law. He harbored my runaway slave."

"Obadiah's like a child. He doesn't have any conception of the law."

"Know it or not, he broke it. . . . Don't you be so insolent and mighty with me neither, Mr. Baynard, suh. It could go jest as hard with you. You got any idea the penalty for harboring a runner?"

"I know the penalty, sir."

Obadiah moaned. "Oh, Lawd, masta. I didn't *harbor* her. Not once, suh! As Gawd looks down on me. Fed her . . . let her lay down on de corn shucks mattress . . . dat's all. Didn't tech her. Didn't harbor her. Swear I didn't. 'Fore Gawd, I swear I didn't, masta."

Baynard nodded. He turned, facing the slave breeder. "You have recovered your property, Mr. Simon. Nothing will be benefitted by tormenting this old man any further. If there's any disciplining of my slaves, I'll do it, sir. You might do well to start back home. It's a long trip to Carthage, Mississippi."

Cold, unrelenting steel underlined every word the elder Baynard spoke. His face remained calm but he was as firmly and immovably set as those huge pillars at his iron-gated entrance.

Simon scowled, but retreated. "They's laws—"

"Once more I say it. And just once more, Mr. Simon. You've recovered your property . . . I bid you good day, sir."

Simon glanced around uncertainly, emptily. It didn't seem settled and yet he knew this man could not be pushed another inch. He shrugged his soiled jacket up on his shoulders, aware that he was horribly hungry and that he had no memory of the last time he had eaten. His voice lashed out. "On your feet, Gree. Get in the wagon."

The mute boy nodded, sniffling. He got up and backed away, head hung down, to the wagon. He climbed into the flatbed and slouched, immobile, staring at the ground. Vinnie remained where she was.

Simon cursed her. "Get in the wagon, you black bitch. Get you home, slut, I sells you to the first coffle passing. Goddamn it. Goddamn it. A wench goes bad, she's bad till she's dead."

Vinnie shook her head, blinking away her tears. She gave him a look of anguished despair, her face empty, her eyes bleak with fatigue. She walked past him. His voice lashed out at her. "You goin' quiet, slut? Or do I need them shackles and spancels?"

She climbed up, using the front wheel spoke as a step to lift herself. She stepped over the sideboard. But the instant she stepped into the wagon she abruptly lunged forward, leaping off the far side, stumbling. She fell, sprawling face first along the stony ground and scraping her knees. She lay a moment as if too beaten to rise. Then she scrambled to her feet and ran down the incline. The hounds went into a frenzy of yelping.

No one moved except Baxter Simon. His reflexes were finely honed, fatigued as he was. He was prepared for anything a slave might do. Whatever she attempted, it had been tried on him before and experience made him wary and it made his reactions remarkably quick.

He ran around the wagon before Vinnie could scramble to her feet. He snaked out the bullwhip as he ran. He seemed to take his time, apparently moving unhurriedly. He brought his arm up and cracked it downward, lashing out with the whip. There was a sharp snap like the static burst of thunder on a cloudless day.

The whip lanced out, seeming barely to reach the running girl. Its tip caught her at the nape of her neck and, like a knife, sliced the pons Varoli—that nerve bridge from the base of the skull to the cervical vertebrae of her spine. Her neck was cleanly severed from her backbone; the nerves controlling her breathing and heart action were cut, and she died instantly.

She took one more long running step and then sprawled headlong, prostrate on her face. She was dead.

Still no one moved. Blackoaks slaves and masters alike were stunned by what they saw. Perhaps every adult had seen death strike before, but never so quickly, impersonally, expertly.

"Bitch." Simon spoke to himself, wrapping the bullwhip about his arm. "She ought to know better'n to run on me again. I tole her what I'd do. Goddamn her."

He glanced about at the people of Blackoaks. Only Styles Kenric appeared removed from the shock of this pervasive horror. He stood slump-shouldered in the path. Ferrell-Junior stared at Simon as if he were some monster from a traveling freak show. Morgan was crying aloud and his body slave was awkwardly trying to put his arm about Morgan's heavy shoulders to comfort him. Baynard seemed to be holding his breath, keeping himself leashed by some terrible inner discipline.

Silently, Simon jerked his head, motioning Gree to the front seat of the wagon. The mute boy moved stiffly. He sat, eyes empty, face muscles rigid. Simon motioned again and the boy took up the reins. He slapped them across the rumps of the horses. The pair strained forward sluggishly and the wagon rattled slowly down the incline. Simon walked beside the horses.

The Baynards had not moved. They did not speak, watching Simon.

Simon knelt beside the girl's body. His face was grayed out, his mouth a taut line. He gazed at her. His eyes blurred with tears. Then he lifted her carelessly, as if she were a croaker sack of potatoes, and stood up.

He shrugged her body over his shoulder with her head hanging down. He walked forward again, braced against the incline. Gree slapped the reins, the wagon rolled downslope. Behind them, the Baynards and the small knot of slaves moved forward too, in a body.

Arriving at the high, split-rail fence enclosing the hog pen, Simon glanced at Gree and motioned with his head. He didn't speak but the boy understood him. The flatbed wagon creaked to a halt.

Simon walked off the path to the hog pen. He stood one long moment watching the snuffling, growling boars milling around in the mud and slop of the enclosure. The stench was fetid and sour. He hefted Vinnie's body and half-threw it over the rough-cut fencing. Somebody behind him yelled out involuntarily in horrified protest. He did not even look around. The dead girl's body struck the broad hams of several swine, was thrown over on its side and tossed around for a moment, the swine squealing. Then the boars, snuffling, slashed at her arms and legs and belly, ripping and tearing and dragging her body down under the thrashing herd.

Simon remained standing rigid, his eyes tightly closed. When he turned at the sound of running feet, he set himself, waiting. He hoped somebody would start something; he wanted violence; he prayed for it.

Young Ferrell and Blade ran at him, too agonized even to realize what they were doing. Ferrell-Junior's face was contorted, rage pulling his mouth down, his eyes distended.

The Fulani was close behind him. Blade's classic face was pallid with horror. His steps slowed, and he stopped running some yards from the pen, as if the sounds of the swine devouring the woman's body paralyzed and incapacitated him. He looked about, terrorized, hearing sounds that never again would be far beneath his consciousness.

Behind him, the smaller Soapy was trying to support the

ungainly body of Morgan, who was doubled over, retching. Vomitus gushed from his mouth and splashed on the path. Kenric retreated, pale and silent, to the rim of shadows at the edge of the barn. He leaned against an upright as if too exhausted to stand straight.

But Baynard moved faster than any of them. His gray face was taut with exertion and inner tensions. A thick blue vein throbbed in his temple. He leaped forward and snagged Ferrell-Junior's shoulder. He bodily hurled his son off his feet as the boy lunged toward Simon's throat.

Simon kept his voice level. He jerked his head indicating the youth on his back upon the ground. "You done a wise thing, suh. I wouldn't-a wanted to hurt him."

Baynard was so shaken with rage he had trouble speaking. He breathed raggedly, but his deep voice was level though crackling with suppressed outrage. "I ought to kill you, you white-trash son of a bitch."

Simon winced, squared his shoulders. His mouth pulled down and he watched Baynard narrowly. His fist gripped the bullwhip until his knuckles grayed, but he didn't speak.

"You best get on your wagon and be on your way, Mr. Simon. And you'll oblige me to make it fast. It is five minutes from here to my front gate. I want you off my property, and that length of time will be most satisfactory, sir."

Simon glanced around him in a show of bravado. Nobody looked at him. He laughed, scalding them with his derision. "What the hell? Why you got a sudden wild hair up your ass? . . . After all, it warn't nothin' but a nigger . . . and it was *my* nigger."

Nobody said anything. Gree sat as if in a catatonic trance on the wagon seat. He stared straight ahead into some lost dimension. Infrequently his whole body would quiver in involuntary spasms. But his eyes were dry now as if he would never cry again.

Baxter Simon took one last regretful look at the young Fulani. Then he swung up on the seat beside Gree and took the reins. No one spoke. The silence deepened across the quarters, the sunstruck barnyard, the upland pastures. The wagon rolled up the incline past the manor house

52

and through the lane of pecan trees to the dusty road beyond the fieldstone wall. The Baynards stood unmoving until Simon turned the wagon outside the gate onto the trail, going west toward Carthage.

CHAPTER 5

THE BAYNARDS of Blackoaks never really forgot
Baxter Simon after his brief, disruptive visit that spring
day. Morgan wakened screaming in nightmares for weeks
after Simon casually threw the body of his slave girl to
the hogs. Morgan couldn't speak intelligibly for minutes
after he was fully awake. He blubbered and stuttered and
his eyes mirrored a horror only he could see. He wept,
shivering with terror, and could go back to sleep only
with a candle burning on the table beside his bed. When
the room and the house were quiet again, Soapy would
creep up from his straw pallet on the floor and crawl in
under the covers with Morgan. He would draw the
trembling stout boy close into his arms, cradling him,
petting him, caressing until Morgan gradually subsided
and finally fell asleep with his arm tightly about his body
slave.

The Baynard men each felt a cold hatred for the very
memory of the slave breeder. Styles hated him most of
all because his distaste was mixed with a sense of his
being covered with vile that could never be completely
washed away. There was too an inescapable sense of guilt
and shame; but mostly there was a violent resentment.
The world seemed muddier and dirtier with a filth thrown
upon him by Simon, a filth that was forever a stigma on
his person.

Styles lay awake in his bed beside Kathy for hours at
night, recalling that hated face. He wished he had killed
Simon. In his mind he could see himself hitting at that
derisive smile with a two-by-four, striking until that cor-

54

rosive laughter was strangled and gone, until nothing remained but a bloody pulp that might once have been a man's head. But the association of ideas led inevitably back to the naked Negro slave. He would recall Blade —the rugged, lean, dark-gold body, the rigid staff pliant and pulsating in his fist, and Styles would cringe, taut, hands clenched and sweated. . . .

Baynard too could not escape the ugly notion that the slave breeder had somehow irreparably soiled and degraded the estate. Simply by walking across its earth, Simon had deposited and left behind a spreading stain of horror and evil that nothing would ever entirely efface. Each night, when Simon was almost lost from his thoughts, Morgan's wild screaming would renew it all. He would never forget the contempt in Simon's cynical eyes—disdain for everything to which Baynard had devoted his whole life—the slaves, the crops, the quarters, the plans for the future. In Simon's gaze it was all doomed, and somehow, without being able to explain why, Baynard found himself unwillingly sharing that dark sense of foreboding. It left him empty bellied, frustrated, and oddly dissatisfied. There had to be something he could do to disprove Simon and everything his evil forecasting suggested, but he didn't know what it was. No matter what Baynard did, said Simon's twisted smile, he and all his works ground slowly and inexorably toward ruin. Damn him! Damn him, he was wrong—as wrong as he was evil, and he'd show him. He'd yet be all right. Things were tough at the moment but they were bound to improve. If the weather gave him a break, he'd be all right, and he could yet prove Simon was wrong—low, contemptible . . . wrong . . .

Ferrell-Junior tried to block the memory of the Negro breeder from his mind because he detested anyone insensitive to the pain of others. He regretted only one thing when something forced him to recall Simon. He hadn't gotten to hit that cold, arrogant face just once, no matter what it might have cost him. He grinned and admitted ruefully that it could have cost him plenty if his father hadn't intervened and hurled him on his backside at the instant he lunged toward that twisted face. He could close his eyes and see the deadly threat in Simon's gaze when he'd said to his father, "I wouldn't-a wanted to hurt him." The hell he wouldn't. Simon would have casually killed him, as insensibly and off-handedly as he had slain that slave girl. Simon needed to kill him, needed the violence upon violence to release inner torments Ferrell-Junior couldn't even guess at. Simon had wanted to kill him. This fact was clear in that swarthy face, in those dehumanized eyes.

Yet, despite the revulsion each man felt separately toward Simon, they found themselves discussing his ideas, even around the dinner table. Baynard admitted to himself that somehow Blackoaks needed to produce another sure money crop or he was in serious straits. He had seen the trouble coming for several years—each time meeting the principle and interest of the mortgage held by the Tallahassee banker, Garrett Blanford Ware, came due; each time almost impossible to cover. He lay sleepless at night going over it in his mind, reaching for elusive solutions, studying and discarding ideas he'd studied a hundred times before, and discarded as often, and trying to ignore the faint fluttering of panic deep in the pit of his stomach. He never mentioned any of this aloud; he tried instead to shield the rest of his family from it. He had always been able to keep it below the surface of his conscious mind until that man Simon rode into the place with his scornful smile and sarcastic, probing eyes.

"Simon provided us one answer," Styles said. "We've got to sell slaves. It's the only way anybody's making anything these days."

"Dear Styles," Miz Claire said from the end of the polished mahogany table. She gave him her warmest smile from her pale-gold face, and fooled no one. The family knew Miz Claire reserved her warmest smile for those moments when she was most vexed or displeased. "Must we talk about such a depressing topic—at the breakfast table?"

Styles's head tilted and he glanced at his mother-in-law along his patrician nose. She was a slender woman, weighing under a hundred pounds, with red-gold hair traced with gray. She wore fussy, print dresses, with ruffles about her throat. "We'd better discuss it somewhere, Miz Claire," Styles said. He had only illy concealed contempt for his mother-in-law's intellect. There was much talk about what a bright, charming, and witty woman Miz Claire once had been, but ever since he had known her, she'd been as empty headed as a gourd, fey and vague. But she was also as rigid as thin steel rods when roused, and one pretended at least to defer to her. Besides, it made it easier to get along with the rest of the family who were extravagant in their protective warmth toward Miz Claire. "The truth is, Miz Claire, Blackoaks has got too many slaves. They multiply like rabbits, but unfortunately, they eat like a plague of locusts."

Those steel rods were showing through Miz Claire's unwavering smile. "Don't we all eat well at Blackoaks, dear Styles? No one ever goes hungry at Blackoaks—master, slave, or guest—and never will."

"They don't," Styles persisted. "But I can't promise you they never will."

Her head tilted, though her smile did not waver. "Still, there's a place for everything, Styles dear, and the breakfast table is hardly the place."

"The place to discuss our problem is where we all are gathered, Miz Claire," Styles said. But he was no longer talking to her, only through her to the male members of the family.

She intercepted him brightly, rigidly. "Well, dear, I simply won't have it. Not at my table, Styles honey."

"We'll discuss it later, Styles," Baynard said from the head of the table. It might have ended but Morgan dropped his fork on his plate with a clatter and burst out, "You can't sell Soapy!"

"Nobody's going to sell Soapy, Morgan," Baynard said gently.

"Of course not, darling," Miz Claire said. "Now will you see what we've done? We've upset poor Morgan. . . . Eat your breakfast, Morgan-baby. Nobody will ever sell dear Soapy, Morgan. Mother promises you that. Why, what in the world would people say if we sold a body slave?"

"Nobody would buy Soapy, Morgan," Ferrell-Junior teased.

"I would," Morgan said. "I'd give you all the money in the world for him—and then I'd set him free."

"Isn't that strange?" Kathy teased. "To look at Soapy, one wouldn't think he's worth half that. . . . And what would Soapy do if you set him free, Morgan? Wander around—a lost little fat boy who can't read or write?"

"If we can't choose some pleasant topic of conversation, maybe we should simply do without breakfast," Miz Claire said, helping herself to scrambled eggs and fried ham. "My . . . I know we'd never have been allowed to talk like this at my mother's table."

"Your mother lived in another world, Miz Claire," Styles said. In his mind where no one could hear him, he added, "And so do you. . . ."

Baynard parried every attempt Styles made to broach the subject of selling slaves. He couldn't say why he didn't want to discuss it with Styles, only that he did not. And yet he needed to talk to someone, and he couldn't talk it over with Ferrell-Junior because the boy was opposed to it. Well, Ferrell-Junior was young, idealistic; he had protected him too much, as he had all his children. He could not bring himself to confess to Ferrell-Junior that he was in increasingly desperate financial trouble. And for some reason that didn't make sense, he didn't want Styles even to suspect the truth. And this he recognized as a self-delusion. He was certain that Styles was totally aware of the true conditions on the estate. There was much about Styles he didn't particularly admire, but his son-in-law was mentally sharp, a clever man. He wasn't likely to be deceived by bright smiles.

"If you do decide to sell slaves," Styles said when he and Baynard sat alone at the dinner table, "it won't get us the kind of returns we're looking for just to sell off the present stock. Some are exceptional, but most are simply bush Negroes."

Baynard studied his glass of after-dinner whiskey. "What makes you think I'm going to sell *any* slaves?"

"Aren't you?"

"I haven't given it any thought."

"Haven't you? I have. We have a resource here at Blackoaks that can be worth a fortune. But if one sold slaves, he ought to do it on some sort of scale—as Baxter Simon does."

"Dealing in human flesh has made Simon an insensitive, almost dehumanized monster."

"But a rich monster." Styles bent forward, leaning on the table, his earnest face reflected vaguely in its gleaming surface. Furnishings, rococo mirror, draperies, wall facings were faintly etched in the table top; this room epitomized the solid, secure appearance of the house. A massive sideboard with ostentatious decorative scroll work in heavy-handed workmanship dominated an entire wall. One felt that this unit of furniture alone would endure forever, even that it might float, it was so carefully and painstakingly crafted. Even the dark mirror above its cluttered top was ornately designed and its frame was elaborately filligreed and polished. The dining table was part of the same leisurely crafted family as were the high-backed tufted chairs.

"We sleep well at night," Baynard said.

"Do we? Have we slept soundly since Baxter Simon paid us a visit? He gave us the answer, Mr. Baynard. Blade. Moab. Fulanis. Both Blade and Moab are purebreds. It is wasteful, foolhardy to throw them away on ordinary black wenches. They could sire fancy-grade slaves—the highest-priced flesh there is. We could name our own price—in New Orleans or out at Natchez. . . . All we need is a purebred Fulani female."

Baynard exhaled heavily. "I've seen only one purebred Fulani woman . . . and Simon slew her and threw her body to our hogs."

"Still. Did you see the way Simon behaved when he saw Blade for the first time—and the prices he offered? And he's not a rich buyer—he's a breeder who knows what the market is hungry for. My God. He offered you $10,000 gold for one black man. . . . Think of it, sir. Think of it. Isn't it worth the effort to find a purebred Fulani female—and soon? . . ."

"That would require a fortune in itself," Baynard pointed out.

"Perhaps. But it would be like the money you spend for peanut seeds in the end. That man Simon was right, you know. . . . Blade would sire the finest breed of black in America. Importing slaves is outlawed. There is only one way to produce Fulanis in this country—breed them. And Blade would sire the top grade. He is intelligent. He has strength. Courage. He's a beautiful specimen —as Moab will be when he is grown."

Baynard nodded reluctantly. "It might be interesting—perfect the breed, improve the bloodline—"

"To bank a fortune, for God's sake."

After a moment, Baynard spoke regretfully. "There are too many considerations, Styles. First is the seed money we'd need for the Fulani woman—"

"Mortgage everything! Don't think twice about it. It's no gamble—you can't lose."

Baynard winced almost perceptibly. He stared for a long time at his mildly burning cigar. "There is the risk of disease. The odds against a black child at birth. I don't know the figures—they must be astronomical."

"The black drops around here survive."

"So do the weeds. But when you breed Negroes— or any fine animal—you're dealing with sickening imponderables. My father always said if there were any way on God's earth without slave labor in the South, he'd sell off every slave. I know you have no conception of just how expensive each of them is, just to keep him alive, to see him through his productive years, and to care for him when he is no longer productive."

"That's the kind of mistake a Baxter Simon would never make."

"All right. Suppose you bred Fulani fancies for the market. They must be handled with incredible caution— against disease, accident, chance. A Fulani fancy on the slave vendue can never betray the weal of whip-bite, the faintest trace of discoloration or bruise or contusion. Smallpox scars would render him worthless. . . . I'll agree. You're right. A Fulani, sired by Blade in a Fulani woman might bring several thousand in New Orleans—in fifteen or twenty years. If it survived the hazards of birth, the risks of simply growing up."

"That's defeatist. Every breath one draws is a gamble."

Baynard laughed. "Perhaps. And yet, ever since Baxter Simon was here I've had bad dreams—nightmares in which terrible things happen to disfigure Blade, or mar him in some way."

"Only nothing's going to happen to him—nothing except our letting his best productive years go to waste by failing to find him a purebred Fulani mate. . . ."

Baynard spread his hands. "I'm sorry to have to say this, Styles. But—just now we can't afford to bid for such a fancy-grade wench on the market. I hate to say it—but temporarily, at least, I'm slightly overextended. Styles, I've gone over and over it in my mind. We'd be bidding against millionaire breeders like Simon—men who can destroy an invaluable human life—as he did here on this farm—to satisfy a transient rage." Baynard shook his head. "Still, he's got us all to dreaming impossible things, hasn't he? He's like some evil genie. Suppose we did go over our heads in debt to find a mate for Blade and Moab. Money tied up for an entire generation. And then what? What if some tragedy did befall any one of the three of them? Perfect, a Fulani is a thing of beauty—a priceless fancy on the auction vendue. Hurt, marred, or disfigured—he might as well be destroyed. He is not any better than a bush Negro. Not as good—because his resistance is less; he's more delicate."

"The important thing," Styles said, "is to think positively. We should consider any option. One comes immediately to mind. Sell as many of our present stock of slaves as necessary to finance the purchase of a Fulani fancy—and then set out to produce the quality we know we could get."

Baynard finished off his third whiskey and set the tumbler down hard. He glared about the room, the shadowed corners, the darkness beyond the drapery-framed windows. He listened for some moments to the sounds of the slaves moving about the house, the night sounds of the farm. He shivered, suddenly and involuntarily. He stood up, his face taut. He clapped his son-in-law on the shoulder and tried to smile. "Well, no matter. No point in discussing it now. No point at all."

CHAPTER 6

THREE DAYS after Simon's unwelcomed appearance and abrupt departure, a sorry coffle of blacks straggled along the road, headed west. The blacks in the human caravan looked diseased, half-starved, exhausted. The ankles of every man, woman, and child bled from the unrelenting bite of their shackles with every step they took. One quickly learned why they kept staggering forward under such conditions of human suffering. When one fell, a whip in the hand of the slave trader laid his back open; he got up and moved forward, or he was cut loose and left to die. The stragglers were silent, morose, but worst of all nauseatingly malodorous. There was a compound of the stench of human offal, of dried urine, the fierce musk of unwashed bodies.

At the head of this train rode a white man with the bullwhip coiled on his saddle horn and a rifle resting in its scabbard. A handgun in holster bulged his soiled jacket out of shape. His face was shadowed under a shapeless hat that had been worn in downpours and dried in pitiless suns. His whipcord trousers were tucked into calf-length black boots, worn at the high heels and turned over at the toes and rubbed gray by the stirrups at the instep.

He cracked his whip as a signal to halt the long line of blacks under the pecan trees some distance downwind from the manor house. He prodded his horse forward and was all the way to the portico before the slaves dared to sag to the ground where they sat hump shouldered, keening, or sprawled facedown, silent in the grass.

The horseman rode to the front steps, dismounted, crossed the veranda, and slammed the iron knocker loudly. As he waited, he contented himself with brushing mud from his boots on the hand-operated mud-scraper beside the door.

The huge door was opened and Thyestes stepped through, closed it behind him, and stared at the slave trader without smiling. Visitors to Blackoaks were infrequent and usually warmly welcomed, but Thyestes had been guardian of this portal for twenty years at least. He recognized white quality when he saw it. He had an unerring eye for white trash.

Thyestes's undeceived eyes took in the slave trader, his fatigue-slavered horse, his scabrous coffle of black derelicts. Tall, weather-roughened, with mud-gray hair streaked with red, the trader emitted a smell of evil along with his gamy body odor. Thyestes' nostrils wrinkled against the stench. "What you want here at my front door, white man?"

The trader wiped away his smile as suddenly as he'd pasted it on. "You watch your tongue, you black ape." His mouth twisted and his gaze raked across Thyestes. "I'd enjoy to git you one day in my coffle, nigger. I'd put a civil sound in your mouth or a hot poker up your ass, one or the other."

Thyestes' expression did not alter. "Well, that jes' won't never happen, Mr. White Man, suh. I'se Mr. Ferrell Alexander Baynard's boy. I always has been. I always will be—and that won't nevah happen."

"Well, nigger boy, my name is *Mister* Eakins Shivers. You tell yore masta I crave some words with him that he might find highly profitable to hisself. Also that I is in the market for niggers—even them that ain't good for nuthin' but smartin' off to they betters. You tells him that, nigger boy."

Thyestes' back stiffened. He nodded tautly. "I tells him. You jes' wait out yondah at the edge of them ole pecan trees. If'n my masta decide he wants talk to you, he'll come out there."

They stood another tense moment, gazes and wills clashing, but Thyestes did not stir; nor was he about to.

He knew what his orders were, and he followed them to the letter. Finally, Eakins Shivers shrugged, called him a snot-nosed black son of a bitch and heeled around. Then he hesitated and spoke coldly across his shoulder. "I offers yore masta a big price for you, mutha fugga, jes' to git you in my coffle."

Thyestes winced slightly but remained unmoving until Eakins Shivers clomped down the wide steps and jerked his horse's reins savagely, leading him toward the trees and the wretched lines of humanity sprawled beneath them.

After some delay, during which Eakins Shivers prowled a small circle restively, the elder Baynard emerged from the house and crossed the yard to the head of the lane. The two men talked for a long time. Gradually the dogs stopped barking in the barnyard and the Blackoaks slaves filtered out of the quarters to gaze in fascinated horror at this unknown spectacle of human misery. The children were held tightly by the wrists, restrained. They too were wordless, eyes wide. There had never been anything like this train of shackled slaves in their world. They didn't understand the terror and revulsion their elders felt, but instinctively they shared it. The house slaves stood back from the windows, shadowed by the draperies, as if superstitiously afraid to be seen by Eakins Shivers or any of his miserable crew.

The Baynards came out one by one to stand on the wide veranda. They did not speak either, but a shared sense of outrage grayed their faces. Chained slaves! They had never seen people like these before, such miserable beasts, of such a low caste. From the youngest to the oldest, the slaves were like animals from whom the last ounce of spirit and hope had been crushed. Some had large, festering body sores and many bled openly and untended. There was no trace of protest left in the strongest of them—they looked ill and dull eyed, not even lifting up their heads because they saw only evil in the brightest day. Miz Claire shuddered. "Oh, Mr. Baynard's got to get those wretches out of there. Suppose some of our friends drove up now—and saw those people out there. What on earth would they think?"

No one answered her. They gazed at the ugly caravan as if it were some fearful apparition from another world that would dissolve from view, from consciousness, from reality. But for the moment the smell, the agony, the pitiful beings were all too real. They could only stand immobile, unable to close their eyes to them; they could not manufacture pretty lies to color it. They could not find a healthy-looking mortal in the long line of blacks chained together at their bloodied, fly-infested ankles. Even the youngest child seemed infected with every known ethnic disease all the way back to kwashiorkor, an ancient nutritional scourge of Africa that affected infants and children, manifesting itself in edema, potbelly, and sickly splotchy changes in skin pigmentation.

Baynard permitted Eakins Shivers and his coffle to spend the night inside Blackoaks property on the banks of a creek a mile below the farmyard. He would not allow them near the quarters, nor would he permit any of the Blackoaks slaves to go near the coffle. With his whip flicking at the slaves, Eakins Shivers rode among them on his horse, forcing them into the creek up to their bellies. Then he tossed lye soap that he had bought from Baynard's commissary stores to the slaves and sat slumped in his saddle until each of them had soaped and rinsed. Then several of the blacks were freed from their leg spancels long enough to build fires and cook grits in lard cans set over open fires. Eakins bought only enough side meat and flour from Baynard's stores to mix with creek water to make a thin red-eye gravy. A tall Negro wearing a stovepipe hat was the only marcher not chain linked and whose spancels sores had healed into gray scars. He was Eakins Shivers' lieutenant and only assistant. He doled out the grits and splashed red-eye gravy over it into cheap tin-plated cups. The slaves ate with their fingers, pressing the runny food into their mouths until it oozed whitely from their lips and drained along their chins.

Night came at last, settling like an impenetrable black cyclorama to shield the plantation from any further view of the travelers. The darkness was infested with mosquitoes and even the sickest Negro in the coffle was harried into impotent frenzy by the insects. Most of them crawled to the edge of the creek and plastered their bodies with wet clay. Then, some of them slept. Others wept, an empty moaning sound that was almost musical in its terrible anguish. Some who sobbed no longer even remembered what they cried for—the faces, the sights, the very substance of a better time in their pasts were lost in the gray mists of endless walking, chained, of hunger never appeased, of every hope denied and sickness never tended.

Eakins Shivers laid his head on his saddle, placed his rifle across his chest, his holstered handgun at his hip. He covered himself with an age-rusted greatcoat and was asleep before the first fire burned down.

The last feeble campfire winked out like a departing firefly and the Blackoaks slaves and masters finally closed their eyes and their minds to their loathsome guests. Across the silent distance, the blacks were swallowed up in the darkness with the snores of the white trader, the stench of body musk, infection, and despair, the fear of the unknowable tomorrow, the muted keening and the unrelieved agony of the ill. This brief rest was not the end of anything and those who looked ahead, or backward, or beyond this painful night, looked in horror. Most would have chosen death to the livid pink of daybreak. . . .

Eakins Shivers and his coffle were gone from the creekside in the darkest hour before dawn. Ferrell-Junior was up at daylight. He saddled his horse in the barn and rode down along the creek. He sagged in his saddle, his horse unmoving in the shadowed creekbed, staring at the tamped ground and trampled weeds, the charred remains of fires, the sure proof that Shivers hadn't bothered feeding them anything for breakfast. The soiled, bald, and scarred creekbank was the last sign of the black train.

His father awaited him at the barn when he returned. The yard slaves were awake and Ferrell-Junior swung down from the saddle and tossed the reins to a waiting black. "Jesus. He didn't even feed them this morning."

"They're gone?"

"Yes. They've cleared out. Thank God."

Baynard sighed tautly. "It's one of the ugliest sights on God's earth."

"How does he hope to sell any one of those diseased, half-starved wretches?"

They walked slowly, shoulder to shoulder up the incline. Baynard was silent so long that Ferrell-Junior jerked his head around to be sure his father was all right. "He sells where he can," Baynard said. "A farmer with a crop that's ready, needing fieldhands desperately—"

"My God. That desperately?"

"Shivers sells cheap. That's about all he's got going for him. Or he trades for the malcontent, the renegade—even the insane."

"Why does even a man like Shivers want to be shackled with the dregs of this rotten business?"

"He doesn't. He keeps moving—going in what looks like a directionless wandering. But he knows where he's going—when he's finally unloaded the sorry best of his culls. Every year at cane-cutting time he's in the Mississippi delta—or the Louisiana wetlands. He sells off the last of his coffle there."

Ferrell-Junior shivered involuntarily. "And then starts out again?"

"And then starts out again."

Ferrell-Junior laughed in a chilled, mirthless, and uncomfortable way. "I know that man Simon has nothing to do with Eakins Shivers and his black culls—Simon's at the other end of the business, selling and breeding the fancies—and yet, it seems to me as if Shivers and that stinking coffle of his followed Simon here like the moon follows the sun—as if Simon brought vile to Blackoaks and that's just the start of it. I know it sounds insane, but I can't get it out of my mind. Am I crazy? Or do you feel that too?"

"I try not to," Baynard said.

They walked together on up the incline in silence. It made no sense to blame that man Simon for the filth of Eakins Shivers, and yet one couldn't escape the sure feeling that if Baxter Simon had not come here, Shivers would not have shown up either. Ferrell-Junior glanced around at his familiar world, troubled and apprehensive. Cabin fires poked gray fingers of smoke up from the quarters. Cattle, horses, and sheep grazed in the dew-wet pastures. Smells of hot, freshly baked breads floated down from the kitchen of the manor house. It was the same old well-acquainted world, and yet, somehow, inexplicably, it was no longer the same at all. . . .

Breakfast was being served in the large family dining room off the kitchen. Thyestes met Baynard and Ferrell-Junior at the door to announce that the family was at table, waiting for them. "Miz Claire's waitin' to ask the blessing, masta, suh."

Thyestes tried to smile but tension pulled his long face taut. He asked hesitantly if the coffle was gone, and not until Ferrell-Junior assured him that it was, did the saddle-brown face relax. It was as if Thyestes had been holding his breath and now could breathe normally again.

Tension awaited Baynard and Ferrell-Junior in the dining room. Good-scented steam vapors rose from the bowls of hot grits, the platters of ham, fried chicken, and eggs, the napkin-covered baskets of biscuits and hot buns, the containers of scalding hot coffee. But even after Baynard asked the blessing, no one touched the food. From the kitchen came a sound of uncontrollable sobbing against the incredible slamming and clattering of metal ware.

His face pallid with rage, Baynard got up from his chair and strode toward the kitchen. He was not unreasonable, but damned if he would tolerate such insolence, such utter and complete lack of discipline in the kitchen. They took advantage of him, as all slaves did of their masters; and he permitted it, within reason. This was all out of line and he would let Jeanne d'Arc know it.

He was stopped in mid-step by his wife's vague voice, which carried a thin steel edge. "It's all right, Mr. Baynard. I prefer you don't go into the kitchen just now."

He paused, then returned to the table. He looked about at them, but no one looked up at him except Ferrell-Junior, who was as puzzled as he. Baynard shook out his napkin and placed it precisely across his thighs. "Miz Claire, I will have discipline. They know better than to slam pots and pans around in there. I suppose it's because Jahndark is in bed and can't oversee—"

"Jeanne d'Arc is in the kitchen, Mr. Baynard," Miz Claire said.

Kathy laughed nervously. "Jeanne d'Arc is the one slamming the pots and pans around, papa."

Baynard frowned, incredulous, and moved to get up again. Once more, Miz Claire's taut voice stayed him. "Pass the food, Mr. Baynard, if you will. Everything is getting cold."

Baynard hesitated and then sat back in the tense silence that was accented and underlined by the lamentations and the clatter from the kitchen. Damn it all. You thought yourself the master when you owned slaves, but in a hundred ways you were the mastered. This was undeniably true when they wanted to let you know they were aggrieved.

When Baynard looked up he saw that Morgan was crying, stifling his sobs with his linen napkin pressed hard against his mouth. Tears welled in Morgan's pale eyes and spilled along his cheeks.

Morgan stared at his father, his eyes accusing and terror stricken. "Obadiah," Morgan sobbed, "Obadiah and Narc are gone."

The wailing from the kitchen increased in intensity—they were listening to every word from out there. "Who in the hell is that carrying on with that sobbing in the kitchen?" Baynard demanded.

"Please, Mr. Baynard. I'll thank you not to curse at my table," Miz Claire said.

"It's Rosa-Monday," Kathy told her father.

"Rosa-Monday is Narc's mother," Miz Claire said.

"I know who she is."

"Rosa-Monday's been in that kitchen since daybreak, crying and beating her head against the wall," Styles said. "Her carrying on woke me up."

"It woke up the whole house," Kathy said. "They've been carrying on like that in the kitchen ever since."

"They're saying you sold the boy Narcissus and old

Obzadiah to the slave peddler," Styles said. He watched Baynard narrowly, with a new respect. "Did you?"

Baynard ignored him. He spoke sharply to Morgan. "Morgan, you can stop that damned sniveling this instant, or you can leave the table—"

"Mr. Baynard, please. This is a respectable household. Or it was. I've already asked you kindly once—"

"What's all the wailing about?" Ferrell-Junior said. "Nobody would sell a human being to Eakins Shivers."

Morgan stopped sniffling, watching Ferrell-Junior's face hopefully. "You think they'll come back, Ferrell? Obadiah and Narc. You think they'll come back?"

"I don't know, fellow. I just know papa. I know papa wouldn't sell anyone to Shivers."

"They're gone," Morgan said. The chorus of wails rose as if on cue from the intensely silent kitchen where the house slaves sat, straining now to hear every word from the dining room.

Ferrell-Junior placed his arm about Morgan's stout shoulders. "You know ole Obadiah's not right in the head, Morg. And Narc is always following people. He probably followed that coffle because he'd never seen anything like it before."

"He'd come home to breakfast," Morgan said in a thoughtful, troubled tone. "Maybe he can't, Ferrell. . . . Maybe Colonel Ben Johnson's got him."

"Who in the world is Colonel Ben Johnson?" Miz Claire asked. "Is he anyone we know?"

"He's nobody we know, mother," Kathy said.

"He's a madman." Baynard spoke in sudden savagery. "Colonel Ben Johnson is an abolitionist, Miz Claire. He was a planter, well-to-do and respected over near Chancellor. Then he went away for a while to fight the Creeks with Jackson. When he came back, he acted as if he was touched in the head. Suddenly up and freed all his slaves. Now he farms over there as well as he can with hired black help. They say he sneaks runaway blacks north on the underground."

"Why would a Southerner do a thing like that?" Miz Claire said.

"I told you. He's a madman."

71

"Nobody has ever proved he helps runaways," Ferrell-Junior said.

"But there's suspicion. Plenty of talk," Styles said. "And you know if there was the slightest shred of proof, he'd hang. You can be sure of that."

"Oh, my goodness. Can't we find pleasanter things to talk about at my breakfast table?" Miz Claire wanted to know.

Morgan burst into tears again. "But I'm mighty worried about Narc and poor old Obadiah."

"You don't suppose that Shivers could have stolen them, do you?" Ferrell-Junior asked. "I can understand his stealing Narc. Fourteen years old. Strong as a bull. Worth more than the whole rest of his coffle. But Obadiah?" He shook his head.

The wailing rose from the kitchen. Morgan pressed his napkin hard against his mouth but his sobs erupted through it. Baynard wadded his own napkin in his fist and hurled it onto his plate. He stood up abruptly, knocking over his chair. His face was gray and a blue vein throbbed in his temple. He spoke loudly, his voice purposely pitched to carry through the walls to the blacks wailing in the kitchen. "We'll stop carrying on like this. Right now. All of us. Of course, if Narc and old Obadiah are lost, we'll try to find them. If they don't show up soon, we'll go out looking for them. Meantime, goddamn it, I won't have another instant of this carrying on."

Miz Claire stared up at him, whitefaced. "Oh, Mr. Baynard, I'll ask you, please. Don't lose your temper at my breakfast table—like some—some common trash. What on earth will people think of us?"

CHAPTER 7

A WEEK PASSED and there was no word from the young slave Narcissus or from the aged and addled Obadiah. Gradually, the tensions lessened, the lamentations subsided and Blackoaks returned to its regular routines, though with less than accustomed warmth. But there was work for everybody and sometimes hard labor is an antidote for melancholy. The three shifts for each twenty-four hours continued to distill whiskey at Baynard's elaborate still. The fieldhands worked at their own unhurried pace, and yet their numbers and their continual, if grudging attention, kept the crops weed free and finally got them harvested, processed, and canned. There were unceasing rounds of repairing, repainting, planting, cooking, cleaning, candle-making, wood-cutting, cattle-tending. Around the manor house and along the lane of pecan trees and in ornamental flower beds, crews of black men tended cushion chrysanthemums, perennials that blazed in reds, yellows, pinks, purples, and bronze —spreading basket sized. Carnations, brightly hued or freshly white, glittered crisp and fragrant. Rose beds were bordered with clusters of creeping phlox.

Rosa-Monday calmed down slowly from an incapacitating hysteria to uncontrollable sobbing, finally to dull-eyed silence. Then word reached Blackoaks that the skeleton of what was believed to be a male Negro had been found near Elba. Authorities over there deduced that the man had been attacked and killed by a rogue panther. He was not identified. Rosa-Monday, with

Jeanne d'Arc beside her, came into Baynard's office-den in the big house. Rosa-Monday tried to speak but sank to her knees and was unable to speak coherently. Jeanne d'Arc was compelled to speak for her. Rosa-Monday, Jeanne d'Arc said, pleaded with the master for permission to go to Elba with her man Septimus, there to look at the remains of the dead slave.

"There are only bones," Baynard said, shaking his head. He was angered, becoming almost violently repelled by Rosa-Monday's continued hysteria. He tried to control his tone. "There is no possible way to tell whether it is Narc or not."

"I'd know. I'd know, masta," Rosa-Monday sobbed.

Baynard stared at his clenched fist on the desk beside him. "There's no sense talking about it, Rosa-Monday. You cannot go. If there were the least chance that it was Narc's body, I'd go with you. But I know better. It is not your boy. And I warn you now, Rosa-Monday, we cannot chase down every rumor that floats through here. Do you understand?"

"It's my boy, masta. I know it's my boy." Rosa-Monday wept. "I done spent my whole life working for you, masta. I'se loved you and I'se worked for you. My Septimus. My chillun. We'se all worked. We never made you no trouble. We never asked—"

"And don't ask now. I tell you, it is not your boy over at Elba. I want to hear no more about it. If you keep carrying on like this, Rosa-Monday, I'll sell you off—the first time some dirt farmer comes looking to buy workers."

"You wouldn't do that, masta." There was a quality of abject terror in Rosa-Monday's voice, but there was cold defiance in it too. After all, she'd been born on this plantation. It was the only home she knew; she felt secure in it; she belonged at Blackoaks as much as anyone, white or black.

"I warn you, Rosa-Monday. Put this business out of your mind. I don't want to hear about it again."

His tone rattled the knick-knacks on the mantle. Jeanne d'Arc stared at Baynard, her dark eyes pained and shocked, as though she were looking at a stranger. Bay-

74

nard glimpsed her expression and he winced, but nevertheless he gestured downward curtly, waving them from the room. He could hear Rosa-Monday muttering and sobbing all the way to the kitchen.

The morning star had barely paled in the sky over Blackoaks when the first lamplight showed in the oversized kitchen. Jeanne d'Arc, yawning and sleepy eyed, supervised the cooks, bakers, dishwashers, meat-handlers, scrubbers, maids, and pantry boys. Though she was an *os rouge*—a cross between a black and an Indian—the Negroes loved and accepted her. She was slender, languidly beautiful with black hair severely parted in the middle, her body supple and shapely. Bread dough, which had been rising all night, was kneaded again and placed in the brick ovens to bake—along with rolls, hot buns, and pastries. The hot buns were Jeanne d'Arc's specialty prepared each morning for the elder Baynard. Yeast dough was sprinkled thick with cinnamon, laced with raisins and sometimes with currants or pecans, and spread with drippy sugar icing as soon as the buns came out of the oven.

For these moments in the kitchen, the helpers and others had their only free period until the middle of the afternoon. They lounged around the kitchen table, or on cold days congregated around the huge wood-burning iron stove, talking in guarded whispers, gossiping, drinking coffee with the fresh buns or hot breads.

A country kitchen was the most utilitarian, most unusual, and often the best-managed sector of the big estates like Blackoaks. Jeanne d'Arc's kitchen was larger even than the formal room where the Baynards held dances and entertained. It had a pitcher pump and porcelain sink with direct drain to the ground beneath the kitchen. There was a short stone stairway down to the cooling room built below ground, a walk-in pantry with shelves to the ceiling, all packed tightly with carefully labeled canned and preserved foods, spices, condiments. Next to this was a walk-in broom and mop closet with tubs, buckets, a chamber-pot, which a small black boy emptied several times a day. The boy assigned to carry the honey-pot had the lowliest job on the place.

Stained-wood cupboards were hung about the upper walls along with racks for heavy knives, spoons, ladles, forks of every shape. The drainboard work space on each side of the sink was extra deep as were the cupboards below it. The large, iron wood-burning stove sat out from the wall; in winter at least three or four black children under five slept behind it. Near the oversized screened windows—the paned insets of which were shoved up even in the coldest hour of winter—was the large, scrubbed pinewood table. The two chairs at each end once graced the formal dining room, then the family dining room. On each side were pinewood benches where the helpers ate.

There were three other doors leading out of the large kitchen, one to a narrow stairway to the upper floors, a second that opened into the family dining room and through it to the formal dining room beyond. A screened door, incessantly opening and slamming shut, springs squealing like a scalded cat, led out to the overhung back stoop where the wood was stacked several times a day to stoke the insatiable iron monster.

While the cinnamon buns were still finger-singeing hot, Jeanne d'Arc personally carried a linen-napkin-covered tray of them, along with a silver pot of coffee and cream and a heavy drinking mug, into the second downstairs room, in which a light showed—Baynard's office-den. She found him dressed, shaven, washed up, and already at work on the books. The room had shelves for the books he seldom read. She found that nobody read them any-more except Styles Kenric, and he found them boring and dull. A thick-glassed case housed Baynard's collection of guns. They were one of his passions, along with falconry. She knew he had even taught Miz Claire—at a happier time in their marriage—to use a handgun. He'd been proud of Miz Claire—she had become expert. Jeanne d'Arc hated the guns; she hated what they stood for; she hated what they could do. But she also knew they were almost like a symbol of manhood to her master.

She closed the door behind her, leaning against it until

the lock clicked and he put aside his account books and looked up smiling.

"You look tired," she said.

"No. I'm all right. How do you feel?"

She shrugged.

"No complications? You've recovered, have you—after the baby?"

She smiled in her cool, distant way. "I was recovered —that first morning when you came in to see us."

He bit down on his underlip. Pain flashed across his pale border-Scot eyes. He reached out and covered her slender hand under his on the desk top, holding it gently, but tautly, almost as if clinging to her. She drew a deep breath. "Have you heard anything about Narc or old Obadiah?"

Barnard's mouth tightened and then relaxed. He moved his shoulders in a way that dismissed the subject. "We're not going to hear from them, Jahndark."

Her eyes clouded and brimmed with tears. "Never?"

"Narc is not coming back, Jahndark. Nor is Obadiah. That trader. He needed a strong young boy like Narc. He wanted him badly enough to take old Obadiah. He made me a very generous offer, Jahndark. . . . The way things are, I couldn't have refused—even if I'd wanted to. I'm sorry. They are not coming back."

The tears welled deeper in her black eyes but did not spill. He watched the squared planes of her jaws tighten. She sighed and withdrew her hand from his, but she did not move away from him. "I'm sorry," he said again. She did not reply. The old grandfather clock ticked loudly in the early morning silence.

In this fragile quiet, they could hear the shuffling sound of the field crew moving past toward the planted acreage from the quarters. Bosworth Pilzer, the Dutch overseer, fat bellied, already sweated, slouched in his saddle and brought up the rear of the column. The fieldhands weren't talking among themselves, but the unintelligible sounds they made as they straggled toward the fields were melancholy and troubled, troubling. Jeanne d'Arc called it "lamenting." Then the workers were gone across the plateau to the cotton fields or to the uplands where greening corn stretched mile after mile in precise rows, or into more fallow fields where potatoes and peanut vines were banked in beds because spuds and pinders would grow anywhere. . . .

About three o'clock that afternoon a lightweight carriage, stripped down for speed, painted black and bearing the insignia of the state slave patrollers, raced into the yard. It rolled in its own dust plumes up the incline under the pecan trees and pulled to a stop at the wide front steps. The two patrollers, in their earliest twenties, sun blistered and cocky with arrogance, leaped down from the carriage boot. The patrollers wore black shirts open at the collar, lightweight black slacks and brown boots. Both wore heavy handguns holstered at their belts.

They sent word by a swift-limping Thyestes that they sought Mr. Baynard. By the time Baynard came through the huge front door and across the veranda, the yard was crowded with family and slaves who appeared suddenly from every direction.

"Got somethin' heah for you, Mr. Baynard, suh," the taller patroller said. "Leastwise, she say she's yore nigger —an' she don't say much else."

Baynard's eyes widened with the shock that flared through him, chased by instant rage. He stared at Rosa-Monday trussed in the rear of the buggy along with handcuffs, spancels, shackles, tins of water, and bolted-down rifles. "Rosa-Monday." His voice shook. "My God, what have you done now?"

"Said she was on her way to Elba," the shorter patroller said. He was heavyset, sandy haired, freckled, bullnecked. "Just kept saying that. All we could get out'n her for a long spell. She was on her way to Elba. But it didn't matter where she thought she was going, she hadn't nary no pass to be on the road at all."

"We finally got her to say where she belonged, and we brought her here," the tall officer said. He helped Rosa-Monday to the ground and then unlocked the shackles and cuffs. He tossed them casually into the rear of the buggy. Rosa-Monday stood, slump-shouldered, massaging her wrists. She stared at the ground and would not look up.

"Damn it, Rosa-Monday," Baynard said. "I told you. I won't tolerate behavior like this."

"It's Narc, masta," Rosa-Monday muttered.

"I told you that you could not go to Elba."

"It's Narc, masta. My first born. Oh, I know it's Narc, masta."

"Goddamn it. It's not Narc. You're not going to find Narc. If I thought you could find him, I'd help you. . . . Now, get back to your cabin." Baynard tilted his head and studied the black faces ringing the carriage and set along the drive. "Septimus, you here?"

Rosa-Monday's man stepped forward hesitantly from the crowd. He was a powerfully structured Negro, broad in the shoulders, massive across the chest, wearing denim shirt and onasburg britches. He was deeply ebon, with flat, thick nostrils and wide, full-lipped mouth. He looked as if he had been crying and his voice quavered. "I heah, masta."

Baynard spoke in cold finality. "Take Rosa-Monday to your cabin, Septimus. I don't tell you what to do. That's between you and Rosa-Monday. But, you better understand this—and you better get it into her head somehow —if she runs away again, I won't be responsible for her."

"Yes, suh, Masta Baynard, suh. I understand. I do understand."

"See that she understands. I won't tolerate any more trouble from her. Is that clear?"

"Yes, suh, I most shorely understands, thank you, suh."

"It's Narc," Rosa-Monday whispered. "My first-born. My baby."

Baynard heeled toward her. "I won't have you talking constantly about Narc. He's a grown boy. I won't tolerate it, Rosa-Monday. You're asking for trouble and I hope you understand it this time."

When Septimus led Rosa-Monday through the silent ring of black people, Baynard shrugged as if shaking off a hair shirt. He forced a wide smile toward the two patrollers, a smile that asked them to ignore the rage still darkening his eyes, the tensions jerking at his cheek muscles, the thick vein throbbing at his temple. "Come in and have a drink of my best whiskey before you go back on duty, gentlemen," he said in a tone of forced heartiness. "Thyestes ought to be able to round up a couple gallons of our finest corn whiskey. I'm sure it will be tucked away in the rear of your buggy by the time you've refreshed yourselves, won't it, Thyestes?"

"Shorely, masta. Two gallons of the masta's finest corn whiskey. Yes, suh."

The officers grinned. "Everybody knows they ain't no finer drinkin' liquor in this heah whole state than yours, Mr. Baynard. Why, I'd drink it all the time, if I could afford it," the tall patroller said. "A gift like that. That's mighty generous of you."

"You've done me a great service," Baynard remembered to say. He remembered to smile too.

The rest of the afternoon was quiet. It was a hot day, almost a hundred degrees in the shade, and nothing more than lamb's tail clouds showed on any horizon. The bowl of heaven was faded and empty. Baynard could almost sense the cotton withering sere in the blaze of heat. He paced the long foyer, sipping a cool mint-flavored whiskey and trying to keep Rosa-Monday out of his mind. There was hysterical wailing in Septimus' cabin, but this was deep inside the quarters and the sound didn't carry uphill to the manor house. But the tension remained crackling in the atmosphere, like static in the air moments before a storm.

That tension did not abate even at the Baynard dinner table that night. Morgan stumbled into the dining room, his eyes swollen from crying. Baynard glanced toward the boy and caught his breath raspingly. It was on the tip of his tongue to order Morgan to bed without his supper, but the taut, unsmiling faces of the rest of the family deterred him. Baynard exercised a terrible inner discipline and managed to lower his voice to the gentle tone to which the family was accustomed. They were also cognizant of the fact that he was capable of two totally different voices—quiet, gentle, and filled with laughter when among his friends, family, or equals, those he loved and respected. Less familiar to them, but also in their experience was the harsh, unyielding tone he employed when angered, or issuing orders he expected to be obeyed on the double. They accepted as a part of his total personality that he had matured with only a thinly veiled contempt for those he considered his inferiors. But despite his faults, they had learned to love him devotedly because his innate kindness and charm far outweighed any effects of a fiery temper, stony prejudices, and bullheaded obstinacy when opposed or crossed.

"Narc was Soapy's best friend—his best black friend," Morgan said into his napkin.

"Has that damned Soapy been after you to hound me about Rosa-Monday's boy?" Baynard demanded. "You tell Soapy, Morgan, either he shuts his mouth on the subject, or I'll have Pilzer put the whip to him. I'm not joking, Morgan. I mean this."

"We can't help it, papa," Morgan sobbed. "Me and Soapy. We loved Narc. He made us laugh. All the time. He knew how to make a real bow and arrow. Better'n anybody. We loved Narc, papa."

"You can't love a slave boy," Baynard said. "Try to understand me, Morgan. I'm trying to be kind. I'm trying to be patient. But you must not become attached to the slaves. Things happen. They do go away sometimes. As Narc has gone away."

"Good God," Ferrell-Junior whispered. "You did sell him to that hell train."

Baynard jerked his head around, his eyes agonized. He exhaled as if fighting for breath. He gazed at his older son for a long moment, then he shook his head and spoke instead to Morgan. "Listen to me, son. If you'll be a good old fellow, Morgan, I have a surprise for you—"

"Narc is coming back?"

"Oh, damn it, son. Forget that slave. No . . . you may as well know the truth. Narc is not coming back. . . . I'm getting you a tutor."

Kathy laughed. "You know what a tutor is, Morgan?" she teased.

He hesitated, puzzled, his eyes bleak. Then, "I'm getting

me one." He added in unassailable logic, "Then I'll know."

"Then it'll be too late," Kathy laughed, kissing him lightly.

CHAPTER 8

BAYNARD SPENT a sweated, sleepless night. He prowled his solitary bedroom and thought about Jeanne d'Arc lying in her own bed on the floor above. He felt empty bellied with longing. It was too soon after her child's birth to thrust himself inside her, but this was where he wanted to be with a terrible urgency and fearful longing. Only when he was driven deep into her vagina did he feel fully complete and whole and stronger than God himself. But he couldn't go up to her; he would not force himself upon her. He would wait until she came to him. Then he would know it was all right to mount her, to have her as before. He didn't know when that would be. In the meantime the night was endless, silent and empty—and endless.

There were so many reasons he needed her. She alone could drive away all those ugly imaginings he was prey to without her body pressed close to his. The sure knowledge that he had lost Ferrell-Junior, that things would never be the same between them again; the terrible memory of the moment when the boy had known surely that he'd sold the slaves into inhuman bondage. It was as if Ferrell-Junior's disenchantment showed him most clearly that the only real difference between himself and Baxter Simon, a dehumanized slave breeder, was hypocrisy. Baxter Simon admitted what he was, faced what he did. Ferrell Alexander Baynard lied about it, to the world, to his family, and worst of all, to himself. . . .

But the night that would never end finally ended and morning came on hotter than yesterday, without a promise of rain. The clattering of a buggy racing up the lane through the pecan trees roused family and slaves before ten o'clock. House slaves and family members spilled out onto the columned veranda through the tall French doors with Miz Claire wailing at them to exercise at least a modicum of restraint. "At least a modicum," she cried. "What on earth are people to think of us—that we are backwoods red-necks—running gawking to the yard when company comes?"

But Morgan called over his shoulder from the steps to her as the buggy rattled across the cobbles and halted before him, "Won't nobody think nothing, mama. It's just ole Gil Talmadge and his father."

Gil Talmadge leapt down from the buggy. He ran around it laughing and swung the 200-pound Morgan up easily in his arms. Gil was in his early twenties, built squat and low to the ground. He was about five feet five inches tall, but incredibly muscular. His red hair was so thickly matted with curls that he could hardly work a comb through it, and it grew low in a straight line across his narrow forehead. His freckled face stretched into an unwavering smile, which he played like a spotlight across the Baynards. Only when his gaze reached Kathy did it falter. Gil was an ultimate product of that culture which held that women belonged in two classes—good women, who were elevated to an untouchable status, except perhaps on a wedding night and the first week or so of a honeymoon—and women nobody had to respect. The kind of woman who loved to fuck. This attitude simplified life for Gil—he had yet to discover an exception to his rule. However, his attitude did restrict his easy nature around Miss Kathy—she was an untouchable, plus the fact that she was so fragilely lovely he hesitated even to gaze at her directly.

"My good Lord," Kathy whispered to Styles at her side. "And once I thought that clown was cute."

Styles frowned her into silence, peering down at her along his patrician nose.

Gil bowed toward Miz Claire and then directed his attention where it had been headed all the time. He admired Ferrell-Junior more than any other man alive, including his own father. He wanted to please Ferrell-Junior and wasn't sure just how to achieve this. Most of all he wanted his attention, his approval. "Hey theah, Ferrell-Junior!" He doubled his fist and struck Ferrell-Junior hard on the bicep. "Hey theah, boy! How you been? Where you been keepin' yourself, Ferrell-Junior? Been in town to Avery's Tavern lately?" He struck him again, grinning. "When you and me goin' coon-huntin' again, Ferrell-Junior?"

Gil's father was as unlike his son as it was possible to be; one might even have believed Fletcher Talmadge accomplished this through some deal with the gods. Prematurely gray, his thinning hair was peppered with a memory of faded brown. He was well over six feet tall, winter thin and almost reticently retiring. A courtly man in a freshly pressed broadcloth suit lightened only by a fresh carnation in his lapel, he shook hands solemnly with each member of the family, smiled warmly at the gaping house slaves, and recalled each of them by name. They giggled and lowered their gazes, pleased and excited by his attention. Last, he bent over Miz Claire's fragile hand, touching its almost transparent flesh with the tips of his carefully trimmed mustache. Then he straightened, smiling down at her. "I recall often and most warmly, Miz Claire, how devotedly I once loved you."

She laughed coquettishly. "I have many lovely memories, Fletcher, and more of them than I ought to admit are brightened by your gallant face."

Fletcher Talmadge held her fingers a moment longer. Then the elder Baynard invited him into his study to sample the quality of an aged batch of his special liquor. Fletcher smiled around at the others. "I trust you'll forgive me if I depart into the study with unseemly haste. There's only one place to find the finest, smoothest whiskey to caress a man's palate—and I managed to make it alive one more time despite the fact that I incautiously permitted my son to handle the horses."

Baynard and Fletcher Talmadge talked a long time in the study over Baynard's whiskey and well water. Most of the slaves, Kathy, and Miz Claire returned into the house. Styles remained on the veranda but stayed aloof from

85

the others watching Gil as a scientist might study an unusual specimen in its natural habitat.

Morgan and Soapy found Gil rowdy, bawdy, and fascinating. They followed every move he made, grinning and wide-eyed. Morgan struggled to attract and hold Gil's attention. "Hey, Gil, papa's gettin' me a tutor, Gil."

Gil glanced toward the boy and laughed. "That's great, Morg." Then he shrugged and frowned, puzzled. Laughing, he clipped Ferrell-Junior hard on the arm again. "What's the hell's a tutor?"

Gil couldn't keep his hands off Ferrell-Junior. It was the only way he felt sure he had Ferrell-Junior's attention, by physically assaulting him. "Hey, Ferrell-Junior, how you like them horses of mine? New pair papa bought me. Had them sent down by wagon from Tennessee. They make the girls turn around and look at me, all right." He laughed and pounded Ferrell-Junior on the arm. "How about it, Ferrell-Junior, ain't they no wenches you and me could git down to the creek for a quick swim and a fast fucking?"

"I'm afraid not, Gil."

"Papa'd kill you, Gil," Morgan said.

"You mean you don't pester teenaged wenches around here? That's the best poontang in the world. Sweet. And tight. And close to the bone. Umm. Hmm. Yes, ma'am!" He swung his arm, fist doubled again, but Ferrell-Junior side-stepped it. "You let the black bucks skim off that sweet cream?"

Ferrell-Junior smiled, shrugging. "If they want it—and most of them do."

Gil lunged at him, leading with his left, and swinging wildly with his right. "Don't be a fuckin' hypocrite with me, Ferrell-Junior. You know you crawl them wenches every chance you get. Remember that time you stayed a spell over to our place? We got our share of black ass that time, didn't we?" Then he laughed. "Maybe you don't want Styles or Morgan to know, huh? Hey, Styles, you ride a black wench now and then, don't you?"

Styles didn't bother to reply.

Gil laughed loudly. He danced around Ferrell-Junior on his toes, the way he'd seen black fighters doing in

New Orleans, feinting, parrying, lunging forward. "Hell, don't eat my ass if Styles Kenric lies to me. He comes from a long line of college-educated hypocrites. The Kenrics of Winter Hill. Holy shit. How much snottier can you get than that?" He shrugged, pretending to think it over. "Hell, maybe they don't fuck over at Winter Hill. Maybe they don't even fart."

"Everybody farts, Gil," Morgan said, laughing with him. "Papa said so. Even ladies fart." Morgan and Soapy giggled, wrestling with each other to hide their embarrassment at facing out loud this undeniable but shocking fact.

Baynard and Fletcher Talmadge came out through the front doorway. They crossed the veranda and walked down the steps to the buggy. "Come on, Gil," Fletcher said. He took up the reins and nodded toward the rear.

"You better come along too, Ferrell-Junior," Baynard said, getting into the carriage beside Fletcher Talmadge.

Ferrell-Junior sat beside Gil in the buggy tonneau, their booted legs hanging over. Gil hung his arm heavily over Ferrell-Junior's shoulders. Soapy and Morgan trotted behind the buggy. Fletcher turned the light carriage on the driveway and prodded the horses down the incline toward the quarters.

Ferrell-Junior felt sick at the pit of his stomach with a premonition of terrible wrong, even before the elder Talmadge headed the buggy into the quarters.

Ferrell-Junior swallowed back the bile that boiled up into his throat, hot and sickening. He was aware of Morgan and Soapy, trotting behind them, of his father and Fletcher Talmadge sitting in cold silence on the buggy seat, of Gil shouting in his ear to make himself heard over the clatter of the buggy on the rocky incline. He did not listen to Gil. It didn't matter. Gil was satisfied and happy as long as he had his captive attention, or believed he did.

Ferrell-Junior gripped the sides of the buggy with all his strength, afraid he was going to vomit when the carriage was halted outside the whitewashed shack where Rosa-Monday and Septimus lived with their eight children, all of them under fourteen.

Gil leaped from the carriage as Morgan and Soapy ran

up to it, breathless, sagging on the pine-slab steps, panting, their mouths open.

Baynard and Talmadge swung down from the buggy. Baynard frowned. "What are you doing here, Morgan? If I'd wanted you down here, I'd have invited you. You and Soapy get back to the big house. Immediately."

Morgan loitered; he had scarcely any memory of his father's punishing him or denying him anything; he could not understand the way he had changed lately. But Soapy knew better than to openly disobey or defy Master Baynard. The two boys retreated, backing away into their shadows until the older men went up the slab steps and knocked on the door. Then they crept into the stingy shade afforded by a neighboring shack and crouched, watching.

Ferrell-Junior got slowly out of the buggy and leaned against the porch flooring. He stared up at his father, aware only of the widening gulf between them, the terrible loss of faith and respect that was tearing him apart inside. Once he had trusted his father unquestioningly. Now, he found himself unable to believe anything anymore—a beginning of a melancholy wisdom.

Rosa-Monday opened the door surrounded by her brood.

"Get what belongings you want to take with you, Rosa-Monday," Baynard said without preface.

"Where I going, masta?"

"Mr. Talmadge and his son. They need a cook—someone to run their kitchen. They've kindly agreed to give you that position on my recommendation. I've sold you to Mr. Talmadge, Rosa-Monday."

"Oh, Gawd, no."

"I don't want any trouble, Rosa-Monday. Get your things together."

She shook her head. "My man. Septimus. He workin'. Cain't no way go 'way without my man Septimus, masta. . . . Oh, Gawd, I cain't go no way. This heah is my home, masta. I born here. It's all I know."

"We'll be good to you, Rosa-Monday," Fletcher Talmadge said. "My wife is dead. You'll help me run the house—and you'll be entirely in charge of our kitchen."

"They needed an excellent cook, Rosa-Monday," Baynard said in a kindly yet coldly firm tone. "One as fine as Jahndark. I told them there was none more qualified than you, Rosa-Monday. Nobody bakes sweet-yam pies better than you."

"I dearly dote on sweet-yam pie," Talmadge said. "Get your things. Anything you want to take."

Rosa Monday looked around wildly. "Where's Septimus? Dear Gawd. Septimus got to go too. Septimus got to go with me."

"Septimus is not going, Rosa-Monday. They've got enough blacks over at Felicity Manor."

"The good lord knows we got too many," Talmadge said. "I'm sorry, Rosa-Monday. We can't afford to buy a buck we don't need."

"You take your suckling, Rosa-Monday, and any of your children that are under five plantings old," Baynard said. "That's the law. The others stay here."

Rosa-Monday grabbed the doorjamb, screaming hysterically. She laid her head back, wailing. Women, children, and frightened dogs came running from the adjacent cabins. Men strode up the path from the workshops. Septimus was among them. When he saw the carriage parked before his shack, recognized Rosa-Monday's hysterical wailing, he ran, but then slowed and stopped, impotently, at the rear of the carriage.

Baynard caught the screaming woman by the arms and forcibly pulled her away from the door framing. He caught her arm and twisted it up her back. When Rosa-Monday went on screaming, Baynard wadded up his bandana and crammed it into her mouth and stifled her screams. She struggled, shaking violently, bent over with her head almost touching the floor.

In a regretful tone, Talmadge spoke to his son. "Best get them cuffs and spancels from the buggy, Gil."

Gil leaped to respond. He ran up the steps with the chains and metal manacles. He snapped the cuffs on Rosa-Monday's wrists though her arms were twisted up between her shoulder blades. Then he caught Rosa-Monday's arms roughly and half-dragged her down the steps. She stumbled, fell to her knees, refused to get up. She was screaming mindlessly now, like an animal. Her frantic eyes found Ferrell-Junior. He winced under her pleading gaze, his queasiness turning to nausea. He felt impelled to stop this evil—Gil's handling her as if she were no more than a snarling bitch—but he did not move. He wanted to yell at his father to come to his senses, but he knew he couldn't do that either. These men treated Rosa-Monday as if she were an animal, because to them she was an animal. If he wanted to be accepted by them, he had to learn to think and act and react as they did. Everything his father and his friends had tried to instill in him told him he should be ashamed of his weakness, his lack of manhood. What his father and his friends were doing here was a simple matter of everyday business, an accepted part of their culture—of his culture. His seeing it as heartless abuse of an agonized woman in front of her screaming babies was only a sign of his own weakness, his own unworthiness. He did not meet Rosa-Monday's terrified gaze. He couldn't do that either.

Rosa-Monday's eyes moved on to Septimus. He had to help her. He loved her. He had shared her bed for the past fifteen years. She had tended him in sickness, borne his children, loved only him. He could not stand by and let them drag her away. She tried to speak through the bandana wadded in her mouth. She pleaded unintelligibly with him, but the big man stood helplessly, transfixed with grief and terror. He loved Rosa-Monday more than his own life and he hated to the deepest cranny of his guts what these white men were doing to her. But he recognized that he was Master Baynard's property, as was Rosa-Monday, chattel to be consigned as the white man decreed. He could agonize, he could weep inside, but he couldn't act overtly against what was a nigger's condign fate. His eyes blurred with tears and he felt as if he were being whipped until his flesh was torn and raw. He wanted to help Rosa-Monday. But he knew better. He could get himself killed, and he didn't care about this, but there was nothing he could do that would help her in the least.

Baynard strode down the steps. With Gil's enthusiastic assistance, he hoisted Rosa-Monday into the rear of the buggy. "Best put shackles on her ankles, Gil," Fletcher Talmadge advised from the porch. "She'll be fine—jes' fine—once we get her over to Felicity Manor and settled. Meantime, no sense in letting her run away."

Baynard studied the six small children crying helplessly on the slab steps. He took up the smallest, a crawler in a rag diaper and placed it in the carriage beside its mother. Then he chose three more which he reckoned to be under five years old. In this way, he complied with the law. The six-year-old was unable to speak through its sobbing. It fell heavily from the steps and lay in the dirt, crying helplessly. The next older child knelt over the prostrate tot and laid her hand lightly on its head, caressing it absently.

"We best get on home," Fletcher Talmadge decided, coming down the steps into the blaze of sunlight. "The woman and her suckers will be fine onct we get 'em on home. Come on, Gil. Get in the buggy. No sense hanging around and asking for trouble."

Septimus took one involuntary step toward the moving carriage and then stopped. Ferrell-Junior sank to the ground beside the two children. He placed his arm about the quivering shoulders of the older girl, but he did not speak. There were no words, nothing he could say to her.

The other slaves stood in stunned silence as Gil laid the buggy whip across the rumps of his Tennessee specials, racing them up the stony incline. The elder Baynard jerked his head toward Ferrell-Junior. His son got to his feet slowly and walked beside him along the path. The slaves gazed at them, unbelieving, filled with sudden unnamed apprehensions. Some strange, unknown god had abruptly struck at the peaceful and unbroken security of their lives and but for the grace of those fearful gods, it was one of them carted away in chains in some stranger's van. Perhaps tomorrow it would be their turn. They shrank back, widening the path for the two white men.

"She'll be all right," Baynard said, half to himself. He glimpsed Morgan and Soapy standing transfixed beside a whitewashed cabin. He reached out, gesturing toward Morgan, inviting the boy into the protective circle of his arm. But Morgan stared at him, his eyes wild, then he

91

turned suddenly and loped away between the shacks, running toward the hammock and the creek beyond it. Soapy hesitated a moment and then followed. "Let them go," Baynard said in a tired, sick voice. "They'll get over it."

"Sure. We'll all get over it," Ferrell-Junior said in a chilled, lost tone. "We finally had to admit the truth. You did what we knew you couldn't ever do. You sold Narc and Obadiah to that monster Shivers—but we got over it. Or we will—sometime."

Baynard's voice hardened. "Did Jahndark tell you I sold those slaves to Shivers?"

"My God, papa, nobody had to tell me." Ferrell-Junior spread his hands, frustrated, unable to reach his father across that widening gulf. "All I need is somebody to tell me why."

"I'll tell you why, son. Because I believed it was best. Because I believed it had to be done."

"And Rosa-Monday wouldn't let you forget, would she?" Ferrell-Junior's voice shook. "Are you going to sell off everyone who reminds you of what you did to Narc and Obadiah?"

Baynard did not reply.

Ferrell-Junior smiled tautly, without mirth. "You can't do it, you know, papa. I think it's against the law to sell me."

"My God, son. Wait. Try to understand. Don't turn against me."

Ferrell-Junior's eyes filled with sudden tears. "I don't want to turn against you, papa. Most of all, I don't want you to turn me against you! I never wanted to turn against you. I never believed I could."

"Can't you trust me? Is that too much to ask?" Baynard swung his arm in a helpless gesture. "I'm thinking of only one thing, son. What's best for this farm, for Blackoaks, for all of us."

"None of us would ask you to do the things you've done, papa. We never have sold Negroes before. We don't have to sell them."

"I do what I have to do."

"That's what Baxter Simon said, papa. He cut out a

slave child's tongue because he *had* to." Ferrell-Junior stopped walking at the crest of the incline, some yards from the side entrance to the manor house. The elder Baynard paused, watching him, but Ferrell-Junior did not speak. Finding nothing to say and no excuse to remain, Baynard walked across the yard and went through a French door, which he closed behind him.

Ferrell-Junior glared around the sunstruck yard, feeling lost, not knowing what to do, where to turn. He could think only that he did not want to lose the strong devotion between himself and his father—a faith and love that had directed and informed his entire existence, until now. It was more than simply seeing his father was only mortal, with feet of clay. He saw the evil in him—evil he had never even suspected and which discolored every thought he had. It was as if his father had not walked away across a narrow plot of glass, but rather had crossed a wide gulf that stretched interminably between them— a gulf that could only widen, but could never be recrossed. He shivered in the blaze of sunlight and heeled around, going to find Morgan.

CHAPTER 9

JEANNE D'ARC came at last to Baynard's bedroom.

In the deepest silence after midnight his *os rouge* concubine opened his door just enough to sidle through like a wraith or lovely houri in some heated fantasy. Thank God, he wasn't dreaming. The huge old brass key was turned stealthily and the lock plunged into its socket.

She caught her cotton nightdress in both hands at her waist and pulled the bulky garment over her head, removing it and tossing it behind her in one swift, fluid movement before she reached his bed. She stood naked in the faint moonlight.

He extended his arms. "Oh, God, Jahndark, I've waited so long."

"I know. It's been hell for me too."

"I've wanted you so desperately, even when I've known better."

"It's all right. I'm here now."

"Yes. Thank God, you're here now."

She crawled up on the high, thick mattress on her hands and knees. Her full breasts tipped with moonlight, were suspended like deep brown clusters and he reached for them greedily as she fell forward against him. She lay with the full length of her heated body pressed against his body, feeling his hardness probing against her thighs. For some moments he caressed and fondled her, as if getting to know her again after a long, enforced separation, recalling her rigid nipples, the full roundness of her breasts, the warmth at the nape of her neck, the hot liquid wetness at her thighs. She lay still, accepting his caresses, responding hotly. Her lips parted, her red tongue pushed between them, she kissed his mouth and along his chin, his adam's apple, the lobe of his ear. She closed her fingers over his on her breasts. "They're all full of milk," she said. "They hurt they're so full."

"We've got to be careful, Jahndark. You mustn't get pregnant again. I can't stand it away from you."

"You forgot to be careful."

"You make it impossible."

"Yes. I try to. Because you want me to."

His hand moved down across the rounded planes of her belly, the muscles weakened by pregnancy, the heap of fatty flesh rising where once she'd been so tautly flat. "I'm getting fat," she whispered. "I'm afraid you won't want me anymore."

"Oh God. I'll die wanting you. That bothers me most —that I'll die—wanting you. Unable to get to you."

"I'm here. I'm always here."

"Yes. That's the way it's got to be. From now on."

His fingers moved into the crisp black triangle of hair padding her mons veneris, slipped down between the full, wetly hot lips to her clitoris, which stood marble rigid, mobile under his fingers. His breath hurt in his throat. "Are you sure—you're well enough?"

"We've waited long enough. Too long."

"I don't want to hurt you."

"I think it's all right," she said. Her hand caught his stiffened rod and worked it with a kind of frenzied gentleness. "You can't stand this," she whispered. "I'll go down on you."

"What about you, Jahndark?"

"It's all right. Just hold me. You can make me come a dozen times—with your hand."

"I want it. I love it. But it doesn't seem the same."

"I love it too. I want it. I want it all."

His heart thudded and he felt his staff grow tauter in her hand, engorged with fresh flooding of blood. She slipped down along his body, tracing her tongue across his paps, over the muscled ridge of his belly. She lay her head on his stomach and opened her mouth. He thrust her forward roughly and she took it between her teeth and deep inside, her hot mouth closing, nursing.

His quivering hands closed in her long black hair. His breathing rasped across his opened lips, and it was as if all the sensation in his body was suddenly concentrated in her sucking mouth. "Wait," he pleaded. "Please wait."

She withdrew her head with a faint whimper, staring up at him in the darkness.

"I can't help it, Jahndark. I've got to have it in you."

"I want you to." She rolled over on her back and lay with her knees bent, her legs spread wide. She extended her arms, pulling him down upon her.

He thrust himself into her vagina, gasping. "I have to be in you, Jahndark. Deep in you. Only then—only then —I know you're mine."

"I'm yours. Forever. Harder. Do it. Harder."

His hips battered, flogging her. He heard as if from great distance her soft moans, felt her legs encase his waist, her ankles lock fiercely at his back. He could scarcely breathe; for that instant he felt as if his heart stopped. He was conscious only of the fearful beating of the pulses in his temples. He thrust himself up into her as deeply as he could and lay still, gasping for breath. He had difficulty speaking. "If I ever die—like this—" he tried to laugh "—doing it to you—"

"Oh, you won't—"

"If I do, you walk away from me . . . don't worry about me then . . . no sense in your being mixed up in it."

She shivered slightly. "No sense—anybody knowing— what—we've been doing—all these years."

He drove himself into her as hard as he could, pleasing her and punishing her in the same instant. He worked his hips faster and her head rolled back and forth on the bed and she whispered in a muted ecstasy, "I'm sorry . . . I didn't mean it . . . I didn't mean it."

"You're my life, Jahndark," he panted. "I couldn't live without you. You know that."

"I know that." Her own hips flailed upward in a savage rhythm, matching his, increasing the tempo, faster, faster until they lunged together with a ferocity that was more like hatred than love, more like a wish to destroy than to share, a totally unbridled passion.

She sagged beneath him, spent, and felt the full weight of his 230 pounds lowered in helpless exhaustion upon her. She opened her eyes and in a flash of panic bit back a scream.

The panic and fear flared through her. Victim of ancient superstitions of her peoples, she thought in terror that she and Baynard had been cast into hell. The room was brilliantly, garishly lit with an unearthly red. Deepest shadows were pools of fiery reds. Fingers of scarlet played like demons across the ceiling in terrorizing patterns. And now she could hear people running and calling to each other in the house and in the distance the frightful screams—fire, fire, fire. . . .

Baynard lunged away from her, his crimson-shadowed face stricken. He leaped from the bed, grabbing at his trousers. Fists pounded on the locked door. Ferrell-Junior's voice shook the walls. "Papa! Are you in there? Papa! Fire! In the quarters!"

"Get down there," Baynard ordered. "I'll get there at once. Get them started with the buckets—save what you can."

They heard the pound of Ferrell-Junior's boots as he ran along the upper corridor and down the wide staircase. Baynard sagged for a helpless moment against the thick mahogany bedpost, breathing raggedly.

Jeanne d'Arc sat up, naked, on the bed. "Are you all right?"

He nodded and fought his feet into the boots, watching the light from the fire play across her bare flesh. He felt that trembling need start inside him again. "You stay here. I don't know when I'll be back, but I want you to stay here."

"Yes."

The fire made liquid pools of red shadows of her eyes. He caught her hands in his and pressed them against his face, then strode from the room, buttoning his shirt as he went. . . .

Septimus' shack was a blazing inferno by the time Baynard ran down the hill to the quarters. The total population of the slave settlement was routed out in various stages of undress. Bosworth Pilzer was there from his fieldstone cottage on the knoll beyond the quarters. He had the bucket brigade in two lines and functioning smoothly. His Dutch voice roared above the flames.

He ran forward when he recognized Baynard. He shook his leonine head. "We can't save the shack, Mr. Baynard. I got them niggers wettin' down everything on both sides —to save what we can."

Baynard nodded, but he felt numb and he stared toward Septimus' shack, which suddenly imploded, the cypress shingled roofing sinking into itself and feeding the blaze. Through the crash of timbers and explosion of the fires a screaming raging could be heard above the thunder of the flames. The sound came from within the blazing shack. Baynard stared, shuddering.

"Septimus," Bos Pilzer said.

"He is in that shack?"

"Yes. We tried to save him. Might have. Before the fire got out of hand. Got up on the porch. Hotter than the hole beyond hell. Fire already spewing out the windows . . . but the door—was barred. We couldn't believe it either—at first. We kept yelling to him that we'd get him out. And all the time he was screaming in there. Just as he is now. And by Jesus—we couldn't batter that door in—and we had to back off, the fire was too bad."

Baynard felt as if his underpinning had been knocked from under him, as if he were going to fall, simply sag to the ground because his legs would no longer support him. He looked about the quarters, lit like high noon by the blaze of fire. He stumbled to the nearest slab steps and sat down, staring sickly up at his overseer. "My God, Pilzer. He's killed himself."

Pilzer winced. "A hell of a way to die—even on purpose. Takes guts I know I ain't got."

Baynard nodded but did not speak. He knew the truth, it had taken more guts than Septimus had to go on living as he had to without Rosa-Monday. He wanted to cry aloud in protest, in agony, but there were no tears either. It was as if the fierce intensity of the fire boiled the tears from his eyes. He slumped on the steps watching the buckets being passed along the lines of black people, the ineffectual sprays of water dashed against the walls and roofing on both sides of Septimus' burning cabin. The flames fed on themselves, consumed themselves, finally weakening, lowering, graying. Baynard did not move. Septimus' screams and wild raging sobs rose from the charred shack long after he should have been dead. . . .

CHAPTER 10

AN ATMOSPHERE of malaise settled like a miasma over Blackoaks. . . .

Styles awoke with a hard-on. He lay taut, flat on his back and kept his eyes tightly closed. It was asinine, of course, but he was afraid Kathy might awaken and read in his guilt-shadowed eyes the lingering memory of the dream that had affected him so profoundly. Though he was fully awake, the dream remained clearly defined in his mind. Wasn't this unusual? Didn't most dreams ordinarily dissipate like the gossamer wisps of which they were compounded? He stirred slightly, disquieted. Had it been totally a sleeping dream—or had he lain, victim to half-waking hallucination?

The dream had begun as a wish-fulfillment of a long-held desire to administer the business affairs of Blackoaks efficiently and profitably, as they were obviously not being handled presently. Baynard could smile and conceal his concern. But Styles was a Kenric of Winter Hill—a life experience of feinting with the creditors, stalling the mortgagors, robbing Peter to pay Paul, stretching every available dollar to delay the moment of inevitable collapse. He had seen that collapse coming from the earliest moment of his awareness; yet, somehow he had made it through the university. He alone of the entire family here at Blackoaks understood why Baynard had sold first Narcissus and Obadiah to the slave trader and then broken up Septimus and Rosa-Monday when old

Talmadge needed a cook-housekeeper. Only Baynard's faint but unquenchable hope of breeding Blade and Moab to some as yet undiscovered, unpurchased Fulani wench had kept him from grasping at the incredible offer of 10,000 in gold Baxter Simon had made for Blade. What a gut-twisting conflict must have roiled inside Baynard: the fearful need for money, the fabulous offer in cash, against what? A groundless hope that Baynard could not discard.

The dream had started on this high plane but had quickly sunk into a heated mire that troubled Styles, even while it intoxicated him. Was he losing his mind? Why such thoughts that he had never even permitted into his consciousness before? His thoughts strayed and he felt his breath quicken. New freshets of blood boiled into his distended staff. An ache of painful pleasure suffused his body from his loins to his temples. The memory of Bax Simon and the aborted deal for Blade brought his thought associations full circle—to the way he and Simon had handled the slave's extraordinary genitals, the way his mind had clouded out, blotting out time, place, bystanders, the passions roused by his grasping Blade's rigidity in his fist.

His face grew heated and he stirred uncomfortably. Kathy whispered, "Styles?"

He caught his breath, suffused with sudden sharp impatience. He pretended to be asleep. The morning sunlight lanced through his eyelids. He forced himself to breathe regularly, as if he were sleeping. He felt Kathy turn toward him on the bed, felt the roundness of her full breasts on his bare arm with only the mayfly-fragile fabric of her gown covering them. He closed his mind to her, wanting to pull away from her touch. That sick-sweet dream still impelled his thoughts; he couldn't escape its powerful hold on him; he didn't want to.

Waking, he'd felt that old ingrained sense of guilt, the puritanically taught need to deny that he'd dreamed heatedly of fingering Blade in the privacy of this room with the doors locked. Now, his pulses racing, he felt no such inhibition. His first interest was in perfecting the Fulani bloodline, wasn't it? He wanted to find a Fulani woman with which to mate Blade and Moab. This was the true route to great riches—the kind of fortune Baxter Simon's family had amassed out in Mississippi. In his dream, he'd been making progress toward the accomplishment of his commendable goal. But here the motivation grew fuzzy. In his fantasy he had ordered Blade up here, locked the door, and commanded the slave, in Baxter Simon's words, to "shuck down." From there the sexually oriented images heated to unendurably guilty and passionate depravity. He saw himself milking down Blade's rigid penis at his leisure and, under the avowed pretext of testing its fluidity, he saw incredible, unbelievable visions of himself going to his knees, taking the great penis in his mouth. . . . He shook his head, sweated, anguished, repelled, and transfixed. All these overwhelming and forbidden *tableaux vivants* whirling inside his mind that he would have died before he admitted aloud, and yet couldn't deny or erase from his thoughts.

He felt Kathy stir against him. She pressed her parted legs upon his hips so the rounded eminence of her tumescent mons veneris caressed him like fevered lips. Her hand slid across his stomach. He heard her astonished and gratified gasp as she caught his upright tool in her fist. Her breath struck his face hotly. He drew away from her. "Don't," he said. "You're as forward as a whore."

She caught her breath sharply. "I wish I were a whore! Maybe you'd pay attention to me then."

He tried to draw away from her touch. "I won't have you talking like a common tart."

Her voice sagged, quavering. "What do you want of me, Styles? I beg you. I try to excite you, try to be what you want. What do you want?"

"I don't want anything."

Her fingers closed tighter on him, but they both felt him go flaccid under her grasp. "Styles, please. Don't you love me?"

"I'm married to you, Kathy. We've been married almost three years. I see no reason for you to act like a stupid bride on her wedding night."

"Why did you marry me?"

His jaw hardened. He knew why he had married her,

all right. She had been a most important facet in the plan for his successful life—the life of a gentleman planter of the South, much as Jefferson had lived—with servants, money, leisure, surrounded by creature comforts. He'd had a plethora of the genteel poverty that had been a way of life at Winter Hill. He had determined early to possess great wealth; marrying it was the easiest course he knew. He'd been the handsomest man in his class at the university, voted so by his peers. He'd also been one of the least popular, but there had been no open poll on this. He had taken a certain pride in knowing he was hated as a snob; no law required that he endure inferiors, and he found many of these in the school. He had set the pattern for his future achievements while at the university. There he had the best of everything; he had been driven by a compulsion to excel, to be first in all competition. He planned to marry the most beautiful girl—he would marry into a wealthy family; he would find one of those rare females with both prerequisites, great beauty and great wealth. He would, through his own mental superiority— and the sure sense that he was indeed one of God's chosen—increase those fortunes thus afforded. Well, it hadn't worked out that way.

He'd first seen Kathy Baynard laughing across the dance floor at a Governor's Independence Day Ball at Montgomery. There had been no doubt from the first instant; she exceeded his first requirement—she was the most beautiful girl he had ever seen. The huge hall buzzed with whispers about the fragilely, blondly lovely little Kathy Baynard, approving, envious, astonished. Astonished? She was that lovely; her laughter dimmed the crystal chandelier. His inquiry elicited the information that Kathy Baynard's father was well known, highly regarded around the state—and extremely wealthy: land, cotton, slaves, timber, and an exceptionally good-tasting whiskey, which he sold in huge casks to commercial vendors.

Well, it had been a mésalliance, that was all. He had married beneath him. On his honeymoon, he had realized that her beauty—a body the hue of fresh new peaches, touched at the pelvic triangle by a red-gold

103

fabric of soft hair—was not enough to arouse him, or excite him enough to satisfy her. In those weeks he had difficulty in responding to her loving ministrations. He took refuge in a sarcastic fault-finding that dissolved her into helpless tears and relieved his obligation to copulate with her. He told her mordantly that it seemed to him she thought of little else except sex and that he found this somehow disgusting, common, and even repulsive. He preferred to pursue, he said, he preferred to have her behave like a lady, as difficult as this might be. He discovered an impelling, erotic need to degrade and debase her. At first, he was able to grow tautly rigid when he was forcing her into anal copulation, fellatio, or flagellation. If he hurt her in some way so that she cried out, he grew hotly excited and responsive. This did not last. Kathy wanted what he wanted, no matter how much it hurt her physically, or should have—in his view—abased her as a gentlewoman. There was nothing ugly or unacceptable to Kathy in their relations—no matter what he forced her to do. And force was the operative word in his algolagnia. If he didn't have to force her into what he considered deviate sex acts, if he didn't in some way humble her or inflict pain, he derived no pleasure, was unable to respond or perform.

Perhaps half a dozen times in their three years of marriage, Kathy had thought she was pregnant and she was ecstatic. When her period was only delayed and she menstruated, she wept inconsolably.

Styles spoke to her in withering disparagement. She was convinced that if she could bear Styles a son they would be happy together, he would love her again. He let her believe this, because he honestly didn't know what might alter their relationship. But he accepted the weaponry she provided him. He belittled her because she could not bear him a son. He wore sarcasm and disapprobation as a shield against her loving advances. He disdained her love of dancing, horse-back riding, partying, swimming, and picnicking, as flighty, stupidly childish, and completely bourgeois. She didn't even know what that meant, except that it implied contempt. She tried to read to please him, but books were not a habit with her, and she grew bored.

She had run free on the plantation all her life, playing with the black children until she was eleven. She loved people, excitement, physical activity. "Talking with you is like conversing with a child," Styles often told her. "And not a very bright child."

"Tell me what to do, Styles," she pleaded helplessly now. "All I want to do is to please you. Please tell me."

"Let me alone. For a start. Why don't you behave like other married women? They don't expect a hothouse romantic honeymoon atmosphere all the time."

"All the time? When? When do you love me, Styles? When do you ever want me? And those fool women you pretend to admire, such hypocrites! Too nice to let their husbands touch them. Maybe they don't love their husbands as I love you, Styles. I've loved you since the very first moment I ever laid eyes on you. Is it something shameful? Well, I'm not ashamed! I saw you across that ballroom floor and I felt all empty and scared and happy inside—like the night before Christmas, when you want everything, and are not sure you'll get anything at all. I knew if I didn't have you, I didn't want anyone."

"That's very pretty. Very penny novel. But it's time you grew up, Kathy."

She choked back tears. "What does growing up mean to you, Styles?"

"Accepting life as it is. Seeing that there is no over-heated flowery romance between us anymore—"

"Was there ever?" she demanded.

"Well, there isn't now. That's what you've got to grow up and face."

"Maybe you ought to grow up, Styles." She was crying now, in anger, not self-pity. "Maybe you ought to realize I've given you all my love with everything that's in me—and when I take it away, it'll be the same—I'll hate you with everything in me."

Styles' mouth twisted into an ironic smile. "How I look forward with longing to that day of peace and quiet —and respectability."

"Is that what my life is to be, Styles? Denied, rejected, empty? Oh, God, Styles, I'm twenty years old. I was made to love—I was made to be loved." She sobbed helplessly.

He spoke in a low, cutting whisper. "Will you shut up that stupid sobbing, Kathy? Whatever our problem, it's between us—"

"I don't have any problem," she sobbed. "You have the problem. I'm not ashamed to cry. I love you. I don't give a damn who knows it."

She wept helplessly, sitting up in bed, her face splotched, eyes swollen and red, her nose running. "Oh, God, help me," she sobbed. She saw herself—in all the hot, empty succession of days—restless, unhappy, lost. She understood now that silent resignation and tight-lipped frustration she saw in the faces of so many young wives she knew.

And yet, was it the same at all? If any of these miserable young women spoke of their married lives, it was in the same despairing tone—the brutal, brutish demands of insensitive men. These men didn't reject their wives, they were demanding, sex driven. Would God this were her problem. But Styles didn't want her. She couldn't make him want her. Nothing she could do could rouse him enough so that he could satisfy her—or reach an orgasm for himself. She saw him daily grow to hate her when she forced herself upon him, and yet she could not live without his caresses. He didn't want her. What did he want? If only there were some way she could know.

But Styles wouldn't talk to her about it, and there was no one else to discuss it with, no one to whom she could mention her misery, her doubts, her ignorance, her needs, her failure as Styles' wife. She did not know where her faults and her failures lay. God knew she loved Styles with all her heart and mind and honest passion. She did not dissemble, or attempt to hide her devotion. There was nothing she would not do to please him. Yet nothing about her pleased him.

She cried out, "I feel as if I am chained, Styles, unable to do anything—for you, or for myself. . . . I could be freed from this terrible paralysis of will if I could only know what you really are like inside—what you really want—from me, from yourself."

Styles laughed in contempt. "Free? Is that what you want? To be free? And what would you do if you were free?"

She shivered, hugging her arms across her breasts. "I don't know, Styles. Leave. Stay. Love you. Hate you. I don't know."

Styles swung out of bed, sweated and raging inwardly. His voice was savage, but icily under control. "Pull yourself together, Kathy. That's my advice to you. You sound like a sex-crazed black wench, not a respectable young white married woman."

"I'm not respectable," she sobbed. "Damn you. Don't you understand? I'm me. Me. Me."

Styles finished dressing, taking his time. He checked himself in the full-length mirror and splashed cologne on his face and scrubbed his hands together until the chilled liquid evaporated. Kathy lay on the bed, watching him desolately.

He walked to the corridor door, glanced over his shoulder. He spoke without the faintest trace of interest in his voice. "Are you coming down to breakfast?"

"I'm not hungry."

He shrugged. Then, "Shall I have Jeanne d'Arc send up a tray?"

"They don't put what I want on trays."

His handsome face tightened in chilled disapproval and he braced his wide, slender shoulders against her. He stepped through the door and closed it sharply after himself, expressing his extreme distaste for her hoydenish behavior.

Styles went down the steps, adjusting his cuffs, shrugging his freshly pressed broadcloth jacket into a snugger fit on his shoulders. He came off the wide polished stairs, turned across the foyer toward the family dining area. The door to the office-den next to the formal front parlor opened so abruptly that he suspected Baynard had been waiting behind it, watching the stair through the narrow slit of an opening. Baynard gave him a brief, taut smile. "Good morning, Styles. Could I talk to you a moment?"

"I'm on my way to breakfast, Mr. Baynard. I'm not

much of a listener until I've had coffee." He tried to smile. He felt faintly uncomfortable, intuitively sensing Baynard's sudden hostility. He never wanted to face the man when he was angered—certainly not on an empty stomach. Baynard was a wonderfully warm and gentle person, but he was a formidable enemy.

"Please." Baynard held the door open to his office. He made the word a command.

Styles shrugged and walked past his father-in-law into the office-den. His gaze raked across the books spread open on the desktop, the red-ink entries. On a shelf above was the row of books of poetry Baynard collected. Hard to reconcile Baynard's love for poetry with his passion for guns, falconry, hunting, his almost insensitive attitude toward his slaves or other inferiors. His gaze came down to the tray of iced cinnamon buns, the almost empty carafe of coffee. He spoke with a faint chill. "It's very convenient, isn't it? Having Jeanne d'Arc serve you—in here—before anyone else is awake or up."

He gave the word "serve" its own special inflection, endowing it with double meaning. But if he hoped to put Baynard on the defensive with the unsubtle suggestion that his father-in-law's inappropriate affair with the *os rouge* slave was known at least to him, Styles failed. Baynard merely said, "Jahndark's a good woman. I don't know what I'd do without her."

Styles sank into a wingbacked chair, pinking his trousers carefully above his knees. He faced Baynard who sat heavily in the swivel chair beside the cluttered desk. He noticed that Baynard had closed the door to the foyer, perhaps locked it. He said, persisting, "According to Baxter Simon, you might breed salable slaves by breeding Jeanne d'Arc to carefully selected black bucks. Do you know yet who the father to her sucker was?"

"No." A shadow flickered across Baynard's eyes, almost like a flash of pain. Styles wanted to laugh. Bull's-eye that time. Baynard wanted no black men covering his *os rouge*. He wanted no one to use her—no one else! Baynard said, "Well, maybe we can discuss that some other time. Right now, I'd like to talk about my children."

Styles tried to smile. He hadn't secured any advantage

to himself. The premonition of wrong deepened. "Before breakfast?"

Baynard didn't bother to smile. "I suppose every parent loves his children. And thinks he loves them beyond the capacity for love of any other parent. On the other hand, I know damned well I love my children far beyond the love of even doting parents. My children are my life. They are all I have to live for, to work for. My love includes you, Styles, as if you were my natural son—as are Ferrell and Morgan."

Styles spoke to the backs of his own manicured hands. "Thank you, sir."

"There is this one slight qualification however. I suppose my love for Kathy goes beyond love—it becomes a protective obsession. I know this isn't the smartest course, but it is a fact of my life, and I hope you can understand that."

"No, sir. I don't know exactly what you are saying."

"All right . . . Kathy is not only my first-born, but also she is the person I hold dearest on this earth. I won't bore you by telling you what an exalted sensation the love of a sweet, gentle, and blameless child can be. That will come with your own first born. . . . When Kathy was very young, I was actually beside myself with fear that something might happen to her, some harm befall her. I warned God every night in my prayers. I told Him I'd follow His laws as faithfully as I could, accept with patience and forbearance whatever He dealt out to me, but that if He permitted any evil to happen to Kathy, He had better destroy me in that same breath and burn my remains forever in the hottest hole beyond hell—or I'd get back at Him. Somehow, I'd get back at Him." He laughed ruefully. "I suppose in an inverse way I was pleading with Him for her safekeeping."

Styles stiffened and sat straighter in his chair. The direction of Baynard's discourse was becoming brilliantly and deadly clear.

"I suppose many fathers feel like that about their daughters." Styles was proud of the calm chill in his tone; it was precisely correct.

"I don't know about that. I don't know whether they

do or not. But what I've said was not intended lightly. I'm a God-fearing man. I believe He has His purpose for us on this earth. I don't believe it's all a colossal accident that somehow made man and mosquitoes. His purpose is so far beyond my ken that I accept it without question. With that exception I just mentioned." He tried to smile. "I believed He and I had to have an accommodation—a meeting of the minds on that single issue . . . and that's what I want with you this morning—a meeting of the minds."

"Sir?"

"Styles, I've accepted you here and loved you as my son. And there is only one thing that can possibly change this, or alter my deep affection for you, my loyalty to you. I'm trying as kindly as possible to warn you— who hurts Kathy no longer exists as a human being for me. I might even understand your actions. But whether I did or not, I would never forgive them. I could not. I would be an unforgiving, unyielding enemy."

"I'm not sure I know what you're trying to say, sir."

"I think you know, Styles. I'll say only that so far as I know, Kathy is blameless. I believe her to be a gentle, lovable, and loving person. She is filled with love, a delight in people, and inner goodness. The thought that anyone might harm her—or break her heart, or her spirit —even you, Styles, fills me with unspeakable rage."

"Why would I want to hurt Kathy?"

Baynard held Styles' gaze unflinchingly. "I heard her heartbroken sobs this morning, Styles."

Styles shrugged, dismissing its importance. He forced a smile. "A misunderstanding. Between Kathy and me. After all, sir, marriages may be made in heaven, but—"

"Styles, I'm being patient. This is not the first time, nor the tenth time I've heard Kathy cry heartbrokenly in that bedroom. I do not mean to pry, intrude, or interfere—"

"But that's what you are doing—"

"A bride's tears are not very important. A wife's crying is her husband's affair."

"Thank you, sir." Styles moved to stand up, to end the interview. Baynard's sharp downward gesture arrested him and he sagged back, stretching his neck uncomfortably in his high collar.

"You and Kathy have been married three years. This is the first time I have ever intruded in your marriage. I hope it can be the last. But Kathy's sobs were those of a miserable and wretchedly heartbroken woman, Styles, and I won't have her hurt like that. Not by you. Not by anybody."

Styles started to speak three separate times, each time bit his lip and refrained. Finally, he said, "I share that hope, sir. I do hope this is the last such scene between you and me. Frankly, I feel you are entirely out of line. You are intruding, and I don't feel you warrant a reply—"

"I don't ask a reply, Styles. I demand a change in whatever is going on between you and Kathy to break her heart like this."

"In order to promote some basis on which we can continue living under the same roof, I'm willing to discuss something which I deeply feel is none of your affair. Kathy and I did have a bitter disagreement this morning. It has been building for a long time. Frankly, Mr. Baynard, I'd like to have a son. I've done everything I can, but Kathy has not become pregnant."

Baynard exhaled. "Sometimes these things take time. Patience."

"Three years is time. I feel I have been patient. I'm sorry but I'm afraid I told Kathy this morning what I have come to believe for some time—that she is barren."

"Are you insane?"

"I don't think so. I'm sorry to be forced to say this to you, sir. Your son Morgan is retarded—"

"Morgan almost died at birth. He was born breach. He almost strangled on the umbilical cord about his throat. It was some moments that oxygen was completely cut off from his brain. For some time they could get no response—they thought Morgan was Miz Claire's third stillborn—"

"Miz Claire is vague. That's the kindest way I know to say it, sir."

Baynard stared at his hands. "Miz Claire was a lovely, charming girl. Much like Kathy. I know you find this difficult to believe—seeing her today in her vagueness, her loss of memory, her obsession with religion. But it is true. She suffered two bloody and traumatic miscarriages before Morgan's birth. We believed Morgan was dead at birth. With each miscarriage her health failed. I know certainly her illness is related to her physical infirmities, the miscarriages, the loss of the chemicals in her body, debilitation. I understand your suggestion. You are saying genetic weakness may well have affected Kathy's ability to conceive . . . but that won't wash, Styles."

"Nevertheless, sir, I believe Kathy is fallow."

"Is she? Or should you look to yourself?"

Styles' face blanched. His eyes narrowed. He stood up, offended, his manhood questioned. "I don't have to sit here and listen to such talk."

Baynard gazed up at him coldly. "You can't make irresponsible and baseless charges against my daughter—against my family—and then walk away from it, Styles. . . ." He laughed in that cold tone. "We can arrange a test which won't prove anything about Kathy, but in less than three months will completely absolve you from any blame in this unfortunate situation."

Styles remained standing, his head tilted. He did not speak.

"In the next day or two, Styles, you are to choose a girl from the quarters—"

"A Negress?" Styles' lips twisted.

"A virgin black. She can be anything over twelve years old. We'll have Dr. Townsend check her to warrant that she's untouched, undefiled—not deflowered. A virgin. She will be yours to use as you wish. We will arrange to bring her here into the house with you—as quietly and as inconspicuously as possible, of course."

"I unequivocally and absolutely refuse."

Baynard stared up at him in cold rage. "That's up to you, Styles. But until you do submit to such a test, I won't tolerate a word—a suggestion—a hint—that Kathy is at fault. And I go beyond that. I will not tolerate another session in which Kathy's poor, uncontrollable sobbing is heard throughout this house by family and slaves. Is that clear?"

Miz Claire came into Kathy's bedroom. She wore a negligee with high-standing ruffles concealing her throat and flowering about her mules. The soft pastel hues highlighted her face, made her look younger. Her hair was carefully brushed, each strand in place. "Baby?" she called. "Kathy? Where are you?"

"I'm in here, mother." Kathy dabbed hastily at her eyes and was busily applying powder to her cheeks when her mother came in to her dressing room where Kathy sat before her mirror.

Miz Claire studied her reflection in the lamplit glass. "Are you all right, dear?"

"Yes. Of course. Why wouldn't I be?" Kathy remained busy at the vanity. She did not meet her mother's eyes in the mirror.

"I heard your sobbing this morning—at daybreak. It broke my heart."

"I'm sorry. I'm sorry you had to hear me."

Miz Claire sighed deeply. "I hear a great deal that goes on in this house. I don't sleep well. I never have— since your father and I took separate bedrooms." Her eyes darkened. "Many people would be surprised at the things I hear in this house—at night. . . ." She waited but Kathy did not pursue this with her. She exhaled and brushed her fragile-looking hand across her face as if physically dismissing the thought. "I worry about you, Kathy . . . I'm afraid you're not happy. This isn't the first time you've wept like this."

"People can't be happy all the time, mother."

"Is Styles cruel to you? Does he make—demands?"

"Demands?" Kathy bit her lip to keep from laughing cuttingly. She shrugged. "It's nothing like that."

"I hope not. I can tell you—the unspeakable things I endured—from your father. The ugly, depraved things men demand of women. I thanked God when I became ill —yes I did!—and your father moved out of my bed, out of my bedroom."

Kathy twisted slightly on the vanity chair, staring up at her mother. "You—didn't like to—go to bed with father? Ever?"

Miz Claire shuddered in revulsion. "I loathed it. I hated having him touch me. . . . It was ugly. Filthy. . . . I'll put up with anything—as long as I may have my own bedroom—and my own person. . . ."

Kathy turned back to the mirror, concealing her face from her mother. Is this me, twenty years from now? Remembering even the good moments in revulsion? Oh, God, not me. Please, not me.

"I couldn't bring myself to tell you some of the things I had to endure," her mother persisted.

Kathy nodded, but didn't speak. She knew about her father and Jeanne d'Arc. Her sympathies lay entirely with her father; they always had. She had always felt a deep compassion for him in his loneliness. His loneliness she now saw as her loneliness, and she believed herself the loneliest soul on God's earth. Without Styles, she had nobody, and she was coming to accept that she had nobody. Now, she heard, shocked, that her mother had hated sex from the first—even in the beginning it had been something *endured*, something *forced upon her*.

Oh, God, Kathy thought, you sound like Styles. . . .

CHAPTER 11

FLORINE PILZER wakened at four o'clock that morning —as she did every day at this dark hour. Her eyes stung with tears of self-pity. Loneliness? Nobody on God's earth knew what loneliness was as she had learned here at Blackoaks.

She heard her husband prowling in the kitchen, making his own breakfast, snarling in his guttural tones, expending his predawn hatreds and frustrations on the kitchenware or a hapless chair that got in his path.

Florine did not move. She lay, counting the minutes until Bos slurped down his coffee, wolfed his cornmeal mush and milk, his four fried eggs and thick slabs of ham. God, a meal like that at this hour. The thought nauseated her.

Mary, mother of Jesus, how she hated him. Yet Bos Pilzer didn't deserve her hatred. He was as kind as he knew how to be, as gentle as his stern upbringing permitted. She fingered the diamond-studded cross on its gold chain about her throat. God only knew how much it had cost. The gold was almost pure, the diamonds were real. It was a gift from him to her, brought back from a slave-buying trip to New Orleans for old man Baynard. Bos tried to give her what she wanted; it was just that he never could, not in a million years. He drew her to him like a hairy bear in bed at night and kissed her moistly, thrust his fingers into her vulva, her anus, her mouth, and scrubbed at her small, firm tits until he was pulsing, rigid. Then, without further delay, he drove it fiercely into her. Nothing about the ceremony

115

ever varied, not even the incredibly short span of time it took him to shoot off inside her. Three or four frantic battering jabs with his tool, which was almost lost under the lapping folds of belly-fat, and he was finished, gasping for breath, falling away from her, turning his back, snoring with that same terrible abruptness. He always left her frustrated, in the lurch, agonized with need aroused but never satisfied. Never. Mother of Jesus, how she hated him.

To compound her loneliness and her restless frustrations, she was a soul in purgatory as far as this plantation was concerned. There was no one to whom she could turn—not relative, friend, child, or lover. She had none of them. She had no one. She was a victim of Bos Pilzer's occupation. He was a hired overseer and as such respected and accepted. As his wife she had no place—not in the exalted heaven of the snotty Baynards on the high plateau, nor among the black women in the lower world of the quarters. She belonged in neither world. The Baynards spoke to her pleasantly enough—when they had to—along their noses. The black women in the quarters were afraid of her. They might have been friendly enough at least to visit—on the path or the roadway between the commissary in the quarters and the fieldstone cottage on the knoll where she lived with Bos—but she was the overseer's wife and he was their enemy. They didn't trust him; most of them knew that when Obadiah and Narc were sold off to the trader, Baynard was not actually involved. Bos Pilzer had dragged Narc off to the creek-side camp. They were afraid to trust Bos's wife. They bobbed their cornrow-pinned heads when she passed; they agreed it was a nice day; they fell silent until she moved on.

On Sunday mornings she drove Pilzer's buggy along the roadway that skirted the quarters, climbed the incline, and crossed the plateau where the big house stood. Often she saw the Baynards going into the chapel Mr. Baynard had built to please his wife when she turned from the Baptist religion and embraced Catholicism. Florine's mouth twisted—translated, this meant when the old girl went off her rocker.

116

Florine never had stopped at the chapel, likely she never would though many of the Negroes attended services there. Negroes were allowed church services as long as whites were present. It was just that they were forbidden to have churches of their own which might become centers for conspiracy. No one ever invited Florine to the chapel and she rode by, eyes fixed straight ahead, going alone into Mt. Zion to the Baptist church where she sang louder, reached higher notes and held them longer than anyone else in the congregation.

She heard Bos plod heavily out the rear door and slam it behind him. Her breath quickened, dry and hot in her throat. She felt the glycerinelike wetness bubble hotly into the lips of her vagina. She laughed. If only she had a lover, she would be ready for him before he ever got into her bedroom!

She went on, lying unmoving until she heard Bos on his horse, clopping down the path into the quarters.

First daylight dimly illumined the bedroom by now. Florine kicked back the covers and gazed down at her shapeless gown, her orange-shaped tits, the flat plane of her belly, her long, well-turned legs. She was proud of her legs. She wished she could show them off without getting herself arrested.

Now, she thought. Now. This was her happy hour of the day, the only time when she wasn't lonely, when she had her lover—in her imaginings. God, if Bos ever even suspected some of her wild fantasies, he'd have her committed. To Bos, sex was something a woman endured, but never enjoyed, wanted over as quickly as possible. It was something shameful, done in the dark. Mother of Mary. . . .

She drew her gown slowly up over her thighs, feeling the fabric tickle her bared flesh. Then, arching her back, she pulled it all the way up under her armpits, exposing her breasts, the nipples as taut and hard as marbles.

Breathing raggedly, she fondled her breasts with her left hand, caressing, massaging, squeezing. She pushed her right hand down into the trim patch of dark hair between her legs. She extended her index and third fingers, working them with a firm, circular pressure upon

117

her clitoris. She bent her knees and spread her legs as wide apart as she could. Come on, she whispered, inside her mind, come on, come on.

She lay, throat parched, fingering herself, making up in tenderness to her body all she'd endured last night from Bos Pilzer. Her fingers flashed faster and faster. For a long, frustrated period she'd had trouble finding someone to dream about. She'd for a while imagined the young minister at the Mt. Zion First Baptist Church naked and mounting her with the zeal and fervor and vigor he expended upon his sermons. It had been briefly adequate. She even got so she sat in a half-trance during his Sunday sermons, seeing him in her mind's eye, naked. Her inner passions mounted as his sermon rose to its hell-and-damnation climax. Static crackled when his voice thundered across that silent auditorium. She often left church weak-kneed, exhausted. But he seldom spoke to her when he stood on the church steps visiting with his exiting congregation. He reserved his warmest attentions for those members who tithed. Her weekly dime didn't buy her much more than a brief nod and a dead-fish smile. Gradually, her fantasies rejected him, the fantastic size she'd endowed his staff in her dreams diminished until no matter how hard she tried to conjure him up in her mind, she could not work up any excitement over him.

She'd never encountered anyone handsomer than Kathy Baynard's husband, the arrogant and aloof Styles Kenric. She'd like to break him in to what sex could really be like. He became her early morning dream guest until one day she met him outside the plantation commissary. He gazed along his nose at her, almost pained, as if she were one of the black women.

She shuddered, remembering, hating him.

She might have been doomed to suffer anguished failure in her morning daydream for lack of a viable mental partner, except that Bos sent a boy to wash the cottage windows one morning without advising her in advance.

Her fingers moved faster on her clitoris as she remembered that morning. It had changed her life. It had set her upon orgiastic fantasies unlike any she'd ever experienced. But that particular morning she'd almost fainted in shock and terror.

She been lying just like this, finger-fucking herself as hard as she could, squeezing her breast mercilessly in her tightening fingers. But her images would not jell— she tried in desperation to dredge up some man from her past, some stranger, a man somewhere who'd pay her to whore for him, anything to fuel her fevered dreams. Only, there was nothing. She felt doomed to failure, to lie in anguished need, unfinished as Bos left her every night.

Then she'd felt hackles at the nape of her neck without knowing why, a strange discomfort, an instinctive sense that she wasn't alone. Sweaty with frustration, she'd slowed her fingers, opened her eyes.

She saw that face at the window, the bare-chested body, dark golden brown in the first sunlight. He had lifted a soapy sponge to the window pane, but now stood transfixed, watching her. She had no idea how long he'd been there.

Her first instinct was to scream and to keep screaming until he was secured in shackles and spancels. A hot wave of terror flashed through her body, left her quivering. But she was innately free of fear and she recovered instantly. Panic was supplanted by rage. She looked around for Bos's gun, something to throw. Then her confusion subsided. She remained another moment, knees bent, legs parted wide, fingers dipped into the dark liquidity at her thighs. Then she jerked her gown down, lunged off the bed, and bounded across the room. She saw terror in the boy's face now. He looked around wildly, ready to run, but for the moment paralyzed by fear. She jerked the window up.

"I ain't done nuthin', ma'am," he blurted. "Ain't done nuthin'. Ain't seen nuthin'. No, ma'am. Nuthin'."

By now the significance of the soapy sponge and the bucket of water cut through her outrage and confusion. She stared at him, the thick cords of his pectorals, the wide shoulders, the beautiful face set in terror—and the huge bulge at his fly. Her voice lowered, calm but cold. "What did you see, boy?"

"Didn't see nuthin', ma'am. Nuthin' in the world. No, ma'am. Jes' washin' windows like Master Pilzer said. Master Pilzer, he sent me. Yes, ma'am."

"Don't lie to me."

"No, ma'am. I ain't lyin'. I never lie. Hardly. You ast anybody, ma'am."

"I'll tell you something, boy. You ever mention one word of what you saw through this window—to anybody—I'll tell Pilzer you grabbed me. They'll string you up and cat-o-nine-tails you."

"Don't do that. Please, ma'am. I didn't see nuthin'. Nuthin' I can remember."

"Yes, you did. But you are not to tell anybody—anybody. Or I'll have you whipped half to death."

"Ain't goin' to say a word, ma'am, to nobody."

"I know how you niggers gossip."

"Not me, ma'am. Not about white folks. I never mix no way in white folks' doin's. No, ma'am."

"All right. What's your name?"

For a moment he was afraid to tell her. Finally, he whispered. "Moab . . . ma'am."

"All right, Moab. Get on away from here."

"Got to do these windows, ma'am, or I get whupped anyhow."

She laughed, a brutal sound. "How you expect to do windows with that ear of corn you're wearing in your pants?"

Blood suffused his dark golden face. His eyes looked stricken with guilt. He was afraid to look down at himself, but he couldn't meet her gaze either. She bit back a smile, no longer afraid at all. He was built like a young god, but he was just a baby. "Go on, get out. And keep your mouth shut. I'll tell Pilzer you did the windows. If he believes me, you won't get whupped. Now go on, get out of here."

He nodded, retreated, bumped a tree, spilled the bucket of water down his front, backed around the tree, tripped over a rose bush, turned and fled.

For a week, Florine suffered the agonies of the damned. She waited sickly for Pilzer to come home each night. If there had been talk among the Negroes, it would have reached him. She watched the faces of her black female neighbors below her in the quarters for the knowing look, the derisive smile, the leer. It didn't happen. Gradually, she forgot her anxieties and remembered only the beautiful boy. She thought of a hundred excuses to have Pilzer send Moab back to perform chores for her. Chores! Oh, God, the chores she'd have him perform! But she was afraid even to speak Moab's name aloud. Pilzer was sharp, astute, and as jealous as a mongoose. She could ask for as many "boys" as she wished, but she could not ask for "that boy." And the odds against Pilzer's sending the Fulani youth again to work around his place were formidable. It wouldn't happen. She could only fantasize about him. But at least she was no longer lonely, no longer frustrated for an imaginary lover to share her fevered fantasies. She summoned him in her mind; she watched him enter through the window, bare chested, golden as toast, innocent as a baby, built like a rampant ram. She writhed under the circular whirling of her fingers, erotic scenes exploding across her mind's eye—all the fascinating, forbidden, lovely things she would teach him; the way she would hold him, nuzzle and lick him, taste him, nurse him; she would drive him insane—as insane as the thought of him drove her, alone in her bed. She had now a lover who wanted her as wildly as she wanted him in her imaginings, a young, untouched boy who'd stood transfixed with desire, his pants bulging with need. "Oh, Moab," she whispered, her head rolling back and forth on her pillow, her back arched, her hips flailing. "Moab . . . oh, God, Moab . . . Moab. . . ."

Moab walked at the edge of the cotton-chopping crews. He yawned, scrubbing at his eyes with his fists. Like his older brother, Blade, Moab was the golden brown of the Moor, the light chocolate of the Fulani. He was not as handsome as Blade, but he showed promise of being bigger, more muscular. At fourteen, he was solidly built, bared to the waist, wearing only onasburg britches and turned-over leather-work moccasins. Moab was tall for his age, and slender, his wide shoulders and arms corded with supple muscles. He wasn't a man yet—maybe three or four years from full growth, but already his chest was thickening, deepening. He was indeed Blade's full-blooded brother, with that shared Fulani ancestry, and the innate quiet nobility of bearing. He hadn't Blade's classic profile, but his features were shapely hewn, delicately finished. His body shone with that soft chocolate sheen. He had crisp black hair, gentle black eyes, and glittering white teeth. He laughed easily; but he was by nature a serious-minded boy, and he had already learned to fear the unknown world ruled by white men beyond the secure limits of the shack he shared with Blade in the Blackoaks slave quarters.

He shuffled his feet through the powdery dust, his head lowered. He didn't care that the trees glistened with mists, that clouds banked thickly against the pink morning horizon or that meadowlarks sang from the hammocks. He had rolled out of bed unwillingly. He hated to see the sun rise high enough so that the slaves could discern cotton plant from wire grass. He felt an inner rage that burned like acid low in his stomach. He did not see how he could spend another long hot day bent over a hoe in the sunstruck fields. Bosworth Pilzer, the overseer, cursed at them from the rear of the column. Moab quivered at the sound of the despised voice. He turned his head slightly and spat toward it and cursed it, praying upon it all the evil of his ancestors' grisgris.

The columns moved through the last shadows cast by a stand of short-leaf pines. The shadeless field stretched before them in the shimmering morning heat. Moab caught his breath, feeling stifled. Even in the protection of the umbrellalike pines, the fiery blaze from the cotton field was already dazzling. Before noon it would be hotter than the Negroid plains of hell.

He shuddered, remembering his last moments in his corn-shucks mattress. He had awakened with a blue-ribbon erection. Peeing against a chinaberry tree hadn't relieved it. He needed a girl. Involuntarily, his lips pulled back from his teeth in a taut grin. What he really needed was a woman—the kind of woman fat old Pilzer possessed. A woman who knew what she was doing and wasn't afraid of everything, even the swollen size of one's blood-engorged staff. He would even have settled for five minutes with his fist—release at least from tensions. It was nothing to compare with the wetness of an eager, pulsating woman, but better than a splitting headache. Only there had not been time for this manual relief.

Moab sweated. There was no way to make those not driven by his brand of compulsion understand the stomach-grinding, gut-aching desires that drove everything else from his mind. It was as if his brain were in his loins.

He chopped cotton in the mumbling, back-bent slave lines for only ten minutes. It seemed at least an hour to him. He dropped his hoe and waved his arm toward Pilzer in the signal that meant he was going into the bushes for physical relief. Pilzer's thick Dutch voice called the attention of every man and woman in the field to Moab. "Why can't you niggers shit before you get to the fields? Hurry it up, goddamn you."

Moab entered the hammock, putting a parapet of underbrush between him and the workers in the field. He reached down to unbutton the sweaty onasburg pants. He lowered their musky wetness below his knees. His rod had already stiffened, springing up instantly when it was free, pulsatile.

He squatted across a log, the prickly roughness of the dead bark biting into the soft flesh of his buttocks. God! it was pleasant to be free like this even if only for a few minutes, his pants down, his staff captive in his fist, the pale body of the Pilzer woman already materializing, naked, liquid, fascinating, behind his eyes. He wanted her more than life. He could laugh at this idea because it would be worth his life even to go near her, to look straight at her. Negroes had been hung for no greater crime than looking directly into the face of a white woman. Ay! That terrible consequence didn't keep him from dreaming about her. Nothing could. If he had to die to possess her, he would die willingly, bravely, his head held high, and his pecker at attention. What was a life of labor in the sun-crisped fields compared to having that body under his for one hour in some quiet, cool hideaway? Make it two hours, gods of my people, and we've got an ironclad deal! The thought of the accomplishment of his maddest dream, the hot sense of anticipation of something that could never be, drunkened him. If he could have her, he would be stronger than a lion, braver than the bravest warlord of the ancient jungle. And he would submit to death quietly, willingly, if first he could grab that warm flesh and fulfill the throbbing needs that exploded through him. His hand tightened on his hardness and he reveled in its rigidity. He was a lion. There was the spirit and the power and the savagery of the lion throbbing through his veins. His fist worked, faster, faster.

As if from some distant galaxy he heard the faint roar of thunder, felt the slicing bite of lightning. Shock, pain, and panic whipped through his body, confusing the messages from his nerve centers. Sperm spurted white and thick from his tumescent tool in an agonized premature ejaculation. Pain wiped his mind clean. He recognized Pilzer's thunderous yelling, felt the terrible cut that whip had sliced along his back. He lunged upward from the log, screaming in fright and pain. He lunged forward and broke through the bushes into the open field—anything to escape that vengeful white man on that horse behind him. His trousers, wadded about his ankles, tripped him. He plunged forward on his face. He scrambled up and grabbed at his pants in the same movement. His rigid member still spurted helplessly. Around him, like screaming banshees, the other slaves raged with laughter. They dropped their hoes, staggered over the banks of cotton, and bent double with the agony of uncontrollable laughter. They laughed until they cried. They pounded each other helplessly, laughing. They fell down laughing.

CHAPTER 12

THYESTES LIMPED into the family dining room. He stood, nervous and slack shouldered beside the elder Baynard's chair. He fidgeted, first on one foot and then on the other. Baynard was aware of the butler's presence but he also disliked being disturbed at a meal. Thyestes knew this; maybe it was time to refresh his memory. Baynard went on eating—scrapple, three eggs fried sunny-side up, grits, and his own carafe of steaming hot coffee. Miz Claire glanced disapprovingly at Thyestes, but said nothing. Styles, taut faced, pushed food about on his plate. He stared through Thyestes and did not see him. Morgan ate with his head lowered and did not look up. Finally, Ferrell-Junior said in a kindly tone, "What's troubling you, Thyestes?"

"Please, suh, masta." Thyestes looked at Ferrell-Junior, eyes stricken, but spoke pleadingly to the elder Baynard. "I knows purely how you hates being pestered at your breakfast, suh. But it's powerful important, masta."

Baynard set his heavy sterling silver fork and knife down on the side of his bone-china plate in a ringing way that told Thyestes better than words how displeased his master was. "All right, Thyestes, what is it?"

Thyestes looked as if he might cry.

"It's Masta Pilzer, masta, suh. Yes, suh. He shore is upset. He outside—on the veranda, suh, and he shorely craves to speak with you this minute. Hit won't wait, he say. I promise him I tells you, or I never disturb you in this world, masta."

Baynard nodded curtly. He took two more large bites

of scrapple, washed it down with a long swig of coffee, and got up from the table, mopping his mouth with a linen napkin. Miz Claire's head jerked up. She watched him narrowly and he remembered to say, "Please excuse me, Miz Claire."

"Well, I do hope so," she said. "What will people think of us if we don't observe proper etiquette?"

Ferrell-Junior also got up. He grinned, excused himself, and kissed Miz Claire lightly before he followed his father. Morgan bobbed his head toward his mother and trailed after his brother. Styles excused himself from the table and joined the Baynards and the overseer on the sunlit veranda.

Pilzer's sun-leathered face was gray, his eyes troubled, but his shoulders were set stubbornly and his head tilted in an air of righteousness. What he had done had gone wrong, but his intentions were totally in the interests of the master of Blackoaks. "I come straight in to tell you, Mr. Baynard. I had a little trouble with one of the niggers in the field gang."

"Which one, Bos?"

"Moab."

"The Fulani boy?" Baynard frowned. "He's no troublemaker. What's Moab done?"

"What's the Fulani boy doing working in the fields, anyhow?" Styles demanded.

Baynard glanced at his son-in-law impatiently, then recognized the logic of the question and nodded in agreement. "Moab should not be working with the fieldhands."

Pilzer flushed. He swung his arm in a gesture that said some decisions were best left where they belonged, with him. "Moab don't know nothing else."

"Well, teach him something else," Styles said. "The fields are no place for that boy."

Baynard nodded. Then, "What happened out there this morning, Bos?"

Pilzer gestured. "Reckon I lost my temper there for a minute . . . but that nigger's been pushing me—he hates the fields—don't work worth a shit unless I ride his tail every minute. . . . I made a mistake, and I come right to tell you, but I was pushed."

"Well, what did you do, for Christ's sake?"

"I come right in to tell you—soon as I cooled off a little. I laid the whip on the boy."

The four men stared at Pilzer, their faces rigid. Baynard shook his head in disbelief. "Why? For God's sake what could he have done to make you do that?"

"That black buck was sittin' in the shade blamming his meat," Pilzer said.

"Masturbating?" Baynard said.

"Yes, sir. Rest of them niggers workin' out in the sun, he's a sitting there beating his dong. He went in the woods to take a crap. He stayed so long I rode in there and seen him—squattin' on a log, with his bare black tail hanging over it, beatin' his meat, big as you please. Well, that was just plain the last straw. He's been nothing but trouble. I lashed out with that whip."

Ferrell-Junior's voice shook. "We've told you, Bos. Never use that damned whip. And never whip a Fulani—never mark one. Everybody on this place knows that. I'll bet you my mother can quote you that one. You mar a Fulani, you've ruined him."

"I know that, Ferrell-Junior." Bos Pilzer nodded. "I told you. He's been pushing me. You gotta make niggers obey you."

"Then you'll have to find some other way to do it." Ferrell-Junior strode down the steps.

Baynard called after him. "Where are you going, son?"

Ferrell-Junior spoke over his shoulder, taking up the reins of Pilzer's white mare. He swung up into the saddle. "Out to check on Moab." He turned the horse, then flung over his shoulder, "For God's sake, Bos. Beating his meat. I bet your back would look like mince meat if you'd been flogged every time you beat off your pecker."

The overseer stared after him. He didn't want Ferrell-Junior, or anyone else to take his horse, but he knew better than to protest at this moment. He called, "Not me. No, sir. You beat your meat, you get hair in the palm of your hand."

Baynard laughed, despite his rage, when Morgan surreptitiously checked his palm. But Morgan nodded seriously. "That's true, papa. Lose your memory too. Minister told us that in Mt. Zion's Boys' Bible School. Told us about this fellow who was just obsessed with the need to flog hisself. Plain pure lost his mind, this pore fellow did, the minister said. Said he met that pore misguided fellow a few years later—he had come back here to Mt. Zion— looking for his very own self!"

Ferrell-Junior rode through the hammock and out to the cotton fields. A few slaves chopped weeds desultorily; the rest leaned on their hoes, still laughing among themselves about the picture Moab had made running out of those woods like wasps were after him, squirting pecker juice with every step he took and tripping and falling over his own pants around his ankles. When they saw the white mare, most of them leapt guiltily and pretended to chop weeds. But when they recognized Ferrell-Junior they relaxed again. They looked up and bobbed their heads, grinning, as he approached on the overseer's horse. "Mornin', Mista Masta Ferrell-Junior, suh."

Ferrell-Junior reined in, staring along the long line of blacks. "Where's Moab?"

One of the grinning men pointed toward the hammock. "He squattin'—over in yonder bushes, masta, suh."

"Again?" Ferrell-Junior turned in the saddle. "But Pilzer just whipped him—"

The man laughed. "That boy Moab got b'ilin' hot blood, masta, suh. He hotter than a stud horse with the scent—"

"Gawd knows he could have he pick of wenches in the quarters—"

"Shorely he git enough wenches—"

"He git enough for *you*, Jonah! Dey purely ain't enough fo' him!"

They laughed and talked again, emboldened by Ferrell-Junior's smiling. The chopping ground to a complete halt and the hands pressed closer, vying for a moment of the white youth's attention. Jonah, a short, stocky Negro, laughed knowingly in a high-pitched tone. "Moab, he git him a wench ever' chance he git to grab one—and then he beat his meat in between—that Moab!"

Ferrell-Junior found Moab slouched over a log just beyond a beige fringe of wild plum bushes. But Moab was not masturbating. He was slumped over round-shouldered, staring at the ground between his legs. Ferrell-Junior saw the boy's back was sliced open, from his shoulder across his spine almost to his hip bone. "Jesus," Ferrell-Junior muttered. He leaped from the saddle and ran to the boy.

Moab looked up. When he moved, flies scattered from his bloodied back. Moab's face registered fright, guilt, and then pain when he correctly read the concern in Ferrell-Junior's face. "I in bad pain, masta," Moab said.

"All right. We're going to get you in to a doctor. Get up behind me on the horse. It's going to be all right, Moab."

Moab was uncertain what was going to happen to him next, but he was thankful for this attention to what he considered a fearful injustice. "I shore hopes so, masta." His voice quavered. "It feels like I on fire."

Baynard, Morgan, and Styles were still on the veranda when Ferrell-Junior rode across the drive to the steps with Moab on the horse behind him. Moab's arms were locked about Ferrell-Junior's waist. Baynard strode down the steps and reached up to help Moab dismount. Baynard swore when he examined the whip-cut across Moab's back. "God almighty, Bos. How could you have done such a thing?"

Baynard ran his fingers tenderly along the boy's back. At this sudden and unexpected gentle treatment and deep concern, Moab dissolved into tears. "I in pain, masta. I in bad pain."

Baynard sent a black house servant running to the barn to have a buggy hitched, double-time. In minutes, a horse handler came up slope, driving a black, single-seat buggy.

"It's a clean cut," Pilzer said in his own defense. "I seen a lot of cuts like that. It'll heal clean."

"It damn well better, Bos." Baynard spoke curtly across his shoulder. "If a weal forms, or a welt rises, you've cost me up to $10,000. I may as well tell you, Bos, I'm gut sick about this. You should have more sense. Your damned dense Dutch temper is going to ruin you yet."

"I got a big job, and you can't make them niggers—"

The buggy rolled into place beside them on the steps and Baynard slashed his hand downward, cutting Pilzer off in mid-sentence. "Now, listen to me, Bos. We got one chance. You get Moab into Mt. Zion to Dr. Townsend. Don't you take him to the vet—"

"Dr. Townsend ain't going to take a nigger into his office," Pilzer protested.

Baynard stared at him coldly. "You better pray he does. He'll take Moab. You tell him I sent you. You show him Moab's back. He knows a Fulani, he'll take him. You stay there. Right there. Doc will probably sew Moab up—I don't know. Whatever he says has to be done, you plan to do it. When you get back, I want you to fix a cot for Moab in the tack room at your place where you and your wife can look after him—twenty-four hours a day if you have to—"

"My wife can't—"

"Your wife can't tend a *nigger*, Bos? Is your wife going to pay me $5,000 for a ruined Negro? Or maybe you got that much to pay for what you've done to Moab."

Pilzer sighed and spread his hands. "We'll take care of him."

"All right. I mean like a pet. I mean you be sure that cut is tended—greased, oiled, bandaged—whatever Dr. Townsend orders. Then, when the boy is well—and that cut is completely closed—you can put him to light work in the commissary with his brother Blade. Under no circumstances is Moab to go back to the fields."

Moab stared at the white man, unable to believe his own ears. He wanted to scream out his wild ecstatic pleasure. But he knew better. He kept his head lowered, kept sniffling as if in agony and scrubbed at his nose as Baynard and Ferrell-Junior helped him into the buggy beside the chastened Pilzer. Moab wished he could sob aloud to guarantee that this concern would last, but he could summon up no tears. The cut along his back suddenly didn't hurt anymore, though he'd never admit that to anyone. He pressed his hands over his face to hide the smile twisting fiercely at his lips. There was no pain, almost no memory of pain. Maybe he was through with the hot fields and hard work and pain for the rest of his life. It certainly looked like it.

CHAPTER 13

THE TRAIN wound irresolutely south and west through flatlands, hills, swamps, hammocks, and uncounted villages. The trip that had drawn him so promisingly as the prudent response to the devilish problems suddenly and dangerously besetting him, turned out to be a tiresome, dirty, soot-smeared, and boring excursion into a strange and unknown world.

Hunter Campbell stared out through the open window across the hot, sun-crisped land. The trees—scrub oaks, jack pines, and cypress—sagged, parched. The towns lay heat-prostrated, desolate, poverty-stricken pockets of unpainted houses, scabrous buildings, and short, potholed streets leading nowhere. Dull-eyed faces stared up as the train slowed and rolled past their station and out of their ken. His mouth twisted with distaste. Not only had he never encountered such privation, he'd never suspected this ugly destitution existed in states united contiguously with Massachusetts. He wasted no compassion upon these impoverished crackers. He'd always believed, and his education at Harvard had reinforced his theory, that human beings succeeded in direct proportion to their energy expended, productivity, and disciplined intelligence. It was obvious these Southerners had been born in penury and never lifted a hand to better their lot. He stared down at them in contempt and amused, disdainful curiosity.

He did experience a distinct flash of shock. His mental images of the land south of the Mason-Dixon Line had always been of huge manor houses, rolling lawns shaded by magnolias and scented with jasmine, tended acreage, and starved, whipped, and brutalized blacks. Infrequently, from northern Maryland south, he did glimpse the roof or a bright wing of a far plantation villa. There were so few of these estates compared to the numbers of small, impoverished, one-mule farms, the blighted villages, the shacks stewing in a few acres of laboriously cleared and plowed land. He had inattentively heard that there were actually two Souths—distinct in economic character—that had existed since colonial times. This information had not impressed him then and he had disregarded it. In astonishment he saw how true it was. There was, in fact, a considerable percentage of blacks living in shacks in villages and along back trails, if not free, not enslaved, not belonging to anyone. Most of the small farms had not even a single black at work. The whites he saw in the towns were not slave holders; they were backwoods people eking out an existence barely above the starvation level. The hell with these destitute whites; they got about what they earned. The plight of the enslaved blacks was something else. This angered and infuriated him. He had come down here hired as a tutor, and he'd do his job too. But he wanted to do something about the slaves. He had no idea yet what he could do. There must be something; he would find it.

Most importantly, despite the heat, the peppering cinders, the soot, and the discomfort, he had escaped a murderously jealous husband. He had lost Addie too, in the bargain, but that couldn't be helped. He had run away without attempting to say good-bye to Addie, and she would never forgive what she would see as an act of cowardice and which he considered pragmatic prudence. He had lost a beautiful love, a warm bed companion, an exciting and forbidden alliance, but at least he was still alive.

A smile twisted his mouth. There hadn't been anything too honest about their affair from the first. She was his cousin's bride, and he had stolen from a Harvard roommate the love poems which had entranced her and brought her naked and quivering into his bed. She had been good, willing and anxious to please him. But worth dying for?

Hunter Campbell was a man who believed in evading

physical violence at all costs and where he could. Compromise, accommodate, or clear out! This was the tenet by which he had lived well and securely and unbruised through military school and Harvard. Now, roaring south via trains from the Boston station, he had followed that safe course again. His cousin had precipitated his abrupt decision and hasty departure. He'd stared Hunter in the eye, challenging him to fight. "I've let it go on because our families are involved, Hunt. But no more. You'll fight me —and no one need know our fight concerned Addie— and we'll settle it that way. You can continue to see her under those circumstances, knowing in advance I'll beat hell out of you every time you do. Or, if you try to avoid me, and go on seeing Addie, I'll kill you. You won't just put me off and go on as you are. You won't get away with pretending to be above violence. I'm not above violence. You're not above it this time. You tried to take my wife from me. Now you'll fight me for her like a man—or I'll kill you as the sneak you are."

Until this disagreeable scene with his Cousin Lodge— who was, after all, a Yale man and very physical, outdoorsy, and pipe smoking—Hunt had been vacillating between two tutoring positions. He had delayed accepting either because Addie was so extraordinarily fancy in bed. He had leaned in preference toward the offer in Boston —a widow with three preteen children—because New England was home and he was a Puritan to the marrow of his bones. Besides, the Boston position offered more money, and when a man reached twenty-seven after five years absorbing culture available only at Harvard and two more years in graduate school, immediate income was of paramount importance, even though his inheritance covered his basic needs adequately. The only reason he had not rejected out of hand the position offered to tutor a backward teenage boy in some godforsaken southern Alabama town was that he felt so strongly against slavery. There had to be some way to help relieve the terrible burden on those miserable wretches. But his humanitarian instincts had been tempered by his profit motive. Only Lodge's insanely jealous threats of violence had tipped the scales and sent him scurrying south.

He had departed Melrose in the deepest night, going from an unlighted room to a black, shadowed street. He had checked nervously over his shoulder all the way to the depot. He had remained in the concealment of the baggage room until the train was ready to pull out of the station. Then he had run out and leaped aboard, tossing his suitcases ahead of him.

There had been a steady drizzle and the accustomed spring damp chill in the air when he'd departed Boston. As the train crossed New Jersey's meadows, eastern Pennsylvania into Delaware and Maryland, the air warmed and the first green showed in the woods along the tracks. People in the coaches threw off their heavy coats, then their jackets and ties as the train crossed the Carolinas into Georgia. The heat was oppressive, but Hunt remained as correctly attired for travel as he had set out.

The soot-frosted glass of the windows showed him he was quite presentable, even though people around him slouched wrinkled, sweated, and in various stages of dishabille. His erect tallness was accented by the stovepipe black hat, which was almost required wear in Harvard Yard. His face was freshly, if agonizingly and uncomfortably shaven. His forehead was rounded, his brows lifted in a habitually imperious disdain. His blue eyes set above chill-burned pink cheeks met the gazes of others with the practiced aloofness that kept strangers at a distance. His pince-nez was secured to his waistcoat by a black satin cord. His nose was straight, but rather sharply chiseled in an almost bargain cut, with slightly flared nostrils of which he was inordinately proud. His mouth had a natural, tight-lipped set, but his chin was well shaped, even tilted in a faintly arrogant way. The sedate ascot—a broad stock looped under his chin and set precisely between the wings of his starched collar so the ends were laid flat, one across the other—was decorated with a stickpin. This was one of the most extravagant gifts lavished upon him by some forgotten relative during his Harvard undergraduate years. His heavy wool, oxford-gray suit, customed tailored and less than three years old, fit his wide shoulders snugly and set off his polished boots and matching vest with its single adornment, a gold watch

135

chain worn rakishly across his solar plexus. He smiled, self-satisfied. The clothing he wore was a part of his entire corpus, obviously. Its fashionable, yet unostentatious correctness told the world instantly who and what he was—a gentleman, born, reared, and educated. However, to his dismay, by the time the train headed southwest out of Atlanta, he was the object of secret smirks, snickers, elbow-jabbing, and ill-bred pointing.

He sat silently, withdrawn and aloof from the man on the aisle seat beside him. He might have completed his long, arduous journey without exchanging a word, but finally the man—stout bellied, middle-aged, sardonically smiling—spoke to him in a taunting and baiting tone. "Come down here to set the slaves free, have you, Harvard?"

Hunt winced. The bastard was intrusive, offensive, and yet he was pleased. He felt impelled to destroy the boor with a sharp verbal parry and thrust. This was his forte. He had excelled in ripping inferiors into bleeding humiliation all through Harvard. By now, words were sharp-pointed darts, his weaponry. "Has it taken you a hundred miles to perceive I'm from New England, my good man—that I am indeed a graduate of Harvard?"

"Hell no. I saw that when I walked in here and sat down by you. But there wasn't no place else to sit. And I enjoy specimen like you. Always wonder what makes 'em tick."

"Good breeding and self-discipline, I suppose," Hunt said, gazing along his nose.

"I reckon." The man laughed. "I suppose you define ill breeding as my thrusting myself, uninvited upon you."

"That's as clear a definition as we need."

The man smiled and winked. "But good breeding, by your reckoning, is your coming down here with bleeding heart to set the South right on the way it exists?"

"We send missionaries to the heathens, sir."

"So we do. My God, don't we! My name is Luther Perkins, sir. I'm an attorney. Never had the advantages of the Ivy League. Went to a little old university down here you never even heard of. One of the only laughs we ever got was a lecturer telling us how fortunate we were never to have been exposed to Harvard's predigested culture. I didn't see the joke as well then as I do now."

"But you see the gut-aching laughter in raping black women and whipping black men, and tearing black babies from their mother's tits? Is that a fair exposition of red-neck humor?"

"As fair as anything else you people believe, Algernon."

"My name is Campbell."

"Thank you. Pleased to be introduced to you—even if I did have to force you into it. Don't let my teasing upset you. Don't mean any harm."

"No. I suppose you people don't mean any harm in any of the vicious things you do."

"What vicious things are those, Mr. Campbell?"

"I'm sure I don't have to enumerate your crimes against human beings for you. Despite that clabber-mouth accent and good-ole-boy smiling, you're clever enough to recognize right and wrong."

"Slavery really eats your ass out, don't it?"

"It is a filthy evil that may well haunt this nation as long as it exists."

"It may that. Why don't you people up Massachusetts way put an end to slavery?"

"We may have to reluctantly make the decision to do just that—in a violent and unrelenting way, sir."

"Great. You are going to end child labor in your Boston factories, eh? What slavery exists more cruel than that? Seven-year-old children working from dawn to dark. Dying of lung disease without ever knowing a moment of childish laughter. I agree with you, Mr. Campbell. It tears my heart out too."

"I certainly don't defend child labor. But I don't sit grinning pretending that two wrongs ever equal one right."

"I was only suggesting that if we all cleaned up around our own front steps we'd never know what goes on in the neighbor's yard, Mr. Campbell."

"You people cannot be permitted to go on exploiting black slaves. Prattling about a minor wrong in New England doesn't change the heinous terror of your red-neck crimes."

"Denying a seven-year-old sunshine, time for play,

decent food—is this a minor wrong in your lexicon, Mr. Campbell?"

"I only say you're dodging the true issue. You sit satisfied, red-necks without understanding of the moral wrong of human slavery."

Luther Perkins laughed. "Before we come to blows, let's agree. Slavery is morally wrong. Morally unjustifiable. But don't close your eyes. Child labor is slavery. You fellows have plenty of bleeding you can do up north without coming down here spreading your abolition shit. You New Englanders don't have to go to war to end slavery. Force your establishment—the textile manufacturers, the shippers, the money people—to pay a fair and reasonable rate for raw cotton. These huge cotton farms can produce only because of slave labor. And slave labor is enforced by the prices paid by New England and English and other textile people on the world market. It's simple enough that even a Harvard graduate ought to be able to understand it."

Hunt laughed cuttingly. "The devil can find justification for anything he does. Look at those slaves working in that field. Can you tell me they have the right to the least human dignity? Can you say they are not mistreated, whipped, starved, and sold at random?"

"Yes. I could tell you that. But it would be like talking to a blank wall. You people have never heard anything except what you already are prepared to believe. The blacks in that field are better fed, better housed, have better medical treatment than millions of whites in these southern states."

"You plantation owners are just overflowing with the milk of human kindness," Hunt said, mouth twisting.

"Some are. Me. I never owned a slave. Never yanked a black baby from its mother's tit in my life. It's only common sense, Mr. Campbell. If common sense doesn't offend you. Slave owners cannot run their huge plantations without cheap labor. Slaves provide the cheap labor—in the short term. Plantations are mortgaged and failing—even with slave labor."

"Thank God."

"Thank your New England industrialists. They're

nearer. Often these plantations go down to mortgagors because slaves are so incredibly expensive—over the long haul. Hold your nose for a moment, Mr. Campbell, and pretend you are a slave-holding plantation owner. Slaves are your only farm implements. Does it make sense to want them whipped, discontented, beaten, ill? They want them healthy. In simple words, this is because only if they are healthy can they work well in the fields, houses, crafts. Nothing else makes sense. They've got to feed them well to keep them going. They give them the best housing possible because this is conducive to good health and all possible contentment."

"And they sell them on the auction blocks, ripping families apart without regard for human emotions."

"That's propaganda shit put out by Quakers. Slaves' families, where there are young children, are protected by law. Mothers with young can't be separated from infants or young children. It's the law, but facts are so awkward when they destroy accepted theories in predigested culture."

"If it is a law, it's another one red-necks break with impunity."

"Shit. Most laws are broken, whether the man breaking them is a red-neck or a blue-belly." The stout attorney went into a long dissertation on slavery. Hunt closed his mind to him. This was easy because he had not opened it very much from the outset. The lawyer agreed that powerful voices of intellect, politics, and religion were raised against slavery since the days of ancient Greece. On the other hand, slavery was an economic, political, and caste-system fact of life that had existed since the beginnings of recorded time. Though people protested against slavery, business, commerce, agriculture, and established society didn't always listen to the chorus of their consciences, or respond to their exhortations. In the eighteenth century, blacks were being advertised and sold in London, Liverpool, and Bristol, without public outcry or protest. By 1788, the House of Commons received over 100 petitions against the slave trade, petitions instituted, at least, by the Quakers. The antislavery sentiment rushed onward on a rising tide, and the British slave trade was abolished in

1807. Eventually, England abolished slavery itself across its possessions. By the 1770s, the debate over slavery was intense in the American colonies and in France. Serfdom, however, intensified during these same years in Russia. The new United States pledged, as they established themselves as a sovereign nation, to suppress the slave trade. Abolitionist movements North and South were already strong and vocal. But almost at once the founding fathers found themselves forced to compromise the issue in order to gain any kind of federation of the states. And nobody knew what to do about the slaves anyhow. Jefferson abhorred slavery, but owned slaves which were freed only upon his death. Almost 10 percent of the South's Negro population was freed in the forty years following the revolution. Freed blacks, in order to survive, remained carefully apart from and subservient to the surrounding whites —in New England and the North as well as in the South —from the northern Quaker as much as from the southern Baptist. The French revolutionists emancipated all slaves in that troubled land. Napoleon immediately reenslaved them. The Quakers, who kept their wives and children in a rigid bondage, fought bitterly North and South, against enslaving blacks. In England and New England, men found no hypocrisy in crying out against black slavery while they enforced child labor in their filth-ridden factories. "But I'll give you this, Mr. Campbell. You abolitionists got yourself an emotional issue in the slavery of blacks. The fodder that feeds the propaganda tracts of the Evangelicals and the Quakers was the horror of the ocean passage, the cruelty toward black men, the rape of black women, the inhumanity toward the insane and the physically ill, the atrocity of the slave blocks. But this is an imperfect world, Mr. Campbell. Abolitionists have made a big business and a huge profit of the politics of protest. I don't reckon I know which is rottener, living off the sweat of unpaid blacks, or growing rich exploiting that slavery."

"I can tell you which I believe is rottener," Hunt said.

"You don't have to tell me. I can guess. I only expounded so long on the history of slavery because I truly enjoy hearing myself talk. Reckon that's why I turned to courtroom law. I get captive audiences there. I can harangue 'em as long as it amuses me."

"You are never disturbed by the right and wrong of an issue?"

"Rarely, Mr. Campbell. Rarely. I recognize this as an imperfect world. I try to make my way across it causing as little harm to my neighbor as possible. If we could get the North to share my credo, we could avoid bloodshed."

"There'll be bloodshed." Hunt assured him. "We'll make you people give these black slaves equality."

"Yes. I can see how a war between a backward agricultural economy such as the South's, and an onrushing industrial economy such as rules the North will surely end." He laughed. "Meantime, Mr. Campbell, let me give you a little friendly advice. Soft-pedal your abolitionist talk while you're down here. Not for the good of anyone else. But for your own welfare. I've seen a lot of young bluebellies ridden out of a lot of communities wearing nothing but hot tar and feathers. You don't need a bath like that to heat up your New England blood."

"Outrage heats my blood, sir."

"Sure it does. Too bad. Puritan inhibition denies any emotion except outrage. That's why you fellows are so cold you got blue bellies. But take heart, Mr. Campbell. You'll warm up after you been in our sunshine awhile. Soon as you've changed your luck with a hot-assed little black wench or two, you'll see a lot of things differently."

CHAPTER 14

NEVER BEFORE in her life had Florine Pilzer been caught up in a more anguished state of ecstatic anxiety. She lay rigidly unmoving in the bed beside Bos, afraid the clatter of her heart against its rib cage might waken him. As usual, he had climbed into bed, stroked her roughly, mounted her, and almost at once let go in that swift, useless ejaculation that may have relieved him, but did nothing for her. Tonight it was worse; it honed the sharp edges of her tension unbearably. He had fallen away from her, grunted something unintelligible, and in seconds was snoring loudly. Florine had lain beside him, breathless with need, apprehension, and a tormenting anticipation in conflict with fear. She had not slept but had drifted into a half-consciousness in which she lost all conception of time or place.

She went over in her mind the incredible events of this unlikely day. She'd been bent over the steaming wash tub, scrubbing at the sweat and grime ground into Bos's denim shirts, when he'd appeared, driving a buggy. She'd stopped working, drying her soap-wrinkled, heat-pinked hands on her apron. She brushed strands of her hair back from her sweated face, watching the buggy roll into the yard. The small one-seater was almost beside her before she realized that the Negro swathed in spotless white bandages was the young Fulani, Moab. She experienced a sudden emptiness in the pit of her stomach.

Pilzer swung down from the buggy. He glanced at her, scowling. He greeted her even less warmly than usual. "Damn," was all he said.

"What's wrong?" She watched the young Fulani narrowly but covertly. He did not look toward her but she saw that his toasted-gold face was pallid. He was agonizingly aware of her presence, all right. "What's happened, Bos?"

"Goddamn," Pilzer said. He jerked his head and the boy got down gingerly from the buggy. Pilzer watched him, face drawn taut, eyelids distended, until he was safely on the ground, supporting himself against the buggy wheel. Pilzer jerked his head again and strode off toward the barn. The boy hesitated, then followed. He had not openly glanced toward Florine, but she knew he was sweetly-painfully aware of her; only they existed in this moment and place; it was as if Pilzer was not even there.

Florine stood squinting in the sun watching Pilzer throw open the door of the tack room. Then he stepped inside, pushed out the wooden window, and braced it with a pole. The boy leaned against the wall of the barn, waiting in silence. Pilzer plodded out of the tack room without glancing toward Moab, walked past where Florine stood. "Is something wrong, Bos?" Florine persisted.

"Goddamn," Pilzer explained. He entered the house, returned with a mattress, which he placed on a wooden cot in the tack room. When this was done, he jerked his head toward the Fulani boy again. Moab stepped inside the tack room. After a moment, Pilzer walked out. He stalked toward Florine, jerked his head in a gesture commanding her to follow. He entered the house and let the door slam behind him.

She found him slumped in a kitchen chair and leaning heavily against the table. His face was rigid but she knew he was seething inwardly with suppressed rage. "What happened to the nigger?" she said. She had learned how to talk with Pilzer; she knew the attitude toward blacks he appreciated. He hated anything with a black skin; he asked no more, no less, of his wife.

"Goddamn," he said. He stared at his fist. It was clenched hamlike, quivering at the end of his thick arm. After a moment he added to that. "Bastard. Goddamn bastard. . . ."

Florine smiled in the darkness, coming fully awake. She was so wide awake, in fact, that she was certain it was almost 4:00 A.M. It had to be Bos's usual waking time. She could not stand this tantalizing anxiety any longer. She was still unable to believe the impossible good-fortune that had befallen her. She didn't know what she'd done to deserve this beautiful opportunity, but she prayed her credit in heaven was substantial. For some reason known only to Him, God had decided to smile upon Florine Pilzer. Perhaps it was all those unappreciated dimes in the collection plate at the Mt. Zion First Baptist Church. Perhaps God felt compassion because she was caught between the two worlds of the rich and the poor in the American South. She stood between those two worlds, belonging to neither. Maybe God pitied her for all the nights she'd suffered Pilzer's sexual assaults with all the excitement and emotional gratification of washing the supper dishes. For whatever reason Moab had been sent up here to rest, recover, and recuperate, she was thankful. She didn't ask questions.

Pilzer went on snoring. Distantly she heard the nocturnal cry of some other wild she-animal prowling the forests. The plantation was quiet. No light winked anywhere. There was no night breeze; it was as if everything held its breath, waiting in the hot stillness. She felt tension like static in the very atmosphere. She thought about Moab's lying on that mattress out in the tack room. She *knew* he was awake. He *had* to be as wakeful as she. Waiting. Listening. Hoping against hope. Her breath quickened.

She waited for what seemed hours. The seconds crawled past painfully, etching out each separate minute. She grew restive and sweated in the bed. She had to know the time. Cautiously, holding her breath, she turned back the covers and swung her legs over the side of the mattress. Pilzer stirred, mumbling. "What's matter, Florine? Where you going?"

"Just going to the thunder chamber," she answered. "Go back to sleep."

He was snoring again, almost at once. She sighed, realizing she'd been holding her breath. She tiptoed across the floor, barely aware of its roughness against the soles of her feet. She crept into the kitchen, found a long-stemmed sulphur match. She struck it and held its yellow flare up before the face of the massive Swiss-made clock which had been in the Pilzer family longer than Bos had. Her heart sank. It was only 1:00 A.M.

She sagged against the pinewood kitchen table. Her eyes stung. Three eternal, sleepless hours before Pilzer would crawl out of bed and clatter around the kitchen. She stared through the rear window. She saw the deep shadows of wisteria vines, the chinaberry tree and the barn beyond, the tack room window braced open. The Fulani boy was out there in the darkness. He might as well be on the far side of the moon. She swallowed hard, drawing what response she could from his actual physical nearness. She felt the thunderous arrhythmia of her heart. In her mind's eye she could see Moab across that ebon-shadowed yard. He lay naked in that cot, his belly flat, his chest corded with muscles, his manhood rigid and unyielding as a dagger waiting to be driven into its white sheath. . . .

The Baynard family was up, dressed, and at the breakfast table before seven that morning.

Kathy was the last to arrive at the table in the family dining room. She was pale, her easter-lily cheeks taut, eyes encircled in dark shadows. She'd worked frantically to erase traces of her silent crying. She had lain awake in her bed all night trying to adjust to what she saw as her existence as Styles' unwanted wife. She could not blame Styles for turning away from her. After all, like every proud man, Styles wanted a son and she was barren, empty, a failure as a wife, a nothing, less than a woman. This was the bitter truth she had to learn to live with, and there was no easy adjustment. She had loved Styles so deeply and so passionately. She had been so proud just to be seen with him. She'd been the envy of every girl in the state, and this exalted her because not only was Styles perfect to look upon, she loved him completely, and they were as happy as jealous people feared they might be. The sound of his voice reading to her could turn her hot and liquid down there. She had wanted him shamelessly from the first. There was no unhurtful way to face the fact that she could not have Styles anymore because he did not want her.

She lay on the sweated, rumpled sheet swallowing at the aching lump in her throat. What had she to live for? She no longer wanted to live, but she hadn't the courage to end even a life that had become ugly and depressing for her. She didn't want to cling to Styles when he no longer wanted her, but she lacked the courage to tell him he could be free. She clenched her fists at her sides. If he asked her for a divorce, she would agree without protesting. She could salvage her pride, her self-respect. These seemed small coin from all she had treasured in her marriage with Styles.

She faced an even more frightening eventuality. For many reasons, Styles was not going to divorce her and she would be condemned to a succession of lonely and empty nights and days for all the rest of her life. She writhed, as if trying to break the hold of fetters.

She heard the family laughing and talking at the breakfast table. She slowed as she entered the family dining room. She didn't see how she could eat without throwing up. She felt a sense of release when Shiva, one of the maids, told her, giggling, that Miz Jahndark's new baby was being displayed in the kitchen. "She a Scandal, that baby," Shiva said, giggling. Kathy went into the kitchen instead of to the table.

Jeanne d'Arc's new baby lay in a wicker basket on the bare, scrubbed white-pine table. Kitchen workers and house maids crowded around, chattering. They stepped back, making a place for Kathy.

Kathy bit her lip. The baby was kicking its feet, as naked as the instant it was born. Its beauty, the miniature perfection of its old-gold colored features, the bright black eyes, moving to follow every movement, struck Kathy like a blow in the solar plexus. She was happy that Jeanne d'Arc's baby was so perfect, so lovely, but the sight of it underlined her own emptiness, her barren uselessness. She could not think of anything she wanted more than a baby

146

of her own. She glanced around, sick. Everyone else was so happy and she was so miserable. "Oh, Jahndark," Kathy said. "She is so beautiful."

"She a Scandal, all right," Shiva said.

"All babies are beautiful," Jeanne d'Arc said, her creamy chocolate face suffused with warm pleasure and pride.

"I wish she were mine," Kathy whispered.

"Jahndark, she let you take care of Scandal, much as you please, Miss Kathy," Shiva teased.

"Kathy." Styles' voice reached for her from the dining area doorway. She turned, nodding, her eyes brimmed with tears. His chilled voice raked her disapprovingly. "We're ready to leave, Kathy. Are you having breakfast?"

Kathy reached behind her, letting the tips of her fingers touch the baby's crib. "I'm not hungry," she said.

Styles shrugged and turned his back. He spoke over his shoulder as if she were a recalcitrant child. "Then get ready to go. Now."

Laus, the coachman, rode on the high seat atop the formal carriage. Two black footmen and a doorman accompanied him. The formal carriage was the best on the plantation. It was kept under wraps in its own carriage house stall, polished, oiled, brushed, in shimmering readiness. An enclosed coach, it had three seats across inside, with a space in rear for trunks or other baggage. It sported two doors on each side, a fringed top and curtains to lower at the windows against dust or inclement weather. The high seat where Laus sat with the doorman was so high they were provided with stationary ladders up each side to navigate to and from their elevated perches. The footmen, resplendent in their uniforms, stood up on the rear baggage rack.

The formal carriage was waiting at the front steps when Kathy came out on the veranda wearing a wide-brimmed straw hat and fragile veil. It was a brilliantly sunny morning, the sky flecked with fleecy cotton-boll clouds. The carriage attendants in polished uniforms stood like marines at attention, fighting to hide their self-conscious, prideful grins. Morgan writhed with anticipation, shifting from one leg to the other. "We're going to get it right now this morning, Kathy," Morgan said, trembling with excitement.

"Get what, Morgan?" Kathy teased.

"My tutor. Papa said he was gettin' me one. It's coming in on the train this morning. Soapy's going with us. Soapy ain't never seen one neither."

"Quite an occasion," Ferrell-Junior said. "The whole family all gussied up—uniformed attendants—the funeral carriage—"

"The formal carriage is not a hearse," Baynard reproved him, but he smiled indulgently.

"—and Soapy with his face washed—all for what? Going in to town to meet the new tutor."

"It's the least we can do," Baynard said. "After all, he is a stranger—coming to live with us."

"On the other hand," Styles said, "the man is nothing more than a servant."

"Yes," Baynard agreed. "A servant. With a PhD degree. Certainly not a slave. I'm sure he should be considered more on the level of a guest—perhaps a distant relative—"

"A paid guest," Styles said.

"Anyhow, not really a servant at all," Baynard insisted. "More like one of the family."

"Your family," Styles said. "Not mine. I count no relatives, thank God, among those cold-blooded, blue-bellied yankees. I never met one yet who wasn't a nigger-lover. I doubt this one will be any different."

Moments dragged past on the sunstruck veranda. The attendants standing at attention beside the carriage, sweated. Their collars wilted; perspiration formed in marble-sized beads under their high hats and careened down their faces.

Baynard paced back and forth on the veranda impatiently, checking his fat pocket watch. Twice he sent Thyestes limping in to inquire when they might hope Miz Claire would join them.

She appeared at last. She wore a wide-brimmed straw hat trimmed with artificial flowers and fruit. Her veil covered almost all her face and flowed across her shoulder.

Her high-necked silk dress rustled when she walked. In her wake came Jeanne d'Arc with a hamper of food Miz Claire had ordered prepared and a bottle of water, an under-butler carrying a small trunk of her dresses and petticoats, a maid with her case of make-up. "We're only going to be gone a few hours, Miz Claire," Baynard reminded her in frustration.

Miz Claire glanced at him, but stood imperiously on the steps until the trunk, case, hamper, and other impedimenta were loaded. Ferrell-Junior laughed. "Well, we're overcrowded now, and we don't even have Morgan's tutor in there yet. . . . Maybe I could follow in the carriage."

"No," Miz Claire said. "How would that look? I want all the children with me. The rest of you may care nothing for appearances, but I do. What will the young man think of us?"

"If there ain't no room when we get the tutor," Morgan said, "me and ole Soapy'll ride in back with the bags and hang our legs over."

"You'll act like a gentleman," Miz Claire said, "if it kills you."

CHAPTER 15

THE THREE LONG, interminable hours dragged past. Florine lay exhausted with tension and sleepless fatigue by the time Bos finally pulled himself out of bed at 4:00 A.M. He struck fire to a lamp wick, turned it down, and sat for a dull-witted moment on the edge of the mattress, huge and round shouldered as a bear. He growled against his fate, against Negroes in general, and Blackoaks Negroes in particular. He scratched lingeringly at his crotch, finally got up and dressed. Florine kept her eyes closed. He took up the lamp and plodded into the kitchen, the light seeming to iris yellowly through the door as if sucked along in his wake.

She was left in the breathless dark. She heard Bos preparing his breakfast. Everything was as usual; only she knew better. This night, this morning were unusual on God's calendar—she was convinced of this. There was nothing in her experience to prepare her for this moment. There was a sick emptiness in her solar plexus; her whole body ached as if she suffered with the recurrent flashes and chills of the ague.

When at last Bos was gone from the house, the light in the kitchen extinguished, a numbing terror assaulted Florine, incapacitating her. She had thought she would leap from her bed and call out to Moab—as she had called out to him through scores of fevered morning fantasies. But she did no such thing. She heard Bos saddle his white horse, heard the animal clop downtrail toward the slave quarters, and still she did not move. It was as if the muscles of her arms and legs would no longer obey the messages from her brain. She lay in a kind of lassitude, knowing she could not get out of this bed because she dared not. Oh, God, there turned out to be such a terrible latitude between one's inner fantasies and reality. Dreams arose hot from a fiery crucible with all fears burned out.

How could she have believed she would have called out to summon that Negro boy into this room, into her bed? And yet she had believed it; she had dreamed on it when she had nothing else to make life worth living except her passionate dreams. But in those sublime fantasies her marriage had no significance, her vows were all conveniently waived. Her marriage? She stirred uncomfortably on the wrinkled sheet. She existed in a marriage in which she was neglected, left night after night in a constant state of frustration and need by a man who did not know or care what he did to her. Vows that cannot be lived with in a day-by-day, hour-by-hour existence are never set forth— or even anticipated—in advance.

She breathed raggedly, pressing her body down into the heated mattress as if seeking a return to warmth and protection. If that boy came boldly to her window now, what would she do—shoot him? She wanted to reach out for Bos's handgun and the reassurance its awkward solidity would afford her. She did not move, but went on staring at the shadowed ceiling.

If Moab came near her and she didn't kill him, Bos would kill her. If she spoke in a kindly tone to the Fulani, Bos would kill her. This truth acted as no deterrent: Bos was killing her anyway. The choice was not all that dramatic; it added up merely to either a quick death spat from a gun, or a slow death from neglect. One consideration she had not looked at before: Bos would kill the boy if he suspected that Moab had come near her when Bos was away. She didn't want Moab's murder on her conscience, did she?

Her mouth twisted wryly as if she'd tasted bitter persimmon. Bos would not kill Moab alone if he found them together—or suspected they had been in the same bed, the same house. Nothing would cleanse Bos Pilzer's besmirched honor and pride under those circumstances except the violent death of both her and Moab. There was no sense worrying that Moab's death at fifteen would be on her conscience. If Moab died, she died too. Bos Pilzer could not have it otherwise and go on living with himself —a white woman once violated by a black man was no longer any good to a white man. God knew, that was the code of the South.

Florine shuddered, chilled. Black on white. The subject of sermons in Baptist churches, of horrified whispers wherever three or more white women gathered. An abomination before God. Part of the training of every Southern white child—and, be honest about it, every Northern white child too, despite the hypocritical denials. She'd been born in Pennsylvania and her earliest memories of blacks were her father's estimation of "those black apes from Africa. They ought to be freed from slavery. But they ought to be kept down south where they belong— where them cracker slave-owners had brought them in the first place." Black on white. Well, this whole controversy left her cold. She had no such prejudice, no such inhibition. Moab was the most beautiful human being she had ever seen. . . .

She swung out of bed. Her heartbeats increased into a trip-hammer tempo. She told herself she'd make coffee— she'd do anything, she couldn't stay in bed any longer, and of course, she could not go near that black boy in the tack room. What kind of overheated madness had ever made her imagine that she could?

The lampshade was still hot. She burned her fingers when she lifted it to light the wick. She didn't even consciously feel the lance of pain. The lamp sat where Bos had left it on the kitchen table. She watched the fire flare up yellow and blue, then she lowered the wick and set the shade in place. She looked around the room; the litter Bos always left behind for her was strewn about—used plates, soiled cups, greasy utensils. A fire still glowed in its coals inside the iron wood-burning stove. But she didn't make coffee. She stood staring at the back door. She walked across the room to it. Her throat felt dry, hurting. Her legs were weak and her fingers trembled as she pushed the door open. She spoke in a low tone and yet she knew her voice would carry to the barn in the dark silence before dawn. "Moab. . . ."

He appeared at once in the doorway of the tack room. He wore only onasburg britches. He was an ebon shadow in the blackness, but she saw him clearly. Her heart lurched. He had been waiting, lying there, waiting for her. . . .

"Come here, boy," she said into the darkness.

He came across the yard to her. Her fingers dug into the doorjamb. She stood in her cotton gown, the light behind her, the door partly opened. She watched him come close. He was covered by bandages wrapped over one shoulder and tightly around his chest. "Yes, ma'am?" he said.

"You feel all right?" she said.

"Yes'm."

"Why weren't you sleeping?"

"Masta Pilzer woke me, I guess."

"You're lying. You haven't been asleep, have you?"

"No, ma'am."

"What have you been thinking about out there?"

"Nuthin', ma'am. Jes' lyin' there, I reckon."

"With a hard-on?"

"Ma'am?" His voice shook.

"You got a hard-on now."

He didn't speak.

"Haven't you?" she persisted. She waited. He didn't say anything. "You think you're going to see me—naked—the way you did the other time, don't you?"

"No, ma'am."

"You didn't tell anybody, did you? Seeing me like that? What I was doing—to myself?"

"No, ma'am. I swear. I never told anybody."

"But you thought about it, didn't you? You think you're coming in here now—and get in my bed, don't you?"

"I never thought that! Before Gawd."

"Don't lie to me. I reckon you'd run and tell that to your nigger friends, wouldn't you?"

"I'll never tell nobody, ma'am."

"You do think I'm going to let you do it, don't you?"

He was breathing raggedly, but he made no attempt to speak.

"Would you—keep your mouth shut—if I let you—look at me again?"

"I swear."

"Just look at me—nothing else."

"Yes, ma'am."

"No. Don't come in this door. Come in the window."

"Yes, ma'am."

Her heart battered in her rib cage. He didn't have to ask which window. He knew—as he'd known in all her frantic fantasies. She turned away, closed the door, trembling visibly. She didn't turn down the wick in the lamp. She was afraid to touch it, trembling as she was. If she knocked it over, she'd set the goddamn house on fire. Things were hot enough.

The lamplight trailed dimly into her bedroom. She pulled her gown over her head and threw it behind her. She walked naked toward her bed. She saw Moab standing beyond the closed window. Her voice rasped. "Open it, damn you. Come on in."

Moab opened the window and stepped through it. She lay down on her side of the bed, aware of her nakedness as she had never been before. Her body quivered, gooseflesh standing over it. She ached in a delicious sense of agony. He closed the window behind him and stood looking at her. His quivering fingers worked at the thick buttons on his pants. He dropped them about his feet and stepped out of them. She stared transfixed at his blood-engorged penis, pointing upward like a lance, trembling in its rigidity, his hanging testicles, the muscular legs. Her hips writhed involuntarily, and she felt the gushing of hot liquid at her thighs. "I'll bet you've beat it off all night," she accused him. "You won't be any good."

He came to the bed, stood beside it, frightened, shaken, but driven by compulsions too fierce for him to fight or understand.

"Well, lie down," she ordered. "You're no good to either one of us standing there like that."

He got into the bed beside her. His dark flesh glowed against the white counterpane. She reached out. His hands were icy cold. She drew them over against her breasts. She felt his chilled fingers close on their taut fullness, and her hips grinding spasmodically already, she moved to him. "Did you know I was going to let you do this to me?" she said. She took his rigid staff in both her hands, running them over it, caressing his testes. He whispered half in ecstasy, half in protest, through clenched teeth. It came out like the beseeching prayer, "Oh, Gawd. Oh, my Gawd. . . ."

"You knew I was going to call you in here, didn't you?" she whispered against his face.

"I prayed, ma'am." His hand moved between her legs, into the liquid wetness. "Gawd, how I prayed. To every god Blade ever told me about, I prayed."

"What am I going to let you do to me, Moab?"

"Ma'am?"

"Say it. Out loud. Damn it. Say it. I want to hear you say it. What are you going to do to me?"

"Fuck you. . . . I'm going to fuck you."

"Say it. . . ."

"I'm going to fuck you." He pushed her legs apart as they had been that other morning. He rolled between them. She held his rigid penis, guiding him.

Her voice rasped against his face. "One thing I better warn you. If we are caught, I'll scream rape. You understand me?" Her voice rose. "I'll scream rape, and I'll keep screaming it until you're hanging from a tree."

He had gone too far now to care about such an inconsequential matter as life or death. He drove himself into her. She gasped with delight and caught his slender hips inside her legs. She locked her ankles, feeling an ecstasy not even anticipated in her wildest fantasy. She had what she wanted, she had what she had to have to live at all, and she could think only how she was going to keep him. She knew one thing: his recovery was going to be remarkably protracted—slow and long delayed.

The lamp was still burning brightly in the kitchen at ten o'clock that morning.

The conductor pushed open the heavy door at the end of the day coach and stepped through, fighting for balance against the sway of the train on the rails. "Mt. Zion, next stop," the conductor called. "Mt. Zion."

Hunter Campbell felt the tension mount when his destination was named. Five eternal days and suddenly the trip ended. He stuck his head out the window, squinting against the scatter-shot cinders that peppered his face. He saw nothing ahead. He should have been relieved and pleased that the long journey was ending, but the sense of strangeness, the threat of the unknown, and a shift in the very attitudes of the people around him made him long backward to New England with regret and melancholy. He'd have been killed if he'd stayed up there. That violence was behind him, but ahead stretched a new life among people he didn't understand, in temperament as well as accent, in a hot, violent land, upon some plantation so far in the backcountry that it was likely the sun set between it and the civilization he'd known. His old life flashed before his eyes replacing the dry, copse-crested sand hills—contemplation, reading, stimulating conversation with one's equals, Massachusetts Hall. Harvard. Cambridge. Addie. He'd never see Addie again. How long before he'd walk the familiar, crooked Boston streets? For no good reason, he envisioned the old houses of Boston decked out for the Christmas season. Then he remembered that first Christmas—a year and a half ago!—leaving Harvard Yard, hurrying in the light snow along the uneven bricks of Massachusetts Avenue, going in the side street to the small house he'd rented to find Addie waiting there ahead of him. How nervous she'd seemed at first until he undressed her before the fireplace, the bright flames glowing and reflected in her peach-bloom flesh. Naked, how wild she'd become. All the good he'd had with Addie, lost forever.

The deeper into the south backcountry the train raced west of Atlanta, the sharper grew Hunter's sense of disorientation, his apprehensions. Since he'd left Atlanta his mode of dress—so elegantly correct in Boston—had seemed extreme in contrast to the casual, rough clothing of the people who shared the day coach. The other passengers grinned at each other, nodding toward him, setting him apart. Thank God he didn't belong to this herd. Still, for the first time in his life he was the object of ridicule.

Yesterday morning, a beefy white man had boarded the train leading a burly Negro runaway in shackles, handcuffs, and a restraining leash about his throat. The Negro sat beside the window, rage seething in his black eyes. He looked surly and he looked dangerous, but Hunt felt only compassion for him. He was a huge man, outweighing his strapping captor by fifty pounds at least, but the chain leash looped about his throat was far more than an equalizer. The white man had only to give it a jerk and he could choke his captive, cut off his oxygen completely. If he yanked hard enough, he could break the Negro's neck. They both knew this. The slave sat, sullen and silent. His nose, wide and flat across the nostrils had been broken and rebroken at the bridge. His body betrayed the grey scars of old knife cuts. The white man and the captured slave sat across the aisle from Hunt where he could neither ignore nor forget them. Negro passengers, Hunt learned, were not permitted in the white day coach; a black captive was something else; he rode with his jailer.

Hunt could feel the hatred and tension like something filthy and tangible across that aisle. He could also hear the snickers of ill-bred children and teenagers around him. Small boys held their circled fingers at their eyes, imitating his pince-nez, and strutted with their heads tilted back. He sweated, miserable in the unbroken humidity and heat. Why had he come to this godforsaken land?

The train slowed, the cars buckling against each other. Mt. Zion was just ahead. Hunt sweated.

The entrance of the Baynards into Mt. Zion aboard their gleaming formal carriage created almost as uncommon a stir among the townspeople as the twice-a-week arrival of the limited. Smaller local trains of the Atlanta, New Orleans & Natchez Line puffed through more frequently. But the twelve car special came all the way from New England—five days over many lines, through many towns and climes. It carried strangers, unusual cargo, and infrequently, it discharged a passenger at the Mt. Zion depot.

The entire citizenry of Mt. Zion turned out twice each week for the event. Many—especially the teenaged girls—dressed in their Sunday best, promenading the plank walks along Birmingham Street, or clustering on the depot platform under bright sun parasols as the train coughed in and halted. On those days—like today—when they were released at noon from their jobs at the mill, the stores, the lumberyard, the smitty, or the cotton warehouse, the young townsmen tanked up on beer at Avery's Tavern and made it a holiday. Older people wandered to the station from the side streets and the town square in the half-hour before train-time. On a sunny day most of the town's 800 population were out to greet the arriving locomotive.

Laus touched the whip to the four carriage horses, perking them up as they turned past the square going toward the tracks and the depot. He watched in pride as the carefully groomed animals responded like show-beasts, pricking their ears and stepping lively. At the rear of the coach, the footmen held on tightly, standing rigid and looking straight ahead, faces set seriously, as if on some urgent mission.

The townspeople paused, turning and staring as the polished carriage rolled past, as if they had never seen it before. Any envy was heavily tempered by local pride—the Baynards were fine people. There were no finer folks in the state that Mt. Zion knew of.

Laus pulled the carriage into a narrow shaft of shade near the Whites Only Waiting Room at the depot. Loungers and the stationmaster ran out to open the carriage doors, but the doorman leaped to the ground and haughtily motioned them to keep their distance. Even the town youths, drinking their beer and sweating in the blazing sun, quieted. Townspeople pushed nearer, wanting to be among the first to exchange greetings with the Baynards.

Pegasus, the doorman, opened the door and dropped the carriage steps. Then he straightened, ready to assist the elder Baynard, who was the first to alight. Several older men called out to him and Baynard smiled in return, exchanging greetings and brief comments on the weather —the heat, the slim possibility of rain and what it was doing to the crops. "You folks goin' out of town for a spell, Mr. Baynard?" somebody called. Baynard shook his head and smiled again. "No, just meeting someone." Miz Claire stepped down next. Many of the women spoke her name, nodding, vying for her attention, but she looked at them in faint annoyance. She recognized none of the faces though she'd been born in the community and spent most of her life in it. A woman of Miz Claire's age hurried over from the rim of the crowd and extended her hand and smiled intimately. Miz Claire stared at her blankly. "Why, Claire, don't you recall me? Imogene Smothers." Claire nodded and smiled in a way that was more rebuff than recognition. Imogene Smothers somehow retreated into the faceless mob without further wounds.

The young townsmen fell against each other, sobbing, moaning in simulated ecstasy, grinning, exchanging blows, or howling like coyotes when Kathy Baynard Kenric stepped from the carriage. The young girls under their parasols pressed closer together as if to be compared with Kathy's fragile beauty only as a group. Kathy's pale face suffused with blood and she hurried into the waiting room with her mother. Morgan stumbled getting out of the carriage, awkward and ungainly and followed closely by his body slave. Townspeople clucked their tongues sympathetically. Morgan wasn't bright; he was a cross the Baynards had to bear despite their wealth and social status. Somehow this was an equalizer for the ordinary townspeople and it removed all resentment. Money couldn't buy everything. Styles followed the boys from the carriage. He exchanged nods and an aloof smile with any of the townspeople—the bank president, a lawyer, a minister—who knew him well enough to speak.

Ferrell-Junior was the last out of the carriage. The townsmen yelled at him and he waved; he knew all of them by name. Some he liked casually, but most of them he disliked because no matter how hard he tried to be one of the boys, he found it impossible to share their interests —getting drunk and riding horses up and down Birmingham Street, playing practical jokes that sometimes left victims maimed or without reputation, harassing the shacks of freed Negroes, or hazing "persons of color" who passed through town. He wanted to be accepted among his peers, but he found it increasingly difficult rather than easier.

His gaze touched at the girls in their colorful dresses and bright parasols. Their eyes fell away under his. He moved his own eyes over them and then stopped at the face of a girl so lovely she looked out of place among her ordinary sisters, like a gardenia in a bouquet of black-eyed Susans.

She was different—and bolder too. Her gaze clashed upon his and held. She didn't smile but something glittered in her pale eyes that he couldn't give a name to—but to which he responded instantly. He felt a sudden tightening in his loins, an emptiness in his belly, felt his face grow warm. He fought in his mind for her name. She was three or four years younger than he—though her pale eyes were as old as coquetry. Lorna June. Lorna June Garrity. Something about her and Gil Talmadge. Looking at her, he found this hard to believe. God knew, she was far too lovely, too gentle looking for Gil.

The train whistle, the sound of its steam engine, a screech of brakes, and a clatter of wheels on rails sent the crowd scurrying around the station to the platform. Lorna June Garrity hesitated one moment longer and then she whirled the parasol like a curtain between them and went away with the rustling, giggling crowd of girls in flowered dresses.

Ferrell-Junior exhaled heavily and strode through the shadowed station waiting room. The big train had slowed to a stop and the conductor was setting the steps into place. Ferrell-Junior joined his family. Idly, he looked for Lorna June in the crowd but could not find her. There were two passengers debarking at Mt. Zion. A traveling salesman—a short, ostentatiously dressed clothing drummer—was first. He stepped down, looking around. Then the tall, erect young man in black top hat, pince-nez, tailored suit, and hand-made boots, was next. A buzz of excitement was ignited in the gaggle of teenaged girls; it flared through the older people and erupted into guffaws and catcalls among the youth of the town.

"There he is, Morgan," Ferrell-Junior said.

"Is that my tutor?" Morgan said.

Ferrell-Junior laughed. "What else could it be?"

CHAPTER 16

WHEN HUNTER CAMPBELL stepped off the train at the Mt. Zion station, he was struck simultaneously by the pitiless blast of the sun and the drunken hoots and guffaws of the milling young townsmen and boys at the edge of the platform. The heat was overwhelming and enervating. The obscene yells of ridicule were like offal flung in his face. The day-coach porter handed out Campbell's two large carpetbags. Hunt set the bags down on the planking and stood, irresolute, wanting to retreat into the locomotive car.

The Baynards moved forward to welcome him. Morgan ran, lumbering ahead of the family. "You Mr. Campbell?" Morgan asked, beaming.

Hunt nodded stiffly, and the very rigidity of his movements set the rowdies to yelling and pushing each other, pointing toward him in scorn. "There! I tole you. That there's what a real blue-belly looks like!" Hunter tilted his chin to convey how totally their verbal abuse was beneath his notice. They found this funnier than anything he had done so far. "I am Hunt Campbell," he told Morgan.

"We knowed it was you," Morgan said. "Recognized right off you was my tutor when you stepped off the train."

"No sensational deduction, really," Baynard said. He extended his hand to Campbell and put his arm about Morgan's shoulders. Soapy stood at Morgan's side, staring open-mouthed at the tutor. "After all, Mr. Campbell was one of only two men to get off the train, eh?"

"You sure look like a tutor," Morgan told Campbell. "Is that the way all tutors dress?"

Hunt glanced around uncomfortably, but managed to smile. "It's quite acceptable attire for Harvard, I assure you, Morgan."

Baynard introduced Campbell to his family. The townspeople stood silently staring at the young man in pince-nez and formal top hat. In their experience, only funeral directors dressed as this stranger did—and then only on the occasion of the actual burial ceremony. They had never seen anything like him. No one in the crowd left the station. This was more excitement than had stirred the imaginations and curiosity of Mt. Zion in months. Baynard motioned his carriage footmen to take Campbell's suitcases. The black men hurried forward.

"You don't have to do that," he told them. "I can carry my own bags."

The town rowdies pressed closer to hear all this. "Nigger-lover," one of them yelled, almost choking with laughter. "It's a goddamn nigger lover."

Baynard tried to ignore the whistling, shouting youths. He gestured and the footmen took the bags and hurried through the waiting room to the carriage. Baynard said, "Well, Morgan, here he is. Your tutor. All the way from Harvard University."

Morgan studied Hunt carefully. "Do I git to finger him, papa?"

Ferrell-Junior and Kathy burst out laughing. Miz Claire frowned, shocked. Even Styles smiled in spite of himself. Hunter scowled, completely baffled by the word. The townspeople pushed nearer in order to hear more clearly. Baynard stared at his son, amazed. "Whatever gave you such an idea, Morgan?"

"That's what Mr. Simon done—when he's thinking of buying Blade."

Now Baynard laughed, relieved. "Mr. Campbell is your tutor, boy. Not your slave."

"I shall try to be your slave, Morgan," Hunter said in a prim attempt at humor. "I'll try to bring you all the wonders of knowledge."

Morgan stared at him now, baffled, and Baynard warned, "Don't expect too much."

One of the town boys stepped from the laughing group

and yelled, "Hey, blue-belly. You down here to free all the slaves?"

Hunt tried to ignore the raging eruption of laughter, but his shoulders straightened defensively and he winced. They knew they were getting under his skin, annoying him. He tried to hide his irritation, but the very way he stood, erect and braced against them, betrayed him to them.

"We better get to the carriage," Baynard suggested. "These young fellows really don't mean any harm. You're new to them. Unknown. They've never seen anyone quite like you before. They're also beered up—and there are all these pretty girls for them to show off to. . . . Sometimes they can get pretty rough."

Kathy walked on Hunt's left and Miz Claire on his right. Morgan and Soapy danced ahead, walking backward, watching Hunt in fascination. The three Baynard men followed, setting up a rear guard between the new tutor and the town roughs who now surged forward, following them through the waiting room. The remainder of the townspeople hurried around the station building. They grouped about in the sunstruck street to watch. The gaggle of girls, their crinolines squealing, knotted together under their parasols, giggling.

Laus, Pegasus, and the footmen stood beside the carriage, nervous and sweated. The raging drunken laughter of these young white men portended trouble and struck terror in the slaves' minds. Horror had erupted from milder beginnings than this in their own memories. All they wanted was to get the family safely into the carriage. Laus was already planning ahead in his mind how he would force the four-horse carriage through the crowd no matter how obstreperous they became. A Negro could be hung for daring to strike a white man, even when he had been struck first, but a Negro, as a white man's driver, could run down anyone who tried to stop him, as the white man himself might do to protect life or property.

Pegasus helped Miz Claire into the carriage, and then lightly touched Kathy's arm to assist her up the folded-out steps. A growl of protest erupted from the throats of the young drunks. They saw that the blue-belly would be next into the carriage and the fun would be over before it began. As one, half a dozen youths suddenly rushed forward, pushing the black footmen aside and trussing Hunter against the huge front wheel of the carriage. Hunter lost his hat and his pince-nez slipped from his nose, bouncing at the end of the silken cord, as he toppled.

"Here! You men. Behave yourselves. Are you insane?" Baynard roared.

His commanding voice rattling in the silence may have stopped them, but Hunt straightened, pressed against the wheel, his face white with terror. This was like the hot taste of blood to the crowd of drunks.

Hunt bent over to retrieve his top hat. One of the town boys kicked it beyond his reach. Hunt straightened. "That's ill bred and boorish," he said. "Completely uncalled for."

"We're all ill-bred boors, blue-belly!" someone in the crowd yelled. "Ill-bred crackers, blue-belly!"

Hunt moved to retrieve his hat, which was now dusty and dented. They let him almost touch it, then another boy kicked it out of his reach again.

"Hit him, Mr. Campbell!" Morgan yelled. "Hit the son of a bitch!"

Morgan's swearing brought Miz Claire's head plunging through the carriage window, but she took one appraising glance at the mob of drunks and didn't reprimand Morgan. The youths took up the chant. "Yeah! Hit him, *Mister* Campbell. Hit the son of a bitch, blue-belly."

Hunt made one more attempt to recover his battered top hat. This time it was booted high. It sailed into the blinders of the right horse. The animal lunged in its traces, squealing.

Hunt straightened his jacket and turned back toward the carriage, clinging at least to his aloof dignity. There was now a wall of red, jeering, taunting faces between him and the Baynards. He stared along his nose at the young thugs and replaced his pince-nez. This was the worst possible of all moves he could have made. It set them off, wilder than ever, laughing and pointing and yelling.

"Hey, blue-belly. You really got a blue belly?"

"Let's see your blue belly, blue-belly."

"Yeah. Let's look at his blue belly."

"Ain't never seen a real ice-cold blue belly up close."

"Always wanted to see me a real blue belly."

Hunt walked forward, erect, face pallid but set. He was taller by some inches than the biggest of his tormentors. He moved straight ahead, looking beyond them, refusing to see them, refusing to hear them, refusing to admit they existed as human beings.

They grabbed at him. They caught his swallow-tailed coat at its collar and jerked it downward, tearing it. He flinched, tried to hold his arms rigid against them, but they were too strong. They ripped the jacket down his back and tossed it over their heads, yelling. He stood, in travel-wrinkled shirt, galluses, and carefully knotted ascot.

"Come on, blue-belly," they shouted into his face like small dogs yapping upward at a whippet. "Show us your blue belly."

They grabbed at his suspenders, jerking them from their buttons and ripping them off. Hunt threw up his arm to protect himself, but made no attempt to strike back.

Morgan howled in rage and thrust himself into the melee, striking out wildly with his big fists, but with a complete lack of physical coordination. "Oh, God," Baynard whispered to nobody, "he'll be killed."

Morgan stood, swinging his arms wildly, yelling at Hunt to fight back. "Hit them sons of bitches. Hit them sons of bitches."

Soapy pushed his way into where Morgan was surrounded. He knew that he could be killed for hitting a white man, but he could think only that he had to get to Morgan. He didn't make it. The sight of a black face was all the mob needed to go out of control. Two men struck at Soapy from both sides, hitting him in the temples and about the cheeks and eyes as if trying to destroy his black face. Morgan screamed, swinging harder, trying to fight his way to Soapy who went down to his knees, still being clubbed by white fists.

"Stop this, damn you!" Ferrell-Junior grabbed the man nearest him by the collar. He wheeled him around and while the fellow set himself, Ferrell-Junior struck him full in the face with all the strength he could muster. He broke the man's jaw and sent him reeling against the carriage.

For one instant, this put a stop to the brawl as the townsboys turned to face Ferrell-Junior. They'd seen him before roused with rage. The youth sprawled on the dirt, half under the carriage, his jaw sprung. He howled in an agony that took much of the courage out of his friends. These boys knew Ferrell-Junior as the mildest mannered youth in the state, with the worst temper south of Atlanta when roused. They hesitated.

Morgan was able to clutch Soapy in both his arms and try to pull him up to his feet. Ferrell-Junior pushed his way forward toward Hunter Campbell, grabbing at the men nearest him. They retreated, just out of his reach. As Morgan got Soapy to his feet, a youth beside him kicked the Negro boy viciously in the crotch. The boot was driven upward and Soapy doubled forward, vomiting.

Styles said, "Oh, goddamn it." He strode forward with his cane raised. He brought the cane down across the neck and shoulders of the man who had kicked Soapy. Kathy leaned out of the carriage, her tiny fists clenched, screaming at Styles. "Kill him, Styles. Kill him."

Styles kept hitting the man until his cane broke. A youth behind Styles struck him on the shoulder. When Styles spun around, the stub of the cane raised, the youth lunged upward and hit him in the face. Styles stood immobile for a full second and then toppled against the station wall and crumpled to the street.

Ferrell-Junior was entirely surrounded by the mob now. Baynard lunged forward, thrusting the youths aside. He caught both Soapy and Morgan by the arms. He yanked them out of the crowd. Laus moved toward him. "Get them in the carriage, Laus," Baynard ordered. The big Negro nodded. He used his knees and elbows. Technically, he hit no white man, but he got the boys to the carriage and into it. He reached upward then and took the heavy buggy whip from its socket.

"No, Laus," Kathy called to him, shaking her head. "No. They'll kill you."

Laus hesitated, holding the thick-stocked whip in his fist. Hunt had retreated to the wheel of the carriage. He stood braced against it, unmoving. His pince-nez was gone, his shirt ripped. Baynard stared for a moment at the toughs mauling Ferrell-Junior from both sides.

Ferrell-Junior's face was bleeding. A gash over his left eye spurted blood. Kathy screamed. Miz Claire pushed her head further out the window, watching Ferrell-Junior fighting against the overpowering odds. "Oh, my God," Miz Claire wailed. "Oh, my baby. My God, Mr. Baynard. Help my baby."

Baynard grabbed the whip from Laus. He plowed forward into the mob, swinging the lash back and forth, cutting, slashing, putting all the strength of his 230 pounds together with the rage of his Scottish temperament behind those savage strokes. The boys fell back, some of them cut, most of them sobering swiftly.

Baynard was almost to where Ferrell-Junior was trapped, fighting. Two of his attackers retreated under the sting of Baynard's whip. The third suddenly yanked a handgun from his belt and thrust it hard against Ferrell-Junior's bloodied eyes. "Hold it, you old bastard," the boy said.

Baynard stopped, the whip raised. His voice shook with outrage. "Put away that gun, you moron."

The mob was silent now. The drunken sense of a pleasurable holiday was gone; the mob fragmented, no longer one brutal, insensitive glob of idiocy that didn't know where to stop. The yelling died away, only a sick residue of horror remained. Everyone stared at that gun rammed inches from Ferrell-Junior's blood-smeared face.

"Put down the gun, Travis," one of the townsboys said. "You don't need to murder nobody."

"Ain't murder to kill a snotty son of a bitch," Travis said. He jerked his head, indicating Baynard. "Nobody takes a buggy whip to me."

Travis pushed the gun forward. A girl screamed. Older men pushed forward, but everything stopped as Travis pressed the trigger.

The hammer fell and clicked. The rimfire had missed. Ferrell-Junior reacted in that flash of time. He caught the gun, yanked it from Travis's hand. He smashed the gun against the station plankings. Three of Travis's friends clutched Travis and half-dragged him into the station waiting room. The other boys, chastened, retreated.

Baynard handed the whip to Laus. He touched Hunt's elbow. "You better get in the carriage now, Mr. Campbell."

Hunt nodded. He walked forward unsteadily as if the ground rolled beneath him. Pegasus helped him into the carriage. Hunt sagged into the seat and sat, staring at the flooring.

Styles got up groggily. He shook his head to clear it and crossed the shaded area, still shaken. Laus and Kathy helped him into the carriage. Baynard and Laus went to where Ferrell-Junior stood, dabbing at his bloody face with his handkerchief. Baynard put his arm about his son. Laus took Ferrell-Junior's elbow, guiding him. There was taut silence around them, an ashamed, repentent quiet. They helped Ferrell-Junior into the carriage. Baynard followed, speaking over his shoulder, "You may drive home now, Laus."

The footmen leaped up on the rear of the carriage. Laus and Pegasus mounted the ladder with alacrity but with great dignity. Clearly, they were not running. The carriage rocked and then sprang forward, creaking.

Inside the carriage, Kathy clung to Styles' hand. He did not pull away from her. "Oh, Styles," she said. "I was so proud of you."

"We all were," Baynard said.

"Isn't the word astonished?" Styles inquired with a faint, puzzled smile. "Nobody was more surprised than I to find me in that street brawl."

Morgan said, "Sometimes you just got to fight, Mr. Campbell. A man's got to fight for his honor."

"It's all right, Morgan," Baynard said. "Mr. Campbell has his own values."

Hunt tried to smile. "I don't believe in physical violence, Morgan. I don't believe it truly settles an issue. I have never yet seen anything important enough to fight for—"

"They were going to strip you down," Morgan said. "They meant to hurt you."

Hunt winced, but persisted. "I—believe violence is a kind of madness."

Kathy reached out and laid the backs of her fingers gently against Ferrell-Junior's bruised face. His cheeks

169

were pallid, but he managed to grin. "Why do you keep touching me?"

"I can't help it," Kathy said. "That—man—almost killed you. . . . I just have to keep reassuring myself that you're all right."

Ferrell-Junior was badly shaken. Reaction had set in by now. He realized how nearly he had come to death. He forced a smile. "I had no idea you cared, Kathy."

She matched his smile, pressing his hand tightly in hers. "Neither did I."

Ferrell-Junior's teeth chattered as though he were cold. "I always knew that guy Travis was insane. But—he would have killed me. He wanted to. He meant to, but that gun misfired." He closed his eyes trying to shut out the fearful memory. After a moment he forced himself to smile and he said, "When I thought I was going to die, Morgan, *your* life flashed before my eyes."

Morgan laughed, puzzled. "My life?"

"Yes. I didn't have time for mine," Ferrell-Junior said.

Morgan grinned happily. "How 'bout that. My life flashed before Ferrell-Junior's eyes."

"And I can tell you one thing, Morgan. Your life's sure been dull, so far."

Morgan laughed and glanced around. He said, "I was pretty good out there, wasn't I?"

"I was proud of you, son," Baynard said.

"And Soapy too," Morgan said. "You were real brave, Soapy."

"My belly aches," Soapy said.

They laughed and patted him reassuringly. He managed to smile. Only the new tutor said nothing on the long drive. He sat erect, rigid, staring out of the carriage like a man lost out of time and space.

Baynard sat braced against the rattling sway of the carriage. He tried to focus his gaze on Ferrell-Junior but everyone was vague, fuzzily outlined. His chest was tight. He felt he could not get a full breath of air. Rage. That was what did it. Rage against that obscene human predator with that handgun. How close that thug had come to killing Ferrell-Junior—and with him everything Baynard lived for and dreamed ahead to. Filth like that brutal, in-

170

sensitive Travis should be locked away from decent society rather than permitted to run free and spawn more of their kind. In time of war, the best of the breed like Ferrell would be killed off first, while rejects like Travis would be left behind to breed. What was ahead for mankind under such conditions? How could he have endured the agony if Ferrell had been slain by that trash? In every nightmare he would see that gun thrust into his son's face, hear the fearful click as the gun misfired. A low moron with a gun had come a misfire away from killing his son. How could he have gone on living if Ferrell were dead? What would he build for? What future was there for Blackoaks? How would they exist without his son's laughter and love in the house? If anything happened to Ferrell and Styles were left to run the plantation, it would be lost. Styles had the education, every qualification except the quality that might keep the farm viable and productive.

The huge posts of Blackoaks welcomed them home.

CHAPTER 17

THE SUITE PROVIDED for Hunt at Blackoaks was far more luxurious and comfortable than he had dared to hope. He faced the fact honestly, it was all much more splendid than he'd ever experienced before—even in the homes of very rich New Englanders. He had met many extremely wealthy families through classmates at Harvard. Bostonians, though, even when they lived well, demanded value for every dime invested. Utilitarianism won out over creature comfort or visual attractiveness every time. A room, a corridor, a stairway, was as large as it had to be, no larger. Here at Blackoaks, spaciousness was a component of pleasant living. His sitting-room study was comparatively small, but high-ceilinged with shelves and cabinets for his books and papers. A glossy-finished desk had been cleared and awaited his use. The chairs were wingback, overstuffed, inviting, and glistening with polish. Tall, narrow French windows opened on a green vista, a blue-misted hammock beyond, and his own private patch of Alabama sky. The bedroom was large enough to sustain a cocktail party easily; its high ceiling made it cool and its tall windows could be thrown wide open to admit the least breezes in across a small, semicircular balcony. The view was less imposing—the workshops in the valley and the depressing whitewashed shacks of the slave quarters beyond as a constant reminder of where he was and how he abhorred this whole cruel stratified existence. It was as evil as the formality of the slave-owners' lives was empty and artificial. He would never be at home here among these insensitively, unconsciously, and uncaringly cruel people, never really be comfortable in this opulence acquired at the expense of human beings in wretched slavery.

He put away his belongings and felt lost in the sumptuous suite. His own dressing room! He gazed at himself in his full-length mirror, remembering the cramped quarters he'd shared in Harvard Yard, the small cottage he'd rented as site for his rendezvous with Addie—the whole layout hardly as large as this bedroom. He missed Addie. The eager way she awaited him, always there ahead of him, always waiting by firelight, wearing her prim dress, but no underthings. The daring recklessness of the lies she told Lodge in order to escape to him. Emptily, Hunt stared at the huge four-poster bed with its goose-feather mattress and hand-sewn counterpane and mosquito-net ceiling—and he wished for Addie.

Despite the luxuriance of the bed, the unbroken night stillness, pillows which seemed to ease against his face, he didn't sleep well. He was awake by four; he could stay in bed no longer than five. He got up, bathed, shaved, and dressed in dark trousers, morning coat, high-collared shirt, and conservatively colored tie. When he heard movement in the first-floor kitchen below him, he stole from the room, tip-toed down the rear stairwell.

He paused at the door of the kitchen, stunned by the activity and happy chatter he found there. The place smelled like a bakery—buns, cakes, rolls, and bread baking in a brick oven. Freshly ground coffee bubbled on the huge stove. Behind the stove small black children played happily with three puppies less than a month old— with names like Slingshot, Silly Sally, and Butterball. There were half a dozen helpers moving about swiftly under the direction of the half-Indian, half-Negress he'd met the night before. Jeanne d'Arc wore a cotton-print dress and a flowered apron, but she looked like some princess from the days of the caesars.

All activity ceased when Jeanne d'Arc, turning from the stove, saw Hunt in the doorway. The helpers stopped working, those sipping coffee and eating iced pecan buns at the table leaped to their feet guiltily. This tableaux held until Jeanne d'Arc ordered the children to get the puppies out of the kitchen. The children wept, but she was adamant. She apologized to Hunt. "Them pups are all that's left of a litter. Morning chill is bad for them. I let them come in for a little while."

"It's all right," Hunt said. "Don't send them out because of me."

But she seemed not to hear him. "Get those puppies out of my kitchen, this instant." The toddlers took the squirming puppies up in their arms and trooped out the rear door. It squealed on its hinges and slammed behind them.

"Is there something we can get you, Masta Campbell, suh?" Jeanne d'Arc said. "Afraid the family won't be up for breakfast for three–four hours."

"I'd like coffee," Hunt said. "Maybe one of those pecan buns."

"Of course. You go in the breakfast room through that door and I'll have La Ment come right in and serve you, masta," Jeanne d'Arc said.

"Couldn't I just eat at the table in here—with you people? Less trouble."

"It wouldn't be seemly, Masta Campbell," Jeanne d'Arc said. The other slaves looked uncomfortable, as if he'd suggested they commit some crime.

"I don't mind if you don't," Hunt said. "In fact, I insist."

He forced a warm smile that reached out to each of the helpers in turn. They lowered their gazes under his and stood immobile. He knew his smile lacked warmth; not that it wasn't sincere, it certainly was. But he was not naturally a warm person among his social inferiors. He laughed and sat down at the table. "You just go right ahead," he said. "All of you, finish your breakfasts."

"Reckon we through, masta," La Ment said.

"Reckon I not be hungry, masta," Shiva said. The helpers took up their cups, carried them to the sink where they pumped water on them and set them waiting to be scalded and run through hot soapy suds. Hunt sat at the table alone. La Ment placed a cup of steaming coffee and a platter of fresh hot pecan rolls before him. Shiva brought fresh whole cream and cane sugar. They placed the food before him and backed away.

"I hope we can be friends," Hunt said. "I want to be your friend."

"We all right busy this time of day, masta," Jeanne d'Arc said. "We hopes you can fo'give us."

One of the small children came through the rear door, slamming it behind her. She was weeping and scrubbing at her eyes with her grimy fists. The child had grit in its eye and was sobbing frantically. Jeanne d'Arc sat in a rocking chair near a window, took the child in her lap, and sent La Ment running for a hair from a horse's tail. Hunter watched in shocked silence and fascinated horror as Jeanne d'Arc made an eyelet of the horse hair. La Ment held the child immobile and Shiva spread the child's eye wide. Hunt came to his feet protesting as Jeanne d'Arc drew the hair across the child's eyeball. He stopped in midstep as the child, freed, jumped up from Jeanne d'Arc's lap, blinking. After a moment a wide grin spread across the child's chocolate face; the grit was gone from her eye.

Hunter shook his head and smiled. "To think I spent six years at Harvard and never learned that technique."

Jeanne d'Arc looked up at him. "Lots of folks that chase after the uncommon, Masta Campbell, miss out on a lot of the ordinary good things in this life."

"My God, Jeanne d'Arc, you're a philosopher too."

She shrugged, returning to her work. "If you say so, Masta Campbell, suh."

Hunter returned to the table and his coffee. The room was uncomfortably silent. The children gathered behind the stove, the helpers moved silently about their chores.

Hunt smiled at them whenever they looked toward him, which was only infrequently. He finished his coffee. He told himself he couldn't expect a friendly response immediately from a race that had been enslaved in this country alone for almost 200 years. They were accustomed to being treated as if they were dray animals. He'd give them time to get accustomed to him, to accept him as a friend. He thanked them for the breakfast and went through the quiet house and out the front door. Lamplight showed around the facing of a door near the formal parlor, but the door was tightly closed and Hunt did not hesitate.

The huge estate was something entirely foreign to

Hunter's experience. He had never seen anything like it before. He stood on the wide terrace, struck by the first rays of the morning sun on its tessellated block flooring. He watched a potbellied white man in slouch hat riding a white horse, herding the fieldhands like animals toward the cotton acreage. He listened to the almost melancholy sighing of the morning breeze in the pecan trees along the lane. He sat for a few moments on a low wall of native fieldstone, with jasmine growing from freshly tended beds and creeping over it—green and yellow tendrils softly fragrant—the faint odor of cow dung from the flower beds. Cypress-wood chairs were set about the terrace, pillowed, the parasol-shaded cypress table already set up for people who might spend as much as five minutes idling out here. He stared across the rolling grassy yard, the fields, the bearded rim of the hammock beyond, and distantly a poor-white's chimney smoke, a gray wisp intruding against the serrated sky.

He found himself drawn by the architecture of the small fieldstone chapel set apart from the house on a small knoll. He left the terrace and walked up the grassy plot toward the small building. A couple of dogs ran at him, sniffed at his legs, wagged their tails, lost interest, and chased a butterfly downhill. The sun glittered in the silver cross that topped the bell tower. He recognized that this building had been erected with great care, attention to detail, and at no small cost. One of the polished mahogany doors was ajar. He walked toward it to enter, but heard someone inside. He was astonished that anyone except himself was abroad at this hour of the dawn. He retreated, backing away. He turned and walked down the incline.

"Mr. Campbell."

Hunt paused and turned. Miz Claire emerged from the chapel. She wore a shoe-length dress and a fragile scarf over her head. He was faintly disturbed at the sight of her —she wasn't beautiful anymore, but there was about her the aura, the memory of great beauty. It saddened him. Baynard had felt impelled to explain last night that Miz Claire was "vague," though by that time an explanation was unnecessary. Miz Claire's conversations consisted entirely of what she was wearing, how it looked on her, what

176

her children were wearing, what she expected of them, and what people would think of them. God knew, he had met women like her before. New England repression and inhibition created lost-eyed, addle-pated, shallow, vain, and eccentric females who were hidden away like skeletons in family closets.

"Good morning, Miz Claire," he said. "I had no idea you were up at this time of the morning."

She smiled vaguely. "I don't sleep well anymore. I like to come up here—early. I feel perhaps God has time for my prayers—at a quiet time like this."

"It should work."

"Are you Catholic, Mr. Campbell?"

"No. I'm not." He knew she would wait for him to name his denomination, but he did not tell her he was an agnostic. Ne sense turning her against him the first time they met alone.

"I was in the Baptist church," she said. "But it seemed to leave me—I don't know the word. Incomplete. I felt empty all the time. I had so much—sadness. . . . Well, we won't talk about that. But my church was no help to me. . . . Someone told me that God said to St. Peter, 'On this rock I'll found my church.' That's the Catholic church, you know."

"That's very interesting."

"Would you like to take a short walk with me, Mr. Campbell? I'm afraid it's some time before breakfast. . . . Mr. Baynard is in his study. But I'm afraid he wouldn't appreciate our intruding."

He walked with her through the small family cemetery beyond the chapel. A low fieldstone fence set it apart. A basket of flowers and another of vases half-filled with water had been set beside the plot entrance. Miz Claire took up the flowers and asked Hunt to bring the basket of vases.

She placed fresh flowers at each of the graves, pulling up any weeds from the grass that the slaves might have missed. She took her time and Hunt realized there was no reason to hurry on this huge estate. She spoke of her dead children—stillborn. Her eyes filled with tears with each memory. He saw the tears were for her loss, not for what those traumatic assaults had done to her fragile health.

"You are very courageous to carry on like this," he told her, "even to be physically able to carry on so well."

She looked up from the graveside and smiled wanly. The sun lay across her pale cheeks. "We Seatons and Henrys persist," she said. "That's my side of the family, you know. The Seatons and the Henrys. Fine old families, Mr. Campbell."

"I'm sure they are."

"The Seatons of Savannah. A very respected name, Mr. Campbell. My mother was a Seaton. My father was a Henry from the Carolinas. Patrick Henry was a distant cousin of mine. We have strength. We persist."

"Yes."

"God gives us only the burdens He knows we can bear, Mr. Campbell. Women like me—we seem fragile. Maybe we seem to bend with the wind like reeds. But we persist. . . . The Seatons and the Henrys. We persist. . . ."

Miz Claire parted from Hunt on the terrace. Her nervousness seemed to increase as they approached the manor house. She touched his arm briefly at the terrace wall, thanked him for helping her with the flowers, and then she hurried away, around the side of the house, her scarf trailing in the breeze. Hunt stood staring after her. He felt he would always recall her like that, hurrying from something he was not even privileged to understand.

He walked in through the wide French doors and found the house loud and alive with people going in to breakfast. He crossed the sun room and turned into the corridor, going toward the family dining area. The study door opened and Baynard stood in it, smiling. "Could you come in a moment before we go in to breakfast, Hunter? I believe we've time."

Hunter entered the study. "I've been out looking the place over. It's truly beautiful."

"Thank you. We're very pleased to have you here. We hope you'll be happy and content. However, Hunter, I'm afraid I'll have to ask you not to attempt to fraternize with the slaves."

"They're human beings, Mr. Baynard, the same as we are."

"Yes. We're well aware of this. But we won't be pleased to have you disseminating abolitionist ideas, Hunter. With them, no matter your intentions, you'll only hurt the slaves. You can't possibly help them with such—"

"They must be taught to help themselves."

"Yes. Well, they can't. It's unfortunate. But we both know they can't. But you can get them into difficulties they can't cope with—when you make them think about situations they cannot alter."

"On the other hand, Mr. Baynard, they can hardly think at all unless someone teaches them to think, can they?"

Styles was lounging in a wicker chair on the terrace when Hunt walked out there in the middle of the afternoon. The sun on the yard was like the breath of a furnace, but in the shade of the eucalyptus tree where Styles sat, a cool breeze soothed him. Styles looked up from the book of poetry he was reading and peered along his thin, patrician nose at Hunter. He laughed, "I hear you're wasting no time arousing the slaves. Perhaps you'll do as thorough a job on poor Morgan."

Hunt stared down at Styles. "I can't understand it. A man like you—of some education, breeding, obviously. How do you reconcile the way you live? On the misery of enslaved people?"

"They're better off at Blackoaks, my dear fellow, than they would be in the African bush, or the jungles of Harvard Yard."

"Does it make you feel superior to denigrate the cultural center of this country?"

"You mean that institution which requires only six years to prepare a man to teach the basics of reading and writing to a retarded boy?"

"You sound as if you're convinced you can boast a better education."

"I certainly can. I do. Of course, I'm talking about higher education. I mean the University of Virginia."

Hunt smiled in a chilled way. "I'm afraid I don't know

much about these smaller Southern schools."

"Don't apologize for your neglected education, Mr. Campbell. But again, I'm afraid we're talking on different levels. I don't mean to disparage Harvard. The rest of the country will never take it as seriously as it takes itself, but I'm not talking about ordinary schools. I'm talking about the advanced education available to gentlemen of the South."

They both laughed. Styles had pushed the ridiculous argument one step too far for either of them to keep a straight face anymore. "I hope you'll be happy here, Mr. Campbell."

Hunt could hear the voices of the slaves toiling in the blazing heat of the open fields. He knew he would never even be comfortable in this strange new world. But he managed to go on smiling. "Oh, I'm sure I shall be—even if I can't understand the odd dialect of your natives. . . ."

Life moved leisurely, smoothly and undeniably pleasantly at Blackoaks. Hunt found his chores as tutor for Morgan simple and easy, if not challenging or promising. At fifteen, Morgan was ready for the simple primers used in the first grades of urban schools. Hunt found his conversations with Styles Kenric stimulating and challenging. They could never be friends; there was friction between them from the first—they were too much alike, egotistical, self-centered, both extremely handsome young men and both extremely aware of it.

There were saddle horses to ride, and slaves to guide him along lovely hidden trails. There was an extremely tasty whiskey distilled on the plantation. There was Miz Claire when he wanted to relax, close his mind, and listen to her talk about her children, her family, her relatives, the parties she'd once held here at Blackoaks. When he wanted to gaze on beauty, there was Styles' wife. He had found the love poems that had brought Addie naked to his bed. He decided he'd use the stolen poetry to amuse and perhaps entrance Kathy Kenric. But Kathy grew quickly restive. She admitted she had no taste for poetry. She suggested they were lovely poems and that Hunt should read them to Styles, who could appreciate them.

Hunt found himself sinking unwillingly under the spell of the good life of Blackoaks. He no longer awoke before daybreak. Often he was the last one down to breakfast. He found himself yawning in the middle of Morgan's lessons. He found himself pouring a drink of Baynard's whiskey neat in the middle of the day. Sometimes he wandered in a warm haze through a quiet afternoon, not even sure where the time had gone.

He lay in his bed after midnight wishing he had a drink. The quart that Jeanne d'Arc had sent up yesterday was somehow empty. He was ashamed—and a little timid—about asking for more so soon. Baynard was scrupulous about the number of drinks he consumed in one day. Miz Claire detested all liquor and thought it should be abolished. Styles drank, but in moderation. Ferrell-Junior would drink with him at any time of the night or day, but never seemed to drink alone. He lay restive, sweated, and thirsty. The woman's screaming from the slave quarters across the narrow valley brought him upright in his bed, shaken.

She screamed again and Hunt threw back the covers. He got out of bed, pulled on his trousers, a sweater, and stepped into his boots. She was still screaming when he let himself out into the silent corridor and ran down the rear stairwell to the kitchen. Baynard had warned him to stay aloof from the affairs of the slaves, and the old boy was probably going to be angry, but he couldn't stand idly by and listen to such wails of torment. The woman sounded as if she were being tortured.

Dozens of dogs ran out from under the whitewashed shacks barking at Hunt as he ran up the path toward the lighted cabin. He panted, going up the steps and pausing at the open door. Inside the cabin he saw Baynard, Laus, Jeanne d'Arc, and a Negro woman, obviously a midwife. On a bed a black woman was in the thoes of agonized labor.

Baynard glanced over his shoulder. Recognizing Hunt, he scowled. His face lightened. He walked across the room, trying to smile. He put his arm about Hunt and led him out on the narrow porch. "Her screams were bad," Baynard said. "Must have upset you. . . . Too bad, it's a wicked delivery. Baby outside the womb. Don't know if they can save the mother. She's a good woman. It's too bad."

"Can't you get a medical doctor?"

"Why? Minerva has delivered hundreds of children. Nothing can happen that Minerva hasn't dealt with before."

The woman on the bed screamed again, a sound that shook Hunt to the marrow of his bones. Then she was silent, and her silence was even more disquieting. After a long moment the midwife came to the door. She carried a large new-born baby completely swathed in a ragged blanket. She did not smile. She said, "Masta?"

Baynard nodded and crossed the porch to her. Hunt followed, standing at Baynard's shoulder. The woman said, "A monster, Masta Baynard. I seen 'em like this before."

She turned back the cover and Hunt gasped. He almost vomited before he turned away. He walked over to an upright and leaned against it. He heard Baynard speak softly. "Knock it in the head, Minerva. Have Laus bury it before Clyetes wakes up. Tell her it was born dead."

Now Hunt did vomit. He clung to the upright until Baynard touched his arm. "Come on, Hunter. We'll go home now. There's nothing we can do here."

"You spoke—as if it were an animal—"

"It was worse than an animal, Hunter. It was a monster. It would have been more cruel to have let it live—let that mother see it."

Hunt did not answer. They walked up the incline to the house. Baynard invited him in to his study for a drink, but thirsty as he was, Hunt refused. This was barbaric. Unconscionable cruelty. To hell with them and their gracious and genteel lives. He felt as if he were caught in the slime and putrefaction that nurtured the fragile hyacinth. That's what life in this place was, and damned if they would seduce him into it ever again. Never for an instant.

CHAPTER 18

THE SERENE TEMPO of life at Blackoaks speeded up suddenly. The dry spell ended with a vengeance, a season of thunderstorms set in. After the rains, the earth itself seemed to sizzle and steam under the blinding glare of the afternoon sun. It was hotter than ever after the storms. But what happened to the plants growing in the fields was most remarkable to Hunt Campbell. One day the only cotton visible were green buds tipped with a hint of fleece. Abruptly, with a fury during the night, the bolls seemingly burst like popcorn. That morning the vast fields lay glowingly white as far as you could see. Every available Negro on the plantation was pressed into service picking cotton. They went willingly into the wavy white fields. There was something thrilling and challenging in those white-blanketed acres. Cotton had always been the staple crop at Blackoaks, and bringing it in was everybody's business. Every other activity ground practically to a standstill as each slave was issued a double-length croaker sack with a sturdy shoulder strap sewn into it. They slipped the straps over their shoulders and hurried, laughing and chatting, out to clean the fields.

Bos Pilzer awoke that morning and, sitting on the side of their bed, spoke over his shoulder to Florine, "I'll take the nigger along with me today. We need him to help pick cotton."

Florine's heart lurched. She wanted to cry out in protest, but she merely shrugged. "Sure. Take the nigger. Get him off my hands." As Bos dressed, she said, "It'll be a welcome relief to me to be shed of him—and the responsibility for curing up those cuts. Of course, it's you I'm sorry for."

"Me?"

"It means all those chores the nigger's been doing for you around here will be waiting when you come in tonight."

"Can't be helped," Bos growled. Then he was silent for a few moments, dressing. Florine turned on her side, facing away from Bos and the lamplight, as if she'd said the last word on the subject. Bos said, "Moab's a good nigger."

"He's all right, I guess." She yawned.

Bos chewed on this. In the weeks Moab had slept in the tack room and they had daily tended his whip cut as Dr. Townsend had prescribed, a change had occurred inside Bos Pilzer. He found himself actually liking a nigger as a person, almost like a human being. Moab was quiet, he responded quickly, he never talked back, and he worked around Bos's overseer cottage like a crew of slaves. Bos had never had it so good, and he admitted it. There were no chores awaiting him when he rode in sweated and exhausted at night. Moab tended the kitchen garden and expanded it to a full acre. Plants seemed anxious to grow for the kid. Wood was chopped, livestock watered, leathers mended. Jobs were completed that Bos had postponed simply because there was too much to do.

He found Florine less shrewish, easier to live with, more fun in bed. Before she had lain unmoving when he mounted her, as if waiting for him to spend himself and dismount. He supposed all good women were like that; none of them really enjoyed sex; they endured it, unless they were whores and in the business. Then they could pretend to be excited. Now when he mounted Florine at night, there was a response. He could sense she found no pleasure in the act, but she tried to please him, and this was beautiful. "Why not?" she said. "With the nigger to do the scrubbing, toting, and washing, I'm not dead tired anymore when you get home."

"Yeah. He's a good nigger, Moab is." Bos sat down on the bed and pulled on his boots. He did not suspect that Moab was tending chores for him far beyond the call of

184

duty. He would have doubted it if he'd heard any rumor of it. The best reason for disbelieving it was the way the kid worked around the place. There was no time for sex, or anything else. Besides, Florine felt about niggers as he did. They were slightly above African apes, but not much. "Is Moab's whip cuts clearing up?" he said.

"They coming along," Florine said. "Just so you're careful with him out there. We've worked damn hard—you and me—to bring him around to suit old Baynard. Those welts get pulled apart now, we never will get rid of scars. Baynard might raise hell. But it's not our fault. Got to get that cotton in—and you and me—we've done all we could."

Bos stood up. He was silent for some moments, his thought processes grinding it out inside his mind.

"The hell with it," Bos said at last. "I don't give a damn what Baynard says. I'll let the kid sleep in today. Try to get along without him. He's no good in the fields. Never was. Hates it. Anything happens to that back—and Baynard's on my tail again. . . . Anyhow, Moab's worth more to me right around here—and damned if I want that scar tissue broken open now."

Florine sighed and pressed down into her mattress. She smiled into the concealment of its feathery softness. She'd known all along that Moab wasn't going into the fields with those slaves. . . .

Twenty eternal minutes dragged past after Bos had plodded downtrail to the quarters on his broad-rumped horse. Florine lay in the bed as long as she could stand the silence and the waiting. Panic fluttered like disturbed hornets in the pit of her stomach. Maybe Bos had changed his mind and taken Moab to the fields after all. It was not like Bos to change a decision once he reached it and got it cemented inside his thick skull.

Her heart battered. Where was Moab? He came through that window sometimes only minutes after Bos rode out of the barn. It frightened her that he was so reckless. Why wasn't he here by now? She looked ahead in dread and frustration to the long day without Moab. Damn that Bos Pilzer. Goddamn him. If he had been stupid enough to take Moab out to the fields, she'd get even with him in a way he'd never forget. He'd regret this, she could promise him that.

For some time now she had ceased being always half-sick with fear that Bos would return unexpectedly and find Moab in bed with her. Given any warning at all, she could get him out the window. He wore only those onasburg britches. He could don them swiftly, or carry them in his hand if he had to.

She twisted, miserable and uncomfortable on the bed. Her thighs ached, heated, and there was a sick sense of frustrated anticipation in her loins. She prayed feverishly.

She had begun praying each night after Bos had mounted her, grunted in release, and fallen away to his side of their bed. "Don't let me get Moab killed," she prayed. "Don't, God. Please . . . don't let me get him killed, God. I couldn't live without him."

She threw back the covers and swung out of bed, trembling. She had prayed about how she would be desolated without Moab, but she had not fully realized how bereft she'd be without him, until now. She ran across the dark room in her bare feet. In the kitchen, trembling with panic, she found a sulphur match, struck it, and lit the lamp. The yellow glow opened up the room. She turned and Moab stood just inside the kitchen door. He was grinning at her.

Weak with conflicting rage and relief, she braced herself against the table. "Damn you, Moab. What are you grinning about? Where have you been?"

He came to her, bare chested, that beautiful bulge at his crotch, but with that infuriating grin pulling at his lips. "Jes' wanted to know sump'in," he said. "Wondered how much you still wanted me."

She gasped and straightened, shocked and enraged. Her hand came up and she struck him as hard as she could across the face. "Goddamn you," she said, trembling. "Don't you ever do that again."

He shook his head to clear it. The imprint of her palm was livid across his dark-gold cheek. "It's all right," he said, voice gentle. "I knows now."

Florine wept suddenly and toppled against Moab, pressing her face against his bare, salty-tasting chest. Her arms closed fiercely about him. She couldn't get him close enough, she wanted him inside her. She stroked her cheek as hard as she could upon his rigid pectoral muscles. Her tear-heated lips parted and she nursed at his paps furiously. His rod stiffened, growing harder. His breath was loud in the room. He laid his arms upon her shoulders, without pressure, but it was the force she wanted. She sank slowly to her knees, her arms about him sliding along his body. She pushed her face against the rough fabric of his onasburg britches at the fly, her hot breath burning him through the cloth, but she waited until he reached down, loosened the buttons of his fly, and took out his pulsing staff. He held her head and pulled her upon it, pressing its head against her lips. She opened her mouth and he thrust it harder, forcing her mouth apart, understanding suddenly that she was wild with desire to suck him; but she didn't want to take it of her own volition, she wanted to submit to him. This proved nothing to him, but he saw it proved something very important to her. He didn't care. It was the first time she'd done it for him. He gazed down at her on her knees to him and he felt mightier than any of his people's ancient gods, stronger than a lion—and, God knew, hornier than a goat.

When she'd had it, and he sagged, so weak at the backs of his knees that he would have fallen had she not supported him, arms about his hips, face pressed against him, he stepped out of his trousers, which were now wadded about his ankles. He knelt and took her up in his arms. She whispered against his throat, "You know how crazy I am about you now, don't you?"

Moab didn't answer. He carried her into the bedroom and laid her down upon it. He caught her gown and pulled it up over her head. He tossed it behind him. Then he knelt over her, braced on one arm and knee. She reached for him, working him with her fist to arouse him again. He saw her hips writhe involuntarily. This quirk of hers—this inability to wait until it was inside her—still had the power to drive him out of his skull. It thrilled him that she was so wild for him that she began that savage thrusting helplessly even before he could mount her. She really loved it. He was one nigger with his own white woman and she really loved it. Sometimes he teased her, by playing with her clitoris and her breasts, but delaying the moment he mounted her, until her hips quivered in that spasmodic anticipation.

The diamond-studded gold cross bobbled on its fragile chain about her throat. The faint lamplight from the kitchen was refracted in its facets, winking at him. He took the cross in his palm, gazing at it. She smiled up at him, still pumping him down there, caressing his testes, feeling him grow rigid in her hand. "You know how valuable this cross is?" She reached up and pressed the diamond-encrusted ornament against his lips.

"No."

She kissed his paps, working her hand faster. She was breathless with anticipation. "It's not half as valuable as your cock."

He grinned, pleased and vain. "That would make it mighty valuable."

"Maybe. To somebody. But not for me. It's not to me what you are. It can't fuck."

Hunt found himself growing steadily more taut drawn, irritable, and even unstable. He tried to tell himself it was the raw change of atmosphere after a life spent in the sanity of New England. He soon discovered to his heated discomfiture that sex and sexual activity were as natural as other bodily functions at Blackoaks, and seemingly everywhere one looked. Late afternoons, when field hands were in from chopping cotton, the young girls freed of their duties, they paired off, giggling, tussling, shoving, grabbing, and drifting off into the hammock. He sweated, watching them, and he could not stop watching. Dusk was a lingering, prolonged interlude on the plantation. Time seemed to hang suspended. The sun appeared to pause patiently for an extra hour or so of musky daylight. The balmy evenings were totally unlike those in New England where it was abruptly dark, suddenly, finally, and blackly night. Darkness settled drowsily here, perfumed and downlike. From the shadows laughter arose or there erupted a sharp, ecstatic cry of agonized delight forced across the lips of some impassioned wench.

Hunt watched, listened, suffered. It was not only a mental but a physical discomfort. Excluded, his thoughts heating, he would remember Addie waiting naked before that New England fireplace, anxious to receive him, eager to enthrall him. He walked around in a constant state of satyriasis. If he took a long stroll to clear his mind of its heated images, he was astounded at the incredible spectacle of a stallion mounting a mare. God! there was fearful violence to match an earthquake. Those horses would kill to get what they wanted, once aroused. And after a week or two, Hunt understood how they felt, how driven they were. In the Blackoaks barnyard, the roosters seemed hardly to take time to eat between chasing down a fresh young pullet, forcing her to the ground, getting a beak sunk into her tuft, and battering away.

No matter where he looked, the pleasures of sex were being exploited, whether it was the black boys luring a lusty wench into a corn crib, the rams at the ewes, the bulls lumbering up awkwardly on the hindquarters of a cow, or the hogs wallowing and squealing in the sump; there was something for everybody. But not for him. He would not have been able to make it through the overheated nights except for the punishment he gave his fist. Nothing was less satisfactory. Nothing stirred his sense of guilt more. Nothing made him seem more depraved in his own eyes—sinking swiftly to the degraded depths of these red-necks. There was no way to reconcile a New England conscience and immoderate self-abuse or the moral values of these crackers. And yet, in this languorous, overheated atmosphere, he would see animals copulating, or blacks pairing off, and find himself excusing himself from his classes to hasten off to his room—and his fist—and release.

He had no idea his agony was apparent to any but himself, until one evening after supper Thyestes came to the wingback chair where Hunt was attempting to read by unsatisfactory parlor light. "Masta Hunter, suh?"

Hunt looked up. His eyes ached, his thoughts had begun to stray northward to a naked Addie. He pressed his fingers against his eyeballs and tried to smile.

"Masta Baynard say he lak talk with you, suh, you be so kind as to come to he office when it convenient."

"How about right now?"

"If that convenient, masta, suh."

The elder Baynard looked up and smiled when Hunt closed the office door behind him. Baynard invited him to sit down and poured him a stiff drink of his prized whiskey.

He waited until Hunt had taken a long sip. Hunt felt the liquor burn its way down his throat. Baynard said, "I've noticed you've been—well, rather taut drawn and nervous lately."

Hunt flushed, wondering if Baynard had noticed how often during a day he excused himself and locked his bedroom door to relieve attacks of satyriasis.

"I've never believed it was healthy for a man—young or old—to be too long denied a sexual outlet." Baynard's tone was kindly. He paused. "You don't resent my talking to you this way? I don't embarrass you?"

Hunt shrugged, waiting.

"I don't know how you feel about copulating with a black girl? How do you feel on the subject?"

"I don't know. I never have. I don't think they should be forced—because they're black and slaves. . . . I don't know, sir."

Baynard smiled. "It's an unparalleled experience, Hunt. If it will be of service to you, I'll arrange for you to be served tonight."

"Tonight?"

"Would you rather not?"

"Oh, no. . . . I appreciate your consideration. Thoughtfulness. Tonight would be—fine. . . . I am simply taken by surprise. . . . Am I to go down to the quarters?"

"Oh, no." Baynard stood up. He no longer smiled. "Never do that. Never. It might be dangerous . . . it might well be fatal. . . . The quarters—belong to the slaves. A jealous young buck—oh, no. No. You let me make arrangements. . . . I'll have a young girl bathed and—made ready. She'll be in your room when you retire."

"Here? In the house?"

"Naturally I expect you to be circumspect—"

"Oh, of course—"

"Discreet—"

"Certainly—"

"And reasonably quiet. What the good ladies of this household don't suspect will never harm them . . . and I don't hold with abstinence—continence—or any substitute for a healthy young man. I want you satisfied, and able to put your full mind to the teaching of my son. I don't want you suffering from unfulfilled needs of the body. Too long without a woman can be bad on a man. That need—denied—can make itself felt in many ways—many of them detrimental to the health and the actual ability to function at full efficiency. . . . On the other hand, I have no wish to offend you—"

"Oh, no, sir. No offense, I assure you. None. No, sir."

Baynard changed the subject with an ease that left Hunt barely able to follow the direction of his conversation. Baynard spoke of Morgan's studies, of the repeated and unsuccessful attempts to teach the boy the fundamentals of reading, writing, and arithmetic. "You won't have an easy job. I want to make it as easy as I can." Hunt sat stiffly, nodding. His mind wheeled. He had no idea what was going to happen, and he looked forward with eagerness and dread at war inside himself. He tried to converse naturally with Baynard, but he was barely aware of what either of them said. He felt a sense of relief when Baynard finally excused him with a paternal smile and a solid pat on the shoulder.

Hunt tried to return to his reading in the parlor but it was hopeless. He heard Kathy playing a love song at the spinnet in the sun room. He stood at the door a moment, listening, watching her, but he was afraid they could read in his face that he was in a turmoil inside. His mouth felt cottony dry. He went into the kitchen to get a drink of water. Jeanne d'Arc gave him a knowing, conspiratorial smile. His face reddened to the roots of his hair. He replaced the glass on the drain without drinking and backed from the room. Old Thyestes grinned at him, and he thought wildly, they all know! They're all in on it and they're all laughing at me. He wanted to go up to his room, but it was so early he felt this was too obvious. He didn't want to seem as anxious as a callow boy. Anyway, he didn't know how this assignation might be arranged. Obviously, Thyestes and Jeanne d'Arc were in on the plan. God knew how many others. He sweated. Perhaps he'd be taken to one of the third-floor cribs, secretly, after midnight. He was not even sure he could go through with it. Here he was, among the hated enemy, exploiting the helpless slaves with them. Suppose, with his nerves on edge like this, he couldn't perform. It wouldn't take long for that little secret to spread—Thyestes, Jeanne d'Arc, the black girl herself, old man Baynard—the whole black community would be laughing about the blue-belly teacher who got a black wench naked in bed—and then couldn't do it. . . .

He considered returning to Baynard's small office and telling the planter as lightly and casually as possible that he had been considering the matter of the bed wench, and had decided against it. Perhaps later. Some other time. . . . He knew better. Baynard was doing something special for him. Obviously, Baynard thought he needed the release. He knew he needed it. If he backed out now, Baynard might say to hell with him, and that would end it. He certainly didn't want that. He didn't want a string of empty, despairing nights. He didn't know what he wanted. But the thought that somewhere in this house a slave girl was being prepared for his pleasure rendered him empty bellied, weak in the legs. He walked out on the terrace and stared at the soft white underbelly of the night sky. Behind him, the piano music ceased, trailing off, Kathy's lovely voice died away, the sun room lamps and candles were extinguished. The family was going up to bed. He could now go to his room without seeming hurried, rude, or driven.

He stood a few moments longer, letting the soft night breeze dry the sweat on his forehead. His heart thudded erratically, seemingly at the base of his parched throat. He glanced up, startled. A lamp glowed in his bedroom window. My God, was she already up there? Was it all arranged, waiting?

He inhaled deeply, wiped his splayed hands along his thighs, turned, and reentered the house.

"Good night, Mr. Campbell."

Hunt leaped as if he'd been ambushed. He heeled

around, wild eyed to find Miz Claire watching him oddly. "Are you all right?" she said.

"Oh, yes," he heard some stranger's voice assuring her. "I'm fine, Miz Claire. I was just startled. I thought you'd gone up to bed."

"Sleep well," she said.

He nodded, thanking her, and waited until she ascended the wide staircase, carrying a long candle, the light flickering across the cavernous upper hallway. It seemed somehow indecent to walk upstairs with her; knowing where he was headed—under her roof.

Thyestes locked the huge front door. He carried a flickering candle. "Good night, masta," he said with a wide smile. "You care for this candle to light yoah way?"

"No. Thank you."

Thyestes nodded and stood with the taper held aloft as Hunt went hurriedly up the wide stairs and along the candle-lit upper hallway. He hesitated at his own door, sucked in a deep breath and stepped inside.

A lamp burned on the bedside table. His thick-mattressed bed had been turned back, and he saw a form in a cotton gown lying on the bed, only partially covered. When he closed the door, panting as if he'd run a mile, the black girl turned on the bed, pushing off the covers.

For some moments they stared at each other in awkward silence. He saw that she was young—criminally young. He had no idea how old she was—there was no way to know for certain a female's age between fourteen and eighteen. But he was sickly certain she was nearer fourteen. God. A child. He didn't want a child.

Her eyes, her quivering fingers betrayed to him that she was frightened. But there was a calmness about her— perhaps a resignation. She was far less nervous than he.

He saw, finally, that she was pretty—a lovely brown little doll, really. She was tiny—petite as far as he could tell in the shapeless cotton gown she wore. She was dainty. She looked fragile. In the lamplight her skin had the look of light, liquid chocolate. He didn't know who had selected his bed wench, but whoever had done it was a connoisseur of dark beauty. Her crisp black hair was brushed back from her freshly scrubbed face; her eyes were huge and black. Her nose was well formed, narrow across the bridge, wide at the nostrils. Her lips were bright against the glittering white of her teeth. Her delicate face was almost heart shaped. There was a gentle beauty about her that distressed him almost as much as her tender age. She looked too gentle, too young, too vulnerable for what he needed so fiercely. But even as he was thinking this, something happened inside him. It was as if something flipped over in the pit of his stomach and he felt himself aching in the groin. He had spent his life abhorring slavery, but suddenly he was seeing what *enslavement* meant to this girl. This fragile, gentle-looking young girl, beautiful in the lamplight, was his to use as he wished. She was his slave. There was nothing his rampant urges could demand of her that she could—or dared—to refuse.

"Ise Sefina, masta," she said at last. "They brought me here—to pleasure you, masta."

He walked toward the bed, feeling himself grow hard. But her gentle beauty, his hatred of slavery, warred inside him. He said, "How old are you, Sefina?"

"I don't rightly know, suh. I think I was born fifteen plantings ago."

"Have you ever—done this before, Sefina?"

"Like this—no, masta."

"My God. Fifteen. Are you a virgin?"

"Has I ever had a man in me before?"

"Yes." He could barely speak the word.

"Yes, masta. Once, when I was a young girl—maybe ten or so. Uncle Harley. He usta sit me acrost his lap. Hurt at first when it pushed up inside me. But hurt good. I used to sneak over to Uncle Harley's cabin when nobody else was there. I'd let him shuck off my pants and sit me down on it. Purely come to love it, masta. But they—sold Uncle Harley away. I nevah had no more. . . . They tole me I was to do what you wish. Whatever you wish, masta."

He sweated, looking at her. Her matter of fact recital of her life with Uncle Harley had almost caused him a premature ejaculation. He said something—admitting inwardly that it was hypocritical. But he had to say it because he was what he was—a New England abolitionist. But he admitted he was lying. He didn't mean the unctuous

194

words, "You don't have to do this if you don't want to."

Her eyes widened. She looked frightened. "You don't want me, masta?"

"I didn't say that. But you are a young girl. A very young girl. You don't have to."

Her voice was soft, but breathless. "I has to if you wants me to, masta. . . . I wants to pleasure you. . . . I couldn't stand to—tell them—you didn't want me."

"You're a beautiful girl. Of course I want you. But do you know what I'll do to you?"

"Yes, suh. Miz Jahndark done tole me Ise to do what you tells me. Ise not to cry. Ise not to say no. . . . Ise to undress you if'n you want—"

"No . . . all right. Yes. I want you to."

Sefina smiled and crawled across the bed on her hands and knees. She slid off the thick mattress and pulled the cotton gown over her own head.

Hunt caught his breath at the sight of her gleaming, naked body. The lamplight glistened damply in the high-standing rise of her full young breasts and rimlighted the dark triangular down at her thighs. Streaks of yellow warmth shimmered along her shapely legs. She stood un-self-consciously naked, and Hunt realized he had never encountered anything like this in all his life. Loving and being loved was as natural to this black child as eating, sleeping, growing. She came from a world completely alien to the inhibited, repressed, sin-conscious land in which he'd been bred.

He reached out awkwardly and took the round, taut breasts like tender fruit in his hands. The heat of her body seemed to penetrate into him, burning away the last of his inhibitions. She had his shirt unbuttoned. She could not manipulate his belt buckle. This was something she would learn in time. He was forced to loosen it for her. He sat on the bed, his staff rigid before them while she pulled off his boots, his stockings, his trousers. She looked up and met his eyes, smiling timidly. "You mighty purty, masta. Mighty purty. I proud to be chose to pleasure you, masta. Proud."

Naked, he faced the second crisis of threatened prema-ture ejaculation. She was lovelier than he had imagined a young girl—black, white, or yellow—could be. Her eager, heated hands on his body inflamed him almost unbearably, drove him out of his skull. He bit down hard on his mouth and managed to wait until she lay back on the mattress, her arms and legs, bent at the knees, open to him. "You want the light out, masta?" she whispered.

"No." He came down upon her. She thrust her hips upward to receive him. He gasped at the fiery liquidity of her. He thrust himself deeply.

Sefina gasped. "Oh, Lawdy, masta. That so good."

Suddenly she shifted her hips inward and battered wildly, digging her nails into his back. He clung to her, aware that she was shuddering in an orgiastic trance. They were spent together. She held fiercely to him, and in the burning liquid of her thighs, he felt himself grow rigid again. And again. He had no idea how many times they rose to that shattering, mind-numbing peak of ecstasy. He knew at last that she was exhausted, physically beat. And yet he could feel no compassion, he could not stop. There was—with everything else—the terrible enchantment of that word—*enslavement*. Never before had he possessed a female who was his vessel to use in any manner he wished. The thought flared into his mind, churned in his loins when he was certain he was too drained, too depleted to move. He felt himself growing hard again, reaching for her, using her. . . . The lamp burned low, flickered out. She whimpered once, like a tired child, but when he pushed her head down between his legs, she accepted him quietly, nursing hungrily.

He had it all—he had everything he'd ever contemplated in his most heated fantasy, ever heard in whisper or bawdy story. The exalting sense of possessing her drove him in the darkness, long after the lamp glass had grown cold. He did not know when he fell asleep at last, only that they lay close together, sweated, wet, hot, clinging. He knew that she slept first. He remembered hearing her deep, exhausted breathing—and then he slept.

Daylight wakened him. He lay for a moment recalling the incredible night, and then he was aware he was growing tumescent. He reached out for the fiery little brown body. His hand found nothing. He opened his eyes. Sefina was gone. He didn't know whether someone had come and spirited her away in the dark hour before dawn, or if she had gone of her own volition. He felt empty, bereft. He needed her. It was going to be hell, getting this night out of his mind. And even after the long and torrid night, he had to resort one more time to his fist for a final hurrah. Then he fell face down across the mattress and slept until noon. . . .

Hunt, Morgan, and Soapy suffered a slow, unproductive afternoon with Morgan's lessons. Five apples today were not necessarily five pencils tomorrow, as far as Morgan was concerned. His attention span was extremely short. His mind wandered. He fidgeted. Hunt yawned and suggested they take a break by going on a trail ride.

He was amazed and gratified, despite himself, that the wish was the father to the deed at Blackoaks. Within minutes after he proposed a ride, horses were saddled and brought to the terrace for them. He wondered if he had only to request Sefina to be serviced as he had been last night?

They rode downslope, and with Soapy riding ahead, they skirted the quarters. Hunt found himself looking for Sefina in the cottages. There was no sign of her. They followed the wagon trail that led upward past the overseer's fieldstone cottage on the knoll. They rode past the house and Hunt saw a woman—evidently in her late twenties—at work sweeping on the porch. She straightened in the shade but did not bother greeting them. Neither Morgan nor Soapy thought it unusual that she did not speak; she belonged in neither of their worlds.

Immediately beyond the house a golden-skinned Negro boy about Morgan's age sweated, hoeing in a meticulously kept kitchen garden. Soapy called, "Mornin', Moab."

Moab looked up and smiled. He would have returned to work but Soapy reined in his horse. "This here is Masta Hunter Campbell, Moab. He Masta Morgan's new tutor. Moab's a mighty fine nigger boy, Masta Campbell, suh."

Moab grinned and leaned on his hoe, looking up at them. Sweat rolled in huge glittering marbles out of his crisp black hair, along his face and from his armpits, down his rib cage. Hunter paused, impressed. Moab's smile made him beautiful—a barbaric prince from some ancient empire of the Sahara. The boy bobbed his head toward Hunter.

"A tutor—that mean he a teacher," Soapy said to Moab. "That's what a tutor is—a teacher."

Hunt saw that the young woman had stopped work on the shaded porch and was standing with her hands on her hips, watching them. The boy straightened and turned to hoe again. "My God," Hunter gasped.

The three boys reacted to Hunt's shock. Moab heeled around; Soapy clutched the reins tighter, and Morgan shook his head, troubled. "What wrong, Mr. Campbell?" Morgan said.

"Come here, Moab," Hunt said. Moab glanced toward the woman on the shadowed porch, then walked nearer to Hunt's horse. "Turn around," Hunt told him.

Moab turned and Hunt shuddered at the unhealed wound slicing across the boy's bronzed back from shoulder to belt line. These damned Southern slave owners. They seduced you with their juleps and their smiles into believing their lies: they cared about the welfare of their slaves; they protected them. "How did you get that cut?"

"A whip, masta," Moab said.

Hunt gripped the reins so hard that his knuckles grayed. He hated this place of hypocrisy and lying. All the pleasure went out of his heated memories of Sefina in his bed. "You're not going to have to endure this inhumanity, Moab. Not forever. I swear it. I don't know how—but somehow I'll free you from all this." He swung his arm, indicating Blackoaks and all slavery.

Now Moab's head jerked up and the horror in his eyes matched Hunt's. Freed. Being free meant he would be forced to leave Mrs. Pilzer's house, his bed in the tack room, and an existence so perfect that sometimes he was afraid it would turn out to be just a protracted wet dream. He was still afraid he would wake up some morning in the shack he'd always shared with Blade and none of this would be true. Freed meant the end to this life at the overseer's cottage. Freed meant being no longer a slave, but it also meant working—and working harder than ever just to stay alive, and nobody responsible for your welfare. And it meant no beautiful white woman to go down on you at four o'clock in the morning, or four o'clock in the afternoon—whenever you wanted it. His voice shook. "Please, Gawd, masta. Not me. Please. Free some other pore nigger. They needs it. I ain't worth it, masta. Please, Gawd, don't free me."

Hunt stared at Moab in shocked disbelief. In the name of God, he couldn't believe what he was hearing. These Southern slaves were as stupid and ignorant as their masters.

CHAPTER 19

BY MIDSUMMER Hunt had begun to regret having ever come south of the Boston Commons. He had discovered rifts in the carefully postulated gentility of Blackoaks as wide as that thick-posted entrance to the estate itself. The ugly hidden substrata was substantial enough to drive a span of horses through, and yet the Baynards persisted in the gracious pretense of elegance, refinement, and felicity. Hunt didn't deny for one instant that there were fearful skeletons in most Boston closets, or that the Brahmins of that cold land attempted in every devious manner to disguise and conceal their shameful secrets. But the difference was enormous between the way of staid New England life and the hothouse existence of these vast plantations. Bostonians hid their lies, but these people built their whole culture on them.

As the first weeks passed, Hunt forgot his initial dislike of the aloof and self-centered Styles Kenric. Styles turned out to be good company. He was reasonably well educated, though not particularly erudite in any particular discipline. He had received what was regarded—and highly regarded—as a gentleman's well-rounded education in arts and letters. But he was proficient, for example, in conversational French. His idiom was stilted and amused Hunt because Styles' French had a definite Southern-accented cast. They talked for hours over salted fried pecans and whiskey on the terrace in French—polishing, practicing, and refining the use of the gentleman's language.

However, Styles was coldly covetous of the control of this estate, and he made no secret of it with Hunt, especially when they sat talking French in the veranda lounge chairs. Hunt didn't welcome, condone, or appreciate these confidences, which didn't deter Styles in the least when he'd had more than two whiskey neats. Management and improvement of Blackoaks was Styles Kenric's favorite subject. Hunt felt it came damn near being an obsession. Kenric faulted Baynard on every point in administering the estate, and explained in detail how he could improve, upgrade, and expand, given the opportunity. Hunt found this boring, even in French.

They were together constantly during the day. Kathy said she was happy Styles had someone with whom he could exchange ideas, though Hunt felt she didn't exactly exude enthusiasm. Miz Claire found close companionship between two handsome young men inspiring and beautiful. She encouraged it. Styles was an expert at fencing. This was an art he had learned well at his university and Hunt was pleased to learn and sharpen his techniques. In the morning, often before the rest of the house was up, Styles would tap on Hunt's door and they would fence, sweating and grunting, for an hour or more on the knoll beside Miz Claire's chapel.

But, sometime during those first months at Blackoaks, Hunt was awakened by a vaguely formed sense of dread and melancholy. He thought he heard the sounds of muffled sobs and cold, cutting, accusatory tones overlaying that stifled weeping. But he could not be sure in the thick silence of the old house. Was it a trick of the night wind in the eaves and the gables? The unhappy sounds were repeated again and again—the bitterness came from some hidden place in his own mind. No. He knew better. He would fall asleep, doze fitfully, only to awaken to the muted weeping—a sound he had half-consciously been waiting for, as troubling as an unexplained and inconstant dripping of water. He realized emptily that there was a deep discord between Styles and Kathy. Her laughing face no longer seemed so bright and innocent and untroubled. It was more a mask over inner misery. He saw the shadows concealed deep in her pale eyes even when she smiled her loveliest. He tried, but he could never draw Styles out on the subject of his marriage. Styles deftly parried any hints

201

and managed to change the topic of conversation. Hunt had to admit that, like everything else he did, Styles dissembled with great charm.

Hunt could not suppress his growing curiosity and concern. Why would the young wife endure insult, injury, assault—whatever drove her to helpless tears deep in the night—unless she found in it some queer painful pleasure? Sometimes, though they were too distant, the walls too thick, Hunt was sure he heard her pleading, begging—for what? One factor remained constant—Styles' voice was unvaryingly contemptuous, with a cold, reserved fury and sarcastic flavor that must have been more galling to a sensitive ego than physical brutality. Styles could verbally abuse Kathy, and then there would follow sounds of the helpless, strangled weeping. Was there any reason for a young woman in these enlightened times to submit to such abnormal cruelty unless she drew her own warped enjoyment from such abasement? He lay uncomfortable, thinking about her, and eventually he drifted into sleep; but he was aware that the young woman down the corridor seldom slept, because he would waken during the night and he could hear the wakeful and restless sounds of her distress.

After listening unwillingly and sweatedly night after night, Hunt came gradually to pity Kathy and to hate Styles and his refined brand of casually inflicted brutality.

However, no matter how miserable the long night, Styles appeared in the morning fastidiously attired, coolly insolent and reserved, with what he must have considered a smile of guarded warmth for Hunt. Remembering the unhappy sounds of the night before, Hunt found it hard to swallow back the bile of his outrage, and on the knoll enshadowed by the chapel, he put vigorous thrust into his parries and lunges. But Styles only laughed, far too expert and quick for him. And Kathy managed somehow to find laughter in the morning—a sound that came to be music to Hunt. He found her courage and her blond beauty matchless. Whatever problems divided her and her husband, Hunt held her blameless. It was almost impossible to believe that a girl so freshly lovely, so alive with gentle, infectious laughter, could enjoy cruelty, or deserve it. All

202

this simply added to the indefinable aura of evil and hypocrisy that hung over this place. He felt increasingly uncomfortable and anxious to escape before he himself was holpelessly mired in its quicksands of grand pretense and self-delusion.

Hunt found in Miz Claire's vagueness a deep psychic hurt, depression, and a courageous concealment of betrayal too agonizing to be consciously endured. One of the first secrets of Blackoaks that was made apparent to Hunt was that Jeanne d'Arc, the *os rouge* slave, was the true mistress of the plantation. How much power she truly exercised may not even have been clear to her, or to the elder Baynard, whom she controlled through the surest means available to a woman. Hunt knew for sure only that Jeanne d'Arc went with coffee and fresh hot rolls religiously into Baynard's locked study an hour before dawn every morning and that they were together in there for at least three hours, undisturbed. The old man had his own Sefina! What he and Jeanne d'Arc did, or discussed, behind that locked door, he could guess, but never know. Perhaps Jeanne d'Arc stole into Baynard's bedroom at night. He didn't know this either, but he suspected it strongly. The sad part was that, unknown to her family and her husband, the vague Miz Claire was totally aware of the whole affair.

He wondered if she found a kind of self-protection—a retreat, and an armor against hurt—in her vagueness and her vapors?

Lying sleepless in the humid, languorous nights, Hunt would think about the old man and his *os rouge*, about Kathy—and inevitably, about Sefina. Poor Kathy. Obviously she was being denied sex and passion—she was an incredibly lovely young girl and she was being starved. Lying in his bed, empty-bellied, dry of throat, he would think about her writhing, sleepless and miserable, on her rumpled bed. He would think about her full, rounded breasts, the color and texture of fresh, ripe peaches. He shivered. He was certain Kathy's whole body was that same warm, mind-bending color. He warned himself against following this chain of thought. He was a little better than a slave. A little. A paid guest. A barely tolerated tutor. A yankee. Blue-belly. An outsider. He would be summarily fired, casually slain, maybe quartered, for daring to reach out to Kathy—no matter how terribly she needed a man. His mind recognized the dangers, but his body would deny no need—he wanted Kathy violently.

He'd get up, sweated from his bed, and pace the floor. There was one answer. He had to have Sefina brought in to him on a more satisfactory basis. He needed release. He needed to use Sefina's body or his uncontrolled desires for Kathy Kenric would push him until he did something they'd all regret. He even considered explaining his predicament to old man Baynard—as circumspectly as possible, and without any hint of his need for Kathy, of course. . . .

No one mentioned Sefina to him. Finally, Hunt could stand it no longer. He stopped Thyestes in the hall, glanced both ways to be certain they were not overheard. He said in a whisper, "How do I arrange to see Sefina again?"

"Sefina, masta?" Thyestes said.

Hunt winced, motioning the old man to lower his voice. "The bed wench," Hunt said. "Don't tell me you don't know. Mr. Baynard had it arranged for me—some time ago now."

"Oh, yes, masta. I recalls."

Hunt exhaled, nodded. He leaned toward Thyestes. "I'd like her again. Sefina. Brought to my room. You know. Again. Like before. Is that possible?"

The old black man merely stared at him noncommittally. Hunt supposed, raging inwardly, that the old fellow had passed the age of compulsive needs. All Thyestes' emotions were centered on his aching feet. Hunt said anxiously, "Is it possible to have Sefina brought to me again?"

"If de masta say so, Masta Hunt. Maybe not the same gal . . . maybe he say a new one."

"No. I want her."

"That up to the masta, suh."

Hunt nodded, frustrated, and let Thyestes go past him. He felt helpless. He knew Thyestes would not bring the matter before old man Baynard. And how often would old man Baynard permit a wench to be brought into the house to one of the second-floor bedrooms? And if not, how else could he see Sefina? Baynard had warned him against ever visiting a black woman in the slave quarters. He could see this would be much like grabbing a black female in the Congo—an aroused black man and trouble. No. He couldn't go down there. Could he then confess to old Baynard that he was morbidly driven to sexual needs, that one young black girl, no matter how extraordinary, was good only for one night, and his hungers kept renewing themselves, heated, day after heated day?

In his consternation, Hunt found Morgan increasingly difficult to teach. It didn't matter to Morgan that today *A* was for apple; tomorrow *A* might well stand for zebra, if this were the best Morgan's confused mind could come up with. Morgan learned, but it was a slow and painful process for them both. It seemed to be taking money under false pretenses. Six years of the best Harvard could afford him, and after two months, his pupil could painfully write his own name and that of his body slave.

Soapy was something else again. Soapy was so alert, so quick minded, so anxious to learn, that Hunt found delight in teaching Morgan's body slave to read, write, and figure the cost of cotton by the bale. One day, Morgan was so proud that he had carved out Soapy's name in the etching-like Spencerian hand Hunt painfully taught him, that the boy danced around on the terrace, waving the paper with the single word black upon it. But Soapy said petulantly, with a tinge of jealousy, "Ain't my name. Soapy. My name Sophocles."

"Sophocles!" Hunt said. He clapped Soapy on the back. "That's a beautiful name! Do you know who Sophocles was?"

"Sophocles wasn't *was* nobody," Soapy said. "Sophocles *is* me!"

Hunt laughed. He paced the terrace, telling them about the tragic Athenian poet who had written *Antigone, Electra,* and other plays so magnificent that they had withstood time, vandalism, and even performance by Harvard actors. They didn't smile at his gentle jab at his school, and he hadn't expected them to. But Soapy was entranced with his famous namesake. He wanted to know so much about Sophocles, a man with a sketchy personal history, that within ten minutes Hunt found himself inventing stories to describe the great man. "It'll never do for a man named for Sophocles to be unable to read and write well. We'll have to teach you, Soapy."

Morgan laughed, agreeing. Misery has always doted on companionship. Morgan truly wanted the best for his body slave, whom he loved above his own family. But Soapy was hesitant. "Ain't that against the law? Teachin' a nigger to read?"

"You going to tell?"

"No, suh."

"Well, I'm not. Besides, I won't teach *you*—I'll teach Morgan. If you sit beside him and learn everything he does, we can't help that, can we? We've got nothing to fear but the *ABCs,* eh, Morgan?"

The boys laughed happily, nodding.

Soapy was soon transcribing whole sentences from the blackboard. He was two primers ahead of Morgan in his reading. He could figure the cost of ten and one-half bales of cotton at sixty cents a bale. He knew who was the first president of the United States. He thought, however, that the man was less than clever for owning up, as Parson Weems so eloquently declared he had, to chopping down his father's favorite cherry tree. "Wasn't ole George jes' askin' for trouble?" Soapy wanted to know.

Hunt laughed. "Not much sense in just asking for trouble, is there?"

"But when there is trouble, a man ought to fight," Morgan said. Without rancor, he reminded Hunt that he had not fought that day in town and had almost gotten Ferrell-Junior killed fighting his battles for him.

Hunt exhaled heavily and told Morgan that a man must decide inside himself what is important enough to fight for.

"Honor. Your honor. That's what you fight for," Morgan said. "That's why slaves don't have to fight. They don't have no honor, the way humans do. . . . Only slaves don't fight back. A human has to fight for his honor."

Hunt smiled wryly. He quoted, " 'They are slaves who fear to speak for the fallen and the weak. They are slaves who dare not be in the right with only two or three beside them—' "

"What the fuck does that mean?" Morgan said.

"It means freedom is something important enough to fight for—even for slaves," Soapy said. "It may be different from honor. But it's better."

"Something like that," Hunt said.

The secret of Soapy's reading skills was too wonderful for Morgan to keep. He ran to Baynard with the news of Soapy's incredible progress with the books and the abacus. Baynard patted Morgan's shoulder, scrubbed Soapy affectionately on the head, gave him a shiny new silver dollar, and after lunch, called Hunter into the library.

Baynard was very friendly and courteous about the problem, but Hunt could tell he was obviously seething inside with outrage. "I'm afraid, Hunt, you're wasting your time and my money. We don't want our slaves to read or write."

"What are you afraid of—sir?"

Baynard poured them both half a glass of his prime whiskey, neat, before he answered. "I know you won't belive this, but I am afraid for them. I am not afraid of them. But I know what a little knowledge can do—I know the hurt that can come from half-truths picked up from incendiary pamphlets, for example—"

"Or the whole truth? Perhaps if I were Southern and still taught Soapy to read—"

"If you were a Southern boy, Hunt, you wouldn't have taught Soapy to read. You would have understood—and wanted him to have—the protection of his own innocence—"

"Or the protection his ignorance gives you and your class?"

Baynard finished off his drink in a long gulp, wincing only slightly. "For whatever reason, Mr. Campbell. I won't tolerate it. There is a law against teaching Negro slaves to read. The state legislature passed that law upon deliberation. In many ways it's a good law."

"It is vile. As vile as slavery itself."

"But it's a necessary vileness. A fact of life down here. As slavery is. We are not involved in an academic discussion of theories, Hunt. We are talking about day-to-day living on great farms with the only labor that is cheap enough to make running those farms feasible. Not a plantation owner in my acquaintance would keep slaves five minutes longer than necessary. If you people—abolitionists —are going to come down here telling us how to run our lives and our businesses, you better prove your own smarts first. You better figure a new way to run huge farms without slave labor. You do that, and I'll free the least pickaninny on my land. I'll move them out of houses I'm obligated to keep in good repair for them. I'll stop growing food to feed them, or making fabrics to clothe and cover them. I'll stop tending their ill, doctoring their sick. Have you the least inkling of how susceptible these people are to every disease they didn't bring with them from Africa? No immunity. No resistance. And then there are the ethnic diseases that infect African children because of racial malnutrition and then strike them as adults, making them total invalids. But now they are *your* invalids. They're like children. Backward children. They're like delicate animals. Sometimes it costs more to keep them well and reasonably able to work than they could ever be worth to you. But you are caught in a vicious circle and they're in it with you." Baynard stopped speaking and laughed.

"What's so amusing?" Hunt inquired.

"I just realized that I am talking to myself. I learned long ago that the zealot has only a mouth, no ears."

Hunt smiled. "I admit my mind was closed when I came down here. But I can tell you, since I've been here, it's clamped shut even tighter."

"Shut or open, you'll have to stop teaching Soapy to read. Not only is it against the law. It's against Soapy's best interests. It's against everything I believe is best for that boy and this farm, and I won't have it. You must either promise you will stop filling poor little Soapy's head with this nonsense, or I'll have to ask you to leave Blackoaks."

Hunt took a sip of whiskey. "May I think it over?"

Baynard smiled. "Certainly, Hunter, take as long as you like. Let me know—in an hour?"

They both smiled, but empty-bellied, Hunter knew that Sophocles the body slave was the loser.

He found Kathy sitting alone on the terrace about three that afternoon. He walked out through the French doors and saw her sagging dejectedly in a wicker lounge chair where Styles had abandoned her after fifteen minutes of desultory conversation. Hunt saw she had been crying, but she looked up smiling when she heard his step on the blocks. His heart lurched and he wanted to blurt out how sorry he was for her. But he hesitated—as indecisive as Hamlet had ever been. Her voice was gentle with compassion for him. "I'm sorry about your trouble with father."

"Trouble?"

"Teaching Soapy to read."

He tried to smile in return, but he could not. His voice was stiff, chilled. "Trouble? What trouble, Mrs. Kenric? I can stop teaching Soapy to read, or return on the next train to Boston. I hate those drafty, sooty cars. What does it matter about Soapy? His mind is going to lie fallow—and whatever may have come out of it—for your father's benefit—won't even germinate."

Her eyes blurred with tears. "I am sorry. Truly sorry."

Morgan told him that Soapy had gone up to Miz Claire's chapel. "He says he wants to pray," Morgan said. "I think he wants to cry and he don't want me to see him cry. I'm sorry if I've done something to hurt Soapy, Mr. Campbell. I never meant to."

"I know, Morgan. I'm sure Soapy understands too."

"Maybe he does, but why did he say he ought to beat my big-mouthed ass in?"

Hunter laughed and shook his head. "I don't know, those niggers talk funny sometimes."

Soapy was knotted up in a rear pew of the silent chapel. Hunter paused just inside the rear doors, struck by the candle-lit ornamentation at the altar. He had seen Catholic churches in Boston less elegantly furnished. Christ, frozen forever in crucifixion, slumped on a cross that dominated the sanctuary. Tall candles illumined it and reached flickeringly at the shadowed pews. Soapy's sobs twisted Hunt's insides. He went to the pew and sat down beside the huddled figure. "I'm sorry, Soapy."

Soapy sniffled and dragged his sleeve across his nose. "I don't give a shit."

"That I'm sorry? I don't blame you. It doesn't buy you anything, does it?"

"No. I mean about them books. Who gives a good fuck? I don't. I just figured I could read, it would make me better'n a field nigger. They piss right on the floor. You know that?"

"You are different, Soapy. Don't worry about that."

Soapy suddenly dissolved into tears again. "That one book—I reckon I sure will miss reading in it."

Hunt nodded. "Maybe I can lose it, Soapy. Somewhere you can find it. Only, you've got to be careful. If anybody finds you've got it, they might fire me—but it'll be much worse on you."

"Won't nobody ever find it, Masta Campbell, suh. I surely don't want to get you in no passel of trouble. You been most passing kind to me, masta."

CHAPTER 20

THE LETTER from Garrett Blanford Ware and the arrival of Mr. Cleatus Dennison almost coincided. From his vantage point as employed guest, held carefully at arm's length by the Baynards, Hunt was unable to discern which event had the most powerful and upsetting impact upon life at Blackoaks.

Letters were rare objects at Blackoaks, brought out from the post office in the Mt. Zion general store. No matter to whom the letters were addressed, everybody knew about them. If the epistle was one which could be shared generally, it was. Sometimes letters were read at the dining table after a meal and discussed by the family. No one read Mr. Garrett Blanford Ware's letter except the elder Baynard. He seemed, to Hunt at least, more than usually taut and withdrawn in the days immediately after the arrival of the Ware letter. However, at dinner, he spoke warmly of Garrett Blanford Ware and of his wife. They had inquired about the health of each and sent their warm affection to all. They had been visiting friends in Montgomery and would pay a visit to Blackoaks later in the month on their return to Tallahassee.

This news brought Miz Claire from her reverie. "How nice that they're coming," she said. "Remember how pleasant their visit was last year?"

"And year before last," Kathy teased. "And the year before that. The Wares I remember. Pleasant escapés me."

"I remember the annual Ware visit ever since I've had a memory," Ferrell-Junior said, matching Kathy's tone.

"Not with any particular thrill, though."

"They're lovely people," Miz Claire said. "Don't listen to my outrageous children, Mr. Campbell. They're very lovely people."

"Maybe that's why I don't like them," Ferrell-Junior said. "I never have known what to say to lovely people."

"I don't appreciate that, Ferrell-Junior," his mother said. "Even in jest. They're always welcome in my home."

"Sure they are," Ferrell-Junior persisted, winking at Kathy. "But you must admit, mama, they're *old.*"

"Why they're not as old as I am," Miz Claire said, and then blushed, confused. "They certainly are not *old.*"

"Why do I get the feeling that what we run here is an ordinary inn on the way between Montgomery and Tallahassee?" Kathy wondered.

"That's not true," Miz Claire said. "They go well out of their way to visit us out here at Blackoaks."

"I'd go out of my way too," Kathy said, "if the price were right."

"That's enough," Baynard said. "The Wares are welcome here. Your mother is right."

"Thank you, Mr. Baynard," Miz Claire said. She smiled around the table. "We'll plan a party. A big party that uses both the house and the yard. A barbecue in the afternoon perhaps, and a formal dance that night. Wouldn't that be nice, Mr. Baynard?"

"Yes. Yes, you do that," Baynard said abstractedly. Only Hunt seemed aware that Baynard was lost in some troubling reverie of his own and had barely heard his wife.

After the meal, Baynard didn't linger for whiskey and cigar. He excused himself and walked alone up to the chapel. This truly stirred Hunt's curiosity. He had discovered no earlier indication that Baynard was in any sense a religious man. . . .

The arrival of Mr. Cleatus Dennison was a circuslike event in itself. Hunt was on the terrace, teaching Morgan his morning lessons with Soapy lounging dejectedly to one side. Hunt had just advised Soapy no one could whip him for keeping his mind and his eyes and ears open. Soapy

212

gave him a wan smile but did not come out of his depression until they heard the carriage rattling up the drive under the pecan trees. Soapy leaped up then, expectantly. Visitor! The news raced like flash-fire across the plantation. Hunt hesitated only a moment and he too followed the boys around the side of the big old house. And Hunt stared, almost as gape-mouthed as Soapy. In fact, an awed silence struck all the witnesses who gathered from every corner of the vast farm.

There was an almost obscene opulence about Mr. Cleatus Dennison's entourage that suggested the decadence and creature indulgence of Flavian Rome. The splendor of the carriages and attendants certainly eclipsed any traveling carnival of Hunt's memory. He was convinced the trimmings of the coaches were sterling silver and that the gems encrusting the door handles, coat of arms, and window framing were sapphires at least. The swank of the carriages was ostentatious in a blatant way that almost bordered on good taste. Gleaming new tack, reins, leathers, and hames glittered with ornamentation. The horses were groomed, trimmed, and brushed until they appeared fresh and ready for show after their trip along the trail. Uniforms of the black attendants were of gold lamé and silk. The driver wore squared upon his head a tall and golden top hat, epaulettes of tasseled ermine, rhinestone-decorated boots. His crew was less grandly, but no less expensively attired. The entire caravan presented the immediate impression of a self-indulgent man with more money than he possibly could spend—though he made every profligate effort.

Cleatus Dennison was himself an imposing, but immediately engaging and personable man. He was as tall as Baynard, as thick chested, as self-assured. Here any resemblance ended. Dennison was crowned with a freshly laundered lion's mane of silky white hair, worn collar length. It was so clean it gleamed and refracted the sunlight. His face was flushed, creased and marked with white brows. His eyes were friendly, interested, sun-bleached blue, webbed with laugh lines, and his smile was almost a reflex. He held himself erect, and one suspected that

213

though his laughter welled up easily, he could, when crossed, strike back swiftly and that he consciously held a violent temper under tight leash.

Baynard invited Dennison into the library where he served his best whiskey. Ferrell-Junior, Hunt, and Styles accompanied them. They were sitting in deep leather-covered chairs sipping whiskey before it was revealed that Mr. Cleatus Dennison was a slave breeder. But he was a professional on a level unknown to Eakins Shivers, and only dimly understood by men like Baxter Simon.

Cleatus Dennison admitted with some humility that he owned a Louisiana plantation larger in scope than Blackoaks, dedicated however to totally dissimilar goals. Dennison did, indeed, breed slaves as Simon did at Willow Oaks in Mississippi, but his conversation was on a higher plane. He did not talk selling, exchanging, or auctioning slaves, which was Simon's entire interest. Dennison was like the devoted horse breeder interested only in improving the animal bloodlines. Money was of no consequence. Breeding and mate selection was everything.

They talked at length about Simon's recent visit to Blackoaks, because it was Simon who had told Cleatus Dennison about Blade, the perfect Fulani—"the finest fucking animal in this country today" in Simon's words. Dennison smiled, recalling. "I met Mr. Simon at an auction of slaves in New Orleans. We were both disappointed in the quality of the animals being placed on vendue. Even those beasts with more than half-human blood looked as if they had been conceived in a hurry with weak-sapped partners watching over their shoulders for the police." He waited for their appreciative laughter. He drew hard on his cigar and permitted the smoke to waft ceiling-ward in small round bolls. "Mr. Simon and I were encouraged to sell our fancies at top market prices, but we could not hope to find the quality stock to replace them. It was depressing. When Mr. Simon was through singing the praises of your perfect Fulani, I came hundreds of miles east over execrable roads to have a look-see. As I have suggested, Brother Baynard, money is of no consequence if I can locate the quality animals I seek. I've been told you rejected Mr. Simon's bid of 10,000 in gold for your Fulah male. I admire you for this. You could not be sure how your Fulani's talents might be used at Willow Oaks. Therefore, I will not insult you—I begin my bidding $2000 above Mr. Simon's top bid and vow to you that your Fulani youth will be mated to Fulah stock of highest quality and most perfect physical condition. You will speak with pride of his progeny from *Couer de Façon*."

Hunt was afraid that Baynard was suffering an attack of vertigo. He paled, sat tense and unspeaking. Dennison was tactful; $12,000 represented no considerable outlay to him and he assumed it was not of serious consequence to Baynard. Dennison applied no pressure. They poured more whiskey, exchanged more views, and spent the next four hours discussing the extraordinary quality of offspring possible to a mating of a perfect specimen like Blackoaks' Blade and a Fulah female fancy. Dennison was well versed in Fulani history. He described the incredibly handsome men and women who once had created a magnificent North African dynasty.

Hunt listened in numb horror as they spoke of blacks as animals. This lower species could be improved, Dennison believed, with judicious admixture of human blood. He had found most unique Baxter Simon's theory that the best animal came from mating an American Indian with an African black. Hunt was no longer shocked that these people could deny to blacks the least semblance of human dignity, knock unwanted births in the head as negligently as they might drown a litter of unwanted kittens. They actually believed the monstrous things they said to each other. They were dealing in animals, and Cleatus Dennison would not let them forget he dealt in prime, quality animals only. He kept returning to the subject of the Fulani people, to his open-ended offer to buy Blade.

The conference broke up about 11:00—an unconscionable hour at Blackoaks where the last candle was snuffed out ordinarily by 10:00 P.M. Baynard's last words to his guest, almost a defensive cry, were, "Blade is not for sale."

The contest of wills resumed after breakfast the next

morning. The verbal jousting continued for a week in which almost all normal routines at Blackoaks ground to a standstill. Hunt saw that Baynard accepted Dennison as an equal, and that he sincerely enjoyed the slave breeder's company. Dennison was a charming man with a steel-trap mind and an inexhaustible store of lascivious vignettes, which were more rancid, biologically explicit, and blacker than Hunt had ever heard during a Harvard bull session. Dennison was conducted on a tour of the whiskey distillery. He met Blade, pronounced him everything that Simon had promised. He was not shown Blade's brother Moab because the boy's back had not yet healed satisfactorily. Baynard was ill with apprehension that Dennison might accidentally come across Moab and lose all respect for Blackoaks as a civilized site.

The two men found much to occupy and entertain themselves during the week. Blade was shucked down and Dennison inspected him minutely, unable to discover a flaw. Hunt was faintly amused that Styles betrayed for the first time since Hunt met him aggressive interest in matters outside his immediate comfort and indulgence. Each such session ended with Baynard's weakly repeated, "I'm sorry, sir. As much as I'd admire to accommodate you. My own future program prohibits it. . . . Blade is not for sale."

Dennison smiled, neither discouraged nor discomfited. They laughed together and changed the subject. They casually inspected the best of Blackoaks' lesser slaves, with Dennison discoursing at length on the probable ancestry of each—Hausa, Jaloff, bush bastard. The women were treated as callously as the males, but as indifferently. They were forced to get down on all fours and then pull the cheeks of their buttocks wide while Dennison probed with his middle finger deep into their anus. They were sprawled out on their backs, legs spread out awkwardly while he parted the lips of their vagina and ran his finger around the dilated orifice. Some took the fingering stoically, some giggled nervously or coquettishly, some wept in abject terror. No matter their reaction, the white men inspecting them intimately ignored them as human beings.

Hunt felt ill, sick with self-hatred that he did not protest in their behalf. But he stood aside, silent, unmoving.

When finally Dennison ordered his entourage readied for travel, everyone expressed regret, urged him to prolong his visit a few days longer, to return soon.

It was this moment of Cleatus Dennison's departure that remained forever etched in Hunt's mind. The splendid carriages were readied, attendants accoutred and lined at attention, the spans of horses almost prancing and glowingly groomed. It was at this final instant that four slaves —two well-built men and two pregnant young women were marched up from the quarters in spancels. The women wept, the men cried openly, like small boys.

Hunt retreated as if he'd been struck across the face. He stood stock still, not breathing, staring. One of the women was Sefina!

He had seen the young girl only once since the night she'd spent in his bed—that lovely, marathon night of holy memory! Months had passed and he'd been unable to screw up enough courage to ask Mr. Baynard for Sefina, or another bed wench. He had suffered worse since that night with Sefina because he knew what a bed wench could be made to do, how willingly she accepted her *enslavement*.

Sefina had been that first time on her way with a group of young black girls to do the plantation laundry. Some walked with wicker baskets heaped with soiled clothing balanced on their heads. They walked with incredible poise, backs straight. He'd smiled tautly, thinking how young white girls had to be painfully taught this art of poise and balance in their expensive finishing schools where they plodded long hours with heavy books on their heads—so they'd one day learn to walk like black washerwomen!

Sefina had hesitated that morning, glancing toward Hunt. A brief smile pulled her lips from her white teeth. Then she'd lowered her eyes and moved past him. Hunt might have called out to her, followed her, even when he realized how brutally unkind this would have been—for Sefina. But he did not move because he recognized by the small round protuberance in the front of her dress that the girl was pregnant.

He had turned away, hollow bellied. That slave girl was carrying his child. God knew, only a miracle could have kept her from becoming impregnated during that wild night when he had driven himself into her with all the fury and passion in him. And there had been no miracle.

He had turned and walked dazedly across the fields and into the hammock. Sefina would give birth to a mulatto child—a mustafina. His son. His daughter. Whatever, the child would have his blood, draw from his corpus, and it would grow up a black slave! There would be no schooling, no training except in back-breaking, spirit-numbing toil. Good God! The little half-breed would be an object of white derision, and never truly accepted by the blacks among whom it would have to live. He leaned against the rough bole of a pine, sick at his stomach, seeing a whole lifetime of horror that he had created but was helpless to alleviate in any way at all. . . .

He didn't mention a bed wench to Thyestes or old man Baynard again. But he awoke at night, seeing Sefina, the protuberant belly, the nascent stirring of life inside her, and he had lain awake, sweated, filled with a sense of horror and self-hatred, a guilt that was never going to free him. . . .

Now, watching the four slaves being prodded into Dennison's last coach, he was afraid he was going to retch. His heart sank. The backs of his legs felt so weak he was afraid he would fall. Sefina was one of the slaves being boarded to leave with the slave breeder. Hunt felt his face pale as the blood rushed downward in his body. Almost immediately, his face flushed red, and sweat broke out across his forehead.

Sefina looked lovely, somehow regal, sad and removed from him. Good God, he thought, one night of slaking my miserable thirsts and this girl's whole existence is altered forever. His child! His son! Born a slave! Sold as a slave, to live its life in slavery. He looked about wildly. There ought to be something he could do, but he could not think what it could be. What a hellishly rotten thing—he had come down here avowedly to improve the lot of the enslaved blacks. So far, all he'd accomplished was the compounding of the misery of one helpless black girl.

A stunned silence settled over the crowded yard outside the veranda. Hunt stood, sick at his stomach as Sefina and the three other slaves were shackled in the last carriage and the shades drawn at the windows. Then Cleatus Dennison departed in a final volley of laughter and shouting and a cloud of dust that smoked back over the people left standing in the driveway.

Baynard noted Hunt's consternation. The older man whispered gently, "It's all right, Hunt. She'll be treated well. . . . The mustafina will be more casually accepted at Dennison's plantation than here. There will be fewer questions. Do not concern yourself. Sefina will have a good life. It's all for the best."

Hunt nodded, but he did not speak. He did not trust himself to speak.

Tensions other than his crackled in the atmosphere. At the rim of the drive, slaves wept and called to Masta Baynard to change his mind and bring back the bartered slaves. Ferrell-Junior was the only one who expressed his outrage in words. "Why did you do it?" he demanded. "It makes you—common. It makes us all common. It makes us no better than Baxter Simon—not as honest about our slave dealings as Eakins Shivers."

Baynard gestured downward cuttingly, stopping his son. Baynard's face paled, a blue vein large as a pencil throbbing at his temple. He spoke in a hard, vibrant voice. "I'll tolerate no further discussion of the matter—from family or slave."

The slaves subsided into sniffling, agonized silence. The family stood rigid, wounded and humiliated, and set against Baynard.

And then—to Hunt's astonishment and shock—Baynard turned on his heel and strode up the grassy knoll. He entered the fieldstone chapel and locked the door behind him. Hunt remained standing on the sun-reflective drive after everyone else drifted away. He stared, puzzled, toward that chapel on the green rise. What could that man possibly have to say to God? On the other hand, if Baynard were made in his god's image, they probably had a great deal to say to each other. . . .

CHAPTER 21

"I MAY as well tell you, right out, I plain won't stand for it. I figured the most honorable and neighborly and upright thing was to get myself over here and lay my feelings right out in the open." Fletcher Talmadge paced the front room, outrage making his tall, wide-shouldered body quiver. He shook an extraordinarily long and bony finger at no one in particular, and yet including the gathered assemblage, the Baynard family, Hunt, and Fletcher's son, Gil. "I woke up this mornin' frettin' about it, and knew I'd get myself in a stew, and if I thought on it too long I'd get so carnsarned raging mad I might do something we'd all regret. So I'm laying my cards right out here on the table, as I told Gil I intended doing this morning when I woke up just sick to my belly to think we got a goddamn yankee abolitionist right here in the bosom of our community."

The lean, aging man didn't glance toward Hunt Campbell; he didn't flatter him enough to bother to look at him. Hunt was astonished at first that the planter would discuss him, in front of his face, as though he were no more than a stick of furniture. Less. He realized that these people considered Negroes on a level with the lower primates, but they held yankees in no such high regard.

"A man is entitled to his own beliefs, Fletcher," Baynard said in a mild tone that suggested no touch of criticism. "Even if we don't happen to share those beliefs."

"I don't give a damn—you'll pardon me, Miz Claire—what beliefs a man holds. Even a blue-belly yankee. I figure they've had few of the advantages of gentle people, and I try to make allowances. Let 'em believe what they want to believe. It's when they open their mouths and stir up trouble for me—that's when I get upset."

"What trouble have you had, Fletcher?" Baynard asked.

"That's just it. That's why I'm here. To nip it in the bud. That's what I woke up primed and determined to do. I didn't even eat my usual breakfast. Could hardly choke down two of them fine eggs Rosa-Monday prepares to my exact liking. You ast Gil. He knowed something was bad amiss when I couldn't eat. You ast Gil."

Gil flushed red, unwilling to be brought into the focus of attention. He was always uncomfortable in the presence of gentle white ladies. He didn't want to risk enmity with Ferrell-Junior by openly censuring the new tutor. On the other hand, he knew better than to oppose his father. He gulped and said, "I could purely tell something was amiss, all right."

"That's when I said to Gil, I said to him, we best have a carriage hitched up to a pair of fast horses, so I could get myself over here to let you know my feelings on this very outrageous subject—stirrin' up nigger trouble."

Baynard smiled, kept his tone soothing. "But you've said you've had no trouble at Felicity Manor yet."

"That's right. Not yet. But I don't mean to have none. It spreads like a cancerous growth, and I won't have it. I won't have it infectin' the darkies on my place. I treats them the best I know how. They eat as well as I do—maybe better—they don't have an upset stomach from worrying about their fool ills, the way I do. . . . But I won't have no abolitionist talk on my place—and I mean not even blowing in on the wind. These abolitionist blockheads don't know their—pardon me, Miz Claire, but as you can see, I am purely riled up. They come down here talking from their empty heads to the empty black burr heads, and that equals trouble. Trouble I won't have. I'm gettin' too old, I been working too long and too hard, and I won't have it ruined by some taggle-headed abolitionist that will look at everything but the facts."

"What abolitionist talk is it you've been hearing?" Baynard inquired.

"Don't take that patient, disinterested tone with me, Ferrell Baynard," Fletcher Talmadge said. "We been close friends for a long time. But I got an abiding hatred for stupidity—and once a hate gets in me, it eats away everything else—even the memory of friendship close as brotherhood."

"I understand clearly, Fletcher, that you're making charges against Mr. Campbell here—"

"That's right. This yankee abolitionist. Right here in yore bosom, and you treatin' this treacherous blue-belly like a member of your own family. I can't believe you're deceived."

"I am at least aware of Mr. Campbell's beliefs—without condoning or sharing a one of them. But he is hired here to teach my son. That's all. We—Styles, Ferrell-Junior, and I have had some heated arguments in the evening before bed—at the table after dinner over cigars and whiskey. Hunt feels strongly against our way of life. But I am equally certain he has not caused any trouble among the Negroes, mine or anyone else's."

Fletcher Talmadge snorted. "I swear I don't know whether it's yore lack of understanding of human nature, or yore flat-out gullibility, Ferrell. When you got a snake in yore bed, it's time for one of you to git out and take a look at the situation."

"All right. What is your specific complaint?"

"My specific complaint is that every white family within a hundred miles knows you got an abolitionist at Blackoaks. Your niggers know it, and from them, my niggers know it. One nigger don't never know something that soon all the niggers ain't privy to. So they knows he's here. Then we hear that he been teaching your niggers to read—and goddamn it—you will forgive me, Miz Claire—teachin' niggers to read is not only yankee-stupid, but it's purentee 100 percent against the law."

"That little oversight has been corrected, Fletcher, I assure you."

"Has it? You ever had a little rust in yore cotton one

223

afternoon that's a killing blight by noon the next day? That's the way this here evil spreads. Niggers is naturally lazy critters. A yankee comes along promising them milk and honey and a two-hour working day and the equal right to fornicate with our sisters and wives. You think them niggers ain't goin' to sit up and listen? You think you ain't got trouble—trouble that can come to anarchy— if it ain't pinched off the first minute you get wind of it. And that's what I mean to do."

Baynard stopped smiling. "Are you asking us to do something, Fletcher, or are you warning us of some action you intend to take unilaterally?"

"I reckon they's a mixture of both in what I'm trying to say. I come here looking for no trouble—beyond what it takes to get shed of the threat of niggers in anarchy. I'm trying to be neighborly—something the rest of the folks in this area won't be if this thing gets out of hand. . . . I'm not just blowing off steam to hear my own voice, Ferrell. I'm telling you in confidence of the known sentiments of dozens of neighbors. You ast Gil."

Gil winced and stared at his shoes. After a moment, he nodded.

"Yeah. Gil'll tell you. We've already had some hot-heads talking about a tar and feather coat and a ride on a rail for yore abolitionist. They ain't done nothing be-cause there hasn't been the first flare of trouble out in the open. The minute that comes, it's like the first real hard pain of cancer—it's too late. None of us going to be able to stop them aroused white folks then, Ferrell. It only appears to me it's a hell of a lot easier to stop your yankee—tutor—now."

"What do you want him to do?" Baynard asked.

Fletcher Talmadge laughed loudly but entirely mirth-lessly. "Me? I want him to get his blue belly and his carpetbags on the first train heading north out of here. That's what I want. And not just to make me happy—for his own security and safety of skin. . . . I may as well tell you, we also heard that he's one of these prissy misses who won't fight like a man—but stands by whilst others fight for him. . . . Well, there won't be nobody to fight for him when he stirs these niggers to trouble, and your neighbors come for him with the hot tar and the chicken feathers. But expecting him to see the logic in that might just be expecting too much of the yankee mentality. . . . Failing his taking the reasonable course of a speedy departure back north, there is the certainty that if he rouses one black ape to sass his betters, to refuse to work, to try to rape a white woman—he's a dead abolitionist. . . . If he plans to stay on here, he best speak wisely and infrequently, and to the right people only—and that's asking a lot of a backward yankee."

Baynard glanced toward Hunt and tried to smile. "You see what you're up against, Hunter?"

Hunter tried to reply, but his throat was tight. He was raging inside. He wanted to tell this red-neck where to stuff it. He wanted to slap his face until his scrawny neck wavered like a reed in the wind. But he didn't move. He managed to smile, and he nodded.

Now Fletcher Talmadge stood directly above Hunt, staring down at him. He spoke to the assembled room, but his voice lashed at the young tutor. "No abolitionist is going to come in down here and tell me what to do with my niggers, boy. Them niggers is my property to do with as I see fit. They is my chattel, like my cattle, horses, pigs, nor any other animal. I want to, I grind them up with my corn. I feed them to the chickens. I sells them, or I keep them. But whatever I do, no abolitionist tells me yes or no."

Gil Talmadge was painfully embarrassed by his father's display of rage in the Baynard front parlor. It was not that he didn't agree with every word his father said. And he could not have put it more diplomatically either. Abolitionists were an evil, and demanded strong measures. You spoke out against them as they whispered against your way of life. They stealthily got pamphlets to your slaves; they secretly read those incendiary papers to them; they stirred up dissension, discord, anarchy. You dealt with the treacherous sneaks as you had to. But insensitive as Gil usually was to the injured sensibilities of others,

225

he saw that his father had infuriated the Baynards, though they probably agreed with Fletcher Talmadge, in principle at least.

It was Ferrell-Junior's friendship, the threat of its loss, that honed Gil's awareness of his neighbors' reactions to his father's outrage. He admired and idolized Ferrell-Junior. Everything that was difficult for Gil to accomplish came effortlessly to Ferrell-Junior. Rather than making Gil envious, or jealous, this served to increase his admiration for the handsome young Baynard. Gil had even been at the point of working his hand down into the heated bodice of some town girl's frock only to have her speak worshipfully of Ferrell-Junior. Gil drew a reflected glory being in Ferrell-Junior's company. He liked for people to know he was Ferrell-Junior's friend, that Ferrell-Junior was indeed his best friend, more like a brother. There were other, rougher wild men that Gil enjoyed more. Often he wasn't sure he understood Ferrell-Junior. But he considered this as part of the price for remaining like a satellite in the younger boy's orbit. It was worth it. Gil realized that Ferrell-Junior wasn't entirely one of the good ole boys, but felt that with his help, Ferrell-Junior would be totally accepted by his rough and ready comrades.

When Fletcher Talmadge had delivered his message and his ultimatum, he kissed Miz Claire's cheek, shook hands around the room, ignoring Hunt as if the tutor were a Negro, or did not exist at all. Then the tall man strode from the house. Styles, Ferrell-Junior, Baynard, and perversely, Hunt Campbell walked out to the Talmadge carriage in the driveway with the embattled father and sweated son.

On the veranda, Gil suddenly struck Ferrell-Junior playfully on the bicep. "Hey, Ferrell-Junior, how about we go coon huntin' tonight." He glanced at Hunt and forced a smile. "Maybe your friend Campbell might like to go along and see how we really know how to live down here."

"I don't know," Ferrell-Junior said.

Gil grabbed him in a bear hug, wrestling him across

the stone porch. "Ah, come on. You ain't sore, huh? A few fellows and me. We're taking the dogs out. Tree a couple coons. Have a few drinks. Some laughs."

Ferrell-Junior worked himself free, frowning. He glanced at Hunt, thinking he saw a way out of going coon hunting with Gil and his friends. "I don't know," he said again. "It would be up to Hunt. If he wants to go, sure I'll go along." He flushed, thinking, why the hell do you have to do things you hate, just to prove you're one of the herd?

Hunt shocked him. "It sounds great," Hunt said. "I've never been on a coon hunt."

Ferrell-Junior stared at Hunt, wide-eyed with shock. Styles too peered at the tutor in disbelief. But Ferrell-Junior saw that Hunt believed he had something he had to prove too.

Gil sparred with Ferrell-Junior, shadowboxing and chortling with laughter. "There you are. Hunt wants to go. We'll be by before dark—taking a buggy to haul the liquor and the grub. I tell you, Hunt. You're going to see a life that's new to you."

Hunt was on the terrace when Kathy came through the French doors in a fragile dress of pastel green that made her even more heartbreakingly beautiful. Hunt felt as awkward as poor Morgan, who had just stumbled, going down the terrace steps with Soapy after his lessons, which had been delayed by the Talmadge visit. He could scarcely bring himself to meet her cool blue eyes. He was afraid he'd betray the hot, forbidden thoughts that flared in him, the incipient passions she aroused in him simply by walking near him.

There was no way he could speak out loud to her what he thought with such uncontrollable heat in his heart and loins. It was not that he had learned a lesson of caution in his affair with his cousin's wife. The fact that Kathy was Styles Kenric's wife disturbed him less even than had his relations with Addie. So far as he knew, until he drove Addie out of her reasoned coolness with his stolen love poems, she and Lodge had lived comfortably

227

and smoothly together. He lay through the hot summer nights, listening for Kathy's stifled weeping, even while he dreaded to hear it—the sure sign her marriage to Kenric was on the rocks. He passed her on the wide stairway, or in the corridor, or on the terrace, and knew he had never seen such fragile loveliness, that he was going out of his mind with desire for her—and nothing offered any relief, not even his fist.

He couldn't say a word about his feelings for her because he was in the unenviable position of paid guest in this house. She had never once, by word or gesture, encouraged him. In fact, though he searched for the tiniest sign of interest on her part, he discovered the opposite. She had begun by considering him almost a clown, and now she accepted him indifferently as a casual addition to the household. As far as his need for her was concerned, Kathy didn't even know he existed.

She sank into a wicker chair near him and gave him a wan smile. "I have come to admire you, Mr. Campbell."

"Enough to call me Hunter?"

Her smile widened and it was like a thousand suns played directly upon him.

"You don't like coon hunting. In fact, I think you hate it, or you would if you knew anything about it."

"Probably."

"But you have to show these young thugs out here that you're not afraid to go out hunting in the swamps with them—even knowing how they feel about your abolitionist views."

"Especially knowing how they feel about my views. . . . I can let them run me out of here, or I can stay. But if I stay, I've got to show them that I'm not afraid of what they can do to me."

"That's what I wanted to talk to you about. It's like the coon hunt. You don't know what it's like at all. If you had, you'd never have agreed to go. And you have no idea what they can do to you—if they want to. You won't like that either. But I admire your courage in saying you'll go. Now if you want to be really smart, you'll develop a splitting headache before nightfall."

"I couldn't do that. Remember? Being smart is just asking too much of the yankee mentality."

She didn't smile. "You don't know what you're getting into, Hunter. You'll hate it."

Kathy was right, in spades. The only qualification was that it was so much worse than even she had suggested it would be. The coon hunt was an adventure in mindless horror.

Hunt had supposed that it would be a caravan of rich young plantation men with their body slaves, a carriage of whiskey and food. They would set up an encampment worthy of an Arab chieftan, they would arm themselves and follow the hounds into the swamps in search of the raccoon. They would in due season tree one of the nocturnal creatures, and one of the hunters would quickly dispatch it with a bullet. Whereupon, they would repair to the campsite where slaves would have hams turning on spits, whiskey poured, and food set out.

They did indeed tree and kill one raccoon much in the manner Hunt had anticipated. But this was not the kind of thrill Gil was looking for. Before they reached the swamp, Hunt had set Gil down in his mind as an insensitive boor, the ugliest kind of red-neck, ignorant, cruel, and brutish. But Gil's behavior once the dogs scented a second raccoon, seemed to Hunt to epitomize the casual evil of all these people. The dogs treed the raccoon, but Gil didn't let anyone shoot it. He managed to chase the animal from the bole of the tree out on a branch too limber to support its weight. The raging of the dogs and Gil's maniacal yelling had the raccoon in a frenzy. It fell through the air and landed in the top of a wild elder bush. Gil raged with delight. He forced the Negro dog-handlers to call off all the hounds except two of his. "I want you to see this," Gil yelled. "You never seen dogs kill a coon— not like Raw Meat and Sabre handle one."

The leashed dogs strained at their chains, slavering, baying. Gil ran to the bush with his dogs. They lunged upward at the coon. The harried little animal spat, wavering unsteadily on the high branches of the bush. The dogs leaped but could not quite get their teeth into the raccoon, though the animal did tremble and slap with his paws at them futilely.

Gil found a limb and knocked the raccoon out of the elder bush. It fell on top of his dogs, clawing and slashing. Gil tossed the limb aside, raging with laughter and never taking his gaze off the infuriated animals. The raccoon, squealing, almost broke free, but as it turned, one of Gil's hounds snagged it in the throat, closing its teeth.

The raccoon's scream was like the cry of terror of an agonized woman. The sound went through Hunt, numbing him, raising hackles at the nape of his neck. He stared at the others around the squealing animals. No one else seemed to have heard the terror and pain in the raccoon's scream. The little beast ripped itself free, bleeding, its paws clawing and scratching at the hounds. It ran a few steps, but it didn't have a chance because the other hound pounced upon it. As it whipped around, the first dog caught it again, ripping its throat open. The raccoon screamed, wailing. The louder the beast wailed, the wilder Gil laughed. He was jumping up and down in excitement. "Get him, Raw Meat! Kill him, Sabre! Get him, boy!"

Hunt retreated, backing away. He was almost to the fire where the slaves worked preparing supper before the racoon's wails died on a strangled sob and, with them, Gil's raging laughter.

The hunters settled down to drinking and eating then, lounging on blankets close enough to the fire so the light touched their faces, but far enough removed so they escaped its heat. They slapped mosquitos, drank whiskey, and devoured plates of potato salad, barbecued ham, sweet potatoes, and pickles.

Hunt could eat nothing. He filled his plate and stirred it around with his fingers, sitting removed from the fire and as far from Gil Talmadge as he could get. This meant he saw Ferrell-Junior only across the fire because Gil set his blanket beside Ferrell-Junior's.

Gil was talking, his voice growing louder as he consumed his third glass of whiskey and branch water. "I started them Saturday cockfights in at Avery's Tavern.

Seen 'em when papa and I was in New Orleans. Figured we could have just as good."

Another youth said, "I seen something better than cockfights in New Orleans last spring. You ever seen them stag shows where a nigger wench takes all those different black studs—every position known to man. Boy, them shows put lead in your trigger. That's what we ought to have at Avery's."

"Hell, them blue-noses wouldn't let you run a thing like that. Cockfights and nigger bare-fisted caused enough trouble. Sermons at the Baptist church. The women's club calling on Avery right in his tavern. Editorial in the paper." The man laughed. "Can you believe what would happen if somebody put on one of them fuck shows."

"Maybe we could put it on—just once," Gil suggested.

Somebody laughed at him. "How you going to run the show—by hand? You need bucks and you need wenches for a show like that."

Gil stopped smiling. "I ran the cockfights," he said petulantly. "I can do what I set out to do."

"Don't dare him," somebody said. "Remember that yankee abolitionist? The fellow who bought a farm near Gil's place?"

Gil laughed. "I fixed that son of a bitch, didn't I? Got me some good ole boys together when that yankee had picked all his cotton, but before he sold it. Burned the son of a bitch's barn!" He slapped his leg, laughing. "Bastard. Coming around down here, stirring up trouble with the niggers. We showed that yankee what trouble really was."

"Gil's a caution," somebody said, belching. "He don't care much what he does."

"Not as long as I get me a laugh," Gil said. "Hell, what else is there? Remember the time they had that big political rally in Mt. Zion. People coming in here from the north. Jed-Tom and few other good ole boys we decided to steal their ice cream."

"We got away with it," Jed-Tom broke in. "With the ice cream. But just then a couple guys come out the back door of Avery's Tavern. They was wearing guns. Scared us silly. We ran but ole Gil had been trying to get close enough to snitch a baked ham and he had to fall down in the tall grass to hide."

Gil rolled on his blanket, laughing, pounding Ferrell-Junior's arm in his merriment. "Them bastards wasn't looking for us. They come out to piss. I had to lie there in that grass and they peed all over me. Then they turned around and went back inside. Hell, I don't care. Never laughed so much in my life."

When the laughter subsided, Gil sat up. "Another time I near busted my gut laughing was when we fixed old Harley Driscoll's wagon! You remember, Jed-Tom."

"I remember. Aye God, I thought I'd bust laughing."

"Old Harley thought he was the town Casanova," Gil said. "Sneaking around laying anybody's wife he could get his hands on. I remember he was sneaking in Blair Plummer's back door and bedding Blair's wife—"

"Gladys Plummer? Hell, I'd like some of that myself."

"We all would. But ole Harley was the tomcat that was gettin' it regular. He'd get off work down at the mill noon on Saturday. He'd go home, wash up and get pretty smelling, then walk about a mile around about to sneak in Gladys's back door. Well, a few of us that knowed what was going on, we was drinking over at Avery's Tavern—way we do Saturday afternoon. We got the idea of fixing ole Harley's clock."

"It was yore idea, Gil."

Gil bleated with laughter, nodding. "I got to admit it was one of the best ideas I ever had. Few of us went over to Harley's wife—Bessie. We told her that Harley had been taken real sick and sent us to fetch her running. So we took ole Bessie through the street, with everybody in town staring at us, and wondering what we was up to now. And we took her right to the house were ole Harley was hosing it into Gladys Plummer. That there was the best one we ever come up with because it was like a string of fire crackers. Once you got it started, you couldn't stop it."

Gil choked on his own laughter. He took a long drink

of whiskey and branch water. "Bessie had hysterics with half the town looking on. . . . She up and left ole Harley. Went back to her folks up in Tennessee, I think. And Blair Plummer, he put a real cap on it, he did. He didn't find out about the party at his place on Saturday— folks scared to tell him to his face, I reckon—and he found out about church time the next day when ole Gladys wouldn't go out and face their neighbors. When Blair found out what had happened, he got a gun and killed Gladys. . . . I tell you, you can say what you want to, we've had some high old times around here."

Hunt felt he'd seen enough evil to last forever, but it had only begun. Gil stood up, waving his arms. "You fellows ready?" he yelled. "Got something you ain't never seed. We found us a real grotesque." He looked around, snarling at his slaves. "Where's the Geechee nigger gal?"

From a wagon removed from the camp two black men brought a teenaged Negro girl in a square-cut cotton dress. She wore nothing else. Though she was barely in her teens, her breasts were overdeveloped, bulging against the faded fabric. Hunt shuddered when she entered the firelight. She was a grotesque, the ugliest creature he had ever encountered—like a nightmare in this hellish swamp. Her eyes were badly crossed, her nose flat and wide against her face, her lip contorted into a harelip. Her hair was pinned in tight corn rows. Her empty grinning exposed pointed, jagged, and sparsely yellow teeth.

The man beside Hunt whispered confidently. "Don't never let a Geechee nigger bite you. Bite's poisonous as a rattlesnake."

The slaves gave the girl a push and she walked crookedly close to where Gil stood. Her massive breasts quivered on her spindly, rickets-wasted body. She suffered advanced pellagra too.

Gil let them get a good look at his latest find. He said to her, "You want some candy, Gora?"

She slavered. "Yas, suh, masta. Yassuh."

"Want yo to do something for us first, Gora."

"Yassuh. I do what you tells me. You gimme candy?"

233

"Want you to take that ole dress off, Gora."

She stopped smiling, puzzled. "Fore all these white folks?"

"You do what I tell you, Gora, or you don't git no candy."

"Yassuh, masta. I do want that candy."

"Then git that ole dress over yore head."

The girl nodded. She hesitated, then pulled the much-washed frock over her head and tossed it behind her on the ground. She stood naked, her enormous breasts quavering. The men yelled and whistled at the size of her breasts. Gil told her sharply to stand up straight. She nodded, trembling, whether with fear or night swamp chill, one could not tell. The firelight softened the creamy chocolate of her skin. Everytime she moved, the melon-like breasts bounced. Most of the white men moved nearer, circling around her, hooting. They yelled with laughter and elbowed each other roughly.

"Where in hell did you find this, Gil?" somebody called.

"I got her," Gil said. "Jes' wait."

The girl said, "Does I git mah candy now, masta?"

Gil laughed. "You want one lil ole piece of candy for taking off yore dress so you could show these fine gentlemen yore tits? You like showin' them tits, don't you? How would you like a whole poke of candy of your own?"

Her jagged teeth glittered. Her eyes seemed to glitter. "A whole poke, masta? Nevah had a whole poke of candy."

"All right. These white gentlemen want to see you whip that nest between yore legs. But you got to whip it good and hard or it don't count."

"Ain't nice, masta. Gits whupped for beating my nest."

"It's nice to do it for us white folks. It's nice if'n you do it nice. You like to do it, don't you, Gora? Want to show these folks how you can whip that nest. And nobody fusses at you. Gives you a whole poke of candy too."

Her hand slipped over the slight rise of her belly and touched at the hairs of her mons veneris. Her fingers moved spasmodically. The men laughed, nudging each other.

Gil said, "You sprawl down on that blanket 'fore the fire, Gora. We gonna let you whip that nest all you want. Nobody gonna stop you. Lie down. That's right. Now spread wide. Wider, Gora. Spread them legs wider so everybody can see you whip that nest."

The girl lay down on the blanket with the fire lunging across her nude body and glittering weirdly in her deep, crossed black eyes. Her fingers moved tentatively on her clitoris.

"Do it, girl," Gil said. "Do it!"

The strange eyes stared, the girl's hand moved faster.

"Do it, Geechee! Le's see you whip it," called one of the good ole boys. They crowded closer, holding mason jars, bottles, and earthenware jugs of corn whiskey. Sweat on their faces reflected the fire. Plumes of the flames danced in their eyes almost as weirdly as in the black girl's.

Gil crouched a few feet in front of Gora, his voice pitched to a sing-song monotone. "What'd the ole man do to you, Gora? What'd the ole man do?"

Under the hypnotic influence of Gil's voice, the girl responded. With her left hand she pulled the mons labia apart. With the index and third finger of her right hand, she moved in wild circular motions, her arm flailing faster and faster. "What'd the ole man do, Gora?"

She began to wail, spittle foaming from her mouth. "Ole man count de hairs on mah nest—ole man count de hairs—ole man count de hairs."

She grew breathless, chewing at her thick underlip, gasping for breath. Her enormous breasts bounced wildly.

"Yee haw!" somebody yelled.

"Beat that black thing, nigger!"

"Beat it off, nigger girl."

The voices of the frantic white men incensed the girl. She wailed aloud, frothing at the mouth, whipping her body about on the ground. Suddenly she began screaming, choking, shaking helplessly. Somebody whispered in horror, "Epilepsy!"

Gil leaped up and down, sweating, yelling at her. The other men grew silent as she choked, almost swallowed her tongue and lay quivering on the ground. Hunt managed to make it across the lighted campsite to the darkness before he vomited.

Hunt was thankful he was concealed in the half-darkness across the fire. The girl was carried away, the stories went on for a while. Laughter rose and subsided, erupted again, and finally ended when two of the good ole boys got violently drunk and fought so furiously they fell into the fire and had to be dragged out and rolled in blankets. Gil couldn't help because he was laughing too hard. He could only roll on the ground, laughing. And across the fire, Hunt sat numbed with horror, feeling as if he had strayed into a random asylum for the criminally insane.

He stared across the lighted space at Gil Talmadge, trying to convince himself that Gil was possibly as obtuse as he appeared. The man was entirely amoral. He saw nothing wrong in anything he did. He felt no twinge of compassion for the epileptic black girl, any more than he had for the raccoon as it was brutally slain. He felt no regret for the horror he had set in motion that Saturday afternoon in Mt. Zion in the name of getting a laugh. Marriages destroyed. A young woman dead. A man's life ruined. Gil had not then or later suffered the least pang of conscience. As he had many times before, he now told the story as a knee-slapping anecdote. Destroying a marriage, causing a murder, creating a scandal. It had merely put excitement in a dull Saturday afternoon. As far as Gil was concerned, people who couldn't protect themselves just naturally got hurt.

Hunt wrapped himself in his blanket and was unable to sleep. He thought about the sane, dull world of Melrose, Massachusetts, of Addie's cool arms. He tried not to think about Kathy. He tried to rid his mind of Gil Talmadge and the agonized screams of the raccoon. He could not sleep. He got up and poured himself a glass of straight whiskey. He found another young man drinking. They sat drinking silently until they passed out.

When Hunt awoke the sun was high through the swamp cypress and the bay trees. The slaves had cleared up the camp. They brought him coffee and then they started home. The rough ride almost killed Hunt. Every time his bottom struck his saddle, he was sure the top of his head was coming off. He was thankful when they left the caravan at a fork in the trail and he rode alone with Ferrell-Junior toward Blackoaks.

"It wasn't the biggest event in your life, was it?" Ferrell-Junior said, grinning.

"Did you like it?"

"I never have liked coon hunts. I don't care for Gil's stories, and I can't even drink like you can."

Now Hunt laughed. "Neither can I."

"Yeah. But you haven't got sense enough to realize it."

Hunt exhaled heavily. "Something I'd like to know, Ferrell. You don't like Gil."

"He's all right."

"Sure. One of the good ole boys."

"That's right."

"And so you suppress every honest instinct you have against the mindless cruelty, every feeling of outrage, every true emotion, just to be accepted as a good ole boy by your peers, don't you?"

Ferrell-Junior rode for a moment in silence. "If you mean do I try to get along with the men I have to live among, yes, I do."

"Why? For God's sake."

Ferrell-Junior gazed at him coldly. "Because if they ever decide you're different than they are, you're lost. They cut you out. You don't belong anymore. You might as well be dead."

CHAPTER 22

FOR REASONS that no one could explain satisfactorily, Hunt and Morgan lost or misplaced so many books and other educational materials, including stylus, slate, and quills, Baynard was obliged to order new supplies all the way from Atlanta. When word arrived that the crate of educational stocks had arrived at the depot in Mt. Zion, Baynard gave it some consideration and finally decided that Soapy and Morgan could take a buggy and make the trip to town to pick up the freight.

Morgan danced awkwardly with excitement. A trip to town meant a day away from his lessons. The idea of his and Soapy's taking a buggy and a fancy-stepping carriage horse alone in to Mt. Zion promised a rare adventure. He was ready to go before he finished breakfast, scarcely able to sit still in his chair. He kept calling in to Soapy at the kitchen table to hurry and stop loitering around; there was a big day ahead. Baynard tried several times to quiet Morgan and make him finish his ham, eggs, and grits. Finally, he capitulated. He said, "Well, soon as they bring up the buggy, you and Soapy can take off. I'll have to give you a couple of golden eagles to pay the freight charges."

"That sure is right costive, papa," Morgan said, shaking his head.

"It's not too much to pay for your education, son," Baynard said, rumpling Morgan's tousled hair.

"Are you sure, papa? For me, it seems a lot, little I'm learning."

"Don't you worry about that, Morgan. How much you can learn, that's Mr. Campbell's worry, eh, Hunt? You just study—and try to keep Mr. Campbell from losing so much material. . . . I'd hate to think where some of that lost stuff might turn up."

"We'll be careful, papa," Morgan said. "Won't we, Mr. Campbell?"

"I'm going into town with the boys," Hunt said abruptly.

Except for the sharp clatter of sterling silver against china plates, the room was unusually silent. Not even Morgan was prepared for this announcement. The Baynards peered at Hunter to be certain they had heard correctly, or that he was feeling well.

"Why would you want to do that, Hunter?" Baynard inquired.

"It's a nice ride. I'd like to go along with the boys— if they don't mind."

"Sure," Morgan said, lunging upward and knocking over his chair. A servant stepped forward and set it upright. "We'd like to have you along—but what about— them fellows—you know. Them fellows we met that day at the depot."

"They've got to get used to me sometime," Hunt said.

"Are you sure this is wise?" Baynard persisted. "You don't have to do something—that may be ill considered— in order to prove something to us, or anyone else, that doesn't have to be proved."

"That's true, Hunter," Kathy said.

He gave her a faint smile. "Sooner or later, there'll come a day for one reason or another that I'll have to go into Mt. Zion. Alone—without a bodyguard. It may as well start today. They have to get used to seeing me, strange as I am, sometime."

"They don't *have* to do anything—not those fellows," Ferrell-Junior said. "You thought Gil and his friends were pretty rugged? They're the upper classes, the educated sons of rich men."

"I could send Laus along," Baynard said thoughtfully.

"No. I don't want you to do that. We're making a big

issue out of this—an expensive trip into town. I don't want that. I figure if I go on in there with the boys, go about my business, they'll finally grow accustomed to my oddness, that I'll overcome their xenophobia—"

"I don't want to catch that," Morgan said.

"Don't worry," Styles told him with a crooked smile. "You've already got it."

"They are working today," Kathy said. "Most of them. They won't be drinking so early in the morning. They won't be part of a mob. There won't be a covey of girls around giggling to egg them on."

"That's my reasoning," Hunt said. "If they get used to seeing me, they'll accept me. I can't be all that strange and unknown to them."

Kathy's laugh was chilled. "Your swallowtail coats will always be—unless they see you at a funeral. And your top hat invites bricks or stones."

Baynard smiled and nodded. "Attire correct for Boston Commons can be outlandish in a small, backwater town, Hunt."

"They might pass you without even recognizing you," Kathy said, "if you wore one of Styles' old jackets, and left off that—ascot. Leave your collar open. It won't kill you."

"Maybe not," Hunt said, trying to joke. "But my mother will turn over in her grave."

"I'm going with them," Kathy announced. She was watching Styles. Hunt saw this, because involuntarily, he was watching Kathy. Hunt understood at once that Kathy didn't want to go; she was merely trying to get Styles to forbid her going. It was like a cry for attention, and it brought a lump to his throat.

Styles glanced up disinterestedly. "Why do you want to ride in to Mt. Zion? You hate it."

"It's not Atlanta," Kathy agreed. "But I could pick up some cloth—I want a new dress for our party."

"What party?" Miz Claire inquired, looking up, smiling.

"The party you're giving for Garrett Blanford Ware and Mrs. Ware, mother," Kathy said.

"Oh, yes, darling. That's a good idea. I'll have to start

thinking about what I'll wear," Miz Claire said, smiling.

"Why don't you take a stroll through a couple of your walk-in closets, Miz Claire?" Baynard suggested. "You might come across lovely dresses you've never seen before."

Miz Claire looked stricken. "I couldn't possible wear something *old,*" Miz Claire protested. "Why, what would people say? What would they think?" And then, her mouth tightening so prune-lines appeared about her lips, she asked in a chilled tone, "Are you begrudging me new dresses, Mr. Baynard?"

He laughed and waved his arm. "Of course not, my love. Buy a dozen new dresses. Another new dress is just what you need. Wear a fresh dress for each dance at your party. I think that would be lovely."

"And I think you're being sarcastic," Miz Claire told him.

"In no way," he told her grandly. "I love for you to look beautiful. It makes me proud of you. It makes other men envy me. It makes other women think I'm not only gallant and handsome, but generous to a fault. No one wants you looking lovelier than I."

"Thank you, Mr. Baynard," Miz Claire said, blushing faintly, pleased.

"Well," Kathy said, still watching Styles. "If we are going we had better get started. . . . You don't mind if I go along, do you, Styles?"

His head came up and he stared at her across the table. He shrugged. "Why would I mind? I think the outing would be fine for you." He got up and excused himself in Miz Claire's direction, and left the table.

Hunt felt his heart sag and knew that Kathy was ill. She had trapped herself into making a trip she didn't want to make. She had proved to herself the last thing she had wanted to know definitely—Styles didn't give a damn what she did. The bastard! The insolent bastard. His dismissal of the "outing" was as insulting to Hunt as it was to Kathy. It made one almost mad enough to fight. Almost.

Hunt exhaled heavily. No, he could never fight Styles

—not even Styles who had the hauteur in his face one loved to smash. But he could hate him. He could loathe him with the irrational passions more usually ascribed to people born and reared in this overheated climate.

Kathy brought one of her father's wide-brimmed, planter's panama hats to replace the stovelid top hat Hunt usually wore when he went outside the house. Hunt couldn't wear it; his head was several sizes too large. "Then go bareheaded," she said, "the sun won't hurt you."

He agreed because she asked it, not because he thought it a reasonable suggestion. He loosed his ascot and opened his collar. "Why, you look almost human," she told him. She gave him one of Styles' casual-wear jackets, a plaid that was tight in the shoulders. Hunt felt an elation because of this simple fact— Styles' jacket was tight about his shoulders. "Now," Kathy said. "You look almost like anybody else. They won't even notice you."

"He still looks like a yankee," Morgan protested seriously.

Hunt laughed. "Well, there are some miracles, Morgan, that not even the witchery of your sister can bring to bear."

"What the fuck does that mean?" Morgan said. But Hunt had to ignore him or reprimand his use of that old unacceptable word in the presence of his sister. Kathy seemed unaware of what Morgan had said. Thyestes announced that the carriage was at the front steps and they moved out through the front door. Kathy took a quick, last forlorn look for Styles. He was in the library reading and did not come out to wave good-bye.

The rest of the family was grouped on the wide steps in the morning sun. The buggy had been replaced with an open, two seater carriage with a fringed top. Soapy leaped up into the driver's seat and took up the reins, swollen with pride and excitement. Morgan clambered up beside him. Thyestes helped Kathy up into the rear seat, and then supported Hunt's arm as he stepped in beside her. "You're sure you can handle the horses, Soapy?" Baynard said. "Maybe I'd better send Laus along."

"Soapy can handle the horses, father," Kathy said. "And if you sent Laus along, it wouldn't help. If there were trouble—and Laus tried to help—he'd only be killed or jailed. Anyway, there's not going to be any trouble. Hunter looks almost human—and nobody's going to notice him."

"Thank you—I think," Hunt said.

"Well—we ready?" Soapy called. He raised the buggy whip high and gathered the lines between his fingers as he'd seen Laus do.

"Just a minute," Miz Claire said. She sent Thyestes limping hurriedly to bring Shiva. "Shiva will have to go with you," she said. Thyestes helped the girl into the rear of the carriage. "You sit between them," Miz Claire said. "Last thing we want in this world is people talking about us. . . . I hope you understand, Mr. Campbell?"

"Oh, I do," he said. "And I'm deeply flattered."

"We don't want people to suspect things that we know aren't true," she said. "The way to avoid suspicion is to be above suspicion. Don't you believe that, Mr. Campbell?"

The carriage horses trotted, their tails like plumes. They moved at their own pace without Laus's strong hands on the lines. The carriage rattled along the narrow trail at a fast clip, but it was not uncomfortable on the thickly padded leather seats. The two boys up front laughed and chatted, with Soapy biting his lips and straining with the effort required to control the spirited animals that were pleased to be out of their stalls. He'd always envied Laus, figuring the big man to have absolutely the best job on the plantation. He'd had no inkling of how hard the driver labored just keeping these beasts under control. They had their own ideas and a man had to let them know quickly who was boss, or they took over. Soapy's shoulders and upper arms ached before they'd gone five miles. His wrists burned, painfully brittle, as if sudden movement would break them off at his numbed fists. But he kept a grin pasted on his face. The last thing he wanted in this world at the moment was to relinquish the reins. And anyhow, to whom would he surrender them? He knew Morgan could never hold the horses under leash, and he was certain the tutor would be unfit by any training to handle this pair even as well as he did. It gave Soapy a sense of pride to realize he was the man in this group, as far as the team and the carriage was concerned. Their safety and their well-being were in his hands. It was a sobering thought, but an exalting one too.

There was no really sparkling conversation emanating from the rear seat of the carriage. Once Hunt observed that it was a lovely day and nobody could dispute this, or add anything to it. Miss Kathy appeared lost deep inside herself and remembered to smile and reply, only when spoken to, and with some effort.

The breeze felt cool and sweet on their faces. The rain that had come up and abated during the night had cooled the hammocks and the sand hills. Puddles, like muddy mirrors in the trail, caught the sun and reflected it in bright yellow lances. Sunlight splattered brokenly through the pines, sweet bay, and wild plum trees. They crossed an arm of the swamp on a narrow shoulder built up of fieldstone, logs, and clay through the black bog. In crooked unmoving creeks winding between thick elders and willows, water hyacinths bloomed lavender against the darkly polished green of their pods. Heron and spindly-legged storks glanced up from stagnant pools— as the carriage rolled past. Squirrel twisted their heads, darting around boles of huge old oaks to get a better look at them. A small deer paused in the trail, head tilted, peering at the horses, and then leaped into the thickets, lost. Above them the sky was a cleanly washed blue, carpeted with clouds fringed with faded gray underbellies. They came all the way into Mt. Zion without passing another wagon or traveler on the trail.

Soapy, with strength he hadn't suspected he possessed, slowed the horses on the potholed town streets. The village dozed somnolently in mid-morning. Old men sat talking desultorily on benches under the elms and oaks shading the courthouse lawn. Cats dozed before closed doors. A few horses batted with their tails at flies at the tie posts along Birmingham Street. The town appeared moribund to Hunt; there was almost no commerce; one might even wonder how the natives made a living at all. The owner of the general store sat, derby hat tilted over his face, slouched on a bag of beans at the stoop. He nodded politely, stifling a yawn.

Soapy pulled the carriage into the space outside the freight loading dock at the depot. A baggage handler came out with a crate of books. Morgan gave the man a golden eagle and painstakingly signed the manifest. It took some moments for him to complete his name. The baggage handler was patient, staring at his nails. Hunt winked at Kathy, smiling in pride at what he had taught Morgan. The man returned the change from the gold coin which was worth about twenty dollars Soapy scowled, reading the manifest, and checking the money in Morgan's palm. "I don' think you gave us the right change, mister," Soapy said.

The baggage handler bristled. He glanced first at Hunt and Kathy who remained unmoving, then he stared coldly at the Negro. "What you say, nigger boy?"

"You ain't give us the right change, masta." Soapy's voice quavered.

"It's all right, Soapy," Kathy said. She sat forward on the seat, took the change from Morgan, and the manifest from the baggage handler. She checked them both and then handed the baggage man two coins. "You were right, Soapy," she said.

"See, I tole you," Soapy said. "It wasn't right."

The baggage man looked contrite. "I'm sorry, boy," he said to Soapy.

Soapy didn't look at him. He loosed his death grip on the reins and the horses pulled away from the depot, turning around in the middle of the street. "That was very nice of you, Soapy," Kathy said. "Even if I was afraid at first we were in for another riot." She patted his shoulder. "That was a very honest thing to do."

Hunt laughed. "Now, Soapy, do you believe that President George Washington once admitted to chopping down a cherry tree—because it was the honest thing to do, even when he knew it would make things tough for himself?"

"I still don' hold with askin' for trouble, Masta Hunter," Soapy said.

Kathy sighed. "Still, that may be what you have done, Soapy. Once that baggage man gets to wondering where you learned to figure change—and better than he could. He'll forget he profited by it. All he'll remember—and tell around town is about the Blackoaks *nigger* that knows arithmetic."

A young girl walking on the narrow planking of the sidewalk called out, "Hello there, Kathy."

Kathy glanced around, and then her face froze as if she did not recognize the girl in the pastel frock and picture hat. Hunt whistled; the girl was freshly beautiful, as softly lovely as anyone he had ever seen. But Kathy did not return the greeting.

"You're a snob," Hunter told her.

She laughed. "So are you."

"But I was taught to be a snob. A Harvard snob. Where did you learn?"

"I don't like her."

"But you do know her?"

She shrugged. "Very casually. Miss Lorna June Garrity. I can tell you this. She can't be seventeen—if that. And she's already got herself a reputation. Not a very *nice* girl."

"She looks nice," he teased.

"Most men think that," she said. Her smile was icy.

"You make her sound interesting."

"Perhaps. If you're looking for the town tramp."

"That beautiful, gentle-looking girl?"

Kathy peered at him across the silent Shiva placed like a bundling board between them—the Alabama version of an old New England custom. Her face was chilled. At first she appeared to be ending the conversation by saying nothing more on the subject. She tilted her golden head. The sun struck her fragile profile, rimlighted her pale hair, bounced on the gentle peach-bloom swell of her breasts at the low-cut bodice of her dress. Hunt shivered, feeling that wave of nausea caused by an overpowering desire to suckle those tits, to fondle that body, to lie close against her. He'd never encountered anyone so lovely as Kathy—

and probably never would again. He had never seen anyone so totally denied to him either. Instead of being a slender little black girl with a bandana about her head, Shiva seemed suddenly to Hunt an insurmountable wall.

Kathy sighed. "I've heard that Lorna June sneaks around with any of the rich young plantation men—the ones you met on the raccoon hunt the other night. She's a social climber. Her whole family is. They're always putting on such airs—and Mr. Garrity is a part-time bookkeeper, wherever he can get a job around Mt. Zion. The way they act you'd think they were the *crème de la crème* of society. You should hear them. Pretending to believe they are just about to inherit some huge plantation somewhere—they even say they once lived on it!" She laughed. "It would be a farce, if it weren't so sickening. Why, they sound like some melodrama they might have seen in one of the tent shows—all about a stolen inheritance."

"Are you sure you don't dislike her because she's the only girl I ever saw who might be thought prettier than you—in her cheap way, of course."

"I didn't notice."

"Maybe you should. This is such a small community—less than a thousand people—this town, the farms and plantations around here. Such a pretty girl. Looks like it would be pleasanter to try to understand—"

"This kind of sermon is certainly out of character for you. Maybe I should not have insisted you come out in the sun, Mr. Campbell, without your hat."

"I was looking at the whole thing from your angle, Kathy," Hunt said.

"My angle? What in this sweet world does a—a girl like Lorna June Garrity have to do with me?"

"That's it. Nothing. She isn't important. But you are. Many things are happening to make you unhappy—even bitter. This seems like a little thing. But you're so lovely, Kathy, that you should grab every chance to smile and be happy."

Her eyes glittered with ill-controlled rage. "Spare me.

Please. Next you'll be lecturing *me* on the evils of slavery—"

"Yeah, Masta Hunter." Soapy called over his shoulder. "Tells us some more 'bout that great 'bolition that's a-coming."

"You just hush, Sophocles," Kathy said. "Haven't you caused enough trouble showing that stupid baggage man that you can count better than he can? What do you need to do in one day to stir up trouble?"

"Don't mean to stir up no trouble, Miz Kathy. No ma'am." Soapy looked miserable.

Kathy jerked her head around and confronted Hunt. "And you're not doing Sophocles any favor either, Mr. Campbell, putting ideas in *his* head. My father is the dearest man in the world—but he's not that tolerant."

Hunt sighed. Kathy was tautly drawn. She was ready to lash out at him and reveal to him—if he didn't already know—his place in the rigid caste system of this social order. He didn't want that to happen. Her friendship was something not casually dispensed, but recalled, it could be forever forfeited. He wanted a great deal more than friendship, but for a man in his position, friendship was something—a base to build on, hopefully. Most of all, he didn't want to hurt her, to add to her hurt. He spoke self-deprecatingly. "You'll forgive me, please, Kathy. I've been called a Harvard illiterate—by a cousin of mine in fact. He suggested there are many of us turned out. The further away I get from Harvard the more I see justification in his—"

"Don't talk like that! You've a beautiful, sharp mind, and you know it."

"Why thank you." His heart lurched at this crumb. "I had no idea you'd noticed."

"I see much more than you think I see. Pull in there, Soapy, before Miss Carter's Notions and Fabrics."

Hunt leaned forward, gazing at her across Shiva. "Well, don't see too much in me, I beg you humbly. I had six years at Harvard, it's true. And now, what do I know? I know for example that Claude Joseph Rouget de Lisle composed *La Marseillaise*. Did you know that?"

Her beautiful smile lit the carriage. "No."

"Well, there you are. I know many such fascinating facts. But how often does this come up in ordinary conversation?"

She laughed. "Well, I'm glad you're here anyway."

"Are you, Kathy?"

"Yes. Styles is much happier since you are here. Someone he can exchange ideas with—someone .educated enough to understand him. Someone to speak with him in French."

Hunt laughed. "Yes. Our French is marvelous to behold. My Harvard idiomatic French. And Styles? His sounds— as Soapy might say—like French that's been dragged through a sack of grits."

Soapy roared with laughter at this. He leaped down from the carriage, hobbled the horses, and ran around to hold out his hand to assist Miss Kathy to the boardwalk outside the unpainted building that housed Miss Carter—Notions and Fabrics. Sewing. Fancy Stitching. Ladies' Remedies.

"Why, Sophocles," Kathy said when he had handed her to the walk. "I'll have to tell father what a great carriage handler you are. Are you trying for Laus's job?"

"Gotta do sump'in, Miss Kathy. Cain't always be Masta Morgan's body slave."

"Why not?" Morgan cried petulantly. "Not never goin' be nobody else's slave but mine!"

"We won't worry about that now, Morgan." Kathy crossed the walk and entered Miss Carter's notions store. Hunt sagged in the seat and gazed without much interest at the sleepy town. Shiva sat primly, her hands folded in her lap. Hunt tried to engage her in conversation, but she was afraid to talk to him. He was an abolitionist and she had heard in Jeanne d'Arc's kitchen that black girls could get in trouble listening to abolitionist talk.

He didn't know how long they had been seated there when he glimpsed Miss Lorna June Garrity. She moved slowly along the walk on their side of the street. Her bright little parasol twirled idly. Her pastel frock was cotton voile, its open weave carefully stitched and sewn to display her charms at their most intriguing. Her dress was just inches shorter that most local girls wore them, Hunt saw, in the style he recognized as chic in New York. Her high-buttoned shoes were visible and she moved along apparently as un-self-conscious as a butterfly. But Hunt knew better. He knew enough about women—thanks to dear Addie—and he'd heard just that soupçon about Lorna June to convince him he was right: Lorna June Garrity was aware that all eyes of the town were upon her, especially those unseen ones behind the pinked curtains along the streets where she promenaded in solitary loveliness.

And she was lovely! She found something of surpassing interest in the cluttered window of the general store, two doors away from where they sat in the Baynard carriage. And Hunt, watching her through the hooded eyes of a cobra, found her a deliciously appetizing little morsel. It was as hard to believe Kathy's sharp estimation of Lorna June as the town tramp, as it was to believe, gazing at her full-blown tits, that she was seventeen, or less. Seventeen going on thirty-six maybe.

She teetered on her heel, gazing into that window as if entranced. Her slender, lovingly structured young body swayed in rhythm to some inner beat heard only by herself. Her hair was brown, with highlights of copper in it when the sun kissed at it. She wore it brushed back under her picture hat. Her clear, unblemished forehead, a perfect, straight nose, uptilted lips faintly touched with color, and a chin with just the suggestion of squareness made her a picture of loveliness. Her eyebrows were carefully formed lines above the clearest, most uncluttered and open brown eyes Hunt had ever encountered. She was not a dissembler, deceptive, a cheat, or coquette—whatever the word for a bad girl was. Her fresh complexion brought to mind dewy flowers in earliest morning before the first sunrays touched at them. He could believe that all the young bucks in the county were after Lorna June Garrity—but that she deserved to be called trash, even by Kathy Baynard, this didn't add up—not even by Soapy's infallible math.

Two things happened simultaneously and, Hunt realized, according to Lorna June's program for the morning. Kathy stepped out of Miss Carter's specialty shop at the precise instant Lorna June lost interest in the general store display and resumed her diurnal promenade. The two loveliest girls in the western hemisphere almost collided in the center of the narrow plank walkway.

"Why, Kathy Baynard. It's just so good to see you," Lorna June said. Listening, Hunt was pleasantly impressed with her voice. Warm, interested, and not at all pulled through sorghum and honey.

"Hello, Lorna." Kathy stared straight into the lovely face without the trace of a smile.

"I've just been dying to tell you, Kathy, how I admired your brother—that day at the depot. He was so brave! Watching him, I just got gooseflesh."

"I'll tell him. I know how interested he'll be."

Lorna June laughed. "Don't you dare tell him. You think I want your brother to think I'm forward?"

"Yes," Kathy said.

The faintest shadow of pain flickered swiftly across Lorna's eyes, darting and instantly gone like a swallow in the dusk. She laughed lightly and Hunt felt a surge of pity for the town girl. He clearly understood the purgatory in which nice people existed when they belonged in neither the rich world, nor the lower depths of the South. Here was a truly beautiful girl caught between those two worlds—one which didn't want her, and one in which she would be lost and miserable. This obviously was not the first time Lorna had been rebuffed by those girls who considered her a social inferior. But there was that suggestion of squared chin. This girl knew what she wanted. She recognized the price tag attached. She was willing to meet the cost, as far as she could. "I've always admired your sense of humor, Kathy," Lorna said. "Even though I wasn't always crazy about your tact."

Kathy gave the girl a chilled smile, stepped directly in front of her, and lifted her gloved hand for Soapy to help her into the rear of the carriage. Hunt sat silently, watching her. Lorna June remained, for one insant like a waif strayed into a hurting situation. Her clear eyes struck against Hunt's, and he bowed, deeper than he had to, with an even exaggerated politeness. He wanted Kathy to see it. And she did.

"You're angry at me, aren't you?" she said. "You disapprove?"

"I'll never disapprove of you, Kathy. Maybe I thought you were a little crueler than you have to be."

"When things climb up at you, you slap at them," she said, her head tilted.

"Yes. Don't you?" He laughed.

"You think maybe she didn't want me to run home and tell Ferrell-Junior how simply divine she thought he was—so brave she got gooseflesh? Why didn't she just tell me to let him know she wanted to go to bed with him?"

"Maybe she did. Maybe not. There is something that is a powerful aphrodisiac about victory in physical combat. The caveman used to come home after slaying a bear—and all the women in the cave wanted to share his rug. Blood-letting in ancient Roman gladiatorial contests got men, women, and children in frenzied oestrus—and lions devouring Christians—that drove them right out of their skulls."

"What the fuck does that mean?" Morgan demanded from the front seat.

Kathy caught her breath. "It means, Morgan Baynard, if you don't quit using that nasty word in front of respectable people all the time, I'm going to break your nose."

"Ferrell-Junior used that word," Morgan said in his own defense.

"Maybe Ferrell-Junior knows when to use it. Maybe he even knows what it means—"

"I know what it means," Morgan began.

"Well, I don't care!" Kathy cried, as if the morning were tumbling in around her gold-blond head. "Get these horses started, Soapy. I'm more than ready to go home."

Soapy's head swiveled on his shoulders. His eyes were bleak, filled with tears.

"Now what's the matter?" Kathy said.

"I—cain't, Miz Kathy."

"You can't what?" she cried.

"No matter how I pulls on them lines, Miz Kathy. Them horses don't gee and they don't ho. They just stands there."

Kathy glared around the sunstruck street helplessly. She caught a glimpse of Lorna June Garrity's standing at the window of Miss Carter's Notions watching around her parasol their reflected woes. This was enough to make Kathy mistress of the situation. She said with chill, "Well, you just get down from there and you lead these horses to the smitty down the street. They'll be able to fix it, whatever it is."

"I'm sorry I don't know anything about it," Hunt said.

She gave him a withering glance. "Oh, what difference does it make?" she said impatiently. "I didn't expect you to know anything about it."

Hunt shrugged Styles' jacket up on his shoulders. As far as Kathy Kenric was concerned, he could well return to Boston on the next train. Not even the fact that Styles' jacket was tight across his shoulders gave him any real elation now. He wondered, in the depression into which her chilled gaze sank him, how any woman could ever find him interesting? What had been wrong with Addie that she had found him delightful? Was it perhaps nymphomania with Addie and no credit to his manliness that she couldn't wait to get in bed with him? He sat silently all the way to the blacksmith shop.

In the shade of the tree outside the smitty, Soapy helped Miss Kathy alight from the carriage. She explained as well as she could to the huge young man who appeared from within the shed, wearing a leather apron and muscles that Hunt told himself were obscene. Hunt felt the blood rushing to his head. This was one of the men who had tried to rip off his clothes the day he arrived in town —the biggest of his attackers, the loudest. Hunt tried to slide down in the seat, to disappear into it. He gazed at the thick-chested man from around Shiva's dark face. But this was no sanctuary. Shiva cried loudly because the

253

carriage was broken and she was afraid she would never get back to Blackoaks alive. "Shut up," Hunt whispered to her. "*You've* got nothing to worry about."

"I want to go home," she wailed.

"So do we all," he told her devoutly.

The young smitty barely glanced toward Hunt. Hunt didn't blame him; the smitty could stand and gaze down at Miss Kathy. And this was what the hulking brute did. He lowered his eyes and kept stealing bashful glances at her, entranced. He was tongue-tied, painfully shy and almost physically helpless. He was sober today and struck dumb in the presence of Kathy Baynard Kenric. So this is what a fragment of an incensed mob is when you get it isolated, Hunt thought wryly—a dullard, blushing and stammering in the presence of a lovely girl.

The blacksmith walked around to the front of the carriage. He caught one of the lines between his fingers and followed it to the checkpiece. He worked deftly and quickly, considering that Kathy stood at his elbow watching with interest. Once the work was completed, the big man was loath to let his audience escape. He followed Kathy to the rear of the carriage, took her delicate elbow in his huge battered paw, and almost hefted her up into it. He still hadn't bothered to give Hunt more than a glance. Kathy settled in the seat across Shiva from Hunt. The slave girl stopped sniffling and whispered, "We gwine home now?"

Kathy ignored her. She offered payment, but the huge young smitty blushed and shook his head. "Shucks, Miss Kathy, warn't nary nothing wrong that a war wouldn't fix."

"A war?" Hunt scowled. "Is it that serious?"

"Wire, Hunter," Kathy said in sharp precise tones. She smiled at the smitty and Hunt saw she was biting back her laughter.

"Oh," Hunter said, nodding vehemently. "A war? Of course."

"Yes, suh, a war," the young smitty said. He stared straight through Hunt, enraged because he felt Hunter was laughing at him in front of the lady. He said coldly, "You sure hell talk funny, yankee."

"I sure hell do," Hunt agreed.

Soapy slapped the reins and the horses pulled away from the shaded area outside the blacksmith shop. Glancing over his shoulder, Hunt found the young brute standing unmoving, gazing after Kathy. Hunt said, "I have the certain feeling that this time I should have fought him."

"Why?" Kathy put her head back laughing. "He would have killed you just as dead this time."

He nodded. The difference was clear to him, if not to her. This time he would have known what he was dying for. He shivered in the bright sun of high noon, finding even that brilliant ball dimmed by Kathy's soft and gentle radiance. How beautiful you are, he thought in a permeating melancholy. You're beautiful inside and out. Maybe this whole damned ugly world is worth it if it nurtures you.

CHAPTER 23

A PEBBLE DROPPED in a pond creates ripples that ride outward and expand forever, says one theory. Nothing spreads faster than contagion, except rumor, says another. Soapy's chance adventure with the baggage master at Mt. Zion depot seemed graphically to illustrate the basic and interlocking truth of both of these maxims. The baggage master was a rotund, balding man of middle age named Turney Hacker, neither a loquacious, nor a taciturn man, and certainly never known as a vicious or vindictive individual; a man who did his work and went about quietly. However, the more Turney thought about a *nigger's* having shown him up before quality white folks, the more it rankled and festered inside him. He soon conveniently forgot that the episode redounded to his own profit, or at least prevented a fiscal loss that certainly would have surfaced when the railroad system's local, part-time bookkeeper, Major Hugh Garrity, went over the bills of lading.

Turney recounted to his wife, Thelma, the incident concerning the "Blackoaks nigger kid" that could work arithmetic in his burr head "without even countin' on his fingers, the way even most educated white folks do . . . probably the black ape can read and write too." Thelma Hacker engaged in no conversations with neighboring women, fellow church members, trades people, or casual acquaintances in the following week that did not include detailed references to the "Blackoaks nigger" who could read the Bible, begats and everything, better than the Baptist minister himself—and not only this—but could multiply three-digit numbers "right in his skull, and lightning fast." Thus do ripples widen, contagions multiply, and rumors burgeon in flight.

Saturday afternoon, over a few beers, Turney Hacker retold his story about the "Blackoaks nigger" exactly as it had happened to him—without the profit or loss figure —to the county men assembled in Avery's Tavern. By the time the story reached the enlarged ears of old Fletcher Talmadge at Felicity Manor, it was a violent tale of secret cells of niggers being secretly taught to read abolitionist pamphlets before voodoo fires after midnight in the Blackoaks slave quarters. At 1:00 P.M. Monday, a delegation of influential and responsible men—plantation owners all, like Fletcher Talmadge who led the group—arrived to wait on Ferrell Baynard, Sr.

Baynard read the fury in Fletcher Talmadge's flushed jowls, bristling mustache, and cracking knuckles. In order not to burden his family with this evidently unpleasant matter, he invited the men—close friends all—into his study where he poured generously from his private stock.

"Won't profit you none to get us all drunk and jolly, and try to joke us out of this thing," Fletcher Talmadge told him.

"I've found that we project to others, motives we ourselves might harbor," Bayard said mildly.

"What the fuck does that mean?" Talmadge demanded.

Lucas Winterkorn, of Mira Vista, laughed. "Ferrell's just saying that because you might use the tactic of getting everybody drunk to reason with them, don't accuse him of the same tactics just because he kindly offers you a glass of the best whiskey in the state of Alabama."

"No laughing matter," Fletcher Talmadge declared stiffly when the others joined Lucas Winterkorn in laughter. They quieted down under the baleful eye of the master of Felicity Manor. Talmadge said, "I tried in a friendly way to warn you, Baynard, about the propaganda and the anarchy being allowed to flourish right under your nose here at Blackoaks—"

"A Negro boy was taught to read by Morgan's tutor— who was ignorant of the law," Baynard protested.

"Nor cared a fuck for the law—our law," Talmadge said.

"The error was remedied, the mistake was not repeated," Baynard said patiently. "What more do you ask?"

"We're through *asking*," Talmadge announced. "We're telling you, Baynard. Git rid of that yankee abolitionist and git rid of that trouble-makin nigger—or we'll take matters in our own hands."

Baynard stood up abruptly, his chair squealing. His face paled and that tell-tale vein ridging his temple pulsed blue, engorged with blood. His voice was level, but deadly. "Just a minute, Talmadge. If this kind of irresponsible, hothead talk came from your son Gil, I'd overlook it because he's young. There's no like mitigating justification for your behavior. We've been dear friends and neighbors for more than thirty years, Fletcher, but when you talk to me about what you—and anyone else—are going to do within the bounds of Blackoaks Plantation, you've already gone too far. Don't ever *tell* me anything you're going to do to *me*—or to my people—for the simple reason I won't tolerate it—from you or anyone else."

"I agree, you've gone too far, Fletcher," said Lambert Tetherow of Pinewood Forest, over near Commerce.

"Just a minute, Ferrell," Lucas Winterkorn said. "And you, Fletcher, subside. Sit down. Have a drink. Cool off. The problem is, Ferrell, that we have it on best authority—"

"White witnesses that was there and seen it," Talmadge's voice rasped.

"—that one of your niggers—Soapy, I think the name was—was down near the Mt. Zion depot reading anarchist propaganda to a group of black slaves—and talking to them about teaching them all to read and take over the farms—"

Baynard burst out laughing. Fletcher Talmadge raged. "Goddamn it, it ain't no laughing matter."

"Sit down, Fletcher," Lambert Tetherow said.

"Soapy is a fifteen-year-old black boy," Baynard said in exasperation. "He has learned to read—barely—one of

Parson Weems's primers. Come on, gentlemen, how serious can this be?"

"This serious," Fletcher said, voice quavering with illy suppressed rage. "We got no place in this country for niggers that read—Parson Weems or whatever—and stir up trouble amongst blacks. And we got no place for yankee abolitionists that shoot liniment up black asses and then stand back like Satan, a-grinnin' and a-watchin' the devilment, the looting and the raping of white women."

Long-term friendships jeopardized. Neighbor fulminating against neighbor. Rumors of black uprisings. Reprisals mounted against a suspect white abolitionist. And so the ripples widened.

"I'll do this much for you, Fletcher, in the name of our long acquaintance and shared interests," Baynard offered. "I'll call in Soapy. Let you see this orating, propaganda-spouting oracle. We'll let him tell you what really happened in Mt. Zion."

"I want no black nigger smartin' off to my face," Fletcher said. "I won't tolerate no nigger denyin' what white witnesses have attested to—and that's all he'd do, deny it."

"In other words," Baynard said, "you want everything but the truth. You don't want facts exploding the lies you've chosen to believe."

"I don't appreciate that kind of talk—even from you, Baynard," Talmadge said.

Baynard exhaled heavily and shrugged. He crossed the study and tugged at a cord on the wall. After a moment, Thyestes limped in reluctantly. The aging butler had heard the voices of white plantation owners raging in Master Baynard's study. These men, Thyestes knew, held power of life or death over black men such as he, and often they had been known to exercise that fearful authority in casual indifference. He entered the study with the same lack of eagerness displayed by early Christians remanded to the lions' pits of ancient arenas. Baynard sympathetically recognized Thyestes' ill-concealed terror and hastily dispatched him to fetch Soapy.

Thyestes returned only minutes later, almost totally unmanned, his bulbous lips quivering, his eyes touched with the moisture of incipient tears. Soapy could not be located. He had disappeared. No one in the house had seen him for the past hour.

And another hour later, the ripples widened—Morgan awoke from his afternoon nap, and when he heard that Soapy had disappeared without leaving word, he dissolved into hysteria, which unnerved the household, broke up the conference in Baynard's study, and sent the plantation owners home to await further developments.

Ferrell-Junior alone was able to quiet Morgan's body-wracking sobs. He promised to find Soapy. Baynard dispatched a house boy to have Ferrell-Junior's horse saddled and brought immediately to the house. In the meantime, the family gathered in the parlor to commiserate with Morgan and attempt to solve the riddle of Soapy's disappearance.

"I think—like Thyestes—he heard the shouting going on in the study and decided to hide until they were gone," Baynard said.

"But Jeanne d'Arc said he left the kitchen very abruptly —and that was before Mr. Talmadge and the others even got here," Kathy said.

"Maybe their visit was a diversionary tactic," Styles suggested.

"What the—what does that mean?" Morgan said.

"I don't believe those gentlemen would engage me in conversation while another group somehow spirited Soapy away," Baynard said. "These men are troubled, and they are actually enraged. But I don't believe they would be parties to such a low scheme. They are honorable men."

"That's how Caesar died," Styles reminded him. "At the hands of honorable men."

Morgan wailed again. "Soapy's dead! They've killed Soapy."

"Soapy's not dead," Kathy said. "Ferrell-Junior will find him for you."

"I'm sure that's true," Hunt said. "Civilized men wouldn't. . . ." His voice trailed off as he realized that *these* civilized men were capable of just such acts against those that threatened their way of life; and any means justified their ends. And more than that, except for the grace of God, it might have been he who was suddenly missing and in the grip of totally implacable men. He said nothing more but laid his hand lightly on Morgan's quivering shoulder.

CHAPTER 24

FERRELL-JUNIOR HEADED downslope from the mansion toward the slave quarters. He let his horse plod at its own gait under him, feeling the slanted rays of the afternoon sun across his shoulders. A dark, fish-tail cloud slid westward hiding the sun briefly and promising afternoon rain. Ferrell-Junior felt a growing anxiety that had nothing to do with Soapy's disappearance. He did not yet believe it was anything more than an afternoon truancy that happened to coincide with the visit of the fanatical old Fletcher Talmadge and friends. No. He'd find Soapy, all right, he was certain. What troubled Ferrell-Junior deeply was the tension pervading the family and destroying the old pleasant existence he'd always known at Blackoaks.

It was almost superstitious, and ridiculous, but it seemed to Ferrell-Junior he could date the start of the uneasiness at Blackoaks to the uninvited visit of that slave breeder, Baxter Simon. His father suddenly sold off slaves as if he were going full-time into this ugly business. Why wouldn't his father even discuss the matter quietly? He talked glowingly of finding a Fulani woman to mate with Blade—to produce superior offspring and improve the bloodlines. But instead of buying, wasn't he selling slaves like a man desperate for quick cash?

Ferrell-Junior was not privy to the financial condition of the estate, but it seemed incredible to him that a self-sustaining farm such as Blackoaks had always been was not even paying its own way. Still, his father lived in a state of tension lately, quick tempered, easily exasperated, refusing even to discuss matters he'd once discoursed on for hours. And God knew what the trouble was between Kathy and Styles, but trouble there was. Kathy—the gentle tomboy, always able to find laughter in everything —suddenly laughed only infrequently and acted as if she were walking a tightrope, and barely hanging on. His father appreciated the progress Hunter Campbell was making in teaching Morgan. But here again, Hunter was treading along the rim of a precipice. The elder Baynard resented the trouble that had come out of Campbell's teaching Soapy to read, and he hadn't forgiven the tutor. His father was polite enough, but one misstep and Hunter was going to be asked to leave. And adding to the tension was the fact that Campbell knew this as well as anyone, but like every zealot felt that *he* was being wronged.

Ferrell-Junior shrugged his shirt up on his shoulders. He found himself looking back in longing for the good old days of last year, of the year before last, to all those easy-going times that seemed forever gone. Once, the whole family had accepted the annual visits of the banker Garrett Blanford Ware as a time of entertaining, of formal parties and long bull-sessions between his father and old man Ware in the study or on the terrace. Mrs. Ware always brought the latest news of fashions in Atlanta or Montgomery or New Orleans, and Kathy awaited her arrival avidly. Now, Miz Claire alone found any pleasure in the prospective invasion of the Blanford Wares. As the day drew nearer, his father's tensions increased, as if the banker's arrival were, in some unexplained way, related to the darkest fears haunting him. Maybe this was overstatement, but it summed up the whole situation at Blackoaks these days—Soapy was lost for an hour and the family reacted in panic, now not drawn closer together, but divided, each with his own thoughts, his own villains, his own suspicions.

He reined in before the plantation commissary and braced his arms on his saddle horn. He called, "Blade? You here?"

The young Fulani bounded from within the shadowed structure as if on springs. He grinned, seeing Ferrell-Junior, and the white youth thought, he is a handsome specimen. That crisp dark hair, the classic lines of his profile, the thick dark lashes some girl would trade her eyes for, and the slender muscular body. Ferrell-Junior smiled inwardly. He wouldn't go as far as Styles and get a hard-on just touching Blade, but the fellow was handsome. Must have all the wenches on the place after him. "I'm looking for Soapy, Blade."

"Ain't seed him today, Masta Ferrell-Junior. No, suh."

"Thought maybe he might be with Moab. He and Moab and Narcissus used to pal around before papa sold Narc."

"Yes, suh. They did. Him and Moab still pretty strong friends."

"Suppose Moab has seen him? Could they be up at your cabin?"

"I don't hardly think so, Masta Ferrell-Junior. Moab, he don't stay up there no more. He lives up at the overseer's cottage now. For some time."

Ferrell-Junior laughed. "Sure! That's where they are! That's why none of the slaves have seen him. They don't hang around up there at Pilzer's place."

"No, suh. Nobody goes up there much, and that's a fact."

Ferrell-Junior smiled and nodded. He urged the horse forward through the path that divided the whitewashed slave shacks. Small dogs ran out yapping. He spoke over his shoulder. "If you see Soapy, you tell him to get his fat ass up to the house, or I'm going to take a whip to him."

Blade grinned. "I'll sure tell him, Masta Ferrell-Junior. When you gits upset enough to say threats like that, hits high time for folks like Soapy to listen sharp."

Ferrell-Junior grinned, thinking about Blade. He returned the greetings of the people he passed without really seeing them. He was aware children and grownups stood squinting after him in the sun. He'd never been close friends with Blade as they grew up, though they were of the same age. In his preteens and younger teens, Ferrell-Junior had spent more time with the young black boys on the place than he had with his own family. Maybe that was why he was so upset when Narc was suddenly sold to a flea-bitten coffle of doomed blacks.

Together with the young blacks of Blackoaks, the whites and blacks of neighboring family estates, he had explored every mile of the surrounding sand hills and swamps. They swam, barbecued stolen chickens in the hammocks, built and drove goat carts, hunted quail, raccoon, possum, and deer, and pestered every unattached female, black and white, they found running free or unprotected. He recalled now that as a gang they had done a hell of a lot of things he disapproved, disliked, and even feared. But he had learned early that to be one of them, he had to go along with the herd. Anything else was unmanly. He had grown up with that conflict, and he hadn't escaped it yet. He wanted to be accepted and approved by his peers, but he also wanted to follow the dictates of his own conscience—which was invariably at odds with the gang mentality. He remembered vaguely the way Jeanne d'Arc would yell at him, "Doan you fool round with them field niggers, Ferrell-Junior. They ain't no good for you." And he realized now that as often as not, there hadn't been fieldhands with him at the time—but sons of rich plantation owners—often Gil Talmadge. He had never listened to Jeanne d'Arc, and neither did the other boys, black or white. But the difference had always been, he had felt he *should* have listened.

He thought about Narcissus being sold to Eakins Shivers' coffle and suddenly remembered how many of those young close friends of his he had lost along the way. For the first time, he realized that often in the early summer one of the boys who had been close to him, a black boy from the quarters, would be gone. He never questioned it after the first day. But the sudden disappearances had troubled him. Narcissus' sale simply brought it all out in the open. His father had been selling off Negro slaves for as long as he could remember—longer, probably. One or two at a time.

He regretted the loss of those friendships. One day they were closest of friends, he and some black boy from the quarters, fighting each other, fighting together against outsiders, giving no quarter, asking none and finding no qualitative differences between sun-baked white skin and burnished copper. He had held his own in fights against any of the black boys, except those few times his uncontrollable Baynard temper overruled his Seaton-Henry common sense, and he let stubborn and unbending pride push him into overextending himself. At those times he lost, and lost badly. It had never occurred to him to complain about these beatings he had absorbed, any more than it occurred to him to demand to know what happened to one of his best friends who was suddenly no longer on the estate. It was a way of life, and he was sensitive enough, he supposed, but not really deeply inquisitive. He accepted things he was told were part of his existence. Loss of those friends was part of it.

His heart beating faster, Ferrell-Junior looked back and saw how many childhood friends he had lost to field gangs, to slave buyers, to sudden, unexplained epidemic. Sickness in the quarters could wipe out whole families, whole blocks of black people. Each time of new loss, he would feel the sharp painful lance of damage that somehow was overlaid by a few words from his father and forgotten, accepted as a way of life. Anyhow, somewhere in his later teens, he lost the last of his black friends from the quarters. He didn't change but they did. They were changed by the way of their lives. He went away to military school for two years, and when he returned, they shuffled their bare feet in the dirt and touched their shapeless caps and refused to meet his gaze. "Welcome home, Mas' Ferrell, suh."

And so that whole, happy and easy time of his life ended. After the brief chill of final loss that could still be summoned—as it passed in a wave of cold through him now—or which came upon him sometimes uninvited, he accepted it, and forgot them and all they had meant to each other in those long hot afternoons of their childhood.

He smiled, remembering Tharus—the only black friend he had with whom he never fought. They would get so raging mad with each other that they'd be trembling and taut lipped. He might say something like, "I can beat the shit out of you, nigger." And Tharus would come back with, "You *say* you can beat the shit out of Tharus—that's what you can really do."

Tharus had that wonderful, comical, common-sense way of looking at everything that Ferrell-Junior always had to laugh no matter how full of rage he was. When he laughed, Tharus laughed with him. Laughing, they found anger impossible to contain. He shivered. Where was Tharus now? What in God's world had happened to that wonderful, funny boy with the common-sense way of looking at everything? What kind of *nigger* had good, wonderful Tharus become? Or was he dead somewhere, lost in some ugly coffle, or sold to die in the Louisiana cane fields? He didn't know. He was gut scared to know. But one thing Tharus had done for him. Blacks would never be animals to him, beasts to be treated callously. This was why every sale of a Narc—or even Obadiah—stretched the tension between him and his father. Every sale of every black was Tharus, sent to die in some godforsaken cane fields where nobody cared about his laughter.

He had never been closer to anyone than to Tharus. When they were very young—before something happened to Tharus—he used to sneak Tharus up the pecan tree and across the courtesy roof and into his window to sleep with him. The first night Tharus visited they had giggled so loudly that it was still a mystery why his father had not come in and thrown Tharus out.

Tharus had stared around the candle-lit bedroom, eyes exaggeratedly wide, as if this was all incredible and new to him though they often played up here on rainy days. "Lordy," he said in exaggerated black accents, "we doan have nuthin' like this at our place." Both saw in their minds the scrubbed barely furnished cabin where Tharus lived, and they giggled. Then Tharus would shake his head and add, "Good thing, too, that we'uns doan't have nuthin' like this. Why we'd need *niggers* to help us keep it shining clean." And in their minds they'd see the crews of cleaners this house did demand—all black —and they giggled. Started, Tharus had to top himself. "Hell, you don't even have a tree to pee against." More giggling. Then, "Hell, my paw says you don't pee against a tree, you don't feel like a man."

They went to bed laughing. Sometimes Miz Claire— she was well and happy and singing all the time then— found them sleeping, kinky black-capped head and brown-haired white head sharing the same pillow. On those mornings she'd slip away in order to help them preserve their desperate secret. She was wise in those years about growing up and growing away from childhood and all its simple wonders and she found no profit in hurrying it.

Jesus, where were those simple and good lost years?

Ferrell-Junior prodded the horse across the front lawn of the overseer's fieldstone cottage and drew rein at the front steps. It seemed to him the place looked neater, better kept than he had ever seen it before. He called, "Miz Pilzer?"

Florine came out on the front porch, letting the door slam behind her. She wore a freshly ironed but aged frock that somehow accented a figure he hadn't realized she possessed. He'd always considered her a slattern, young but slovenly. Her hair was carefully brushed, and she looked as neat and clean as her home. Some unexplained change had come over the place.

"I'm looking for Moab, Miz Pilzer."

He saw her flinch. "Is something wrong?" she said. "Are you taking him back to the fields?"

He smiled, shaking his head. "No. Moab won't ever work in the fields again, Miz Pilzer. It was a mistake he was put in the field gang in the first place. That whip-cut scared us."

"That's just it. We've worked hard—Pilzer and me— on that nigger's back to be sure there ain't no scar. Put him back at hard labor—and—"

"Well, we're not going to, Miz Pilzer. And we really appreciate all you and Bos have done to help Moab. All I want to do is to ask him a few questions."

"He ain't here," she said. She had to hold herself in tight leash. Here it was almost four in the afternoon; Bos would be coming in from the fields and she had been waiting, sick with desire and fear, since noon and Moab had not shown up.

"You got any idea where he might be, Miz Pilzer?"

"I don't." Despite the rage inside her because Moab had kept her waiting all afternoon—very likely had thrown the whole afternoon away because Bos might be coming in—Florine found herself thinking about getting Ferrell-Junior in her bed. No matter what they said about a woman never even enjoying sex, she looked at a man and she found herself wondering—would he be like Bos? Like Moab? Better than Moab?

She felt that young Baynard would be better. He was the handsomest boy in the county—she'd heard that consensus when she'd gone in town to the Mt. Zion Baptist church. He carried his male beauty easily, as if he seldom thought about his looks at all—unless he caught a glimpse of himself in a creek, a mirror, a shop-window, or some passing female's admiring eyes. She had no way of knowing that Baynard was so easy-going because his father had instilled in him early his coming responsibilities and obligations and the humbling fact that if they were ever bigger than he was, he was less than the least field-hand. Ferrell-Junior had the easy self-assurance of who he was, but it was Tharus who had taught him long ago the most humbling lesson of all—never take yourself too seriously. Tharus had left behind the greatest gift of all—laughter.

"It's intolerable hot, Mr. Baynard," Florine said. "Wouldn't you care to come in—and wait till that nigger straggles home? You know how niggers are—unreliable, shiftless."

He smiled. "I've sure heard that, all right."

She smiled with him, empty bellied with a sudden sense of longing. She felt herself growing fevered, hotly liquid down there. "Well, where there's smoke there's fire," she said. "I'm sure—if you'd care to come in . . . I'd try to be entertainin'—much as I can. . . . So lonely up here—seldom have company . . . be most pleased."

"Thank you," he said, responding to something he didn't even understand, a sudden crackling static between them. He was sure that if he stepped off his horse and inside that door, he could be fucking this woman within ten minutes. He felt himself growing hard. "I sure would

269

like to," he said. "It must be lonely for you up here."

"Yes." She stared at him through a haze. "Very lonely." She was thinking she wanted to go on her knees to Ferrell, the way she had to Moab that morning when she was afraid he wasn't coming. Spreading her legs wide no longer seemed the ultimate in submitting to a man—going down on her knees to him, taking it in her mouth, sucking it, this was complete submissiveness. She had never done this to Bos. The first time she'd ever done it was with Moab. The first time she felt a blood-quickening urge to do it was this moment—with this man. "Please—won't you come in?"

Ferrell-Junior hesitated, his belly oddly empty. Then he remembered Morgan's agony and he shook his head. "I'd like to," he said. "I'd really like to. A shame you living right here—and us hardly knowing each other—"

"Yes. That's a shame." I'll suck you, she was screaming deep inside her mind, please, I'll suck you. . . .

"Some other afternoon," he said. "I'll come up and visit you—if I may."

She shrugged. It was this moment—this agonizingly sweet instant that concerned her. If he didn't come in now, he would never come back—or if he did, it would never be the same. God, if he'd only step inside that door with her now, this second, she would show him—he would never get Florine Pilzer out of his mind. The madness she'd learned with Moab would be only the starting place. . . .

"I do have to find Moab and Soapy," he said. "I recall a place on the creek where a boy named Tharus and I used to fish. . . . I'll try that."

She shrugged; she had lost interest. She sagged against the porch wall as he rode away in the brilliant afternoon sunlight.

"Oh, sweet Jesus," Soapy said. "Somebody comin', Moab. I hear a horse in them underbrush."

Moab looked up from the primer reading book. He had been so fascinated, so entranced, and concentrating so hard upon the words Soapy was teaching him, he had been oblivious to the world outside this nook beside the creek.

"Quick," Soapy said in panic. "Gimme dem books. I hides 'em. They catches us with them, they flog us both."

"They don't flog me," Moab said. "They done tole me. Nobody ever lays a whip on my back again—I too pretty, they said."

"Well, I ain't. They'll flog nigger shit out'n me. They'll flog me 'nough for both of us. I hidin' them fucking books."

Soapy grabbed the primers that Hunt had "lost" and that he had "found" over the past weeks. He scrambled to the edge of the chokecherry thicket and began to scrape leaves and debris over the books. "What you scared of?" Moab demanded.

"If you wasn't just a dumb field nigger, you'd have sense enough to know what I scairt of it," Soapy rasped across his shoulder. "They's a law against teaching us niggers to read—and that means one nigger teachin' another nigger as much as a white man teachin' a nigger. It plumb a killin' offense."

Ferrell-Junior rode his horse in through the underbrush into the small clearing on the knoll where he and Tharus had played pirate, fished, fought battles, and camped out. He arrived in time to see Soapy frantically scraping dead leaves over the books. He decided to ignore this. He said, lowering his voice to an authoritative pitch, "What you two niggers doing, laying around out here? Miz Pilzer's looking for you, Moab. And she's plain upset that you've been gone all afternoon and not taken care of your chores."

"Yas, suh." Moab blanched, realizing for the first time how many hours had passed unnoticed while Soapy taught him painfully to read and write. He had believed he would never want anything more than be permitted to crawl in that woman's bed whenever he got a hard-on, and sometimes when he was so tired, it barely stood up. But the fascination of understanding what rows of black letters on a page really meant! My God! She was going to kill him.

He leaped to his feet. "I reckon I best git on home,

Soapy," he said. He raced across the rocky creek, barely touching the water, lost in the hammock.

Ferrell-Junior gestured toward Soapy. "And you. Get up behind me. Morgan's crying, sick at his stomach, afraid something has happened to you."

Soapy climbed up behind Ferrell-Junior, locking his arms about his belt to hang on "Naw, suh, nuthin's happened to me."

Ferrell-Junior kept his voice hard and cutting. "Well, something is going to—if you're not a hell of a lot more careful than you are now."

Moab came across the kitchen garden, sweated and empty bellied. He tried to dart into the tack room in the barn, but Florine Pilzer's voice snagged him like a lash about his throat. "Hey, nigger. Come here."

He saw her shadow in the kitchen door. She was as naked as the day she was born. His cock lunged upward, hurtingly rigid in his onasburg britches. He walked across the yard toward her "Yes'm."

She was crying. "Damn you. Where have you been, Moab? I've been waiting for you."

"I was busy," he said. He stepped inside the door. He reached for her breasts with both hands, but she retreated.

"Busy? Doing what, you bastard?"

"Soapy and me We was down by the creek."

"You and Soapy What you want with that fat nigger? What can he do to keep you all afternoon."

"I tole you. I'm sorry. I here now." He reached for her again, cupping his fingers to fondle her vulva. She retreated again, taut with rage.

"You're here now. Now? You black bastard. I've been waiting for you for three goddamn hours."

His rage flared, matching hers. "You've always got your fingers," he told her.

Her hand lashed out and she struck him with all her strength across his face. The livid hand-mark stood on his cheek and up his forehead. He did not move. Her eyes filled with tears. For a long time they stood unmoving, staring savagely at each other in the hot silence. Flies battered at the screen door, buzzing. She surrendered first, sagging forward against him, clutching him to her. He thrust her down to her knees roughly. Oh, my God, she wailed in a swift half-thought, he owns me—body, soul, mind. . . . He dropped his pants, stepped out of them. He caught her hair in his left hand, holding her fiercely. She stared up at him as he pressed the glans of his rigid mast against her lips, between her teeth, and deep into her throat.

CHAPTER 25

A LIGHT RAIN fell all the next morning. Nonetheless, before ten o'clock, Gil Talmadge galloped his Tennessee carriage horses up the lane under the dripping pecan trees. "Came by on my way to town to inquire about Morgan," Gil told the family assembled on the verandah to meet him.

"Morgan's quite all right today," Baynard said. "Tell your father we do appreciate your courtesy in coming out of your way to inquire."

Gil laughed. "Papa hoped Morgan felt better. Coming by was my idea. Papa was most mightily concerned whether you'd caught that black runaway Soapy."

"Soapy ain't no fuckin' runaway," Morgan said. Kathy slapped him hard across the neck, and Miz Claire looked as if she'd faint at that unaccustomed violence.

"We found Soapy," Baynard said with a slight chill replacing his smile. "He'd wandered off with another darky boy fishing in the creek—just as you and Ferrell-Junior used to do."

Gil laughed and shrugged. His father's concerns were not yet priorities in Gil's mind. He swung suddenly and whacked Ferrell-Junior across the shoulder with his fist. "Hey, Ferrell-Junior, it's Satiday. You know what Satiday means, don't you?"

"No. What does it mean?"

Gil laughed. He looked around. "Maybe not much out here where things are quiet. But us good ole boys got some purentee gut-busting fun planned in at Avery's

Tavern this afternoon. I'm on my way there now. You want to come along?"

"I'm not sure I'm coming into town this week," Ferrell-Junior said.

"Look, now! You come on in! Lord knows, you don't want to miss this. Come on over to Avery's Tavern. Anytime after lunch. You'll be plumb glad you did."

Gil would add no more details, certain he had whetted Ferrell-Junior's appetites and roused his curiosity. Anyone who knew good old Gil Talmadge also was aware that Gil never made an idle promise. He had indeed introduced the Saturday afternoon bare-fisted nigger fights at Avery's Tavern; he'd been the moving force behind the Saturday afternoon cockfights there. He'd tried to import a nude-girl show from New Orleans. This had failed because of logistics and not because he gave it less than total enthusiastic support. But Gil was known always to be stirring things up, one way or another, and when Gil Talmadge promised excitement that was unusual in nature, you could bank on it.

When Gil was gone, racing the thoroughbreds down through the crocheted shadows decorating the lane, Miz Claire said, "I'm glad you're not wild like that Talmadge boy, Ferrell-Junior. Chasing around like a chicken with its head off, drinking, running after women, swearing, chewing tobacco, and making poor roosters fight to their deaths."

Ferrell-Junior kissed his mother's ceramic-glaze cheek lightly. "You're right, mom," he teased. "And you've got the cardinal sins lined up in the exactly correct order —women right in there between drinking and swearing."

Ferrell-Junior spent the morning debating inside his own mind whether to go into Mt. Zion and spend an afternoon and evening drinking with Gil. He recognized in advance that he'd probably have a few laughs. He also realized any of Gil's schemes could lead to explosive trouble, sometimes easier to get into than out of. If he got drunk enough, only the horse would be able to find the way home, and it always took him two days to recover from the monumental drunks he carved out in Gil's company. Before noon, he sent word by a houseboy to hitch one of the fast horses to the lightest buggy on the place. He was going into Avery's Tavern; he'd known this from the first, counting on his own weakness of character. If he hadn't been certain he was going, he'd never have wasted time fretting over it; he'd simply have dismissed it from his mind.

About one o'clock, Ferrell-Junior headed west toward Mt. Zion. The infrequently traveled trace was dimly outlined with wagon tracks but passable, eroded by rocky gullies in places and sometimes almost overgrown by patches of wire grass and fennel. The high-stepping horse followed the wagon ruts as if by instinct. Ferrell-Junior's mind was free to argue inside itself whether any entertainment Gil Talmadge's brain could devise was worth the gargantuan headache that would surely result. Then he thought about Lorna June Garrity and felt a heated, empty sense of anxiety in his loins.

There wasn't much material to build on as far as she was concerned—for one brief instant a raw, naked look in her eyes that morning months ago when the family had met Hunt at the Mt. Zion station. Maybe this had meant nothing except what he read into it. God knew, this could happen. More promising was Kathy's scathing report of her meeting Miss Lorna June Garrity in the street outside Miss Carter's Notions. "You were all she could talk about," Kathy had told him. "How handsome! How wonderful you were—"

"That's interesting," he teased. "But what did she tell you that's new—that we didn't all already know?"

"—fighting all the town toughs like some dog in a street fight."

"Did she say that—dog in a street fight?"

"Oh, no. To her it was *all jus' too—too excitin'*." Kathy exaggerated a honey and corn-pone accent. "You just gave her *gooseflesh* to watch you fightin' and bleedin'. Common amusements for the common mind."

"Did she say that?"

"I said that. I just said it."

"Did she say the good part—about the gooseflesh?"

Kathy's lovely mouth pulled down. She shrugged, but

Morgan said, "She said that part, all right. I heard her. She said that, all right. What the f—what'd she mean?"

"Maybe you're lucky, Morgan," Kathy said from across the table. "Maybe you'll never have to know."

More than a dozen horses, buggies, wagons and mules were hitched to the posts and rails in front of Avery's Tavern when Ferrell-Junior rode along Birmingham Street. This was a sizeable crowd for so early in the day, even on a Saturday. Word of Gil Talmadge's surprise had spread swiftly across the countryside. Negroes, body slaves, and drivers for some of the rich young men already laughing inside Avery's Tavern lounged in the shade. The Negroes slept or talked desultorily, sentenced to wait, three hours or ten without food or toilet. The weather had cleared; the sun was out and the day's excitement arranged by Gil promised a large, free-spending crowd in town today.

Ferrell-Junior pulled left on the lines to turn the horse and buggy into an open space near Avery's Tavern. He could hear the bursts of laughter, the sudden shouts from within the half-opened Dutch door. With a restless sense of indecision, he tugged right abruptly on the lines and the horse moved past the tavern. He didn't really want a drink this early. Sometimes they got to drinking in Avery's just past noon and there were serious brawls before dark. He hated getting caught up in these scrapes, but if your friends were involved, honor required that you wade in— even when it was over your head. He'd never really enjoyed the cockfights either, though he would no more have admitted this aloud than he'd have refused to go to the assistance of an embattled friend even when knives were in play.

Still, now that he was in town, there was little to do except join his friends over beer. The town afforded no other attractions. He pulled the carriage under a splotch of shade provided by an elm. He braced one boot on the splashboard and watched the young girls promenading along the tree-lined walks. Each was pretty in her own fresh, undistinguished way. Their dresses crackled with starch, their crinolines whispered as they walked, and bright little parasols twirled. They strolled, giggling, the teenage eligibles on display.

"Well, hello there, Ferrell Baynard."

He straightened and turned, pushing his planter's hat back from his forehead with the back of his hand. The girl's voice was warm and friendly and he wanted to match her friendliness with his own charming first impression. But shock stunned him into an awkward silence for the space of a couple of heartbeats.

Lorna June Garrity stood in the walk a few feet from him. Her parasol spun idly. Jesus! she was beautiful. Built like something special for Christmas. Right out of a wet dream, but so dewy fresh and gentle looking you didn't dare believe what you prayed might be true. "Well, my goodness," she said, chiding him. "Don't you know me? You make me feel so forward—and brazen. Speaking to a man who isn't even going to return my little old greeting." Her smile illumined the shaded place.

"Hello."

"Well! All that. Hello. Anyway, that's better. Not much, but a little. It'll keep folks from thinking I'm a perfectly brazen little hussy—accosting strangers on public streets. I declare—from the look on your face—I think you don't even remember me. I'm Lorna June Garrity."

"Yes. . . ."

"I'm sure you know my cousins, the Garritys of Autumn Glades."

"Yes. I know them well. Leander. Phyllis. Miss Mabel. . . . I hope they're well."

"I hope so too." She laughed. "We don't have too much commerce with the Garritys of Autumn Glades, I'm afraid. Even though they are my own dearest cousins. And Uncle Leander is my father's double-first cousin—but my father—Hugh—doesn't speak to them at all." She shrugged her incredibly milk-soft shoulders. "Why waste a precious minute talking about them when I do so want to tell you how wonderful you were—that other day— fighting those vulgar drunks who attacked your—servant? You were so—brave."

"Thank you."

"A girl would always feel safe—and protected when

278

she was with you." She shivered delightfully. "No matter the situation. Even a little ole town girl like me that you've met and forgotten—while I think about you—so often."

He grinned. "I'm sorry."

"Since you're so ungallant as to forget, I'll tell you—though I shouldn't—I helped your sister put on the Catholic church bazaar—last Christmas. She did introduce us, even if you are so ungallant enough to disremember."

Ferrell-Junior smiled, remembering. He recalled how reluctantly Kathy had introduced them. Kathy's booth sold chances on Christmas turkeys. Lorna's booth—one she shared with three girls who mostly stood and watched—sold kisses. It was the most crowded booth at the bazaar. Not even bingo drew such a mob. He hadn't gotten to her booth, simply because he refused to stand under a barrage of disapproving female stares in a line that stretched more than halfway around the hall.

"Would you care to take a ride in my buggy?"

"I'd love to," she said. "But you know I can't. You haven't even met my folks."

"I've met your father—Major Hugh," he said.

"It's not the same thing," she said with a faint smile, "drinking in the same saloon with my father, and meeting my mother."

He laughed and leaped down from the carriage. He caught the horse by the checkrein and led it along the street. They sauntered together in the sunlight, conscious of the eyes of the town upon them. Lorna's eyes danced and her parasol jiggled on her shoulder. He felt empty bellied to know that Lorna June Garrity was so lovely, so dainty and so full of laughter—and that she was a town girl that would never be accepted by his family. The Garritys of Autumn Glades were part of his world—and unfortunately Phyllis, who was about Lorna's age, was stomach-turning plain. He had heard his father, old man Talmadge, and even fair-minded Lambert Tetherow laughing and talking about the way the bookkeeper Hugh Garrity pretended to be the rightful owner of the big Garrity estate, Autumn Glades. Young county bucks got old

279

Hugh drunk just to hear his tirade against his cousin Leander.

He personally didn't buy this snobbish attitude. But on the other hand, the minute you weren't part of the herd—one of the boys—you asked for trouble, for yourself and anyone else involved. It was the kind of fight he didn't have the courage for. It was all right to walk along a sunstruck street and laugh with her, but you didn't get involved unless you were prepared to face whispers and derision, and ask worse for her.

Lorna paused before the picket-fence gate of a tall, narrow old house with bay windows, gables, and scrolls. It looked as if it had been built a long time ago by someone who had seen the pattern in New England and tried to keep it pictured in his mind on the long journey south, spilling essential details along the way. The old place was in good repair; it had simply never been a pretty house, too big for its lot and, like the Garritys, belonging neither to the world of the Southern well-to-do nor to the poor. It was a place whose very pretensions made it ugly and vulgar. There were rockers and a swing on the honey-suckled shaded front porch. One could see that Major Hugh liked to putter in the yard. He had a small garden, and the flowers banked against the house were rich and well tended. "Why are you stopping?" Ferrell said.

"Because I live here." She glanced up at him, and away as if afraid to let him look too long into her eyes. He waited. She sighed. "Well, this is where I live. Won't you come in for a moment? We could sit on the swing if you like. It's very cool."

He hesitated. He didn't want to leave her so soon; he didn't want to get involved either. He kept telling himself this was as much for her as for himself. He could tell her quite honestly, and with deep regret, that it would take a minor miracle to make Kathy like her, and another to make his mother accept her. Even his father would be disappointed to learn he was involved with the daughter of Hugh Garrity. His friends would smile behind his back—and the schism between him and the young men he had to live among would widen. As ridiculous as this all seemed to him, he recognized it all as painfully factual. If he smiled, lied, and said he would see her again sometime, what would he do? Spend the afternoon in the bar with Gil Talmadge, wishing to hell he were with Lorna on her cool front porch? And if he walked away now, it would be completely finished with Lorna, no matter that he might change his mind later. She must have been hurt like this before—she must have learned to deal snubs by tilting that beautiful little head and putting the pain behind her. Jesus! When he thought of the way Kathy and Phyllis Garrity and their friends laughed about Lorna and rebuffed her. "Sure," he said. "I'd like to."

He tossed the lines loosely over the hitch rail at the curb side of the narrow board walk. He held the gate wide, bowed, and Lorna laughed up at him as she sailed through grandly.

Lorna was pleased, excited and more than faintly astonished that Ferrell Baynard had agreed so warmly to sit on her porch, meet her mother. Not one other plantation-bred boy she'd known had been so openly friendly. They had been quite willing to sneak around after dark, meet her on corners, go for rides on lonely lanes, but none wanted word to get back to his family that he had been a guest at the town Garritys'.

Ferrell was so open, so warmly friendly and natural. She felt a rush of warmth, looking at him. He was so much handsomer than any of the other county boys. Maybe her mother was right. Maybe beauty did come from within. His innate goodness certainly set him apart. Lordy, how those silly girls must have swooned with envy to see him walking beside her, laughing at everything she said.

She cooled, walking up the steps, drawing taut inside, afraid something would happen to spoil it this time. After all, Ferrell was the sort of boy she should be dating. If her father hadn't been cheated out of his rightful inheritance by his conniving cousin Leander, she'd be living at Autumn Glades now instead of that witch Phyllis—and the boys from the neighboring estates would be flocking around her—openly.

She had been reared from infancy on the importance of

"Society"—and that meant the rich farm and plantation owners' families. Her mother had taught her—along with her potty training—that she belonged only among the "best people." She had been trained to reach out toward the rich, the blue-blooded, the social leaders. "They were always my own dear good friends," her mother said repeatedly. "Until that ugly trouble with Cousin Leander— and we were left with nothing—and your father not at all trained for commerce."

She preferred not even to think about the sacrifices necessary to pay for her tuition, social life, and clothing at the girl's finishing school where she spent three years alternately miserable and happy. She had been invited to the homes of some of the girls at Thanksgiving and Christmas—but somehow they always turned out to be girls like her, with miserable, driven mothers and pretensions to better circumstances. She had begged to be allowed to come home, but her mother insisted that she stay—and prepare herself for the wonderful life that would someday be hers, by right of birth and inheritance.

Her mother was not alone in insisting that Lorna prepare for the kind of life they envisioned for her. "Leander was a smart lawyer. And a lot older than I was," her father would say. "I know that my side of the family was entitled to Autumn Glades and the Garrity money. We were on the male Garrity side—and I was *told* repeatedly that I would inherit. There was the business of a new will, and suddenly Leander had everything—and we were left with a bed chamber and a few hundred dollars. Why, even if I had enraged the old man—he wouldn't have done that to me. That's where Leander made his mistake, and that's why we'll get him. Don't worry. It costs me a lot of money each year in attorney fees. More than we can afford. But I'm working on it, Lorna. I'll never stop working on it."

"It would be bad enough—but it would be bearable—if Leander and Mabel would treat us like family—and invite us to Autumn Glades," her mother said.

"I wouldn't go," Major Hugh said. "I'll never set foot in that place—as long as Leander Garrity is there."

"You'd go," his wife said. "For Lorna's sake, you'd go."

Her father kissed her cheek. "I'd do some hurtful things for my girl," he said. "But—to admit that Leander belongs in that house—"

"There's no sacrifice too terrible to make for Lorna," his wife said.

Many people longed to better their social status in life. But for Lorna June Garrity, ambition for a place among the first families was no longer a driving motivation—it was an obsession for her, and she was pushed ruthlessly by her mother. "You may have to take some rebuffs," her mother said. "But just always remember who you are— you are a Garrity of Autumn Glades. You are as good as the best of them—better. Remember that—and they can't really hurt you." Her eyes filled with tears. "As they have not been able really to hurt me."

Lucinda Garrity must have been watching from behind the front-room drapes. She came out through the screen door almost as Ferrell-Junior and Lorna came up on the porch. She was a slender woman, forty years old, harried and anxious looking. There was the tension about her peculiar to the restless, nervous people abstracted by their ambitions. Her hair was prematurely gray, but she wore it brushed and set with great care and attention. Her house dress was crisply fresh, and she kept darting her hands behind her as if to hide the tell-tale marks of house-work. "So you are Claire Baynard's oldest son? Claire and I were once close friends—when the major and I used to stay at Autumn Glades before Hugh's Uncle Runyon Garrity died. So long ago. I suppose she's forgotten me now." Lucinda's smile was aggressively sweet. "You and Lorna sit down—there in the swing, Mr. Baynard. I'll get some lemonade—I know that'll be welcome after this terrible heat."

"Yes. That would be very nice."

When Lucinda had gone into the house, Lorna said, "You'll have to forgive mother. Talking about the old days at Autumn Glades—as if that's all we have to think about. . . . But she was terribly hurt—by all that happened."

"Yes. I guess so."

"I know it's easy for you to think she may be—silly. But suppose some cousin—some distant cousin from some town—simply came into Blackoaks and told you that it belonged to him. And he had some kind of papers to prove it—the originals of which suddenly and conveniently disappeared soon after the will was probated."

She laughed. "You're so terribly nice and polite. You try to care, but you can't, really. Can you?"

"Not really. I keep looking at your eyes—and wondering what color they really are."

"What color would you like them to be?"

"Just when I think they're green, I see they're blue. And when I decide all right, they're blue, I see they're not really. They're more violet."

"Oh, tell me some more. You make me sound so exciting."

"You're exciting all right—" and then he stopped and stood up when Mrs. Garrity came out on the porch with a tray of lemonade in a pitcher and tall mint-topped glasses. He took the tray from Lucinda and set it on the table. She poured lemonade for them, smiling at him all the time she poured. "It's so good to meet Claire's oldest son after all these years," she said.

This reminded Lucinda that indeed the last time she'd seen Claire was at Autumn Glades when she was *enciente* —she couldn't bring herself to say pregnant—with Ferrell. "How long ago that's been," she said, sighing. "And yet those good times seem only so recent when I think back."

When there was a lull in the conversation, Lucinda would remember some other vivid recollection of Autumn Glades and recall it for Ferrell, who finally had to tell her that he visited the old estate infrequently and wasn't too familiar with it. "I imagine it's not as lovely as it was in the old days," Lucinda said. "Major Hugh could tell you if he were here—how lovely it all was in those years at Autumn Glades. . . . I'm sorry the major isn't here to meet you, Mr. Baynard. He'd be most happy, I'm sure. Press of business. Even on Saturday. He's an accountant you know, here in town. But sometimes he must work— even on Saturday."

Ferrell bit back a smile, hoping they wouldn't notice.

He knew where old Major Hugh spent his Saturday afternoons—getting a snootfull in Avery's Tavern. He supposed the old boy had to lie to the socially minded and probably ultrareligious Mrs. Garrity in order to get away. He was overcome with a terrible melancholy, feeling sorry for all of them.

He realized that Mrs. Garrity was talking to him and had been for some moments. He smiled and nodded. "—only temporary, of course, even though he is an excellent accountant. When the adjustment is made in the will and the entire estate of Autumn Glades is turned over to him, the major, of course, will have to spend his time directing the estate. As he was trained to do, of course."

"It's so stuffy here on this old hot front porch," Lorna said.

"Why, dear, I think there's a nice breeze," her mother said.

"Maybe if we went for a ride in your buggy, Ferrell," Lorna said. "Somewhere—anywhere it's cool would be nice. . . . It's just so hot here in this old town. Don't you think it's just oppressively hot, Ferrell?"

"Whatever you want to do," he said.

Lorna stood up, twirling her small parasol and stretching her arms. "I need a fast cool breeze in my face," she said. "I feel as if I'm just smothering. . . . It would be so nice to get out where it's quiet and cool—even for a little while."

Ferrell stood up. He said good-bye to Mrs. Garrity. She made him promise to remember her to dear, sweet Claire, and to come back to visit them soon. He nodded, and promised. Lucinda laughed up at him and stroked Lorna's arm gently. "You be nice to Mr. Baynard now, Lorna June. You want him to come back again, so you be nice to him."

CHAPTER 26

THEY WALKED down the steps, saying good-bye to Lucinda over their shoulders. She kept smiling relentlessly and telling them to have a good time and for Mr. Baynard to come back again soon. It was only a few steps along a plank walkway across the truncated front yard. They were almost to the gate when Lorna stopped so suddenly that Ferrell narrowly avoided colliding into her and impaling himself upon her parasol.

He heard her catch her breath sharply and her barely audibly whispered, "Damn!"

He stared over her picture hat at the young man about to enter the gate. Ferrell-Junior's first impression was of "ugly." The youth was anywhere between twenty and thirty—he had a pinched Irish face that was going to age slowly. He was no taller than Lorna June, but built broad, squat, and low to the ground, his short-legged body thick and muscular. His hair was a deep Irish-setter red, so bushy with ringlets he couldn't part it. The hairline across his short, straight forehead was a severe, unbroken line. His large ears stood out on both sides of his small head despite the way his thick, curly hair grew out as if trying to cover and conceal them. His suit was cheapest broadcloth, his boots aged and glistening with polish. He carried a bouquet of wild flowers. His reddish brows, red-brown eyes, coppery lashes, stunted pug nose, and wide-lipped mouth seemed ready to fragment. He looked about to cry.

The man's hand was extended toward the gate. He remained frozen, arm in mid-air, staring at Lorna June, stricken.

Lucinda recovered first. She called from the porch. "You and Mr. Baynard go right ahead, Lorna. Have a nice time. . . . Mr. Scroggings can come up on the porch and have a nice glass of lemonade with me."

The sound of Lucinda's voice restored mobility to both Lorna June and Mr. Scroggings. He dropped his hand and retreated a step on the board plankings of the walkway outside the picket fence.

Lucinda moved forward, coming down the steps. As if propelled by outside forces, Lorna walked forward too. Ferrell held the gate open for her. She went through it, barely glancing toward the red-haired boy who stood slumped-shouldered beside her fence. "Oh, Luke," she said. "Hello, Luke."

She walked to Ferrell's buggy. Ferrell followed and touched her elbow, assisting her upward. She pinked her skirts over her shoetops and stepped upon the iron step to sail lightly onto the narrow, leather-padded seat. She settled herself, shaking out the pleats and ruffles and folds of her dress, crinolines whispering. Ferrell walked around the rear of the carriage and swung up beside her. All this time, Luke Scroggings stood unmoving, face muscles rigid. The buggy pulled away from the curb and Luke remained immobile, staring after them, as if ill.

Ferrell-Junior glanced back. Lucinda had crossed the walk and stood at the gate talking gently but insistently to Luke Scroggings, from old habit picking up after Lorna June. Luke was watching the buggy going away from him.

Lorna kept her eyes straight ahead. Ferrell felt faintly troubled by the sad little episode. Clearly, Luke Scroggings believed he had a date with Lorna. Almost as clearly, this had happened to him before. Lorna said, "Poor Luke . . . he just won't let me alone. . . . He has a good job and all. Clerks in the bank. He started as the janitor. Can you believe that?"

"Yes."

"Mr. Leonard Forsythe says Luke is one of the smartest young men he's ever met in banking—and Luke's completely self-taught."

"But he just can't learn to stay away from Miss Lorna June Garrity," Ferrell-Junior teased.

She laughed, nodding to people who paused to gape at them along Birmingham Street. "He just hangs around. All the time . . . I try to tell him how hopeless—as nice as I can."

"And you just told him one more time."

"What?"

"You did just break another date with him."

"Not really. Not a real date . . . oh, I might have told poor Luke something. Anything to get him to stop pestering me, you know."

"Well," he said in some irony. "This ought to tell ole Luke what you think of him."

She shrugged. "It should. But it won't. I don't even know if I really told him to come over this afternoon. I know he has Saturday afternoons off—the bank closed and all. My goodness, even if I said it, I didn't mean it. . . . I was only trying to get rid of him—the pest. . . . Anyway, one thing I'm sure of, I told him I would see him—if I wasn't doing anything else. The same as I always tell him."

Thrilled by the reaction she was getting from the other townsgirls, youths, and the general public, she slithered her trim little bottom over nearer him on the buggy seat and took his arm possessively. Ferrell-Junior reminded himself that only part of this display of warmth was for his pleasure—she meant first to impress her friends, neighbors, and enemies. He said in mocking disapproval, "But poor ole Luke planned all week—and dreamed—and brought flowers."

She recognized his taunting tone and she shook her head, laughing. "Now surely, Mr. Baynard of Blackoaks, we've pleasanter subjects to discuss on a nice Saturday afternoon that Mr. Luke Scroggings, bank clerk."

Ferrell-Junior guided the high-stepping horse and bright-glossed buggy twice around the town square and once more the length of Birmingham Street because he knew intuitively this was what Lorna June Garrity wanted. They made a remarkably handsome couple in the little phaeton, and nobody was more aware of it, or excited by it, than Miss Lorna June Garrity.

"Hello, Lorna June."

"Hi, Lorna."

"Afternoon, Mista Baynard—Miss Garrity."

Mister Baynard—Miss Garrity. And so their names were linked by others in salutation. Lorna shivered in an ecstasy of delight. These obeisances of the crowd were like long-delayed, always deserved accolades—rose petals strewn in her path. For this moment at least she sat where she belonged. She enjoyed what should have been a natural part of her birthright as a Garrity. She, at least, had been born in the big old house at Autumn Glades. This was more than pimple-faced Phyllis, or even Phyllis's treacherous father who was after all, only a second cousin, could say. All the slings and arrows, the rebuffs, the cuts —none of it mattered in this delicious present. This was the moment to which she and her mother had pointed her all the days of her life—transient as it might be.

At last, Ferrell turned his horse out of town on a narrow lane through sand-hill pine hammocks. Lorna June sighed. She moved over on the seat again closer to him. Her trim little hip bumped his. She clung to his arm and the jostling of the buggy sank his bicep repeatedly into the fullness of her breast. It seemed all his sensory perceptions were concentrated in that right bicep. Almost all. She wriggled again and her hip snuggled harder against his. He felt a hot, flashing reaction in his gonads. They seemed to contract and his rod grew hard, standing rigid against the fabric of his trousers. The carriage wheels struck a pothole and jostled them roughly. Her free hand grasped his leg for support. Her hand accidentally closed in reaction on the inside of his leg and her fingers clutched frantically for the briefest instant upon his stiffening staff. He caught his breath sharply, warning himself in the same moment that it was the fault of the pocked roadway; a most innocent gesture. Still, his cock ached, heated where her hand had brushed it so briefly.

She jerked her hand away. Laughing, she blamed him for finding all the chuck holes in the road. He hadn't, he said, but she was right. It was a great idea. She blushed and he was aware how conscious she was of the intimate way her hand had closed upon him. His heart battered in quickened tempo. She knew he was hard. She knew how terribly he desired her. She even had a quick idea of how he was hung down there. "You're just awful," she said. But she smiled and pressed closer.

He breathed out through his parted lips, certain she pressed his arm inches deep into the resilient softness of her breasts. Jesus! such tits on such a slender girl. And only seventeen! There ought to be a law. There probably was. He slowed the horse, letting it follow its own lazy pace.

"Doesn't that glade look inviting?" Lorna said. "Over there." Beyond a copse of new short-leaf pines that almost concealed it from the lane, a small promontory lay deeply shadowed by tall and ancient oaks. He pulled hard on the lines, turning the horse off the road. "Doesn't it look cool?" she said. She sounded breathless. "So lovely and cool. I'm just—burning up. You know?"

He tugged on the lines. The horse slowed and stopped in the deepest crosshatching of shadows. He dropped the lines and turned, pulling her into his arms. She lay a moment with her head against the inner plane of his shoulder. She lifted her arm and stroked his face gently. This movement turned her body just enough so that he found his palm covering an incredibly full and pliant breast. He closed his fingers automatically. Lorna shivered and her breath was hot against his cheek. Still caressing her tit, he kissed her. The shock waves went through him from the creeping hackles across his skull to the weakness in the back of his legs. Her mouth was fresh, soft, and opened to him as vulnerable as a baby. He knew for all his rutting around the countryside, he had really never kissed anybody before. He wanted to get closer and closer, to taste her and enjoy the sensual delight of her gentle, eager lips. She pressed her parted mouth upward for him. She quivered when his tongue pressed between her teeth. He felt the shudder wrack through her entire body.

He pressed her head back against his arm on the seat rest, thrusting his tongue as deeply into her throat as he could. The delicious sweetness of her mouth almost frightened him; it could be habit-forming. The way she simply surrendered herself upset him; she had no defenses; she appeared to want none. His hand cupped her plump, taut breast, lifting and caressing. His cock was so rigid he was in actual agony.

He felt the wild thundering of her heart through the generous insulation of her mammary. She caught his free hand and pressed it with all her strength over her other tit, almost as if begging him to hurt her. She let her head fall away from his mouth enough to speak breathlessly. "I wouldn't do that," she whispered, "for anybody else —but you. . . You make me—so wild . . . I hardly know what I'm doing."

She gazed up at him, her eyes glazed over, like a baby's sleepy eyes. He kissed her lips, drew his mouth along the faintly squared line of her jaw, licked behind the lobes of her ears. She quivered. He slipped his hand in under her bodice and drew her tit out, cupping it in his hand, gazing rapt at its peach-bloom color, its pale pink nipple, its taut fullness. She pressed her face against his neck as he examined her loveliness at his leisure. She did not protest, though he felt the faint shivering of her body as if she were chilled. He drew her dress over her shoulders. She had to lean forward so he could quickly and deftly loosen half a dozen small buttons along her spine. He pushed her dress and underthings down so that both her tits were exposed. She lay back now, breathing through her parted lips, her eyes tightly closed. He could do anything to her in that moment and he knew it, and it gave him a sense of power that was intoxicating. He cupped her breasts, tasted them, sucked fiercely at her small nipples until she whimpered in delight. He ached with need. "Do you like me?" she whispered.

"My God."

"Would you—like to see me—again?"

He laughed helplessly, his throat burning. He wanted to die right here; he never wanted to leave her. "I'd like to see more of you, all right."

Her breath against his cheek was faster, hotter. "You could see all of me if you wanted." He winced as if she'd hit him in the groin. There was no mistaking her meaning.

"If you would be—nice—to me."

"Nice?"

"You know . . . if I were—your sweetheart—if every-body knew that . . . if you took me places—like inviting me to the parties out at Blackoaks."

He went on caressing her lovely breasts—he was help-less—but his hard-on subsided slightly. Oh, God, women. Making deals. At a moment like this. Oh Jesus! when else? They used the ,weaponry available! He was hurt because this removed any lingering doubt about the social-climbing Garritys. Everything his mother and Kathy and all the others had said so snidely about the Garrity women was true. And then, his hand cupping the loveliest tits he'd ever seen, or ever hoped to see, he had to admit fairly, she was bargaining all she had to offer—in order to attain the goals her mother had set for her and so relentlessly pursued. God knew, the exchange was totally fair—her beauty was worth far more than all the dull parties his mother and her friends would ever throw.

"Couldn't you just tell your sister—how nice I am?" she whispered.

"Kathy wouldn't believe how nice you are," he said in complete honesty.

She laughed and kissed him. She arched her back so her breasts reared higher against his fevered hands. "Oh, you," she said. "You know what I mean."

The sickness struck at him vitally again. He knew pre-cisely what she meant, all right. But how could he tell her—now of all times—that there were no words he could say which would influence his mother or his sister? No matter how badly he might want to do it. They would not accept her. If she came to a party of theirs, invited, but unwanted, they would subtly, but certainly, make it unpleasant for her. Why would she want to expose herself to such painful situations? Oh, Jesus. He couldn't tell her any of that. Not now. He could only say, lamely, "I don't really invite anybody to those parties, Lorna. My sister or my mother—"

"You'll tell them you *want* me, though? You could do that . . . if you liked me . . . if you wanted me." She lay back, forcing her swollen breasts and rigid nipples hard against his sweated palms. His throat ached, dry and taut. She pulled his head down to her bared breasts and he mumbled something into the fragrant, freshly sweet cleavage, drowning in uncontrollable desire. If he were thinking at all now, he was thinking with his hips.

CHAPTER 27

"GOOD LORD, LORNA," Ferrell said, wincing. "I can't stand this. . . . I never wanted anyone so terribly."

"I know, dearest." She caught his face in her hands, pulling him against her opened mouth. She kissed him frenziedly, as if sucking at his tongue, drinking him in. God! What a witch! She knew instinctively what most women never learn.

He had worked her dress down over the flat cream-colored planes of her belly. Her frock would go down no further over the flare of her hips. Her navel was exposed. Jesus! even her navel was lovely. He bent down, reaming it with his tongue. Her hips writhed in sensuous delight. He looked up, his eyes agonized. "I've got to fuck you," he said. "I can't stand it anymore."

Unlike every girl he'd ever known who reacted in prim shock at that word, she only nodded, misty eyed. He reached down and pulled her skirts up above her thighs. Her legs were long, trimly turned, with slender ankles and shaply thigh lines. Her panties were lace trimmed, loose about her legs. She lay back on the seat rest, biting her lip. She caught the lace-trimmed panties in her fingers, uncovering the dainty triangle of brown hair at her mons veneris and the liquidly glistening lips of her vulva.

He pushed her down on the narrow seat. She spread her legs as far as possible in the confined quarters. The horse stirred restively and the buggy shuddered. He thrust himself upward into her, clinging awkwardly to the seat rest and to the rolled top of the splashboard. He had the sensation of liquid heat of a fierce intensity—and the sense of shock at her hot wetness speeded his orgasm. He'd felt girls' vaginas which were almost dry, slightly damp, even wet—but never liquid with a heat that flooded around him. She thrust upward in a spasm and it was quickly over for her too. He stayed upon her as long as he could maintain the awkward position. But finally, cramped, he pulled away, cursing himself because this hurried attack couldn't have been any thrill for her. They had shared a hasty orgasm, but nothing else. Neither was satisfied.

Ferrell toppled back against the seat, pulling her up into his arms. Her radiant hair was loose about her face. This gave her a wanton look that set him wild despite his exhaustion. She tried to straighten her dress but he caught her hand. "Don't," he said. "I want to play with your pussy . . . I want to hold it."

"My dress will be ruined."

"Just a little while," he pleaded. He pushed his hand between her thighs, pressing her legs apart. He rolled up her dress as much as possible, working his fingers in the rich, hot liquidity. He heard her breathing increase in intensity and she sagged against him as if surrendering, spreading her legs wide apart for him, no longer caring about her rumpled dress. Jesus! she loved it. She was helpless the moment you touched her.

She lay against him as he probed her vagina with his fingers and worked her clitoris until her hips flailed involuntarily. She reached over and took his limp penis in her hand. She closed her fingers under his glans and moved her clenched fist on him, and all he could think was, Jesus! she'll have me gone again. He grew stiff in her fist and she stroked him faster, watching him grow distended in response to her ministrations.

"Wait a minute," he said. He leaped down from the carriage. From beneath the seat, he took a coarse blanket and tossed it out flat on the sun-speckled leaves. He reached up then and swung her out from the buggy in his arms.

"How strong you are," she cried. "How wonderful."

He laughed. "Right now I'm stronger than God."

"Oh, I hope so," she whispered. "I hope so."

He knelt and laid her down upon the blanket. He

loosened the remaining buttons on her dress, shook it out and tossed it on the wagon seat. She smiled dazedly up at him. When he started to remove her petticoat, she caught his hand, shaking her head. "I'm scared."

"Of what?"

"Of being naked. Out here. In the open. Somebody might come—"

"Somebody will come. Me."

She caught his distended cock in her hand. "I am scared, Ferrell. Can't you do it to me—like this?"

"Do what to you? Say it."

"Oh, Ferrell, I couldn't—don't make me."

He spun his fingers faster on her clitoris; her hips worked. "Say it—do what to you, Lorna? . . . What do you want me to do to you? . . . Say it."

"Fuck me," she whispered. "I want you to fuck me, Ferrell . . . but don't make me fuck naked."

"Listen to me. Look at me. Look at it. See how hard I am—"

"Oh, I do. It's so beautiful. I want it—so bad."

"Well, it's hard again so quick because you're the loveliest thing I ever saw. I want to see all of you. Naked." He worked his hand on her clitoris as he talked.

She sank her tooth into her lower lip and nodded. "Yes," she whispered. "All right—I don't care if someone does come."

"Nobody's coming," he told her, slipping her crinolines and petticoat down her hips.

She kicked her underthings away and lay back with her knees bent and her legs apart as his fingers moved on her mons labia. Her eyes closed and she breathed raggedly, waiting. She sprawled in naked helplessness and he knelt over her, drinking in her loveliness. Her peach-blossom body, touched with pink nipples and a dainty triangle of sunlit brown hairs was so unreal her flesh seemed to gleam with an unblemished ceramic glaze. She looked fresh and new, untouched. Her taut breasts stood full, their nipples like small buds. Jesus! he thought, I'll either die from heart failure or I'll shoot off before I can get into her again.

CHAPTER 28

FERRELL-JUNIOR walked into Avery's Tavern about five-thirty that afternoon. He felt so good he had to keep himself under leash to keep from putting his head back and roaring with laughter. And the real reason he was afraid to do that was because the backs of his legs were so weak if he put his head very far back, he would fall over on his ass, and lie there like an upended turtle, unable to get up. On the other hand, falling over wouldn't be too bad. What he wanted most was two or three hours of uninterrupted sleep. He'd kissed Lorna good-bye before they got in the village limits. They had ridden sedately down Birmingham Street, and he had managed to get out of the carriage and walk her to her gate without falling victim to fatigue. He'd promised he'd see her again next Saturday, but he had not walked her to her door. Lucinda Garrity and Mr. Luke Scroggings were sitting on the front porch, and he didn't have the strength to face that. He'd bowed in courtly greeting to Lorna's mother and wondered what Lorna would find to say to the red-haired, red-faced, red-eyed bank clerk. He yawned. Thank God she had to face the crisis and not he. He would have driven on home to Blackoaks, but he decided he needed a couple of beers and a ham sandwich to build up strength for the ride home. Thank God, he could nap on the trace. The horse knew the way home better than he did.

Ferrell-Junior paused just inside the Dutch door, squinting to accustom his eyes to the smoke and shadowy haze after the brilliant sunlight of the street. A man walked by and bumped him, mumbling a beery apology. Ferrell reached out frantically and braced himself against the doorjamb. The long room had a polished mahogany bar down one side wall, chairs, tables, and benches comprised the rest of the furnishings. Paintings of almost nude women—buxom wenches all, draped in American flags, unfurled scarfs bearing such inscriptions as No Place Like Home—decorated the rough, unfinished walls. The place was thick with smoke, loud with laughter and boisterous talk. Tom Avery, the owner and bartender, had pressed one of his Negro slaves into service as waiter. Every table and most of the benches were occupied. Town youths, many of whom he had fought in the melee at the train station, lined the bar. They grinned sheepishly and waved, speaking his name. He nodded and returned their smiles.

"Get you a table right away, Mr. Baynard," Tom Avery called across the bar. He yelled at his slave. "Gretch, clear off a table for Mr. Baynard."

"Yas, suh," Gretch said and stood immobile, helpless. Clearing a table meant asking some of the townspeople to vacate their chairs in deference to the planter's son. Gretch knew he couldn't do that, but he also knew he was in for big trouble with Master Avery unless he did do it. "Yas, suh," he said again.

Ferrell grinned and ignored the black man standing helplessly with his tray dangling at the end of his exceptionally long arm. Two men got up from a small table near a window and Gretch raced toward it, calling over his shoulder in panic, "Heah y'are, masta. Heah y'are."

Ferrell sat down and told Gretch to bring him a mug of beer, a double shot of whiskey and a giant-sized ham-on-rye sandwich. Gretch nodded, backing away from him. He had never learned if it was proper to turn his back on a gentleman of quality. He wasn't sure how to tell a gentleman of quality from white trash. They were all mixed together in Avery's Tavern this afternoon. Their laughter, their taunts, their jokes, and their cruel pranks were all very similar.

It was late in the afternoon and few new customers straggled in. Some men checked fat watches and said they had to be getting home to tend to chores or eat supper or lie to the old woman. They straggled out unwillingly into the sunshine of the street, shuddering when they stepped into the fresh air.

Gretch returned with his beer, whiskey, and sandwich. He set them carefully before Ferrell and said, "Masta Avery say that be fo' bits." He knew the price and had not checked it with the busy bartender, but it was not seemly for a black man to dun directly a gentleman of quality. "Masta Avery say" was like a shield Gretch wore between himself and his customers. Ferrell paid him and gave him a dime for himself—which he knew Avery would take away from him later. He thanked him, and Gretch smiled. Few ever thanked him for anything. Maybe this was the distinguishing mark of a gentleman.

Ferrell took a quick drink of whiskey and followed it with a long, welcome draft of beer. Jesus! that felt good. He shivered, feeling drained, but stronger, better than he'd ever felt before, complete, gratified. God, she was wonderful. You touched her and she started, and only you could stop her. Sweet Jesus.

He heard a vaguely familiar laugh and he checked across his shoulder. He winced, because he had been right. The laugh belonged to her father—old Major Hugh Garrity. Old? Ferrell supposed Garrity was forty, but already graying, already slumping in the narrow shoulders and sagging into his own round belly. He was not a tall man, red faced with silky white hair carefully shampooed and brushed. There was an almost habitual haggard and harried look about his face, and the laugh that Ferrell recognized was the sure sign that the major had been lapping up the booze until his last inhibition was lowered. They did that to him, Ferrell thought, repelled. They bought him drinks until his exaggerated politeness, his extreme courtesy, and his unyielding smile gave way to a raucous laughter and finally to frenzied tears when he related—to the secret pleasure and hidden winks of his audience—how he had been defrauded of his rightful property and place in life. He put on quite a show, and every week there were people willing to pay to see it.

Ferrell watched the men grouped around the table with Major Hugh nudge each other and nod toward the wavering little man. Ferrell had seen this before. The major's performance was new to nobody who'd been born in the area and ever frequented Avery's Tavern of a Saturday afternoon. But he had never cared before; now he felt desperately embarrassed for Lorna's father. He was making a jackass of himself—a man who during the week was the model of sobriety, polish, and gentility. Ferrell couldn't help feeling contempt too, but his censure was tempered and mixed with a terrible sense of pity, because the old man knew he was the butt of their jokes, but he was helpless to end it once he started drinking with the boys.

Ferrell tilted his glass to drain off the whiskey when Gil Talmadge grabbed his arm and half-threw himself into the chair beside Ferrell at the small, rude table. "Hey, boy! Where you been all afternoon?"

"Hi, Gil. You got any exitement going on?" Ferrell had seen Gil when he entered the tavern. Gil had been sitting at the long table formed by pushing three smaller tables together. The county plantation men and boys gathered there, somehow aloof from the rest of the room. Ferrell had pretended not to see them because in his new excruciating weariness it was pleasanter to be alone.

"Man! I been waiting for you. Listen, finish off that drink and come on out back. You got to see what I got back there." Gil sat drumming his fingers on the table, grinning and watching the men crowded around Major Hugh Garrity, while Ferrell finished off his drink. "Come on, fellow. Bring your sandwich." Gil raised his voice, yelling, "Hey, Gretch, you lazy black ape! Bring me and Mr. Baynard a couple of beers out back. Fast, you hear me? Don't fool around, boy, or I'll lay the blacksnake to you. You hear me?"

Gretch was busy taking orders at a crowded table. He managed to look across his shoulder and smile in wretched servility—a "boy" who was twice Gil Talmadge's age.

Gil threw his arm about Ferrell-Junior's shoulders and convoyed him through the crowd to the rear door. They stepped out into a small yard, walled by one-by-twelve pine slabs, all at least eight feet tall. The ground was wet, muddy, and minced with boot heel marks. There were a dozen white men standing in a semicircle about a nude Negro man.

The Negro was taller than anyone else in the yard, towering over the white men. He was well over six feet tall, with wide, muscle-corded shoulders, which gleamed with oil and sweat. His chest was deep and ridged with muscles, his belly flat, but it was not until Gil had guided Ferrell to the rear of the semicircle that Ferrell saw what the giant's true attraction was.

"My God," Ferrell said, laughing in spite of himself.

"You ever seen such a hugamongus pecker in all yore life?" Gil demanded.

Grinning, Ferrell shook his head.

"He's mine, pecker and all," Gil said. "I bought him. Bought him when papa and me was in New Orleans looking at slaves. Guy sidled to me and asked me if I was interested in something special. Hell, I didn't know what he was talking about, so I said sure. Man took me to this private auction—place where they sold freaks of all kinds. Blacks with four nuts, amorphodites, dwarfs, queers of all kinds—and old Arthur here. Real name is King Arthur—and you got to admit with a hang like that, he's a real king, all right."

The black man stood naked and expressionless, staring straight ahead as the white men approached him, tested his muscles, looked in his mouth, but finally got around to the object of the visit—they hefted his huge cock and the pendulous gonads. Ferrell shook his head; if he hadn't seen it, he wouldn't have believed it. Limp, the black's penis was like that of a young stud horse. He watched the young plantation men fingering Arthur, weighing his balls and his cock in their hands, making side bets as to the weight of each. Through all this, the big buck stood coldly silent, staring straight ahead, unmoved by the betting, the fingering, or the remarks wheeling around him like swarms of June bugs.

"Fellow I bought Arthur from got him right off a slave boat in Cuba. Few months ago, Arthur was sporting that staff around the African bush. Now, he's mine. Cock and all."

One of the men in the crowd spoke over his shoulder to Gil, "How big is his rod when he's got a hard-on?"

Gil laughed loudly. "You wouldn't believe me anyway, friend. That's something you got to see for yourself to believe. Maybe next Satiday."

"I'll sure hell be here," the man said.

Gil caught Ferrell's arm, thrusting him forward. "Go on up close, Ferrell-Junior. Take a good look. Feel them balls, get a grip on that staff."

Ferrell shook his head, resisting the forward pressure. "This is close enough." He tossed his sandwich away into the mud. For some reason he was no longer hungry. Gretch delivered their beers and Ferrell retreated a few steps, drinking from the mug and watching the entranced white men.

"Bigger'n my arm, for God's sake—"

"My God, if my wife ever saw that, she'd laugh me out of the house."

"That nigger's really hung—"

"Like a stallion."

"Hey, Lawtey, here's a nigger what could ream you a new asshole."

"I never in my life saw nuthin' like that. We got us a prize stallion that don't do nuthin' but stand at stud out at our place. He ain't structured no better'n this here nigger."

"I've seen smaller batterin' rams—hell, I got *one!*"

"Hell, I'm better off'n Arthur is. Built modest like I am, at least I can get it into something smaller'n a cow."

"Yeah. What's this buck good for, Gil? He might be great for everything except fucking—he can't dip that stick in nuthin' less'n a washtub."

Gil laughed, moving through the crowd and taking Arthur by the arm. "You wait until next week. None of you bastards don't spoil it by talking too much, we're going to put on a show with Arthur that will curl your toes, and I guarantee that. Gonna cost you five bucks to see it—

and gonna be worth every penny of it. Ain't that right, Arthur?"

Arthur went on staring straight ahead as though Gil were nothing more than a pesky deer fly.

Ferrell turned on his heel and returned to the bar room. He found a table as far as he could get away from the red-faced Major Hugh Garrity and his friends. He ordered another drink. The major was crying openly now, begging for commiseration from his comrades. Defrauded. Cheated. The major wept. Then the lower half of the Dutch door was pushed open and the squat, red-haired Luke Scroggings entered. Some of the men at the major's table cursed Luke and told him to get on home. Luke ignored them, except the set of his wide thick shoulders was warning enough to any intelligent enough to heed it. He bent over the major. His voice was low, but inflexible. "You're coming home to supper now, major. Miz Lucinda sent me to fetch you."

The major protested and the men around him growled, but Garrity got unsteadily to his feet and Scroggings led him from the tavern, half-supporting him. Ferrell winced, watching them. This was one of the chores that went with loving Miss Lorna June Garrity. This was one of the tasks Luke Scroggings performed in order to be permitted to stay within Lorna June's orbit and to buy his weekly rejection every Saturday afternoon. Ferrell took another long pull at the beer and ordered one more double whiskey, which Gretch brought on the run.

"Where'd you go?" Gil demanded, sitting down beside Ferrell and slapping his empty beer mug on the table —a signal to the boy, Gretch. "I worked old Arthur's cock up a few strokes—just to give you some idea—"

"I figured that was what you were going to do."

"Well, my God! Didn't you want to see it?"

"I got a horrible inferiority complex seeing it on a soft," Ferrell said.

Gil laughed. "Yeah. But wait until nex Satiday. Me and some of the old boys are going to try to find three or four black women that think they can take on old Arthur. We're going to fix up a show. Put a mattress out there and Avery's going to set up his chairs. Five bucks from everybody. I reckon to git back most of what Arthur cost me, next Satiday afternoon alone."

Ferrell nodded, but said nothing.

"But it's got to be kept quiet. If some of these Bible-readin' women or the preachers in these churches heard about it, we'd all be dead." Gil's eyes glittered. He appeared intoxicated with the excitement of his gargantuan plans. "You gonna see something next Satiday, Ferrell-boy, that you will recall when your own cods are stone, stone cold."

"I may not be coming in next Saturday," Ferrell said.

Gil's laughter subsided. He glanced around and then nudged Ferrell hard, with his elbow. "Yeah," he said. "I saw you with her."

"Who?"

"The town lay," Gil said.

For a moment, it was as if the shouting, the laughter, the haze of smoke, the smell of beer receded and came to Ferrell only from a great distance. Rage gorged up inside him. He clutched the sides of the table and bit back the murderous anger that welled into his mind. He stared at Gil, sick. But Gil was drumming the table with his fingers, looking around, grinning, unaware that he had said anything that wasn't common knowledge, shared by Ferrell.

Ferrell had to fight within himself to keep from smashing his fist into that grinning face. He reminded himself that Gil had been his friend as long as he could remember. They'd committed all manner of boyish crimes together, most of them hatched in Gil's fertile mind. Anything for a laugh, the thrill of a moment's excitement. Anything to break the deadly monotony of rural life. Gil had once arranged a sex orgy for himself and Ferrell-Junior in his father's barn. Gil had brought in five black girls, the youngest ten and the oldest fourteen. He had been about thirteen then, Gil a little older. Gil had made the girls undress and perform every sex act he'd ever heard of in song, dirty joke, or whisper. They had stolen chickens together. They had lied for each other in times of crisis. There was nothing Gil couldn't say to him.

He tried to tell himself that Gil had been known to lie. But what would be his motive for lying about Lorna? And there was little in scandal, rumor, secret, or concealed crime in this town and this county that Gil didn't know. Ferrell wanted to believe Gil was lying, half-drunk, excited by his black stud, riding him. But sickness roiled in his stomach. Lorna. The town lay. The casual way Gil said it was like a shouted accusation that nobody could refute. He didn't want it to be true. Lorna couldn't be the town tramp. She was too fresh looking, too lovely. She was also so easy that he had touched her and she had submitted. He pushed his drink aside, biting back vomitus.

"Gil . . . that's a hell of a thing to say."

Gil laughed and gazed at him, incredulous. "Bet you got in her pants today. Right?"

Ferrell shrugged. He stared at the backs of his hands, wanting to cry for no good reason.

Gil laughed again. "Hell, if you didn't screw her first time out, you're in a new minority, old pal. . . . Every white guy in Calvert County has had ole Lorna June Garrity—at least once."

Ferrell pushed away the mug of unfinished beer. Somehow he remained outwardly calm though he was raging, screaming and crying and protesting inside. He was shaken with shock and with deflated ego, a strange terrible sense of loss for something that never was, never could be, and was better ended like this. But it was so brutal, so abrupt, so casual, and somehow so irreparably dirty.

"I never heard that," he said, his voie sounding odd and hoarse in his own ears. "I never heard that in my life."

"Well, take my word for it, old son. If you don't git it this time—you'll git it next time. Don't fret about it. Better just hope that ole Link Tetherow never has got her —yet. Ole Link's got the clap so bad he walks spraddle-legged."

CHAPTER 29

FERRELL-JUNIOR walked stiffly out of Avery's Tavern. He felt nauseated, sick at his stomach. He got into his buggy and headed his horse east out of town, letting the animal set its own pace. The phaeton rolled at a steady clip because it was time for the horse to be fed and it recognized the home trail. The sun was lowering beyond a wall of purpling trees, the sky cerise and orange, streaked with angry stria of red and banked with pink-tinted clouds. It would be well after dark before they reached Blackoaks. Ferrell didn't care. He didn't want to see anyone, he didn't want to talk to anybody. He was cold with empty-bellied rage, but couldn't say whether his hatred was directed more at Gil Talmadge or the faithless little town tramp, Miss Lorna June Garrity.

He sagged against the seat rest, bracing one boot against the splashboard. His eyes burned with tears. He couldn't say why except that everything had seemed so beautiful when he walked into Avery's Tavern, and now it was ugly, and as dirty as the whispers about Lorna June Garrity. Strange that he'd never heard those rumors about her. He'd heard she was pushy, a social climber who'd do anything to get herself accepted by what she considered to be "the right people," but never that she was a round-heeled little tramp who put out to anybody who took her to the woods in his carriage.

The hellish thing was that he'd promised her he'd see she was invited to the very next party at Blackoaks. Hell, this had seemed a small price to pay for what he was getting. It would be fun to have her at a party; it would brighten a dull evening. Now, he knew better. The whispers about her were far more sinister than he'd suspected. He could never ask her to a Blackoaks party, and he had to stay away from her before he got too deeply involved.

He gripped the lines tightly. Why did he worry about whether he'd see her again or not unless he wanted her hellishly? Why did he feel somehow betrayed? What had betrayal to do with it? He'd gone out this afternoon with an incredibly lovely girl, who, it transpired, was a tramp. He had let her believe he cared about her, that he would help her meet the people she aspired to know intimately. The scales balanced pretty evenly there. So they'd both lied to each other—he directly, and she in what she let him believe about her. He should feel relief, not betrayal. He sure as hell didn't have to get her an invitation to any parties. And he had been afraid he might get deeply and emotionally involved—it was already happening this afternoon—because she was so freshly lovely, overheated, and habit-forming. Now he didn't have to worry about involvement.

Damn it. Why didn't he feel better? Face it. His pride was wounded. He had spent the most enthralling afternoon of his life—convinced that any man was a liar who said all women were the same once you got their underpants off. Lorna had seemed different, more exciting, more eager to please a man. She had seemed wild about him. It had built up his ego so he was ready to do battle with Kathy and his mother to wangle the invitations that Lorna wanted. Well, his pride was the only real casualty; only his self-esteem had suffered. When you looked at it reasonably, what else should he have expected? He'd had her naked in less than thirty minutes after they reached the pigtracks, and that made generous allowance for stubborn buttons. She was easy. She certainly was not virginal. It followed that if he had had it so easily, so had others ahead of him. Why then had he been so stunned and shocked to hear she was less than chaste?

He shook his head, wanting to deny that she was baggage handled casually by transients. She looked so fresh, so dainty, new and untouched. It was almost as easy to believe that Kathy was promiscuous. Yet, there was Gil's laughter, his knowing leer—"every white man in the county has had little ole Lorna June Garrity—at least once." Jesus. It was just so difficult—damned near impossible to reconcile her gentle loveliness with what Gil said about her. But the truth was, her chastity or lack of it didn't matter. After all, he wanted her for only one reason.

No, damn it, he didn't want to be another of the men who stood in line to get Lorna June Garrity in the boondocks. He would not be. He had to stay away from her.

Why stay away from anything as incredibly lovely —and easy—and pliable? Hell, he ached in his loins, wanting her again already. He could get one hell of a hard-on right now just thinking about her. And the thought that she put out to many men should only arouse new desires. His need for her was matched only by his loss of any lingering wisp of respect for her. Hell, he wasn't going to stay away from her. It was one thing to get emotionally involved. It was another to use a beautiful little slut as he wished for excitement and self-gratification. He'd have what he could get, as long as he could get it. What the hell if life wasn't as pretty as you had hoped it was?

He laid the lines hard across the rump of the horse, speeding along the faintly marked trace. He was running away from something. He could not race fast enough to escape a strange sense of loss and empty-bellied insufficiency. Somehow he blamed Lorna, and he could not forgive her, even when hating her for being good to him didn't make sense.

Lamps, candles, and lanterns glowed brightly all through the big house when he came through the tall gate and along the lane under the pecan trees. Blackoaks was alive with activity. The entire place seemed different to Ferrell, somehow alien, as if he'd been a long time away, and he had changed, and he'd never see anything the same way again.

The banker from Tallahassee, Florida, Garrett Blanford Ware, and his wife, Margaret, had arrived with their three-carriage entourage. Ferrell had always been intrigued and puzzled by the second closed carriage and the oversized blacks who served as Ware footmen. They were huge, glowering men who never replied even when addressed directly. They were always armed, with handguns in holsters at their belts, or rifles held across their massive chests.

The arrival of the banker's caravan had delayed everything. Dinner was being served as Ferrell-Junior entered the front corridor. He excused himself. He said he had eaten at the tavern when, as a matter of fact, he knew he couldn't keep anything on his stomach. It didn't matter what he said to them, he could not endure the Wares just now. He believed them to be the area's vainest, shallowest, most supercilious and self-centered people. He shook hands with Ware who called him "just an outstanding young man." He suffered Margaret Ware to kiss him moistly on the mouth. Then he brushed his mother's cheek with his lips. He found her tense and quivering, holding herself in leash only through some inner discipline you never suspected looking at her frail body, her vaguely smiling blue eyes. He climbed the wide stairway, went into his bedroom, and fell across his bed.

Exhausted, he was asleep, fully clothed, in a few moments. He awoke about 2:00 A.M., hearing the chime of the old grandfather clock in the downstairs corridor. The house was silent. He lay on the bed, aware of nothing really except that he had a hard-on. Perhaps now that he'd met and mounted Miss Lorna June Garrity he'd suffer permanent satyriasis.

He got up, removed his boots, undressed, used the thunder chamber, but found his rigidity remained undiminished. Nothing was going to give him relief until he got back to her. She was deep inside his mind, embedded there. He was fascinated by her, captivated by her. She was inside him and only God knew how to dig her out.

It was some moments before he was consciously aware of the shadows and faint fingers of light scratching at his darkened ceiling. He got up from the bed and crossed to the window.

Stunned, he stared down at the small procession of men with low-wicked lanterns. Scowling he saw that his father, wearing no coat, his shirt open, was leading three Negroes up the knoll toward his mother's chapel. He recognized Thyestes, Laus, and Pegasus in the dim light.

He closed his eyes tightly and then opened them exaggeratedly wide. This couldn't be real. It had to be fabric from a dream. God knew he was emotionally and physically tired enough to be suffering a nightmare. But he was not asleep. He felt the chill of the flooring against his bare soles. Cool night breezes brushed across his sweated face. It was real enough, all right. When the procession reached the knoll, the three Negroes slouched on the small stoop of the chapel while his father took a lantern, stepped inside the chapel, and closed the door after him. There was what seemed a long, silent wait. Then his father came out of the door, carrying bags that he transferred to Laus and Pegasus while Thyestes stood by with a lantern in one hand and a gun in the other.

Incredulous, Ferrell leaned against the sill and watched the men return slowly downslope. They entered the house through the terrace windows. The lights were extinguished and darkness settled over the estate. Only Ferrell-Junior was left, troubled, wide awake, sleepless—and with an aching hard-on.

CHAPTER 30

SUNDAY DAWNED, a time of tension for family and guests at Blackoaks. Father Anthony, a priest from the Catholic Church in Commerce, had arrived the day before to celebrate mass in the Blackoaks chapel. Miz Claire was taut, fine drawn, like a bowstring ready to snap. She had promised a full congregation for the priest. The arrival of the Wares suddenly had kept her from getting word to as many neighbors as she would have liked. She had warned the house servants they were to bathe, dress in their best, and appear on time for the services. She had less success with members of her own family. Ferrell-Junior refused to attend church. "I'm too sick to sit there," he told her. "I wouldn't be able to make it."

Baynard, Sr. also declined to attend services. He needed the time, he told her, to discuss business with Garrett Blanford Ware. Miz Claire trembled, looking as if she might go into hysterics. "I promised Father Anthony." Her voice quavered. "Can't you understand that?"

"Father Anthony doesn't give a damn whether I'm there or not—as long as he gets the kind of donation he will very subtly, but definitely specify—in round numbers."

"You're anti-Christ," she wept. "You're irreligious."

"I'm busy, that's all. . . . I'll apologize to the priest—if I get a chance."

Hunt Campbell tried politely to decline, but at the wild, swirling look that he could define only as panic

311

that struck Miz Claire's eyes, he agreed to go. "Though I am an agnostic," he told her.

"Father Anthony won't care what your religion is. We've even had Methodists at mass in the chapel."

Hunt walked up the knoll with family and guests. He sat apart on the last row, behind the house servants, alone and uncomfortable. He watched Miz Claire on the aisle seat, first row, troubled. She fidgeted, nervous, more vague than he'd ever seen her, as if she were sinking into a serious depressive state. He felt he should tell somebody, but there seemed nobody to tell except God. While the others prayed, he kept trying to get through, with prayers of his own, but he had the feeling he was talking into an empty infinity.

Margaret Ware arrived at the breakfast table, but finally drank only black coffee. She was, she told them, on a restricted diet. All the food on the table was either too greasy, too starchy, or eggs. She was a tall woman, almost six feet, and rawboned. She spoke in a husky, mannish baritone, but according to her detailed account, delivered while the others ate, she had a most delicate stomach. If she ate anything that didn't agree with her, it might just come right back up. She wouldn't think of putting them to the trouble of preparing the special foods her system demanded. Anyhow, only Thelma, the black cook who had served in her mother's family, knew how to prepare the diet correctly. When one traveled, one had to anticipate certain inconveniences. She certainly did not want to be a minute's trouble or concern to anyone.

"She looks like a blacksmith to me," Hunt whispered to Kathy on the way up to the chapel. He was pleased to find himself escorting Kathy when Styles, resplendent in a cream-white suit and silk cravat and white boots, walked between Miz Claire and Margaret Ware, gently touching their elbows to help them over rough places and twigs on the grass. Hunt wondered what Styles wanted, but he didn't mention this to Kathy. She smiled at him, and encouraged, he said behind his hand, "She looks healthier than any horses you've got on this place. But you know what I've learned in living among people richer than I am? A lot of people show you how important they are by finding fault when they're your guests. No matter what you do for them. They find fault with everything. No matter what it is. This puts you on guard, you're dealing with a superior being—and you won't relax until they leave."

Kathy was still laughing when they entered the chapel. Miz Claire turned, her face frantic, and scowled at Kathy across her shoulder. Kathy stopped smiling and sat quietly in the pew beside Styles.

Ferrell-Junior fell asleep sometime during the hours before daybreak. His final decision was to break off with Lorna, simply not see her again. He awoke troubled about his father and that weird scene at the chapel last night. He tried to figure what it meant, but Lorna ate like acid through his anxiety. He stared down at himself, standing rigid. He could exist only if he admitted he was going to see Lorna at the first possible moment. In the meantime, he could get by only because his fist was handy and insatiable. Staring down at his rigid staff, he thought about Florine Pilzer.

I could take this thing up there to her right now and make her a very happy lady, he thought. He remembered the look in her face, the way she had invited him in. They both knew what she wanted, and if she saw this—even restricted at first in his pants—she'd sprawl out on her back. But, unfortunately, this was Sunday and he couldn't go up there because old Bos Pilzer was there, and he'd undoubtedly object. In fact, the Dutchman would probably object violently. And, worst of all, no matter how he tried to tell himself how great she'd be, he didn't want Florine Pilzer. He wanted a particular woman— not any woman. He wanted Lorna. The thought of Lorna drove every sane consideration from his mind, inflamed his body, stirred his memories, and set his blood to pounding in anticipation.

He heard a wagon on the rocky drive and went to the window in his underwear, his rigidity on display. He caught his breath. Florine Pilzer was alone, dressed in her finery—as she did every Sunday—for the drive in to the Baptist church in Mt. Zion. He watched her sitting straight on the carriage seat, handling the team easily. Dressed up like that, she was a comely wench. His mind raced ahead of her. He could slip on trousers, boots, and a shirt, order a fast horse and ride across country after her. He knew every trail and pigtrack between Blackoaks and Mt. Zion. He could overtake her easily, and he could make her forsake her mission. He looked down at himself, wanting to ride after her, wanting to show her what he had for her, wanting to forget Lorna by mounting Florine Pilzer. Hell, doing it with Florine when it was Lorna he wanted would be no more satisfactory than his fist, and it would get him involved in something he truly didn't want, even with a hard-on. . . .

Garrett Blanford Ware was up by daybreak and dressed by the time the room was pink with morning sunlight. Waking at this early hour was an old habit. He awakened by five every morning down home in Tallahassee. Thelma, the family cook, had his breakfast ready by the time he came downstairs and he ate heartily. No sense waiting for Margaret. Her diet and her detailed conversation on her ills depressed him. He disliked starting a morning feeling dispirited. It affected his whole day, and this was not profitable for a banker. He had to be able to smile, even when he turned down an application for a loan, or foreclosed a mortgage. As soon as he finished breakfast at home, he set out walking toward the bank. There were places where a man, if he were discreet, could find an hour or two of diversion at this time of the morning in Tallahassee, if he could pay the tariff. His especial favorite was a mustee woman, named Orange because of the odd color of her hair and her skin. He looked forward with some eagerness to getting back home to Orange. Unfortunately, this annual pilgrimage into Alabama was not a vacation at all; it was strictly business, and it was touchy and time-consuming as hell.

Ware was an extremely tall, extremely gaunt man in his late forties. His dark eyes somehow never burdened anyone by probing. He laughed a lot and he liked to look around when he talked. He believed this put people at ease with him. He dressed neatly, in tailored shirts and suits, which were one of his extravagances. It galled him that he could afford only few extravagances despite the fact that he was president of one of the most profitable banks in the southeast. But he was only the president. Mannsteiner was the owner and he ruled tight-fistedly.

He walked out on the small courtesy balcony and sat down in the rocking chair there. A mild breeze touched his face; he was thankful for the cool of early morning. It was going to be another hot Alabama day—the same kind of heat and humidity that made Tallahassee so oppressive in the summer. Early autumn and Indian summer was little better up here. He had wished for some years that he and Margaret could take a boat trip to the Scandinavian waters for a couple months each summer to escape the heat and the mosquitoes. But every summer it was the same. By July, old Mannsteiner was there going through the books at the bank, growling and scribbling names on sheets of paper. Those names represented delinquent or shaky mortgages, and the complete list would be handed over to Ware. "Investigate these, Ware," Mannsteiner would say, using a tone he might employ in speaking to a janitor. "Look into them. Bring in some satisfaction."

He stared across the green rolling knolls of Blackoaks. This estate had been on his list for the past ten years. Baynard had learned that far back that he could delay making interest and principle payments until the final day of the mortgage note maturity date. And that's what he did. Every year, he showed up here pretending to be a personal friend, on a friendly visit, and this was the way Baynard received him. The mortgage had become a touchy subject between them. Both knew it had to be paid. Mannsteiner would foreclose without thinking twice about it. There was only one way Baynard forestalled this inevitable ending: he could pay principle due, and interest, or he could pay interest and request an extension. This he had done, year after year.

Each year, Ware waited patiently for Baynard to introduce the subject of the mortgage. Ware himself could never mention it; this violated some unwritten code of the magnolia country.

After breakfast, when the family, guests, and house servants had gone up the knoll to celebrate mass at the chapel, Baynard invited Ware into his office-study. He offered Ware one of his best cigars, poured him a glass of whiskey, neat. They sat for a moment, silent.

"Have you had a nice trip this summer, Blan?" Baynard asked.

"Always have to mix a little business in with pleasure," Ware said. "My bank does a lot of business up this way."

"I know."

"You'd be surprised how many mortgages we hold on estates up through here—all the way to Birmingham. A lot of banks don't like to deal outside their own community. Too much risk. But Mannsteiner had a brilliant idea—"

"Mannsteiner?"

"Yes. The Jew who owns my bank. He owns a bank in New York, one in Richmond, one in Jacksonville and in Savannah. Of course, he isn't even listed on the boards of any of them. But I assure you, he owns them. He learned—maybe twenty-five years ago that planters down this way have a—certain pride, shall we say? Mannsteiner sees it as a false pride, but one he is pleased to indulge. No Southern planter wants his neighbors to know that his plantation is mortgaged to a bank. So Mannsteiner set up a bank in one community—and made mortgages through it for estates hundreds of miles away."

"At 10 percent interest."

Ware shrugged. "When a bank makes a mortgage loan there is a great risk factor. Especially mortgages made on property at great distances—in different states. Now, Mannsteiner is very happy to make such loans—but somebody has got to pay for the risk and the loss. If a man wants to go out of his own area to borrow money, he must be willing to pay extra for the service, Mannsteiner figures. He has suggested that we may have to raise our rates up to 12 percent. We've had some delinquents—a few will have to be foreclosed." Ware laughed. "Thank goodness, this is never a problem at Blackoaks."

"Still, you're bound to know I've made no mortgage payments all year."

"Don't think about it," Ware said. "I'm not going to worry about it, if you don't."

"Thanks, Blan."

"What are friends for, Ferrell? We have a business transaction here, but I think we have friendship first. Why, Margaret and I—we have had the privilege of watching your children grow up."

Baynard laughed. "That was never the way I intended it when I first took out this loan, Blan. I thought one good year with the cotton, and I'd pay you off. I never realized 10 percent could add up so overwhelmingly in one year. Because you have been my friend, I've been able to get by—making the interest payments only."

"I've been happy to do it—and more importantly, until this year—Mannsteiner has been happy about it."

Baynard straightened in his chair; his florid face paled slightly. "Until this year?"

Ware frowned, and waved cigar smoke from in front of his face. He let his gaze trail across the books in the shelves. "You don't know Mannsteiner, do you?"

"I've always dealt with you, Blan."

"Of course you have. Wouldn't have had it any other way. But—I have to deal with Mannsteiner. One of the smartest sons of bitches I ever knew. But an implacable son of a bitch. He never misses a thing. Right now, if he were here, and you got him in a conversation—if he would talk about anything but money—he'd tell you that Georgia, the Carolinas, Alabama, Mississippi are all fading, and in time will be the financially, educationally, and productively the most backward states in the country. He could give you a lot of reasons why. But the point I'm making is that nothing escapes him. I would venture to say he knows as much about Blackoaks Plantation as you do—and he's never seen it, never been nearer to it than Tallahassee. He knows your cotton isn't getting top grading anymore at Mobile. He says you have a heavy percentage of slaves who are aging, past their productive prime. They are now costing you a great deal more than they are worth to you. He would tell you depreciation here at Blackoaks is excessive. Why, I told him, you have one of the best-looking estates down this way. But he just shakes his head. He reads nothing but the cost sheets."

"Does he—do you want to close me out? Is this what you're saying?"

"Good lord, Ferrell! That's the farthest thing from my mind. Or from Mannsteiner's. As I said, there are a few delinquents up this way that we'll have to foreclose. But, my friend, put your mind at ease. Your estate is not one of these."

"Not yet." Baynard drew a deep breath.

"Does this mean you agree with Mannsteiner's estimate—that in less than one hundred years, Alabama will be one of the poorest states?"

"Does it matter whether I agree with him or not? He holds the dice."

"You know Mannsteiner's passion. Florida. Oh, I knew that would make you laugh. Nothing down there but palmettos, alligators, rattlesnakes, sand, and mosquitoes. Right? Wrong, according to Mannsteiner. He says right now, in the 1830s, is the time to buy land in Florida. He calls it the coming land of opportunity."

"I've just lost all respect for him. The Indians are still scalping people down there. I thought you came north each summer just to get a taste of civilization."

"Oh, it's a rough frontier right now. Even Tallahassee is south of law and order sometimes. We get a lot of runaway slaves, escaped convicts, murderers, absconders. But there's money to be made down there—in citrus, land, cattle, lumber, phosphate, tourism—"

"Selling guns to Indians—"

"Yes. We're still having some Indian trouble. But Port St. Joe is building a race course to rival Saratoga for the tourists."

"According to Mannsteiner then, I ought to sell out here in Alabama and move to Florida—land of opportunity?"

"According to Mannsteiner."

Baynard laughed. "Tell him I said to go to hell."

Ware laughed with him. "I'll tell him. It'll give him a laugh. But he sent a message to you that I hope you can take with a grin."

Baynard drew a deep breath. He gazed at Garrett Blanford Ware, trying to catch and hold his roving eyes. "Yes?"

"I'm sorry, Ferrell. The new interest rate next year on your loan will be 12 percent. You must understand. The risk. The fact that you have never actually reduced your principal. All these things have to be considered."

"And I am growing third-grade cotton."

"I'm sorry, Ferrell."

Styles found Garrett Blanford Ware sitting alone in a lounge chair on the terrace about two o'clock that afternoon. Styles still wore his creamy white suit, but he had removed his silk tie after lunch. He wore his collar loose and open at the throat. He said, "How nice to find you alone, sir. I had been hoping to get a chance to talk to you."

"I'm always happy to talk with you, Styles. Margaret thinks you're the handsomest young man she's ever beheld. And I'm quite impressed with your brilliance. I take a real interest in highly intelligent young men."

"Thank you, sir. I wonder if you'd care to take a short walk? I'm sure you'd find it—most interesting."

Ware got to his feet with alacrity. "I'd like that, Styles. Everyone should take long walks after the Sunday meals they serve here at Blackoaks."

"They should. But they take naps instead."

Ware laughed. "You might be interested to know I walk to the bank from home every morning at home in Tallahassee—a distance of two miles—and we're almost as hilly in Tallahassee as was ancient Rome."

Styles walked in thoughtful silence beside the tall, lean man until they had crossed the crest of the plateau on which the big house was built. They started down the incline toward the slave quarters. Styles glanced over his shoulder. "I know your bank is—interested—in Blackoaks, sir. Mortgage, I assume. I don't know the amount of the mortgage. But, it seems to me, as president of your bank, you'd be interested in the improved management of this estate's affairs."

Ware spoke stiffly. "I'm afraid that we can't discuss Mr. Baynard's financial transactions or arrangements with the Commercial Bank of Tallahassee, Styles."

"Quite proper, sir. I understand and applaud that. I wouldn't be a party to such discussions—even if you initiated them. . . . My total interest is in a resource of Blackoaks which I feel is not being exploited in a way that might be most profitable—to us and to you."

"Yes?" Ware bobbed his head, almost like a carrion bird, looking the estate over, but his smile encouraged Styles.

"We're certainly not deceiving the bank that the land at Blackoaks no longer has the life or vitality to produce top-quality cotton. For the past two years that I know of, we've gotten a third-grade rating at Mobile. And yet, each year, we pour all our assets and resources into growing cotton that is of steadily decreasing quality. I don't believe we—or anyone else—can go on like that indefinitely. And certainly, if I were master of Blackoaks—and I realize I am not and never can be—we would not go on in this way."

"Go on."

"We'll just go up this path into the slave quarters. I hope you're not easily shocked. You may see—shall we say?—a certain informality of existence up here. They don't mate in the streets in packs like dogs up here, but they don't really try to hide from each other what they're doing either. And slaves relax on their days off—and they have other standards of conduct than ours."

"Don't apologize, Styles. I come from one of the roughest frontiers remaining in this country. But because it's far south, rather than far west, it doesn't get publicized, but life is pretty raw in Tallahassee—the whole state."

Styles said, "We own here at Blackoaks, two of the finest specimen of blacks in this country. True and full-blooded Fulanis."

"Extraordinary. I know a great deal about slave

bloodlines. And I am quite conversant with both the history and the physical and mental superiority of the Fulah."

"Unfortunately, both our Fulanis are male," Styles said. "For a long time Mr. Baynard has talked of buying a Fulani female—"

"They're not that easy to find these days. With the anti-import laws and all. Purebloods."

"And they're expensive."

"You'd enter in savage competitive bidding, all right. You'd have to be well financed to have any hope."

"That's my idea, sir. Precisely. But with the proper financial backing, we could do it. Think of it this way, Mr. Ware. If you, sir, owned two beautiful and healthy male specimen, wouldn't you willingly lay everything—everything—on the line to produce that strain of animal —for sale in the slave markets?"

Mr. Ware's head bobbed on his long thin neck. "I might be tempted. . . . Yes, sorely tempted, Styles."

"Wouldn't you be even more tempted if you knew that your old ways of running your estate were no longer viable, that your estate was depreciating in value alarmingly, doomed to failure—simply not relevant anymore?"

Garrett Blanford Ware said nothing, but he smiled and glanced around, bobbing his head in a way that conveyed to Styles no impression of censure. He followed Styles up the steps of a whitewashed shack. He glanced around, checking for disrepair, deterioration. He found the shacks in good repair, but aging. As most of the Blackoaks slaves are aging, he reminded himself. He watched Styles with heightened interest.

Styles knocked on the door and called, "Blade?"

There were surreptitious scrapings and rapid guilty movements inside the shack. Feet pattered across the bare flooring, someone bumped an article of furniture and cursed in a tense whisper and then evidently went out a rear window, landing heavily on the ground. Blade opened the door, still buttoning up his onasburg britches. His lean, muscular body glistened with sweat. "Wasn't expectin' you, masta," he said.

Both Styles and Garrett Blanford Ware smiled. Styles spoke over his shoulder, "What's your immediate first impression of Blade, sir?"

"A real stud," Garrett Blanford Ware said, and they all laughed, Blade nervously.

"Where is Moab?" Styles asked.

"Moab, he doan stay heah no mo', masta," Blade said. "He live all the time up at Mast' Pilzer's place."

"Yes. All right . . . you can take my word for it, Mr. Ware. Moab is a younger model of Blade—from the same pattern, the same mold, the same blood line. . . . Mr. Baynard bought them and their mother when Blade was five and Moab still a suckling at his mother's teats. Mr. Baynard got them most reasonably, because the mother was suffering deep depression and her owner wanted to get rid of her. She was indeed mentally disturbed—but for emotional reasons. Her man—a purebred Fulani like her—couldn't endure slavery. He had been brought over here on an African slave ship. He stood it a few years—because of his woman, I suppose. Then he ran away. He was run down with bloodhounds—and shot when he resisted. Blade's mother lived only a few months longer after they brought her here—she committed suicide."

"Fulahs are prideful," Garret Blanford Ware observed. "Most as stiff-necked and unbending as some Southern plantation owners I've met!" He laughed in a rueful way, bobbing his head on its spindly neck. "Fulahs don't take kindly to the yoke."

"Blade is not like that, nor Moab. They're gentle, broke in well—"

"I suppose. As long as they're treated fairly."

Styles told Blade to step inside his shack and drop his britches. Blade obeyed silently. Styles and Ware followed. Ware found a straight-backed cane chair and sat down, studying the incredibly perfect Fulani narrowly.

"Blade's a perfect specimen," Styles said. "Mr. Baynard has rejected an offer of at least 12,000 in gold for him that I know of."

Ware whistled between his teeth, rocking on the rear legs of the chair, his eyes blinking, his head bobbing.

Styles pulled Blade's eyelids down, pressed his lips back over his gums, exposing the even lines of white teeth. He struck Blade on the chest with his fist, drew his hands along Blade's lower arms and biceps. Then he pushed his hand down through the crisp pubic hairs and took Blade's still engorged penis in his hand. "See how he is hung?" He turned, holding the staff as he spoke to Ware. His fingers closed and relaxed spasmodically and involuntarily. "You can see—he's perfect. His younger brother is an equally fine animal. I believe we could amass a fortune and make Blackoaks synonymous with top-quality fancy slaves—in a few years. Can you see that, sir?"

Ware's head bobbed. "I can see a great deal . . . more probably even than you do."

CHAPTER 31

BY MONDAY MORNING Ferrell-Junior had made an irrevocable decision: he was not going to see Lorna June Garrity again. Should he chase after a girl that every man in the county had had, at least once? Could he see her for physical relief and release and not get emotionally involved? That first Saturday afternoon had proved to him he could not. She got inside him—no matter what she'd done—and this was a hell of a situation, against everything he had been taught, everything he believed. What gratification or pride came from getting a woman anyone else could get, simply by pushing her over on her back? He had spent the long weekend torn between dashing in to see her, and admitting she was a slut, and that he didn't want her. He felt sweated down, exhausted, physically, emotionally, mentally. It wasn't worth it; he was going to get her out of his mind somehow before he got in so deep there was no way out.

He tried to involve himself in preparations for the huge party honoring the Garrett Blanford Wares. There was much activity; everybody was busy, but there didn't seem anything for him to do. His father was overseeing the selection of ninety-proof, eight-year-old whiskey at the distillery. Nothing but the best would be served at the party. His father didn't need his help or advice.

Smells of parboiling, baking, stewing, frying, barbecueing, marinating, and steaming rose from Jeanne d'Arc's kitchen. She had her underlings on the run in there. Pies, cakes, hams, smoked and barbecued turkeys, geese, guinea hens, and chickens grew in huge mounds. Excitement was contagious and spread from the house slaves to the fieldhands and the craftsmen—everyone looked forward to a holiday.

Hunt told Ferrell-Junior that this elation among the house slaves was the most interesting phenomenon of all to him, "They act like it's their party—their fun and games—and all it really means is harder work than ever, and long, unbroken hours of tending the whims and wishes of selfish, demanding, self-centered white people who look on the slaves as animals incapable of feeling any human emotion, or ever becoming physically exhausted."

Ferrell-Junior shrugged. He had more troublesome problems than worrying about why house slaves shared the mounting excitement over a party. He looked forward to it without pleasure at all. He had given Lorna June his word that she would be invited to this party. But this promise had been elicited before he had Gil Talmadge's dossier on her sex life. The hell with her. On the other hand, this was one reason why he didn't go racing in to see her. He didn't have the guts to tell her he wasn't going to assure her an invitation to Blackoaks, after all. Go fuck somebody, he thought, raging. Go fuck yourself.

He made it through Monday night only by walking down to the barn and ordering Pegasus personally to hitch the fastest carriage horse to his lightweight buggy and have them waiting for him before seven the next morning.

He dressed in the half-light of dawn and went rapidly down the rear stairs, remembering how he and Tharus had long ago raced down these steps on secret errands of boyhood.

"Good morning, Masta Ferrell-Junior," Jeanne d'Arc said as he came into the kitchen on his way to the rear door. "Can I get you some breakfast?"

He shook his head. She was preparing the tray of hot iced buns and coffee she always took in to his father in his study. Usually, he would have taken half a dozen of the buns and eaten them on the way down to the barn. "You want to see me throw up—you feed me something."

Jeanne d'Arc laughed. "Masta Ferrell-Junior's got hisself a girl he wants something fierce." She put her head back, laughing. The other servants around the pine table grinned and nudged each other.

"Yeah," Ferrell-Junior said, going out the back door, "it's hell, ain't it?"

"No, suh," Jeanne d'Arc called out to him. "It ain't heaven nor hell. It's when you is caught between heaven and hell. That's when you can't eat—or don't dare eat."

Their laughter pursued him down the incline in the chill of early morning.

He drew up on the reins, halting his lathered horse before the picket fence at the Garrity house on Birmingham Street before nine that morning. Lorna June was on the porch. He had been sure she would be, though he hadn't known why he was so certain. Maybe only because he wanted her to be so badly.

She was sweeping the porch, and she had never looked lovelier. Her brown hair was brushed back loosely from her soft and gentle face and tied with a yarn bow at the nape of her neck. Her round-necked house dress was brightly printed—something they were doing with cotton in the mills of Birmingham, England. Her complexion was so clear, her eyes so open and fresh, he felt that twist of pain in his belly. Gil had lied about her. The things he said could not be true.

She put away the broom and stood nervously brushing at the front of her dress, watching him. Her face was incredibly alive with her warm smile. He leaped out of the carriage, crossed the walk, shoved the gate open, and hurried toward her. He walked up on the steps, slowed, stopped with one foot on the porch, the other on a lower step. He stared at her. He said, "I know I said Saturday. I stayed away as long as I could."

She nodded. "I hoped you'd come. You're all I've thought about."

"I was pretty sure I was going out of my mind." He stared at her, trying desperately to read in her face some sign. God, wasn't there some way you could tell

326

about women? What they were? What they had been doing?

"I know."

"Could we—go for a ride—in the country—to the hammock?" he didn't want any misunderstanding about where he wanted to go, or what he wanted to do.

Her face glowed faintly pink, and she lowered those eyes under his; but she nodded. He felt the painful contracting in his gonads. He was going to have her. Soon.

"I'll tell mama," Lorna said. She went into the house; the door slammed behind her. She reappeared almost at once, as though she were running toward him as frantically as he sought her. She carried a fragile, wide-brimmed hat and a scarf. Lucinda followed her to the front door.

"Good morning, Mr. Baynard. How nice to see you. Lorna said you were coming in Saturday."

"Yes. I was in town. It's good to see you."

Lucinda nodded. She remained inside the door watching them until Ferrell handed Lorna up into his carriage. He went around it and got in beside her. He glanced back at Mrs. Garrity. How often has this happened? Some man takes Lorna for a ride on Saturday afternoon, and comes running back on Monday—Tuesday at the latest?

He glared at that perfect profile, so fragilely and perfectly cut, that hint of squared jawline and chin. What are you, he raged inside, the angel you look to be, or the hellion I'm sure you are? What kind of succubus are you?

She laid her gentle fingers on the back of his hand. "I'm so glad you came."

He nodded and laid the whip across his lathered horse. "Your poor horse," Lorna said. "You must have whipped him all the way in to town."

"I whipped both of us," he said.

"You sound—different. You sound angry."

"No. I'm not angry. Why should I be angry with you? Maybe I'm just anxious—to get out there again."

"It was—wonderful, wasn't it?"

As soon as he said it, he despised himself for it, but it

327

was too late then. "Did you enjoy it—more than any other time?"

She caught her breath sharply, and her head tilted. From the corner of his eye he could see her pallid cheek, but most of all, he saw the taut squared line of her chin. "Somebody has said something to you about me. Haven't they? Something to upset you?"

He shrugged. They passed the last house on the village limits, going along the infrequently traveled road. Spindly tufts of grass grew in the wagon ruts. He turned and looked at her. "Take your tits out."

She caught her breath, and something like pain flickered across her eyes. She sank her tooth into her lower lip. She turned, looking at him, her eyes misty. "Here? Now? On the road?"

"Yes. I want to see them again. I've thought of nothing else."

"I know. Me too." She frowned faintly, watching him, troubled and puzzled.

"I can't wait, Lorna. I want to see them now."

"Suppose—someone saw me—naked like that?"

His voice was hoarse. "They won't—and even if they did—they wouldn't believe what they saw—I hardly believed it—that's how lovely you are."

She sighed, slightly reassured. She smiled and touched his face with the tips of her fingers. The touch of her hand seemed to burn him. "You're going to ruin my reputation, Ferrell." But, he saw between elation and rage, she was reaching back to loosen the buttons at the back of her dress. "Do you really want me to?"

"Yes." His heart battered erratically. Why did he wish perversely that they might meet somebody on this road so she would see he didn't give a damn about her reputation, that he wanted her debased, that he wanted to prove to himself what she was.

"All right." She glanced back over her shoulder toward the village. Her face was pale. "I'll do it—if you want me to."

She unbuttoned the dress, slipped the straps of her petticoat over her bared shoulders. She let the dress fall so the fabric rested on the full, taut rise of her

328

breasts. She bit her lower lip, waiting, watching him.

He reached over, caught the top of her dress and pulled it down to her waist. She exhaled heavily and sank against the seat rest. Her creamy breasts, tipped with pink cherry nipples stood bared. She closed her eyes and let her head sag against his shoulder. He closed his hand on her breast, caressing, closing his fist until she gasped, pulled her over so he could nurse her nipple. "Oh, God, Ferrell," she whispered. "Oh, my God, you drive me out of my mind."

"Look at what you do to me," he said.

She leaned forward and stared at the bulge in his trousers. She reached over tentatively and closed her fist on it.

"Take it out," he told her.

She looked around, the woods, the road both ways. "Ferrell, are you sure you want me to?"

"That's all I am sure of. Take it out."

"All right."

She had no trouble with the buttons of his fly. He felt his throat tighten. He had been sure she wouldn't; with enough experience every little task was made easier.

She drew it out and caressed it. She sank her head against his chest, stroking him. He breathed in the sweet, fresh fragrance of her hair. The agony was so sweet it was almost unbearable. He put his hand under her bared arm and fondled her breasts. He found that the harder he closed his fingers on her breast, the tighter she held his cock, the faster she stroked him.

He turned the horse, going off the road and toward the hidden plateau under the great oaks. She looked around, recognizing the place and sighed. He said, "Why don't you take the rest of your clothes off?"

She turned her face up and kissed him. "All right."

She took her dress off, folded it neatly, added her underthings, leaving only her lace-trimmed underpants. "Take them off," he whispered.

She caught her thumbs under the top band and rolled them down. When she placed her panties on the neat stack of her clothing, she ran her hands over her belly and down her thighs, fingers splayed. "It feels good," she said, "being naked—for you. Knowing you want it. Knowing you like it."

He stopped the horse and swung down from the carriage. He tossed the blanket out on the ground and then took her in his arms. He knelt and laid her down on it. He slid his hand down her inner thigh to the wetness at her vulva. "Have you been out here often—before?" he said, voice taut.

He felt her body tense, but her voice was soft, "Not —here."

"But you've been out here before?"

"Yes."

"Like this?"

"Oh, Ferrell." She struggled, tried to pull away from him. He moved his finger faster on her clitoris and she relaxed, lying back.

"Have you?"

"Please, Ferrell, don't."

He moved his fingers faster. "I want to know, Lorna. I want you to tell me."

"All right. What do you want me to say?"

"Have you—fucked—out here before?"

She was silent for a breathless moment. "Yes."

"Often?"

"Oh, Ferrell." He closed his hands tautly on her, probed two fingers deeply into her. She gasped, but writhed her hips, involuntarily, pressing them upward, her back arched. "Oh, Ferrell, do it . . . fuck me . . . now . . . please."

"I'll fuck you when you tell me."

"Oh, they have hurt you, haven't they? They've told you—lies about me?"

"I don't know about anybody else, Lorna. I want to hear you say it. . . . You told me you've been fucked here—before. How often?"

"Once."

He moved his hand, driving his fingers into her. "How often, Lorna?"

Her hips worked spasmodically, her head rolled back and forth. "All right. Twice . . . but I wish I never had.

. . . I never liked it . . . never—not until you. . . . Oh, God, Ferrell, that's the truth."

He pushed her legs wide apart. She bent her knees, lifted her legs to receive him. He came down between her legs, pressed his glans into the mouth of her vulva, held it. "You've fucked before—more than twice—you put out, don't you, Lorna? You fuck because you're crazy about fucking?"

"No. No. No."

"You put out?"

"What do you mean?"

"You know what I mean. They come to see you. They take you out—like I did Saturday—and you put out to them?"

She closed her eyes tightly, rolled her head back and forth. The breath burst across her lips. "All right. All right. Sometimes."

He drove himself deeply into her. She locked her legs fiercely about his waist. He covered her opened mouth with his and thrust his tongue between her teeth. She nursed at it furiously. It didn't last but a few moments—they stroked furiously, driven, obsessed, and then they sagged together, clinging to each other as if they would never let go.

Ferrell's eyes burned with tears. Jesus! this was worse than anything he could have imagined. Between heaven and hell, that was the way Jeanne d'Arc described it in her native wisdom. That's where he was. He had his answer. Lorna was easy, because she couldn't help it. He knew what she was. He should be free of her, but he knew he was not. And more than that, he was sickly afraid now that he never would be. She drove him insane, and it was the kind of insanity he'd been seeking ever since he first dreamed of a girl.

They lay close together. He left it in her even when it was limp. She tightened her legs, holding him. She kissed his throat, his chin, his ears. He held her breasts as if afraid she might go away from him and he would never have their fullness and sweetness again. He pressed his nose into her hair, wanting its fragrance and hating the fresh air that ordinary people breathed.

"Ferrell, I won't ever let anybody else—touch me."

"Don't."

"You're afraid I've said that before too. . . . I never have, Ferrell. I was always looking—for somebody like you. . . . I might have made a couple of mistakes—but that's all they were—mistakes."

He felt himself growing hard again. "A couple?"

"Oh, Ferrell, don't." But she was smiling. Her terror and panic were past and gone. She knew someone had said things to him about her, but she also knew how terribly he wanted her—almost as terribly as she wanted him. She felt secure in his arms, nobody else could ever reach her there. No one else could ever tempt her when he was away from her—as long as he wanted her. She wished she could tell him that, but she felt warm and pleasant, knowing it was true. "Whatever I've done—it's past and over—and nobody could ever make me do it—but you."

He began to move in her again, growing rigid. Her breathing quickened and she responded instantly. "But you'd do it—for me, wouldn't you?"

Her heart thudded. "I don't know what you mean—yes, yes, yes, I'd do anything for you, Ferrell—anything you told me."

"I know," he said. He felt stronger and wiser and sexier than Solomon. He didn't have a thousand wives, but he had a thousand women in one in his arms. He controlled her. Whatever he told her to do, she would do. How could he stay away from her now? How could he make himself think of anything except her—except of being with her, like this?

When she drove him to the brink of insanity, he was saved only by the mutual simultaneous release that tossed them, spent, back on the blanket, holding to each other like children. He sprawled on his back, exhausted, afraid he would go to sleep because he was overcome with fatigue. He stared up at the sun sparkling distantly beyond the leaves of the ancient tower of trees. She lay with her head on his leg. She took his limp cock in her hand, holding it gently, studying it. "You're so beautiful," she said. "Did you know that?"

"Sure."

"Limp, it feels like a girl's wrist."

"You keep doing that and it won't be limp very long."

She was silent for some moments, stroking him gently, pulling back the foreskin to expose the reddened glans. She said, "Did you tell your sister you wanted me—at your next party?"

He winced, thankful she couldn't see his face. "Yes." This was a lie, but she would never know it was a lie. He was going to get her invited to that stupid party for the Garrett Blanford Wares. He couldn't get through it if she were not there.

He heard her delighted gasp. He felt her kiss his glans lightly and he gasped. "My God," he said. Then, despite himself, "Have you done that before too?"

She sat up, releasing his penis. That squared little chin tilted, her eyes flashed. "No. I've never done that before. I never wanted to. I never did, and you can't make me say I did."

He laughed aloud. He didn't love her—hell, he couldn't, could he? But he was sure as hell crazy about her. That was it. She had driven him out of his mind.

Then, she added in a soft, breathless whisper, "But I'll do it for you—if you want me to . . . as much as you want."

He felt his staff rising to rigid attention again. "My God, you'll kill me."

She laughed, holding it, stroking it in her fist. It hurt, but the pain was pleasurable. He lay back, letting her do it. "I'm really going to be invited?"

"Yes. Though I'm damned if I know why you'd want to be."

"When?"

"It's this week. Kathy will get an invitation to you. I promise you."

She kissed his glans again, parting her mouth. "Can I tell my mother that I'm going?"

"Yes. Yes. Yes."

"Oh, Ferrell, you just don't know how happy that's going to make her."

"Could you kiss it—again?"

She smiled. "For you—anytime." This time she slipped her mouth over it, closed her lips. He was afraid he was going to suffer a heart attack. She drew her head away. "You're not only beautiful," she told him. "You taste good."

"Oh, God, Lorna. Look what you're doing to me."

"I want to. You're so good to me. You can help me to be accepted by all the really right people—"

"Jesus, Lorna. You're the right people." He sweated. "You are. They're not. That's the honest to God's truth."

"I know they'll like me—if they get to know me—I am truly happy, Ferrell. Truly."

"Why? Because you're going to a stupid party—because you and your mother think you ought to. God, haven't you done enough things—trying to be something —oh, hell, you're a lovely girl—if you'd just relax and be lovely."

She heard only that she was lovely. She kissed his rigid cock again, lingeringly. "Am I prettier than any of the other plantation girls you know?"

"My God, yes."

"It looks like they'd want me at their parties then?"

He laughed, a helplessly frustrated, mirthless sound. "That would be the last reason they'd want someone like you at their stupid parties. They're trying to marry off their ugly daughters—and you'd make them look more like pigs than usual. The girls would hate you—because the boys would all want you."

She smiled. "I'd love to go to those parties, Ferrell— with you—to see the beautiful dresses, hear the music— and know that I am the loveliest girl at the dance."

"I don't know what you think those parties are—"

"Oh, I remember lovely parties, Ferrell. . . . When I was at Miss Amile's Finishing School—your sister Kathy went there, didn't she?"

"Yes."

"When I was there, I had such lovely times. I went home at Christmas with some of the girls. Oh, the parties, Ferrell—the way the boys swarmed around me."

"Is that the first time you fucked—the first time you put out?"

"Oh, Ferrell, don't be mean. Not now."

"Having a hard-on makes me mean."

She held him, stroked him, and chattered on. Her own daydreams and anticipations were about to come true. She didn't believe him that the parties were dull. She didn't want to believe him. Her mind had been closed to anything except the bright excitements her mother had sold her from childhood. He didn't care, he didn't listen. He felt her mouth when she suckled him, her hand when she caressed him. He nursed her breasts and probed her vagina and let her chatter because he knew she was happy, and her happiness pleased him. She sucked him hard, then lifted her head, staring up at him, her eyes brimmed with tears. "Oh, I love you so, Ferrell. . . . You're so good—so good inside."

He drew her down upon him. "You don't know how hard I try not to be," he said.

CHAPTER 32

ON THURSDAY MORNING Miz Claire woke up screaming.

She sat up in her bed sobbing like a child alone and abandoned in the night. Neva came running, waddling from the cubicle next to Miz Claire's bedroom where she slept—and where, since she'd grown older, fatter, tireder, and more pampered, she spent most of her time. She had been Miz Claire's personal body slave since she was eleven years old. She was eight years older than Miz Claire, but looked aged enough to be her mother, with cottony white hair braided in tight corn-rows across her head. She had devoted her entire life to Miz Claire, and it had not been an easy road, not a step of it.

She sat on the bed and took Miz Claire in her arms as if the white woman were still a small girl. "It's all right, honey, Neva's here," she whispered. "It's all right, honey. Doan you cry. Neva's right here—everything goin' be all right."

"Oh, God, Neva. I can't do it."

"You don't have to do nuthin' you doan wanta do, honey. . . . But you tell Neva. Neva doan know one livin' thing her baby can't do if she sets her mind to it."

"I'm old, Neva. I'm ugly and old."

"Honey, now you ain't ugly. You ain't evah gonna be ugly. Everybody gets old."

"But I looked so good, Neva. Just a few weeks ago. I looked in the mirror and I did look nice. . . . I was so proud. . . . But, oh, Neva, the skin on my neck—it's old like a turkey's neck. . . . Oh, God, I can't face people.

I can't have this terrible party, Neva. I'm too tired. I'm too old. I'm too ugly. I won't go down there. I won't let people see me like this."

She wept hysterically. Seeing she could not soothe her, Neva laid her down on the pillow, poured water on a fresh cloth, scented it with cologne, and bathed her cheeks and throat. When Miz Claire's screams and outcries subsided to heartbroken weeping, Neva called Shiva from Miss Kathy's room. Shiva came reluctantly in from the corridor. "You stay right here with her till I gits back," Neva ordered. "No matter what nobody says to you—nobody—you stay right at her side, or I skins you, nigger girl."

"I'm scared," Shiva whimpered.

"Didn't ast you if you scairt or not. You scairt of every blessed thing. A man is heavy hung and you is scairt. A man smiles at you and you is scairt. Ain't nuthin' about this pore little girl here to scare nobody. She just all hurt inside—like her heart's a-breaking. It ain't catchin' and she won't hurt you. You do what she asts, and I be back soon's ever I can."

Neva waddled out the door with Miz Claire screaming her name and Shiva pressed against the wall in abject terror. Neva waddled down the stairs her slippers slapping the pink soles of her aching feet. She yelled for Thyestes as she reached the landing. Thyestes was waiting for her when she reached the foyer steps. "Thyestes, you send somebody for Dr. Townsend this instant."

"Yes'm, Miz Neva. I do it. But we mighty busy—fixing for the party."

She brushed past him almost upsetting him when her shoulder struck him. "Nigger, you don't git somebody started for the doctor right now, you ain't gonna live to see no party. Now jump. When I speak to you, I don't like to speak to you twice in a row. Three times, I likely lose my temper an' bat you crost the head. You tell 'em I said it's bad—real bad—it's Miz Claire, and that doctor is to git out here fast as he can."

She didn't even bother to check to see that Thyestes ran on painful feet to do her bidding. She crossed the foyer and struck the closed study door with her fist. "Mast'

Baynard, I got to see you. Right now."

The door opened instantly. Baynard stood there, face drawn. "I know, Neva. I heard her screaming."

"Whyn't you come a-runnin' up there then?" Neva demanded, glaring at him.

His temper flared, but he bit back any answer. "I'm going up now," he said.

"And ain't a minute too soon neither," she said to his back.

Jeanne d'Arc came out of the study carrying the tray of used dishes. Neva stared at her, mouth twisted. Jeanne d'Arc simply laughed. Neva said, "Why ain't you in the kitchen where you belong, slut?" She went back across the corridor and began the slow agonizing ascent of the wide stairway. She clung to the banisters, but was breathless before she reached the landing. "Damn him," she gasped, pressing her fist between her copious breasts. "He heerd her screamin'. Whyn't he come? Oh, no. Gotta wait till I walk all the way down these heah stairs to fetch him."

Shiva stood, trembling, beside the corridor door when Neva finally made it back to Miz Claire's room. She was waiting to escape as Neva entered. When Neva stepped through the door, Shiva darted past her. Neva swung her hamlike arm, trying to hit her. "Thanks fo' nuthin', you no good little black wench. Lef' up to me, I'd of sold you off years ago. Wouldn't nobody nevah trusted you to be nobody's body slave in my day. A black gal had to know somethin'. Had to be smart. Gawd, the way things have done gone to hell these days—nobody worth nuthin'."

She saw that Baynard was sitting, braced against the head of the bed. He was holding Miz Claire in his arms, assuring her that she would be well enough to attend the party; that she would be the prettiest woman there—next to Kathy maybe; that she looked ten or twenty years younger than all the women she'd grown up with. But the more he talked the more disturbed Miz Claire became, restless, anxious, drawn tighter. Neva dampened a cloth with cool water, yelled to a maid to fetch fresh cold well water at once, and added cologne. She waddled over to the bed. "You jes' upsettin' her something fierce, Mast' Baynard. Bes' lemme talk to her. Bes' lemme explain she doan have to have no party less she wants to. . . . We call off that party in five minutes, if that's what Miz Claire wants."

Baynard withdrew from Miz Claire and stood up, looking relieved to escape. "Of course," he agreed. "Of course we will."

Neva glanced at him in chilled contempt. The nod of her head toward the door dismissed him. "I calls you if'n we needs you."

He stood helplessly a few moments and then retreated, closing the door as he went into the corridor. He found Styles, Margaret, and Garrett Ware at the breakfast table. Styles was eating fastidiously—one egg, two slices of bacon, one-half slice of buttered toast, and coffee. Ware was putting away eggs, ham, grits, potatoes with wheat cakes and syrup on the side as if supplying himself for the winter. Margaret's breakfast had been especially prepared for her, but she returned it to the kitchen for the second time because there was a trace of butter. She hated to be a nuisance, but those blacks simply had to understand her health was too delicate; she could eat no grease. None of them inquired about Miz Claire. Baynard felt the flaring of rage, directing all his frustrations against those smug and supercilious people stoking away the food.

Most of the family visited Miz Claire during the morning. Dr. Townsend arrived before ten. He came into the formal parlor from Miz Claire's sick room. Baynard and Garrett Ware were talking quietly. Styles and Mrs. Ware were engrossed in a game of two-handed solitaire. Dr. Townsend said, "I think she'll be quieter now. I gave her some laudanum. She's quieted. Left some with Neva. Don't give it to her unless she's very disturbed. We don't want to get her depending on laudanum."

"Laudanum, doctor?" Margaret Ware looked up from the card game, brow tilted questioningly as if she'd never heard the word. Damn her, Baynard thought, the rage boiling in him again, she knows what laudanum is. She just wants it said out loud.

"Laudanum's an opium derivative, Mrs. Ware." The doctor glanced toward her impatiently.

"Indeed?"

The doctor frowned. "Well, perhaps a tincture of opium. Term is used loosely. In the sixteenth century a Swiss physician and chemist named Paracelsus used the term to cover any remedy even based on the drug. I guess that's what we do today."

"Poor Claire," Margaret said. "She must be seriously ill."

"It's worse than a headache," Dr. Townsend told her almost curtly. "She's exhausted. Tired out. Too many demands being made on her—she tries to give too much—to people who don't know anything but taking. . . . I bid you all good day." He turned toward the door, then paused. "She's resting now, Ferrell," he said to Baynard. "You might want to drop up later and check on her. If she's—disturbed—you should call me again. We might have to discuss the planned excitement—it might be too much."

"Oh, dear," Margaret said. "It's too late to call off the party. . . . Anyhow, I'm sure Claire wouldn't want to do that. She should just force herself to get up and get about. She shouldn't let herself go like that."

The doctor paused in the doorway, glancing toward the large, rawboned woman across his shoulder. He seemed about to say a great deal, but he said only, "It's never too late to cancel a party, ma'am—even a children's party."

Ferrell-Junior opened his mother's bedroom door about eleven. He found Neva sitting, with one leg braced off the side of the bed, as she had been for almost three hours. Neva was holding Miz Claire in her arms. Miz Claire had just waked up, terribly thirsty, Neva told Ferrell-Junior.

Miz Claire gulped down the cool well water. She smiled up at Ferrell. "There's my baby, Neva. Our baby. You remember when he was born, Neva?"

"Ah remembers everything, honey."

"Oh, it was so cold. The coldest February night I ever lived through. Do you remember, Neva? That long, endless February night my baby was born. My beautiful baby . . . you were worth it, darling. Coldest, longest night in history. Wasn't it, Neva?"

"It was, honey."

"And Dr. Timmons arrived early in the evening. He's dead now. He was in Mt. Zion long before the new doctor came—Dr. Townsend. . . . Poor Dr. Timmons he did everything he knew."

"You was jes' one contrary baby, Ferrell-Junior," Neva said in a soft, gentle voice more to soothe Miz Claire than to inform Ferrell who had heard it all scores of times. "You was goin' come in yoah own sweet time —or not at all. . . . Poah, frail little mama. You didn't care how you hurt her."

"I cared," Ferrell teased. "I kept telling her I cared. I just didn't want to leave her."

"Oh, my baby," Miz Claire crooned. "My sweet baby. My first baby boy . . . and I worry so about you now."

"I'm all right, mama."

"I was just exhausted," Miz Claire said, returning to her memory that had changed from one of agony to one of anguished pleasure more pleasant than the present. "Poor Dr. Timmons . . . he was as tired as I was."

"Tireder," Neva said. "He fell fas' asleep. Couldn't no cannon of woke that white man. He sagged in that chair yonder and he snored up a woodpile!"

"Neva delivered you," Miz Claire said. "All by herself."

"That was a long time ago," Neva said. "I was young and a fool then. Wouldn't do it now. No way you make me do it now. . . . Thought then it was the thing for me to do."

At eight that night, Ferrell was surprised when Thyestes brought word that his father wished to see him in the study. When he got there he found Styles, Garrett Ware, and his father seated in chairs grouped near his father's desk. At his father's feet were two heavy carpetbags. Frowning, Ferrell looked up at his father's face, found it cold, unyielding, and set. "Sit down, Ferrell," Baynard said. "I thought you ought to be here. This does concern you. One day this estate will be yours to manage for the family. I decided you may as well know, firsthand, some of the problems I've faced, the decisions I've had to make, the reason I've followed certain policies, and why I am planning a definite program for our future—the only one that I think is truly feasible."

Ferrell sat down. There was an air of tension in the room that he did not understand; it was certainly not the festive air one associated with the night before a huge party. Except for his mother's emotional upset, he had never found life more to his liking. He'd left Lorna, singing, and he had been singing inside ever since. He didn't know what he was going to do in the future, only that his present was set—he was going to see Lorna as often and as naked as possible. He smiled to himself at this vagrant idea.

"First, I have an announcement which will undoubtedly astound Garrett Ware. I realize you have come to expect me to delay to the last moment my payments to your bank."

"I've never worried one moment, Ferrell," Ware said. His head bobbed and he smiled around the room. "I wish we had more customers as solid and reliable as you and Blackoaks."

"Despite your assessment you made earlier on its doubtful future?"

"What doubtful future?" Styles inquired.

"Our cotton," Baynard said. "It has decreased in quality. I have assured Mr. Ware that when we find the right seed—"

"I'd like to suggest, respectfully, sir," Styles said, "the kind of seed is not important—not as important as the land—"

"My thought precisely," Ware agreed. "Land that is tired, played out, overcultivated, lacking adequate water —fertilizers. . . . I only suggested diversification. . . . I may as well tell you, Ferrell, I am most favorably impressed by Styles and his ideas for making Blackoaks a stud farm for rearing quality blacks—fancies—for the market."

Baynard's face flushed red, then went deathly pale. Ferrell-Junior watched the pencil-sized vein work suddenly blue across his father's temple. With an almost visible effort, Baynard suppressed his rage. He said, coldly, "I'm certain Styles means well."

"Styles has the interest and the future of Blackoaks at heart," Ware said, "as do we at the bank. If you'd take our suggestion—from the bank as an interested party—you might consider Styles' suggestions, and Styles himself as your estate manager."

"Thank you," Baynard said in that deadly soft voice that meant he was seething with anger inside. "But I can tell you, Garrett, as well as my son-in-law, Blackoaks is a cotton plantation. It always has been."

"Sometimes we are forced to change where change is indicated," Ware suggested, smiling. "The bank, as an interested party—and I as an old and, I trust, valued friend—are interested in seeing you change policies which may be outmoded."

"Perhaps the bank—and perhaps you, Garrett—will have no further direct interest in Blackoaks after tonight. I have in these two bags the money to pay off interest and principle on my long-standing loan with Commercial and National Bank of Tallahassee. This should end your direct involvement in its affairs, preclude any further interest in its management."

Ware sat forward, craning his neck in its collar. "You're paying off—the entire debt? Ferrell, if you've made financial arrangements with some other institution, I know I mentioned something about 12 percent interest —we can certainly discuss that. It was never a final figure—we are open for discussion."

"Whatever my arrangements, Garrett, they don't concern you any longer, do they?" Baynard said. He pushed the two bags of money forward with his boots. "I know you'll want to check the amounts. I know you will— before you and Mrs. Ware leave us on Saturday."

"Ferrell, I cannot understand you. I detect an absolute

343

chill in your manner. A finality in your tone. I don't think I deserve that after all these years. I've believed we were close personal as well as business friends. Why, I've made every effort to be of service to you."

"At 10 percent interest, Garrett, I'm sure you found my friendship neither too distasteful—or expensive. Whatever you've done for me—I'm certain you've been amply repaid—at 10 percent interest."

Ferrell-Junior whistled softly between his teeth. Ware craned his neck as if on a witness stand. "I've explained to your father. We are forced into high interest rates— the loss, the risks. We service clients in different states—"

"Well, at least you won't have to worry about returning to Blackoaks next year, will you."

Ware craned his neck and stared at Baynard, stunned. Styles said, "Aren't you being a little rough, sir?"

Baynard shrugged. "Perhaps. Perhaps it's the sense of relief. Perhaps it's knowing I won't have to come up with 12 percent interest next year."

"I told you we could discuss that," Ware said. He mopped at his face. "You'll need capital, Ferrell. May I inquire where you hope to get it?"

Baynard studied the banker a moment, then shrugged. "I have assets I had not realized before—"

"My God," Styles whispered. "Blade. Moab. You expect to capitalize by selling Blade and Moab."

"I'll do what I have to," Baynard said. "As I said before, this is a cotton plantation. I add, with some pride that selling my whiskey commercially—as far away as Atlanta, Mobile, and New Orleans—has become quite profitable." He held up a quart bottle, labeled. "On the market my whiskey is known as Plantation Choice. It's a good whiskey, and often asked for. The label reads only, 'Bottled in Mt. Zion, Alabama.'"

"I congratulate you," Ware said.

Ferrell-Junior said, "So that's why you sold Narc— and Obadiah—and the others—to get up the cash you needed to meet this debt."

His father smiled at him. "I knew when you understood—"

"And you've been stashing it away in the chapel," Ferrell-Junior said, laughing.

"I don't know of a better bank," his father said. "Got the best nightwatchman in existence."

Ferrell laughed with him, but neither Ware nor Styles smiled. Styles said, voice shaking, "You can't do it, Mr. Baynard. Ten—even twelve thousand—may sound like a fortune—but you'd be throwing away a whole future of untold wealth! My God. You can't do it, sir."

Baynard stared at his son-in-law coldly. "We'll discuss it later," he said.

CHAPTER 33

FERRELL-JUNIOR AWOKE the next morning drawn taut with a sense of nervous anticipation. The day was bright with promise and shadowed by dread. The laudanum quieted Miz Claire, and she wakened passive and composed but prey to a hundred baseless fears. Neva had given her more of the drug this morning. Miz Claire let Neva dress her in one of her prettiest morning frocks and said she looked forward to her party. But she would not leave her bedroom, nor allow Neva to leave her.

Ferrell-Junior found the entire household oddly altered. At breakfast, Garrett Blanford Ware was polite, but restrained, vaguely wounded. His wife ate her food without comment and without returning it once to the kitchen. Hunt Campbell appeared nervous. He'd taught Morgan a short patriotic poem which Morgan was scheduled to deliver at the barbecue. Kathy awoke singing. She inspected her three beautiful new dresses made especially for the all-day party, and she looked forward to wearing each, topped tonight by the ball gown of four shades of green blended in the fabric. Most of all, Ferrell-Junior found the world a lovely place—the day promised Lorna.

He dressed, whistling, and thought about Lorna, as he had all night. She was lovely, gentle, and charming. The most caste-conscious had to recognize this. Even these hide-bound, intransigent snobs would have to accept her —because she was his guest at Blackoaks. He didn't give the first damn about any of their opinions, except for Lorna's sake. He didn't want her hurt. He grinned coldly at his reflection in the mirror. He wouldn't tolerate it. One thing he did care about was the impression Lorna would make on Kathy. He loved Kathy; hers was the only judgment he respected or cared about; he wanted Kathy to accept Lorna.

He exhaled. There had been a brief, hot skirmish with Kathy over the invitation for Lorna which would have to include her parents. "I want her here, Kathy. I want you to invite her."

"I won't." Kathy had shrugged, her tone final. "She simply isn't accepted—and for a lot of good reasons."

"Maybe. But I want her invited for only one good reason. I want her here. I'll boycott the whole dull shebang if she isn't here."

"Do you know people laugh at her pretensions? They think her father is a funny little clown? But it's her mother nobody can endure—because she's an absolute pest? I can't expose innocent people to Lorna's mother—people who accept my invitations in good faith."

"Kathy, you know you don't give a damn about those bores, any more than I do. . . . I can't think when I last asked you to do something for me that really meant a great deal to me."

"Ferrell, please don't get involved with her."

"Too late."

"Oh, God, Ferrell. Why?"

"Because she's got beautiful tits—"

She laughed at him. "That's two of the stupidest reasons I ever heard in my life."

He relaxed. She was laughing with him. It was going to be all right. "Is it? I never heard you deny that you were the most beautiful—"

"That's what I mean. Stupid. Pretty. Big tits. That's all people think. Being a nice person is more important—"

"No lectures, Kathy love. Just the invitation."

She gazed at him, troubled, but weakening. He caught her by the shoulders and kissed her. "Oh, damn you," she said. "All right, Ferrell, I'll invite her. But I'm going to tell father."

Every slave on Blackoaks Plantation was awake and busy by dawn. All washed with lye soap, all wore their

347

best. Even those who would come no nearer the big house than the perimeter of the plateau wanted to look their best. Their guests would be the carriage-, baggage-, and animal-handling slaves of the white party-goers. The body slaves would remain in the mansion with their masters and mistresses. Barbecued hams, chickens, and beef would be served in the quarters, along with cakes, pies, sweet potatoes, vegetables, and a second run of corn whiskey from Master Baynard's expanding distillery.

The house slaves all had been provided new outfits in honor of the occasion and as a quiet display of Blackoaks affluence. Thyestes' size-thirteen feet had been expertly and carefully measured and a pair of soft leather shoes had been sewn to accommodate his corns, fennels, wens, and ingrown toenails. Dozens of small boys, trained to bow deeply and often to the guests, wore new suits, identical in cut and color. The boys were under the supervision of Laus and he repeatedly warned them to stand straight, smile often, bow low, take charge of the horses, and never to pick their bottoms, no matter how hot and sweaty they became. Lined along the front steps, almost as alike as bronze coins, they grinned expectantly, stood straight, and tried to remember not to scratch.

Tables had been set in a squared *u* on the terrace and food was set upon it as tightly as possible. Smaller, linen-covered tables to match were stacked with silver, piled high with dishes, plates, platters, and glasses. A couple of barbecue racks had been set up, attended by resplendent black chefs just beyond the terrace. This was for effect, atmosphere, and display. The food was prepared, loaded on the tables, and covered with long bolts of cheesecloth.

The first guests arrived just after seven that morning and continued arriving until noon. The first arrivals came up the lane under the pecan trees, the young men ya-hooing, the young women waving their parasols, the children leaping down to run ahead. They arrived in buggies, light carriages, formal coaches. Their slaves rode behind them in wagons piled with small trunks as if they'd come for a month instead of overnight. The young men rode their best horses, racing in, yelling like marauding Indians.

Early arrivals were in time for breakfast—hot cakes, ham, fried and scrambled eggs, jellies, hot breads, fresh doughnuts, grits, hash-brown potatoes, fried chicken, and coffee, set up buffet-style in the family dining room. Chairs were placed along walls in the entire dining area and the corridor. The place reverberated with shouts and greetings, friends who hadn't met for months.

Kathy, radiant in palest yellow, Styles, and the elder Baynard greeted the guests as they came up the wide steps to the veranda. Each arrival told Kathy she was lovelier than ever, and Ferrell-Junior grinned crookedly when he caught her eye, taunting her. She smiled politely at her guests and secretly stuck out her tongue at him. Styles was 100 percent charm. The young and old females were captivated. But Ferrell-Junior saw that Styles was abstracted, still stunned by Baynard's decision to sell Blade and Moab in order to finance future operations at Blackoaks. Inside his mind, Styles sought some way to stop Baynard, and since there was none, he grew steadily more frustrated and impotent. Baynard himself was almost as charming as Styles. He apologized that Miz Claire was unable to greet them. He promised that she'd surely be recovered enough to attend the barbecue and the ball that night. "You know how she loves to dance," he'd say. "Nothing really serious—just a slight headache."

None of the guests questioned him, or pursued the matter further. Miz Claire's "indisposition" was well known in the region. Even people who didn't know the Baynards except casually, knew Miz Claire suffered occasional "spells."

Ferrell-Junior watched the Leander Garritys arrive in the Autumn Glades formal carriage. The vehicle looked seedy, the attendants less than polished. He grinned to himself, realizing he was being critical. But it was easy to criticize the Garrity cousins—from Leander to his three carbon-copy sons. And Phyllis—at eighteen she'd finally realized she'd inherited the less fortunate features of her rawboned mother, Miz Mabel, and her cockalorum father. Phyllis let her bitterness show in snide cutting remarks about everybody and everything. The boys, Charles, Robert, and William lived under the thumb of their mother, who wanted them to be little gentlemen, seen, but always mannered and retiring, though each was over twenty. It was Leander who interested Ferrell-Junior most, though only casually. Leander resembled his cousin Major Hugh, except that the major was red faced and outgoing, Leander pale, secretive, and withdrawn. Just the type, Ferrell decided, he'd cast in an old-fashioned melodrama as a defrauder, a forger. They passed into the house toward the breakfast area and Ferrell put them out of his mind.

Breakfast was served until ten-thirty that morning. The barbecue was uncovered, the black servants lined inside the u-shaped tables to assist in serving, at eleven-thirty. The meal was loud, boisterous, with people mingling through the crowds, carrying overstuffed plates, visiting as they ate. Garrett Blanford Ware thawed out by the time the lunch was served on the terrace. He had been stiff and withdrawn until other plantation owners of the area arrived. Ferrell-Junior realized after last night how easy it was to identify the estate people mortgaged to Ware's Tallahassee bank. One could recognize the debtors by the effusive way they greeted Ware, the way they laughed at his jokes, smiled obsequiously upon him and Mrs. Ware, and the way they listened attentively to the banker's pronouncements. By the time the meal was over, Ware had forgotten, for the present at least, that his pride had been wounded.

Hunt Campbell was a success with the women and girls, if not with the men. He got Morgan through his presentation and was going to allow Soapy to recite until Styles quickly stifled that idea. Women crowded around Hunt. Only Styles was handsomer, more courtly, and Hunt was a stranger—from New England. During the afternoon, Hunt had only one serious crisis. When the women and girls retired for their afternoon naps, the men lounged around drinking Baynard's best whiskey and smoking his especially imported cigars. Talk turned to the abolitionist named Colonel Ben Johnson who had once been one of them, accepted by them, welcomed into their homes, until he began to say that "niggers was as good as humans, and ought to be freed, and treated as equals. Johnson is asking to be burned out. There is talk of harassing him until he realizes it is wiser to move out of the region." Hunt spoke out in sharp protest, and he was baited, and finally might have been hit by at least two young hotheads had not the elder Baynard intervened, and warned them this was a party—and abolitionist talk was forbidden, even debate.

The married women gathered in Miz Claire's suite of rooms on the second floor. It was crowded, but with the windows thrown open it was bearable, if not really cool. The shouts and laughter of the children, the voices of the men floated in on the breezes. The younger girls were in other bedrooms, supposedly taking naps before the dinner party which began with punch and cocktails at six.

Miz Claire felt stifled. She kept sniffing camphor and sending Neva for cool cloths. She wished these women in hell. Though they said nothing, she was sure they were secretly laughing at her, how old she looked, how ill she was, how wrinkled her neck. She had to bite down hard at times to keep from screaming out. She sat close beside Neva, clinging to the fat, black hand.

Elloree Summerton was in her sixties, the oldest woman in the room. She remembered the first time she ever broke wind in Rube Summerton's presence after they were married—"almost forty years ago now, but I can still remember them terrible stomach pains."

The other women giggled and glanced at each other. Elloree was a caution. She was getting older now and didn't care what she said. She laughed, her double chins quivering. "I tried not to—tried to hold it in. I was so embarrassed I could have died, but my stomach pains were so agonizing I couldn't stand it, I had to do it. I still remember the look of surprise on Rube's face, and his voice was stunned with the shock in it.

"He said, 'Elloree, you farted.'

" 'What?' I said.

"He couldn't believe it. He said, 'You farted.'

" 'I broke wind,' I said. 'I had to. I couldn't help it.'

"He stared at me as if he'd been sold a nag instead of a filly. He just shook his head, accusingly, 'You farted, Elloree. Ladies don't fart.'

"Poor old Rube. He really believed that—along with other fool things our men believe about us women. He was terrible upset about it. He told me later he went to his father and told him about it, and how he felt cheated because I'd broken wind and women didn't fart.

"Rube's father was a good old man. A hellion. A real man. I used to think how much I'd like to go to bed with him, but I knew I never could—a scandal not even the Summertons could live down. But Rube's father told him right off, 'Now, Rube, you've got to have common sense. Women are just like us men—and darkies—when it comes to gas. They get flatulent—it's got to go somewhere.'

"But poor Rube wasn't that easy to convince. He kept insisting, 'But not ladies—' until his father told him, 'Rube, I don't want to hear no more about it. Ladies is just humans in tight stays, son. Their shit stinks, just like yours—even if everybody pretends it don't.' "

Kathy laughed with the other women and tried to hide her shock at Elloree Summerton's explicit language. Though Kathy had been married three years, this was the first time she'd been borne along in the current of matrons converging on Miz Claire's suite. These women —who displayed outrage at the least impropriety in mixed company—discussed the most intimate details of their marriages freely.

Kathy sat quietly, certain she could never discuss her problems with Styles out loud like this. She'd die on the inquisition rack before she'd admit that Styles didn't want her, that even if he did get hard enough to penetrate her, he grew limp inside her. She could never let them guess that only his cruelty to her aroused Styles at all. If he believed he hurt or debased her in any way, he could respond to her—mildly and temporarily at least.

She was thankful her face was flushed with laughter— and astonished perturbation—at Elloree Summerton's frankness. She was afraid they might guess from her agitation the upsetting tenor of her thoughts. To her surprise, they did turn on her at last, making her the target of their salacious remarks, the way hens turn on a bloodied chicken. Their voices clucked, their laughter scratched and clawed. But in the end, it was all in gentle fun. They didn't believe Kathy Baynard Kenric had a problem serious enough to discuss. They even laughed, telling her to enjoy her "perfect marriage" while it was perfect. You'll wake up on all fours some morning wondering what hit you, they told her, laughing. Kathy's marriage, they agreed, was still just like playing dolls, or playing house.

Kathy laughed with them. . . .

Ferrell-Junior sat on the stone wall enclosing the terrace and watched the foot races, the horse racing, the wrestling, horse-shoe pitching, and general horseplay going on across the shaded lawn. The afternoon was wearing away and the "town Garritys" had not shown up. He didn't believe it was like Lorna to miss a moment of one of these parties when finally she'd been invited. He wasn't yet too troubled. There had to be an explanation and Lorna certainly wouldn't miss one dance.

Something struck him hard on the shoulder and he said, without turning, "Hi, Gil."

Gil Talmadge hurled himself hard upon the wall against Ferrell, almost driving them to the ground. Gil said, "Hell of a party, Ferrell-Junior. Couple more drinks, I'm going to have to get me a woman, even if she's black."

Ferrell laughed at him. "If she wasn't black, you wouldn't know what to do with her."

Gil laughed. "I taught you plenty, didn't I? Member that time I got them five prize wenches on papa's place and we had that party—God, my pecker ached for a week." He looked around. "Hey, I heard something funny in town. . . . Heard that Lorna June Garrity's been talking around town that she was being invited to this party— by you."

Ferrell said nothing. He shrugged.

"You been riding that pretty good, haven't you, Ferrell-Junior?"

Ferrell-Junior shrugged again, staring at the games on the lawn before them.

"Hey, come on. This is me. What the hell is Lorna June Garrity—just another town girl. You're not falling for her, are you, for God's sake?"

"You talk a lot."

"Listen. I'm your friend. I tell you. You don't get mixed up with town girls like Lorna June Garrity. That's poison, old son. Where could you take her—except to the woods to flog it off?"

"Don't worry about me so much."

"But I do. You got to learn what people like us can do —and can't do. Hell, the word around town is that Lorna June is wild for you. She hasn't dated anybody else since you went out with her." He laughed raucously, "And her old woman—as far as her mother is concerned, you're unofficially engaged."

Gil laughed so loudly at this that the men on the terrace fell silent for a moment staring at him. Still giggling, Gil lowered his voice. "Look, I been thinking. We can have a party that'll be more exciting than that sex orgy we had with papa's black wenches. Satiday—tomorrow—you take ole Lorna June out to the boondocks. Get her buck naked on a blanket. Hell, you git your hands on her, and she goes plumb out of her mind."

Ferrell bit back vomitus. He had been about to tell Gil to shut up and get to hell away from him, but Gil had said the magic words that made him sick at his stomach. "You git your hands on her, and she goes plumb out of her mind." He knew this. Hell, it was common knowledge. Everybody knew Lorna June Garrity. He shuddered— even Gil Talmadge knew that if you got your hands on her, she submitted to you.

Ferrell slumped on the wall, ill. Gil went on talking enthusiastically, anything for a thrill, anything to break the monotony. "You git her buck naked and have her, and when you've had your fun, three or four of us good ole boys will be hiding out there, just out of sight. We'll take turns. A real gang show, Ferrell. Hell, she's the hottest little mink in this state—once we get her started, she'll be wild for it. Seeing three or four of us riding her will stick in yore mind the longest day you live."

Ferrell stood up. "Go on, Gil. Get away from me. You're full of shit."

"Oh hell, Ferrell-Junior. You standing against your *friends* for a hot-assed little town girl? Hell, the more she

354

gits, the more she wants. She'll go for it as long as somebody's got a hot poker to stoke her fires. What you say?"

"I say you're a stupid son of a bitch," Ferrell told him and walked away.

Gil sat on the wall, laughing after him. "Think about it, old son. You'll see I'm right. Best idea I had in years. You wouldn't want to cheat her out of a swell party, would you? And you know you'd love to see her taking three or four guys in a row—and gittin' hotter every minute."

Ferrell walked faster. But he knew he couldn't walk fast enough to escape the way these people felt about Lorna June Garrity. And he'd thought he could change them, make them see how good and beautiful she was. He saw now—family or neighbors—they were never going to change. He was almost thankful Lorna and her family hadn't shown up here yet. Jesus knew he didn't want to hurt her, and yet if she came here, there was nothing but hurt in store for her.

CHAPTER 34

BY SIX that night Ferrell-Junior knew definitely that Lorna wasn't coming to the party. He wandered the crowded house, the laughter-filled grounds, trying to put some sense into it. Unless something had happened to her, Lorna would be at this party in spite of hell. Nothing could keep her away. This was the kind of invitation she and her mother had been scrounging for all these years. He heard the musicians tuning their instruments. He stood in the wide-open French door and watched Kathy and Styles lead the first waltz. Kathy was glowingly lovely in a gown that was pale, almost gray-green about her shoes, a dazzling deeper shade that set off her pale-blonde beauty at the bodice. Styles had never been handsomer. Ferrell knew this by the sighs, whispers, and titters of the young girls lined near him.

Watching the dancers, hearing the music, seeing the laughing faces, he felt the anger gorge up in him. It was suddenly easy—looking at all the "nice" people having fun together—to know why Lorna June Garrity had not shown up. She had not been invited. He felt the rage seethe and boil inside him, compounded of hatred for these people, for Gil Talmadge, for himself, for all the false standards these people lived by. Jesus! is this what I am? Am I like these people—Cousin Leander Garrity and his boys, old Talmadge?

How could this bunch of country clods set themselves up as somehow better than their neighbors who happened to own fewer slaves, no slaves, or were in commerce— which meant they worked for a living? The fact that Lorna would have been as pretty—prettier—as brainy and charming and full of laughter, and a hell of a lot more fun to dance with than any of these girls wouldn't have been in her favor, it would have helped to destroy her. Still, he couldn't help feeling a kind of relief that Lorna hadn't made it here—and exposed herself to the scorn and contempt of these girls, the snobbish males, the unbending parents. Even these liveried house slaves might have treated her with disdain, for God's sake. They reflected the attitudes of their owners.

He missed her; that was the hell of it. If anyone thought it was clever simply to neglect to invite Lorna, they were wrong. He knew now how much she meant to him, how much he wanted her with him.

He pushed his way through the dancers to where Kathy was dancing with Link Tetherow. Ferrell tapped him on the shoulder. They stopped dancing and Kathy stared at him, wide-eyed, and Link protested. "Hey, this is your sister, Ferrell."

"I know a pretty girl when I see one." Ferrell-Junior managed to smile, though rage roiled around in his empty belly.

Link moved away reluctantly and Kathy held out her arms, laughing at him. "Why am I honored with your first dance?"

"Can we go out on the terrace?"

She laughed. "People will talk."

"I don't give a damn about these people, Kathy." His cold tone warned her that he was raging with anger, illy suppressed. She fell silent, walked ahead of him through the dancers and out on the terrace. There, she turned, and said, "Where is she?"

His voice was sharp. "That's what I want to ask you."

She shrugged, still smiling. "I said I'd invite her. I didn't say I'd personally deliver her at your feet."

"Kathy—you lied to me."

Her face paled. She stopped smiling abruptly and stared up at him for a breathless moment. Then she drew in her skirts and started to walk past him. He caught her arm. "Let me go," she said under her breath. Her rage matched his.

"Kathy, you knew what this meant to me."

"Yes, damn it, I did."

"If you invited her, she'd be here."

She was about to lash out at him. Her cheeks were pallid, her pale eyes chilled. But she hesitated, seeing the agony in his face. She sighed out, compassionate. She spoke quietly to one of the liveried servants, sending him for Thyestes. They stood in taut silence, music and laughter and the chatter of young girls swirling around them in the mellow darkness. The gray-haired butler limped out to the terrace and nodded, troubled, because he sensed the tensions crackling between Kathy and her brother. This was unusual enough to disturb and discomfit the old servant. "Ye'm, Miz Kathy?"

Her head tilted, Kathy said in a soft, taut voice, "I just want you to tell my darling brother something—that I'm not a liar, Thyestes."

Thyestes retreated half a step, looking pained. The last thing he wanted was to be embroiled in a dispute between the white folks, even two he loved as he did Kathy and Ferrell-Junior. "Oh, Miz Kathy. He joking you, that's all. Did he say that, he was jes' joking. Wasn't you jes' jokin', Mast' Ferrell?"

Kathy's voice tautened. "Did you deliver an invitation to Miss Lorna June Garrity in Mt. Zion?"

Thyestes didn't hesitate. He shook his head. "No'm, Miz Kathy. I didn't. I knows I didn't. Cause I didn't deliver no invites into town at all. All them invites went to plantation folks. You can ast Laus—he drive me around. And we delivered the last one."

Kathy's shoulders sagged. "That's all right, Thyestes." She turned to face Ferrell, contrite, but he had heeled around and was walking away from her across the dark lawn.

Ferrell-Junior heard the snickers and whispers of lovers hidden in shadows of gardenias. He heard the swelling shouts and laughter of the slaves at their party in the quarters. He went slowly up the knoll to the shadowed chapel. A pair of lovers grunted and heaved in the darkness

358

at the foyer. He turned away, walking out onto the moon-lit lawn.

"Quite a party."

Ferrell stopped abruptly, startled. He turned and Hunt Campbell grinned at him. "Yeah. We throw real bashes."

"Needed a breather. They dance faster down here, with wilder steps. Even the married women kick up their heels."

"I suppose so."

Hunt laughed. "What are you doing up here alone? You antisocial, or just withdrawn?"

"What the hell are you talking about?"

"You. Of all people. Out here—no girl on your arm—as if trying to get away from everybody . . . I just wondered why."

"I've got to take a leak."

Almost all the party-goers were bedded down for the night when Ferrell came in from the terrace, carrying a glass and what remained of a bottle of his father's whiskey. He crossed the parlor unsteadily and paused at the foot of the stairs, laying out a plan for ascending them without holding onto the railing or getting down on all fours.

"Ferrell." His father stood in the parted door of the study. "Feel like talking a few moments—maybe a night-cap?"

"Sure," Ferrell-Junior said. "All I need is one more drink."

He entered the study and fell heavily into the deepest, most comfortable leather chair.

His father poured him a jigger of whiskey in a glass, saw that Ferrell had his own bottle, smiled gently, and set the tumbler aside. "You weren't at your best tonight, Ferrell. I'm afraid you insulted quite a few of your guests. You weren't hospitable."

"I'm a Baynard of Blackoaks," Ferrell-Junior told him. "If I want to be rude—insulting—refuse to dance, tha's muh perogative. Got lots of perogatives."

His father smiled. "You've a lot of obligations too, old fellow. As you'll learn. These people are our friends. We must be polite, even when we're bored."

"Wasn't bored. Was enraged. Full of rage."

"I'm sorry about that. Anything you'd like to talk over with me?"

"No."

"May I guess?"

"You invited me in. It's your office. I'm your son. It's late as hell. Sounds like I'm at your mercy."

"I love you, Ferrell-Junior. You are my firstborn son. I've been proud of you since the first moment I saw you. Whatever I've done, it has been for you. I'd never knowingly hurt you."

"Tha's very kind of you."

"Son, I've seen something tonight that disturbs me deeply. Oh, not that you didn't ask any of those pretty young girls who had dreamed ahead to this party to dance with you. That you ignored their mothers, were curt to their fathers. They all love you—and they'll forget. I'm disturbed about what you are doing to yourself."

"Tha's very kind of you too."

His father laughed. "So cold politeness is going to be your shield, eh?"

"As Morgan so aptly puts it, what the fuck does that mean?"

"That I want you happy—as possible. That I don't want you hurt—unnecessarily. That I don't want you to hurt yourself. It's all right to have fun with certain—women, Ferrell. I did. But it is not all right to get involved in something you'll regret."

"Her name is Lorna June Garrity, father."

"I know her name. I'm sorry to say this, Ferrell. But your display of rage tonight convinced me that Kathy was right—you are deeply involved emotionally with this young woman."

"Well if I was—you all fixed it tonight."

"Ferrell, I'm talking beyond tonight. I don't want you to make a mistake that will not only harm you, but would hurt her in the long run."

"There's no long run anymore. You don't have to worry about that."

"I've come over the years to the conclusion, Ferrell, that there are two kinds of women—the good and the—

well, less moral. There must be truth in an idea that persists—"

"Stupid people don't ever let the truth get in the way of what they believe, father."

"I must say this. I hope you won't get deeply involved with a girl below you—socially, educationally, financially —in every way that counts. A family you'd grow more ashamed of."

"You too, father? My God, I never thought I'd hear you talk like this. Guess I didn't know you as well as I thought I did."

"I'd do anything to keep you from hurting yourself, Ferrell. You may as well know that. If my ideas sound old fashioned and perhaps not relevant to your world, believe me, I speak from experience—some of it sadly earned. And I speak from a great love for you."

"I know. That's why I can forgive you. That's the only reason."

Ferrell found younger children and boys on cots, mattresses, and folded blankets all along the upstairs corridor. Two young men were already in the bed they were to share with him. One was Gil Talmadge and the other Link Tetherow. Ferrell gazed down at them a moment. Gil slept with his mouth open. Link slept curled in a fetus position. He pulled the comforter off of them and walked out to the small balcony. He slumped in a rocker with the comforter about his shoulders and drank from the bottle.

He was asleep there in the first bright rays of daybreak when he awoke to the sound of frightened sniffling and somebody's shaking his shoulder in panic. "Mast' Ferrell-Junior . . . Mast' Ferrell-Junior. Please wake up. . . . Missy Kathy sent me. Made me come right in this heah room with undressed white gen'mums . . . I scairt, Mast' Ferrell-Junior. No telling what them white men do to me they wakes up and finds me in they room alone."

"Oh, for hell's sake, Shiva, shut up. You haven't got enough money to get them to do anything to you."

"You des doan know that Mist' Gil Talmadge, Masta. You des doan know him."

Ferrell-Junior laughed, nodding. "All right. Tell me

what the hell is wrong and get out of here, or I'll wake him up."

"Oh, please Mast' Ferrell-Junior, 'fore Gawd, doan do that."

"All right. Tell me what other reason got you in here?"

"Missy Kathy. She done send me. I tole you. She say to wake you up—and give you this. She say to tell you she sorry. She say to tell you I found it last night where it fell behind her secretary. She said to say she real sorry."

He took the invitation with Kathy's scrawling handwriting across the face of it, "Mr. and Mrs. Hugh Garrity and daughter Lorna June." He nodded, holding the large white envelope. "All right, Shiva. And you tell Miss Kathy I real sorry too. I real sorry—for both of us—for our whole damned family—and all our friends."

Shiva burst into tears. "Oh, Mast' Ferrell. You want me to try to recall all that?"

"I want you to get out of here. I'll give you to the count of three, and then I'll yell for Gil Talmadge."

Shiva bit the back of her hand in terror and fled.

CHAPTER 35

AT NINE O'CLOCK the next morning Ferrell-Junior was in Mt. Zion. He drove in his light carriage with his high-spirited horse under tight rein. The sun was already intensely hot; the big trees along Birmingham Street seemed parched early in the day. Ferrell pulled the carriage into the curb before the Garrity home. He sat for a moment, shoulders slumped round, staring at the empty street, the silent house whose windows reflected the sun like dead eyes. The quiet about the Garrity house was more than sleepy, early morning silence. There was a deathly stillness about it, as if the people inside it were awake but were not moving around because they found themselves without a goal, without the energy to do anything. Even the heavy pervading odor of gardenias and honeysuckle seemed funereal.

He got out of the carriage and hitched the horse to the post. Carrying the white envelope, he crossed the walk, went through the gate. He hesitated at the steps. The mute quiet of the house was forbidding. He crossed the porch and rapped on the door. There was a taut, extended silence before Mrs. Garrity opened the door. She stared at him icily. "Oh," she said. "It's you."

"Yes. May I please see Lorna, Mrs. Garrity?"

"Haven't you hurt her enough?"

"Yes. I won't hurt her again, Mrs. Garrity. I just want to tell her how sorry I am."

"It's easy for you young no-goods to come around saying—" Mrs. Garrity stopped speaking when her husband appeared at her side. He wore his black coat and derby, on his way to his bookkeeping job. His natural reflex was a smile for the guest. Then he realized who it was and he looked confused, dismayed, unhappy for them both.

Major Garrity stepped around his wife and bobbed his head at Ferrell without actually speaking to him. "Got to get to work, hon," he mumbled to his wife. He scurried across the porch and down the steps and hurried out of the yard, chasing his morning shadow.

"There's nothing you can say to me, Mrs. Garrity, that I haven't said to myself," Ferrell said. "I just want to see Lorna long enough to—"

"You promised her," the mother accused in that flat dead voice. "She told all her friends. She told them all. She bought a new dress—"

"I am sorry."

"Do you think that makes up for anything at all, Mr. Baynard?"

"No. I don't. I don't think I can make it up. I'm not going to try."

"Then why do you want to see her?"

"I would like to tell her—how sorry I am. I won't keep her at all."

Lorna appeared beside her mother in the doorway. She wore an aged housedress that hung loosely on her, she had not brushed her hair, nor put on any make-up. Her eyes were red and swollen.

Lorna sank her tooth into her pale underlip and stood gazing at him, without accusation, without warmth. Ferrell felt his eyes burn and he ached across the bridge of his nose. She had never looked lovelier, even in her nicest dresses and most becoming picture hats. She looked so clean, so beautiful, so incapable of the kind of cruelty he had inflicted on her. He wanted to weep, to cry helplessly. He wanted to take her in his arms. He drew a deep breath. He held out the invitation. "I brought you this. It's no good now. It's too late. But I wanted you to know. It was there. All the time."

Lorna took the envelope and glanced at its face without interest. At last she looked up. "Thank you, Ferrell."

"I can't say how sorry I am." He glanced at her mother,

but spoke directly to Lorna. "I won't bother you anymore."

He bobbed his head toward Mrs. Garrity, gave Lorna a ghastly caricature of a smile, and retreated. Mrs. Garrity's voice lashed out after him. "If it was there, why didn't Lorna get it?"

"It was lost, Mrs. Garrity," he said.

"Lorna's invitation—the only one that was lost?"

He paused on the step. He spoke slowly. "I know. It was *lost* on purpose, Mrs. Garrity. I know that now. What else can I say?"

She looked as if he had struck her. "Why did you come here—to say that?"

"I thought Lorna might understand. It might make it a little easier—though it changes nothing. It was lost. I didn't know it. I wanted her to know that." He bowed again and walked away toward the gate in the blaze of sun.

As he closed the gate, Lorna's voice stopped him. "I prayed all night that you'd come this morning—that there was some mistake."

He turned, gripping the gate pickets. He gazed down at her. "There was no mistake, Lorna. I wanted you there. They didn't. I couldn't change that. I thought I could. I couldn't. I didn't want to hurt you."

"That's all that matters, Ferrell."

"No. That's all that doesn't matter. Your invitation was *lost* on purpose. That's what matters."

"Can't we—go for a ride?" she said. "Can't we talk about it?"

"What is there to talk about?"

"You were hurt once—about what somebody told you of me. I told you the truth—and you loved me. Couldn't I love you—when you come and tell me the truth?"

"I can't tell you anything that won't hurt you, Lorna. I don't want to hurt you anymore."

"I know that. I know how good you are."

"Don't say that. I do hurt you. Everything I do hurts you—or will, sooner or later. There's nothing I can do that won't hurt you."

"You don't want to see me—anymore?"

"What good is it? What does it matter what I want? *They* won't let us. My family. The people who know us. It just won't work. Everything I do ends up hurting you—no matter what my intentions are. No matter what I start out wanting."

She drew a deep breath, placed her icy hand on his heated one. "All right, Ferrell. I understand. Truly . . . but can't we go somewhere—just this once?"

She looked so tiny, so miserable and forlorn. Delaying the break was only going to extend her hurt. But she seemed ready to crumble, as if she'd had all she could endure for one day, enough hurt. He nodded. He opened the gate and she gathered in her skirts and came through it without glancing back toward her mother at the doorway.

He helped her up into the buggy. He turned the light carriage in the middle of the street, heading east out of town. Her voice sounded dead. "Aren't we going—to our place?"

"No." He shook his head. "We couldn't ever go back there again—even if you were fool enough to see me."

"Oh, Ferrell, don't you know I'm fool enough to see you for the rest of my life if you'd only let me?"

He winced. He stared straight ahead but he didn't see the hot sunlit and shadowed trail, he saw only the empty procession of days and nights all the rest of his life without her. But it took no brilliant imagination to see what would happen to them if he tried to go on seeing her. He could still hear Gil Talmadge's hated voice at that party yesterday afternoon, "What the hell is Lorna June Garrity—just another town girl. You're not falling for her, are you, for God's sake? . . . You don't get mixed up with town girls like Lorna June Garrity. . . . Where could you take her, except to the woods to flog it off. . . ." Gil was an ape, a dirty-minded clown, but he put it in plain words for all of them—Kathy, his mother and father, and all the people he had to live among. Gil spoke for them all.

"I'm just not man enough," he said aloud. She had no way of following his thoughts. She laughed helplessly and said, "Ferrell, what are you talking about?"

"Us," he said. "Or I would. If I knew how to."

They rode out of the town limits. Lorna moved over near him, her hip touching his. He felt that emptiness, knowing this wasn't going to happen anymore. No other girl would ever know quite how to move over against him in such a happy little way that went through him and excited him. Such a simple thing, and yet he realized how much it meant.

She laid her hand on the inside of his leg. "Even when I hated you most," she said. "Even when poor mother and I waited and waited—and that invitation never came—even then, I knew I'd want you—always."

"Please don't."

"Don't you want me? I've missed you so, all week."

"My God, haven't I hurt you enough?"

"You didn't want to hurt me, Ferrell."

"I never *want* to."

She moved her hand, touching him. He grew instantly rigid under her caressing fingers. She closed her hand tightly upon him and exhaled heavily as if she'd been holding her breath for an interminably painfully long time. He looked at her. She was trembling. "Even if you're not going to see me anymore, Ferrell. Please. Just this once."

"We can't. . . . There's no place to go."

She stared at him, incredulous. "There's hundreds of square miles of forest—you'll find a place."

"No. No safe place," he said. "Not for us."

She laughed at him. "Oh, dearest sweetheart," she said. "Don't worry about us so much." She unbuttoned his fly, reached inside his trousers, and drew out his high-standing cock. "He wants me," she said, "even if you don't."

"He doesn't think straight. I try to. Somebody might come, Lorna."

She laughed again. "Now you sound like me the day you wanted to undress me on a public road. Now there's nobody in the world but you and me—and you talk like a prim version of me!"

She bent over and took it in her mouth, nursing it. "Oh, God," he said. "Don't do that!" She only nursed harder, taking it deeper. He looked around wildly, troubled. He saw no one along the trail. He saw the dim markings of a logging trace and he turned the horse into the lane, slapping the reins to speed it. She clung to him, her arms tightly about his waist as they rattled along the faintly marked trail deeper into the underbrush.

CHAPTER 36

THE SCENTED pine-forest breezes rushed past Ferrell's face as he drove deeper along the dim trail. Lorna clung to him, loving him with her mouth, jostled by the speeding buggy. At last, she sat up, puzzled. Ferrell's face was taut, strained. He held the lines as if he were running away from something—perhaps himself. "Please, darling, let's stop here."

He nodded and pulled the wagon into a copse of second growth. He glanced back over his shoulder. "What are you afraid of?" she said.

"Nothing . . . we'll do it—in the carriage. All right?"

"Oh, no. Don't be so formal and withdrawn—it's just not like you." She swung down lightly from the buggy, and looked up at him, smiling. When he hesitated, she reached under the seat, found the thick blanket, and spread it carefully on the pine needles. "There," she said. "Am I forward enough for you?"

He swung down from the buggy and caught her in his arms. She put one arm around him, but held his rigid rod with the other. "You do want me."

"I'll always *want* you," he said. He no longer cared about anything else; he had to have her. He had never wanted her so terribly. He held himself in leash with only the strictest self-discipline while he undressed her and laid her clothing across the front seat of the buggy.

She stood submissively while he undressed her, though she did go on holding him in her fist, milking him agonizingly. "Will you believe something?" she said. "I never wanted anybody but you—I never liked it with anybody but you. I wish to God with all my heart, Ferrell, that I'd never had anybody but you."

He didn't speak, removing her lace-trimmed underpants so she stood in the middle of the blanket naked. "Do you believe me?" she persisted.

"Right now, I'll believe anything in the world you want me to."

"Don't be mean. Not now. I wanted—something— whenever I let somebody touch me before. . . . I thought that was one way to get what I wanted from them. . . . I never thought about liking it—hurried and sneaking and empty. . . . But I want—this—from you."

"It's just hard to believe I'm that much different—or better—than anybody else."

She laughed and pirouetted before him on the blanket. "Why? Do you know anybody as pretty as I am? Anybody you want as much?"

Now he laughed with her and caught her in his arms. He drew her down to the blanket. She bent her knees and opened her legs to him. "Don't you want me to—love you —play with you first?"

"I've been crazy for you—for four days . . . you don't need to drive me any wilder. Anything . . . Anything you want me to do, Ferrell, you've just got—to tell me. . . ."

He thrust himself inside her and for a moment they lay still, clinging to each other, nearer tears than an orgasm.

They were so engrossed in each other they did not hear the rustling in the underbrush. It was not until they reached a driving climax, almost struggling off the blanket in their frenzy, and Ferrell fell away from her exhausted, that he saw Gil Talmadge and the others standing just inside the small clearing.

"Get out of here," Ferrell said to her. "Get in that buggy and get to hell out of here. Dress on the road. Anything. Get to hell out of here."

He lunged upward. Lorna turned over on her knees, ready to spring to her feet when she saw Gil and the others. She screamed, "Ferrell!"

"Get out of here," he said again from the corner of his mouth. "I'll hold them as long as I can."

On her feet, Lorna was paralyzed with fear and the terrible vulnerability of her nakedness. Her hand shaking, she reached down for the blanket, and lost her last chance to escape. Gil lunged forward and fell on top of her, forcing her to the ground.

Ferrell caught Gil at the collar and jerked him upward. "Stop it, Ferrell!" Gil yelled. "We goin' do it—like I tole you."

Ferrell hesitated. Lorna stared up at him. He gazed down at her for that long instant, unmoving. In that second, something happened in her face that would haunt him as long as he lived. Something went out of her eyes—they went on staring at him, but now they were dead and flat. Hell, that didn't matter now. All that mattered was that he get her out of this. He flung Gil away from her as hard as he could.

Gil struck on his knees and lunged up, cursing. "Hold that son of a bitch," he said. "He's crazy. . . . Take care of him, Arthur."

The huge black slave moved in from behind Ferrell. Ferrell turned, but this was as far as he could make it. The hamlike fist caught him in the temple and he fell against the buggy wheel. He stayed on his knees a moment, shaking his head, trying to clear it. But when he could see clearly again, he was tied to the buggy wheel, his arms between the spokes.

The other men stood over the rumpled blanket where Gil had Lorna on her back. Link Tetherow. Walter-Roy Summerton. Gil. And the slave, Arthur. They stared fascinated as Gil forced Lorna's legs apart. When she screamed, Gil backhanded her across the face. She sagged under him and Gil fell upon her and thrust himself into her. "Whip it, you little whore," Gil said. "Won't let me have it, huh? Too damned good for Gil Talmadge, huh? Told you I'd get you—and by God, we got you now. We all got you."

Lorna's head rolled back and forth. Her eyes were wild,

371

a look of sickness spread across her cheeks, graying them out. "Oh, Ferrell," she whispered. "Ferrell . . ."

Ferrell struggled and the horse stepped forward. Ferrell stopped fighting when he realized the slave had secured his wrists to the side of the buggy. If the horse was startled or moved forward, his arms would be broken. He held his breath, sagging then. There was a liquid weakness at the base of his spine, as if his backbone had turned to clabber. He bit back a sudden gorge of vomitus staring at them helplessly, watching impotently.

"Help me," she whispered.

Gil fell away from her and Link Tetherow jerked open his pants and thrust between her legs. She had been crying, but she didn't cry anymore. She lay as if dead, supine as Link had his turn and was followed by Walter-Roy.

Ferrell watched through a haze, figures without reality. His mouth tasted metallic, acid. He vomited and it spewed across his chin and ran down his shirt.

When Walter-Roy fell away from Lorna, Gil laughed. "Got me all ready again." He stepped forward, but Arthur caught his arm and shoved him half across the clearing.

"Me," Arthur said. His black staff stood rigid. "Me have it. Me have it now."

Gil yelled at him. "Get away from there, you damned black ape." But he didn't go near to stop him. Link Tetherow took one horrified look as the huge black man covered Lorna, turned and fled.

"Hell, I ain't staying here in this," Walter-Roy said. He turned and crashed through the underbrush, running.

Gil stood long enough to see Arthur reach under Lorna's hips and draw her pudendum up to his rigid penis. Lorna cried out, but Arthur closed his hand over her mouth and held her tightly while he stroked with his hips. Gil turned and ran. Finally, the Negro too was gone, loping through the undergrowth, and they were alone, unmoving in the clearing. . . .

CHAPTER 37

FERRELL WALKED in the earliest dawn light up the knoll toward the chapel. He had been burned out with fever for days and was still shaky. Physically, he was weak, but he was strong in his determination to follow a course he had finally, and agonizingly, set for himself. It had been a hellish two months, but it was over. For the first time he knew what he was going to do. He had reached that place toward which he felt now he had been racing all the days of his life. Every road had led to this moment, every turn and every detour had brought him inevitably here.

Reaching a decision had been agonizing. He had lived in a kind of ceaseless purgatory since that moment two months ago when he finally had freed his wrists after Lorna had been gang raped. His arms bled badly, cut and burned by the ropes as he worked himself free without startling the horse. Lorna had lain unmoving, sprawled on the rumpled blanket. He stared at her in terror as he worked, not even sure she was alive. It had taken a long time but he had gotten Lorna's clothing on her. She was breathing, but in a state of shock. She behaved as if she were in a catatonic trance. He carried her in his arms and lifted her into the buggy. He drove swiftly back to Mt. Zion. It was almost noon when they rode into town; the village was crowded at this hour. He drove through the gawking crowds of the curious lined along the street and the shaded walks. He looked neither left nor right. He drove to Dr. Townsend's office and pulled the rig into the rear of the building. He carried Lorna gently into the doctor's office. Dr. Townsend looked up, stared at Lorna, his face pallid. "Name of God. What monsters did this?"

Ferrell laid her down on the doctor's examination table. The doctor said, "Here, let me look at you first." He quickly wrapped Ferrell's wrists, staunched the flow of blood, told him he'd better wait in the reception room. In all this time, Lorna had not moved, nor spoken. Ferrell said, "I'll get her parents." Dr. Townsend agreed this would be a good idea. Ferrell found Major Hugh Garrity at Avery's Tavern. Gil, Link Tetherow, and Walter-Roy were there. None of them looked at Ferrell. He sent the major to the doctor's office and then drove along Birmingham Street to the Garrity home. Mrs. Garrity was in a rocker on the front porch. Luke Scroggings sat near her. The ugly, squat little red-haired man wore his Sunday best. He stared at Ferrell with chilled and implacable hatred. His face was so pale that the freckles stood in sharp relief like pebbles across his nose, cheeks, and forehead. Ferrell drove them in his buggy to the doctor's office. Mrs. Garrity went into the doctor's private cubicle where her husband awaited her. Luke Scroggings sat stiffly beside the corridor door. Ferrell sagged into a chair. They did not speak. The vomitus on his shirt was an unbearable stench by now—a sick-sweet odor that kept renewing his inner illness. Flies batted against the windows and sounds drifted in lazily from the streets.

At last, Dr. Townsend came out into the reception room. He peered at Ferrell coldly. "You might as well go on home, Baynard. You've done all you can."

Ferrell stood up. "Has she—come out of it yet?"

"For a little while. She's under sedation. She's suffering severe shock. I think it would not help for you to see her now."

Ferrell somehow got home and up to his room. It didn't help to pull off his clothing and throw it away. He showered with buckets of water that the servants brought and poured over him in a porcelain tub. But he was not clean.

He went downstairs to dinner, but when he sat down in the middle of the ordinary table conversation, he felt as if

374

the walls were pressing in on him. He put food on his plate but as he took the first bite he knew he was going to throw up. He barely made it through the kitchen and out the rear door. He sank helplessly on the rear steps. Jeanne d'Arc washed his face with cool cloths, brought him icy water to drink. He couldn't keep the water on his stomach either. He stood up, shivering with chill. She supported him going up the rear stairwell to his room. Thyestes helped him into bed. Alone on his bed, he lay awake, obsessed and horrified by his mind's relentless replaying of the scenes of the rape in that clearing. He kept seeing the light in Lorna's eyes when she looked up at him, he heard her screams. Her cries awoke him when he dozed off.

He kept going over it in his mind, trying to find some way he could have gotten her safely out of there. Even with the black slave concealed from view behind him, he should have done something. The four of them would have overcome him, as they did, but if he'd gotten her into the buggy, the fast horse could have gotten her away from there. If he had beaten Gil while he had his hands on him instead of just throwing him on the ground, this might have stopped the others. Over and over it wheeled and spun in his mind. Every replaying showed him all the things he could have done, the ways out of there. But he had lain helplessly. It was a vile and depraved thing they had done, and he was as covered with their vile as they. He hated those men, but he hated himself as fiercely, and he wanted to atone for the vicious wrong he had done Lorna, and he didn't know how. At every step she had given of herself to him, and in return he had brought her nothing but hurt.

Kathy came in on her way to her own bedroom, but he feigned sleep and did not talk to her. A little later, Miz Claire cracked the door. The corridor lamp light illuminated her there. She stood a long time, gazing worriedly at him. She finally closed the door and went away. He dropped off to sleep and woke up in the blackest dark, covered with sweat, certain he had screamed aloud in his sleep.

He awoke the next morning sick at his stomach. He did

not want to get out of bed. He felt weak and apathetic, unable to sleep and yet too tired to dress. However, all the household dropped in, worrying about him until he couldn't stand anymore. He got up, went stealthily down the rear stairs and out to the barn. He had a horse saddled and spent most of the day riding old trails he'd explored long ago with Tharus. God, it had looked like a different world then—clean, beautiful, and full of promise.

When he came into his bedroom in the dusk, Kathy stood at the window. She turned when he entered. He winced, not wanting to talk to her—or to anybody.

"Something terrible has happened, hasn't it?" she said.

"I don't feel like talking, Kathy."

"Something about Lorna Garrity."

"Please, Kathy."

"I love you, Ferrell. I don't want to see you hurt like this. I'm sorry—about what I did."

"It's all right."

"No. It isn't. We thought it was best. We thought you'd be mad—and get over it."

"I forgive you."

At last, she went away. He fell across the bed and stared, wide-eyed, at the ceiling until he fell asleep from exhaustion. Lorna was there in his dreams, begging him to help her, screaming, pleading, crying, and he lay unmoving. He awoke a little past 2:00 A.M. and tossed sleeplessly until dawn.

The next morning he rode into Mt. Zion. Lorna was at home. Luke Scroggings sat in cold silence on the Garrity front porch. Neither the major nor Mrs. Garrity would see Ferrell. Dr. Townsend came out, dry-washing his thin pink hands. "It won't help *her* to see you, Baynard. I don't see how it can help you."

When the doctor went back into the house, Luke Scroggings spoke to Ferrell for the first time. "Stay away from here. You've hurt her enough. Stay away."

The days after that passed heavily, like stones dropped one after another. Word reached Blackoaks that Major Garrity had sworn out warrants charging Walter-Roy Summerton, Gil Talmadge, and Link Tetherow with assault and rape. No mention was made of the Negro slave.

Ferrell knew no mention would ever be made of Arthur. But he was stunned that his own name was not mentioned at all. Fletcher Talmadge drove up the lane, raging. He strode up and down in Baynard's office with the elder Baynard, Gil and Ferrell looking on in silence. "That goddamn sheriff and his deputies come out. Going to arrest my boy. For what? I ast them, for what? For diddling some cheap town girl that ast for it? What in hell else you suppose to do with them hot-assed little tramps that come around throwing themselves at our boys? Little bitch. Out there with them boys. She was buck naked. What's she think they were gonna do—play drop the handkerchief? I told the sheriff and them deputies, by God, they could arrest my son—reckoned I couldn't stop 'em. But I warned them I knowed more about what that little bitch had done—and with who she'd done it. I tole them they better warn her old man off before it was too late to back out. I tole them I'd blacken that cheap little town bitch till she'd regret it the longest day she lived. Well, they backed down. They went away—ain't heard no more. But, by God, I mean to fight 'em. A boy out for a little fun with his friends—and it ends up with them making a mess like this."

Ferrell got up and walked out. He prowled the plantation, plodding across the autumn fields, wandering along the loneliest pigtracks. Old Man Talmadge said it all for the plantation people. They didn't even consider for one second the harm they'd done Lorna; they didn't care. Three young bucks out for a wholesome good time. So, a town girl got herself hurt in the bargain. Too bad, but not too important—unless she tried to make trouble for her betters.

Ferrell sweated. He felt as if his own skin were too tight, as if he could not breathe inside his own constricted rib cage. Somehow he had to break free of the guilt and the vile and the agony that obsessed him.

He could kill them. He wanted to kill them all. He could kill the slave, Gil Talmadge, Link Tetherow, Walter-Roy. Only this violence would efface the ugliness of what they'd done. As long as they lived to share the filthy secret of that rape, he could not live at peace within himself. He wanted to kill them, but even as he thought this, he saw that it would in no way ameliorate the tragedy, only compound it. This was demonstrated conclusively to him when Gil Talmadge showed up alone at Blackoaks about three weeks later. Gil swung down from his buggy and, laughing, struck Ferrell sharply on the arm. "Don't do that," Ferrell told him. "Don't ever do that again."

Gil frowned, then laughed. "Come on, don't be sore. Hell, my old man says you ain't with us. I told him he was full of crap. So—we were a little rough on you. We didn't mean no harm. We had the hots. There she was naked and begging for it. What the hell."

Ferrell strode away from the house, and Gil trotted catching up with him. They walked up a knoll overlooking the fallow fields. Gil said, "Hey, Ferrell-Junior. You heard the latest—about Lorna Garrity?"

"No." Ferrell's heart sank at the sound of her name.

Gil laughed again. "Ole Lorna got married."

Ferrell bit back hot vomitus. His stomach was wracked with dry heaves. He kept walking, damned if he'd let Gil see him so helpless. He couldn't believe Gil could chat so lightly about Lorna, feel no guilt, no regrets, no compunction—and not a trace of compassion. Gil remembered only a high old time that had gotten out of hand and almost resulted in a hairy scandal for him and his friends. He was laughing now as he talked, the whole thing behind him. "That's right. She married ole Luke Scroggings. The bank clerk. Married in the Catholic church, for hell's sake—like she was a purentee virgin, by God. . . . I know one thing. In the Baptist church, we don't have high masses in Latin and all kinds of confession and hocus-pocus, but we have some idea of decency—no slut like that would be married—after she'd been screwed by a nigger— right in the church. . . ."

Ferrell's fists clenched, his nails digging into his palms. Get out of here, Gil, he thought, raging, or I'll kill you. I swear to God, I'll kill you. But he said nothing. He walked silently, and Gil chattered on, unaware of his seething inner rages.

"We heard about the marriage down at Avery's. Ole Major Garrity has stopped coming in down there on

Saturday. Hell, they say he broke down crying at work and even lost his job. Walks around town talking to hisself. But word comes to Avery's Tavern on just about everything going on around this place. Me and eight or ten good ole boys got likkered up and decided to put on an old-fashioned chivaree for them newlyweds. We followed them home from the church, yelling and singing. Thought old Mrs. Garrity would break down right there on the street. People in town nearly busted their guts laughing. We stood outside the Garrity house for hours. Old Mrs. Garrity pulled down all the shades. They say she ain't put 'em up since—and hardly goes out of the house. Hell, no wonder, people laughing at that slut daughter of hers. About ten o'clock all the lights in the house went out. Somebody yelled. "I'll bet ole Luke Scroggings has got it where nobody has ever had it before!' I tell you, we laughed and yelled till we fell down laughing. Then old Major Garrity comes running out on the porch with a shotgun. He was crying and cursing and carrying on. He started shooting. Loading and shooting wherever he heard a sound. Hell, I got away easy, but Herbert-Ed Onslow and one of them plantation Garrity boys got full of buckshot—the damned old bastard—shooting a gun like that."

Ferrell stopped walking. He stared at Gil. The son of a bitch had no sense of moral right or wrong. Killing him would solve nothing. Just as you might kill a rat for stealing corn in a barn. You'd stop its stealing corn, but the rat would die without any faint understanding of theft, or right or wrong. Where a conscience should be, Gil had only a vacant place. Killing Gil might destroy old man Fletcher Talmadge, but Gil would die without a sense of anything except how wrong and evil it was that he was shot—a good old boy trying to be sure everybody had a laugh. Ferrell said, "You better go, Gil . . . and stay away from me . . . from now on."

"Come on, Ferrell-Junior. This is me. Ole Gil. Hell, you know I regard you highest of anybody I know—"

"Stay away from me, Gil, or I'll kill you. I swear I'll kill you. . . ."

But now he knew that killing wasn't the answer. They might deserve to die—the three of them—but not if their deaths in no way atoned for their evil. Maybe they deserved to live—if only they could be forced to live with a sense and an understanding of their own depravity and evil. This was beyond him. There was no way that he knew to make the insensitive aware, to make the amoral sensitive to his own wrong-doing. Still, he could not go on living in the same community with them and their fearful hypocrisy.

Returning to the house, he tried to go quietly to his own room across the terrace where Hunt and Morgan were studying, and through the sun room. But his father's voice halted him at the foot of the stairway. In his father's study, the elder Baynard motioned him toward a chair, but Ferrell went on standing. "I'm worried about you. Very worried. This business with the Garrity girl—are you in some way involved? You were not charged. But I know something has you physically ill—and emotionally tormented. I want you to tell me—has it anything to do with the assault on the Garrity girl?"

"Yes. I was there."

Baynard retreated half a step. He looked as if his son had struck him fiercely in the solar plexus. He gasped for his breath. "You—were—with them?"

"I was there, with her—tied up."

"You fought them?"

Without mentioning the Negro slave, it was difficult to present a convincing argument that he had opposed them forcefully. "I tried."

Baynard shook his head. "You fought against your friends?"

"Friends? Rapists, vicious thugs?"

"Your own kind, Ferrell—the people you live among. You fought them?"

"I tried to stop them."

Baynard paced the worn carpeting. "You're lucky they haven't turned against you."

"Jesus, papa. I never thought I'd hear you talk like this—"

"I'm trying to tell you about the *real* world we live in, Ferrell. The people we have to live among—not the world of the ideal society—the way we might like to be—"

"Or that we pretend with such hypocrisy that it is—a place where all men have honor, all women are virtuous—"

"Our women are virtuous—"

"Our women! Our women are sisters to Gil Talmadge and Link Tetherow!"

"They are ladies. . . . We protect their virtue, their honor. Perhaps we don't feel the same about town women. We're not all equal, Ferrell—"

"I don't want to hear this. I won't be part of it."

"You are part of it. Be thankful you were born in a superior class. You are part of that class."

"Then to hell with it."

Sometime before dawn he fell asleep. He awoke suddenly with a start, conscious of someone near him. He opened his eyes, shivering. Miz Claire sat on the edge of his bed. She touched his forehead gently with her fingers. Her eyes were troubled. "Are you all right, Ferrell?" she said. "I heard you moving around all night. I couldn't sleep."

"I'm all right, mama. Don't worry about me. There's nothing you can do. Nothing anybody can do."

"Won't you talk to Father Anthony?"

"Your priest? About what?"

"He'll help you, Ferrell. He's helped me—through great evil. Things I could not have stood—without help. Things I couldn't tell you . . . things I wouldn't tell you."

She persisted and he promised to talk with the priest. He would have promised anything to be rid of her. He spent the rest of the week in torment. He kept going over in his mind the way Luke Scroggings had married Lorna at the earliest possible moment. The ugly little red-headed man had done the one thing that showed courage and innate decency—the one thing Ferrell Baynard hadn't even considered. Luke had married Lorna to protect her. Luke loved her.

Ferrell tossed restlessly on the rumpled bed. One truth stood out in painful clarity—Luke Scroggings didn't love Lorna any more than he did. Scroggings had something

381

he didn't have—the guts to face these people for the rest of his life as Lorna's husband.

Ferrell stared at his trembling hands. In God's world, once in an eon two snowflakes *were* identical, and two people were made only for each other. Too late he believed this was true of him and Lorna. No matter what outside forces affected them, Lorna was perfect for him, and she alone. If God had a plan, their being together must have been part of it. The Greek myth had it that male and female once had been a single entity, and now each divided half spent eternity seeking the matching part of his own self. For a little while, he'd found this with Lorna. When he destroyed what they had, he destroyed himself. . . .

He had no answers. Alone, he could find none. Perhaps he could talk to Father Anthony. He had no faith in what Father Anthony purveyed, but maybe somebody in this screwed-up existence could offer values he was able to accept and live by. But when Sunday and Father Anthony arrived, Ferrell stayed in his room and watched the young priest lead the small procession of family, neighbors, and slaves toward Miz Claire's chapel on the knoll.

Ferrell stared down at the priest. Something in the quiet demeanor of the cassock-shrouded man shook him profoundly. Perhaps it was his own inner confusion, his grabbing at straws, but Father Anthony exuded a sense of calm—a serenity that deeply impressed him. He watched the procession disappear inside the church, admiring the tranquil composure of the priest. He wished with all his heart that he could embrace a faith that let you confess, unburden your guilt, cry aloud your anguish, and then go out and start afresh. He envied the young priest, but he had nothing to say to him. . . .

He decided he'd better dress and get away from the house before the services ended and his mother brought the priest up here to him. He turned from the window, reached for his shirt, and doubled over, retching. Intense pains roiled in his lower abdomen. He shook with chill, burned with fever. Nauseated, he reached for the chamber pot beneath the bed. It had not been emptied for the morning and the hot amoniac smells struck his nostrils and he retched again. He sagged to the floor in spasms of pain.

Kathy found him. She summoned half a dozen servants and directed them efficiently. The chamber pot was emptied, scrubbed, refilled with fresh water. The room was mopped, windows opened, beds remade, fresh night clothing awkwardly forced upon him, only to have him heave and vomit again as soon as he lay down in fresh bedding. Kathy simply started the slaves to cleaning again and sent for Dr. Townsend. The doctor arrived late that afternoon, unhurriedly. He walked around Ferrell's bed, checked the fevered eyes and the arrhythmic pulse. He gave him laudanum, finally. When they were alone, the doctor said, "Let's be honest, boy. Kind of sick you are, I can't help you."

Ferrell drew the back of his trembling hand across his dehydrated mouth. "I'm burning up—freezing—at the same time."

"You'll be all right. You'll recover—when you make peace inside yourself. You're throwin' up because you want to throw up. You want to throw it all up, eh? Only you don't know how."

"Help me."

"I wish I could say, I wished I could help you. But I don't even wish that, boy. I figure God has some ills He don't want me fooling with—an' you got one of 'em, far as I can see. I'll leave some laudanum for you with your sister. . . . Maybe in time you'll start to live on that. . . . That's one way out."

Ferrell's head rolled on his sweated pillow. "You can stop, doctor. You can't hate me any worse than I hate myself."

"Hate yourself, do you? Well, maybe that's the beginning of wisdom. . . . But I don't hate you, boy. You ignorant people—and I don't care a damn how educated you are—who think you're better than anybody else because you own more land, more slaves, more horses—I don't hate any of you. . . . I pity you—when I think about you at all —but I don't hate you. . . ."

Kathy came back into the deepening dusk. She brought a bowl of soup from which she tried to feed him. But he threw up the first spoonful. It spewed out of his mouth and he was helpless to stop it. She sent the soup away, had him cleaned up, and then sat in a rocker beside his bed until his breathing convinced her he was asleep.

When she was gone, he did fall into a fevered, fitful, disturbed sleep. He cried out, ground his jaw teeth, and fell from one side of the sweated mattress to the other. He'd waken icy cold, curl under blankets, and finally sleep, only to reawaken, feeling as if he were being parboiled in his own sweat.

He had no idea how long he was ill with fever. The dawns lightened the room, the noon sun heated it, the darkness hid it again, and he lost count of the days because he did not care. Whenever he awoke, Kathy sat near his bed, keeping constant vigil. She no longer tried to talk to him. He withdrew deeper and deeper into himself. He reached the place where he was nearer dead than alive, dehydrated by vomiting, unable to keep food or liquids on his stomach. Miz Claire sent for Father Anthony. But it was in this unreal existence between life and death where nobody outside could reach him that he found a way back.

He would get away. He had to find a sanctuary away from Blackoaks and all the people he knew. His father's values could never be his. He could never accept—or live by—the standards of men like Gil and his good ole friends. From the first he'd had no way of sharing Lorna's world—without a complete break from his own. He hadn't the guts for this totally altered life, or felt the need for it, until it was too late. He had taken her because he wanted her, never considering what he was doing to her. He had hurt her so terribly she might never really recover, but he could not make it up to her. There was no way. Killing Gil and Link and Walter-Roy would in no way replace what they had cost her. He'd wanted to kill them because unless they died he could not live in peace in this place. Theirs was a filthy secret he could not share. But he couldn't kill them. He couldn't kill anybody. He could only somehow take the only alternative left open to him—he could somehow get away from them, somewhere find a sanctuary. Whatever this world of theirs was, it was too tough for him, too ugly, too vicious, too filled with duplicity and casual cruelty. He had to get away; he had to atone, to make amends, to pay terrible penance. Only in this way would he ever find peace—within himself. And so he made his decision that no one could turn him from.

Now, he entered the chapel. It was lit yellowly, with innumerable tall candles, glowing in the early morning. He saw Miz Claire, crouched alone, on her knees in the first pew. She looked so small, so vulnerable, huddled in prayer. He stood for a long time until she finished praying for whatever her needs were. When she sat back, her hands folded in her lap, Ferrell walked down the aisle. She looked up, startled. "Oh, thank God," she said. "I prayed you'd get well."

He took her hands, kissed them. He sank to the bench beside her. "Mama, I want to talk to you. Try to understand what I'm going to do. I'm going into your church—"

"Of course, darling. Anytime. Why, it's your chapel as much as mine. I built it so my children—"

"Mama. Listen. I'm going into your church. The Catholic church. I want you to write a note to Father Anthony for me. I'm going into the seminary—into the priesthood."

She stared at him for a long time, delighted, terrified, already bereft. "How pleased Father Anthony will be," she said at last. "Now he'll know I truly am converted—a part of our church. . . . I'm giving my son—my dearest son."

"Mama, please don't try to make anything like that out of this. . . . I'm not going in for any reason—except I'm running away, mama, from things I can't face."

She nodded. "We all run away," she said gently. "Sometimes that's all we can do—to save ourselves. . . . You'll be a good priest—because you're a good person—"

"Don't, mama. . . . I wish—for your sake—I could honestly say I feel—called—into the church. . . . I don't."

She smiled wanly and nodded. "It's all right. God moves in mysterious ways. . . . Who can say why he does God's will?"

CHAPTER 38

THE CHILL winter rains set in about the time Ferrell-Junior departed from Blackoaks to enter the priesthood. It seemed to the elder Baynard that the winter dankness and his son's leaving him had come in the same grievous moment. He was always cold; it was impossible to find warmth. He had never slept well at night. Now he slept only fitfully, if at all. He prowled the silent house during the late-night hours, not even knowing what he was looking for. Sometimes in the blackest hour before dawn he would find himself standing chilled and desolated in his son's bedroom, simply staring at the carefully made-up, empty bed. The room was empty, the house was empty, the world was empty without Ferrell. His eyes filled with tears, and he let them well and ooze along his cheeks, unashamedly. He wept for Ferrell, but unhinged and unnerved, he wept mostly for himself, his lost dreams and plans that suddenly had no relevance. "I have no son," he whispered in the darkness.

He tried to conceal the emasculating rages and frustrations that simmered deep inside him. He was seldom without a debilitating pain in his chest, cramps in his abdomen, headaches that would not subside. He struggled diligently to keep anyone in the household from guessing the truth, but he was almost incapacitated by impotent anger all the time. Fury bubbled fiercely under the thin crust of his desperately cultivated civility, ready to erupt. He would have cried out in mortal pain and smashed everything within reach except that he never slackened his taut control of his crippling emotions. At the least obstacle, the first sign of friction or counteraction, he felt compelled to yell out in wrath, to weep in exasperation, to snarl in irritation, but he kept it all tamped down. On the surface he was more polite and considerate than ever and he was famous for his genteel and courtly demeanor.

He found temporary surcease only in those two or three quiet hours with Jeanne d'Arc behind the closed door of his study while his family slept at dawn. He could talk to her as he could to no one else. Only she understood the terrible impact his son's departure had had on him. He talked, ramblingly, of his old dreams and future plans that had given his life purpose, and tentatively, he tried to formulate in words his ideas for the future in which Ferrell-Junior could be no part. But even this time stolen with Jeanne d'Arc was a kind of frustration, perhaps the worst kind. She had no answers; he expected her to have none, but talking with her showed him most glaringly how little hope there was now for him, for what remained of the family, for Blackoaks. Though Ferrell-Junior had always been at the heart of all his preparations for the future, he'd never before been forced to face how totally all planning was anchored to his son. Without Ferrell, he could only drift from one empty day to another.

There seemed so little purpose in any of the daily chores he'd always handled automatically. The cold showers with which he'd begun his day for as long as he could remember were neglected. Some mornings he didn't even bother to call Thyestes in to shave him. He was unsettled by baseless misgivings that somehow the plantation suffered from lack of the dedicated management he'd always provided it. He'd get up long before dawn, even in the rain, and ride a horse across the weed-grown winter acreage, driven by apprehensions he could not explain, even to himself.

He could not relax. If he sat on the terrace, there occurred to him some task somewhere demanding immediate attention. He assumed duties best left to Pilzer and handled more efficiently by the overseer. For some reason his stomach always felt queasy though he ate less than he ever had. He seldom even finished one of his favorite hot cinnamon buns which Jeanne d'Arc brought to his study faithfully every morning. He drank more black coffee because he suffered those chronic headaches lately for which coffee was the only antidote.

He would stalk out onto the terrace on good days, or into the sun room during the winter rains, and stand silently while Morgan struggled, trying to read the simplest complete sentences. Baynard's eyes filled with tears, but he was honest enough to admit those tears were only partly for Morgan. He wept for himself too.

One morning when he paused in the sun-room doorway, Hunter Campbell glanced across his shoulder and discovered him there. Hunt told Morgan to read for a few moments to Soapy. He got up and crossed the room toward the plantation master. He was stunned to see the big man look around frantically, as if seeking some escape.

Hunt had reached an impasse—in his career and in his personal existence in this place. He had expended his best efforts for months and for all his dedication he found only minimal improvement in Morgan's skills. Morgan's capacity to learn was strictly limited. Hunt had not been aware of a restrictive puritanical conscience in his own corpus, but he supposed he was so ruled, despite his erotic interlude with his cousin Lodge's hot-blooded wife. He found himself ashamed to take Baynard's money under false pretenses. Morgan could write his own name, read simple directions and door signs. He could travel about without assistance. But to believe Morgan was ever going to enjoy reading books as an avocation, or working the most basic math, was self-delusory.

"I'm tired," Hunt told himself when he saw Baynard standing in the doorway. "Tired and disgusted too. I've been thinking for weeks that I'd reached the logical end of this assignment. I've known I was going to have to chuck this whole thing, this hopeless task with Morgan, this plantation built on the sweat and misery of black people." He wanted to say this aloud to Baynard. He wanted it out in the open. Last week he had written his solicitors in Boston to send his inheritance checks to a subsidiary of a Massachusetts' trading company in New Orleans rather than to Mt. Zion. This was the way he had begun to break his ties here. He wanted to go back north; he wanted to return to the old life he'd known in New England. He was unsure whether he could do that or not. There was no way of knowing whether Cousin Lodge would permit his reentry into Melrose—or even into Massachusetts. Lodge belonged to the vindictive branch of a cold and unbending family.

Most of all, Hunt had to get away from Blackoaks because of Kathy Baynard Kenric. Her gentle, flawless beauty tormented his waking hours. She trailed after him into his sleep and she haunted him there. When he heard her crying so desolately in the night, he felt driven to violence though he'd spent his life training himself that violence was counteraction, never an answer. But he wanted to kill Styles Kenric. That bastard harried Kathy, kept her miserable. And if there were some way to get Kenric out of the way, he could make Kathy happy. He could try with everything he knew, with everything he could learn with her.

But since none of this fantasy was coming to pass in the real world, since the neighbors in this territory were waiting—with bated breath, it seemed—for him to make any overt abolitionist movement, he had little hope of finding a place of promise or security in this community. He could even look back with nostalgic longing to the simple and satisfying existence in Harvard Yard, to the hidden hours in the side-street cottage with Addie. He was obliged, at least, to apprise Baynard of the facts about his son's limited capacity for learning.

He strode across the room. "Mr. Baynard, could I speak with you please?"

He hesitated, stunned at the fleeting panic which whipped across Baynard's flushed face. The heavyset man glanced around, as if trapped. "Sorry, Hunter. Forgive me, I'm—busy. Terribly busy." Realizing this was patently false, he added lamely, "I'll get back to you. But not now. . . . I've too much on my mind."

Before Hunt could speak or intercept him, Baynard heeled around and strode along the corridor toward his study. Somehow, to Hunt, he seemed like a rabbit scurrying in terror for his nest. Hunt stood, incredulous, staring after Baynard until the study door closed loudly behind him. Hunt felt troubled because if he had found one quality to admire in this godforsaken land, it was the inner strength of the master of Blackoaks.

He exhaled heavily and drew his gaze away from the tightly closed door. His eyes trailed across Kathy on the stairs and leaped backward. The world wheeled around him and he felt a rush of dizziness and knew his face flushed, erubescent as any callow boy, at this unexpected glimpse of her. God! she was beautiful. Her own face glowed faintly when their eyes met. His heart lunged. At that moment he wanted her more terribly than he had ever wanted any woman. Her beauty was so fragile, so rare that he could not get her out of his mind, to see her so near was unsettling. Overwhelming desire flared through him, burning out everything else, every sensible consideration as well as the practical realization that he could never have her. He had to have her! He had to have her or he had to get away from the sight and touch of her. She was always so near, yet so unattainable. She was always where he must meet her, speak to her politely, and yet keep a distance greater than that between southern Alabama and Boston. Damn it, he couldn't go on wanting her so desperately, wasting his whole life yearning after a girl he could never have. How long would he remain the staid young tutor from Harvard? When would he, in a fit of passion, break down her bedroom door because he couldn't keep his hands off her any longer? Never had he wanted any woman so fiercely that he abandoned all reason. He had to have her, or he had to get to hell out of here. *Damn it, Baynard, listen to me. . . .*

The raw winter rain seeped down the panes in icy drops. The lamps and candles of the parlor glowed wanly, constricted by heavy shadows in all the corners, like gray fringes lining the drapes and dark platforms around the tables, sofa, and chairs. It was not yet eight o'clock, but winter darkness blotted out the world beyond the rain-frosted windows.

Miz Claire sat in a deep chair under a double-shaded lamp, knitting. Baynard stood at a window, watching the rain, the darkness, the nothingness. Behind him he heard Miz Claire's muted chatter, but he didn't really listen. He had heard everything she had to say many times and had attended it the first time with only meager interest.

He saw Styles enter the room, the tall slender man reflected in the rain-iced panes. Baynard tensed, wishing he didn't have to make conversation with his son-in-law, but unable to devise an escape. He warned himself too that he couldn't hope to run away from everybody, hold himself aloof, no matter how devoutly he might wish it.

"Have you heard recently from Ferrell?" he heard Styles ask Miz Claire. She looked up, smiling. Damn Styles! he knew they hadn't heard, just as he knew his asking would please Miz Claire, endear him. To Claire, any man as handsome as Styles was correlatedly a good and upright man.

Baynard turned from the window. His voice rasped. "We haven't heard. We won't hear. Everything is over between young Ferrell and this house—"

"Don't say that, Mr. Baynard," Miz Claire cried. "Of course Ferrell will write."

"As far as I am concerned, my son is dead."

"Mr. Baynard! I plead with you. Stop such talk."

"All right. He's alive. We both know that. But to what profit—to anyone—including himself? Will someone explain to me why in God's name a healthy, normal young man with everything to live for would bury himself in a place of misfits and queers?"

"Obviously, he didn't find what he wanted from life here," Styles said. He could not pretend displeasure that Ferrell-Junior had entered the priesthood. He did not try.

"I believe you could have helped to dissuade him, Styles," Baynard said. He gestured impotently. "If you had done as I asked you—talked to him. He always listened to you."

"He was not at that time listening to anybody," Styles said.

"He was listening to God," Miz Claire cried.

"Oh, for Christ's sake, stop that superstitious, fanatical religious chatter," Baynard told his wife. "I still believe you could have influenced him, Styles . . . I'm sorry. I can't forgive you that."

Styles shrugged. "Perhaps I thought it best that he go into the priesthood."

"Best? For whom? For you?"

"For all of us. Perhaps even for Ferrell. For this plantation certainly. For the way it can be run in the future—"

"By whom, for God's sake?" Baynard demanded.

"I think it is not too soon to begin to plan to build Blackoaks—as it should be built—without Ferrell in those plans. He's not coming back, you know. We must go on here. . . . It's up to us whether we prosper or decay."

Baynard felt his heart constrict and then pound erratically. He called upon all the discipline within him and managed to remain coldly polite. "I gather from your tone that you're suggesting this success or failure of Blackoaks in the future is somehow up to *you?*"

Styles nodded. "I do believe I have a great deal to offer to the management of this estate. More, actually, than Ferrell-Junior could have provided. He stood between me and any serious projections I might offer you. That's not true anymore."

Baynard took a step toward Styles. His voice quavered. "You're as far from directing this farm as you ever were. . . . Why—if Kathy had borne you a son, I might have felt differently, I might have considered seriously even listening to you. . . . I'm sorry. I am unable to do that as things are."

"I don't see that you have much choice," Styles said in a mild tone.

Miz Claire said, "Mr. Baynard, you're being unfair as well as cruel to Styles. Ferrell-Junior would want Styles to succeed him as the master of Blackoaks someday."

Baynard didn't speak for the space of a long-delayed heartbeat. At last he spoke directly to his wife in a tone one might use on the deaf or retarded. "Ferrell-Junior's desires are not relevant to this discussion. If Ferrell-Junior had given a goddamn about this farm, he'd have stayed here to run it. Whether or not he might support Styles' ideas for running it don't mean a goddamn thing to me."

"Please, Mr. Baynard," she said in an offended tone,

"there's no call for offensive language in my parlor."

"Sooner or later," Styles said in unruffled calm, "you're going to have to put aside your emotional unreasoning and take a rational look at the future. I don't believe it's too soon to do that. No matter what you think, you can't live forever. I would suggest, first, a total shift in your plans for continuing cotton as the major crop of this farm. This simply is not reasonable under present conditions. It is not even logical when you consider the other, more promising resources on tap here."

Baynard's sarcasm should have singed him. "The Fulani woman as the answer to all our problems."

"That's right. Yes. One of the most serious errors of which you have been guilty in the years I've known you has been that of planning to sell two pureblooded, thoroughbred Fulah males for a few thousand dollars cash—"

"I happen to believe—if it were any of your concern— that Blade and Moab—perfect, without blemishes as they are now—are major assets worth at least $20,000 in cash. In gold. I can hold one or the other in reserve. I can sell them outright, or borrow money on them. I can run this farm as it should be run—without going deeper in debt because of usury interest rates."

Styles spread his hands. "Don't you have any understanding that there are other ways to financial disaster than high interest rates on bank loans? To continue to grow low-grade cotton year after year—"

"I'm a cotton farmer, Styles. This farm is built on a cotton economy."

"Perhaps it was. Once. A long time ago. When this earth was strong and fertile, before it was planted out, starved. Maybe in your father's lifetime this insistence on cotton made sense. Today that's all changed. Why, to keep growing inferior cotton, you would take these two perfect Fulani specimen—you would sell them off at what seems to you a good price. Then you sink that money in low-grade cotton—and then what?"

Baynard laughed coldly. His face was flushed and blood throbbed in his temples, but his voice remained level. "For the sake of argument, let's say that I tried to bid—

in an open market, against well-heeled slave breeders—for one or two Fulani females. If I had any chance of getting such females, I'd then be building my hopes, my entire future on Blade and Moab—on the slim chance that they won't be destroyed by illness or accident. What happens if in some accident they are marked, scarred, maimed? Then, I have nothing. Not even assets negotiable at a bank. If a Fulani is perfect, he is an asset. If he is scarred, or marred, he is better off dead because he's not the best laborer among the Africans. He's not really a laborer at all. No. It's too risky, tying up the entire future of this estate on the health and procreative abilities of two young blacks who might fall tomorrow of a dozen diseases."

"But to produce Fulah fancies for the market would only be the beginning," Styles protested. "This is what you refuse to see. You've other good and valuable bloodlines here. If I could, I'd get experts in. I'd find and segregate those pure bloodlines. We could deliver fancy-grade quality black animals at the New Orleans or Natchez auctions a year from now—and every year after that an increasing number. And that's what we *would* do if I ran this place."

Baynard met his gaze, held it. "Well, you never will run Blackoaks. You never will because this job demands a man to handle it, and you're not qualified, Styles—and you never will be."

CHAPTER 39

STYLES AWOKE about 1:00 A.M. He lay tense, sweated, with the sense that something was wrong; he had no idea what. He felt faintly giddy and unsettled after an unsatisfactory two hours of fitful sleep; for the moment he was confused and unsure what had wakened him, and he found it difficult to orient himself. Then he heard the faint whispered sound that had broken into his rest and brought him awake. Someone was catfooting along the corridor. He glanced at Kathy sleeping beside him on the bed, her arm thrown across her forehead. She slept placidly and breathed regularly. Whatever it was in the corridor, it had apparently disturbed no one else. Only because he'd been restless had the noise penetrated his consciousness.

He swung his legs over the side of the bed, holding his breath. The springs whimpered, the mattress rustled. The movement in the corridor ceased abruptly and a breathless hush ensued, as if everything waited. He caught up his bathrobe, swung it over his shoulders and went stealthily across the flooring to the corridor door.

He cracked the door cautiously and peered through. He was astonished to see Baynard standing tautly out there, listening. Styles stared, puzzled. For weeks, Baynard, unable to sleep, had been prowling the house noisily at all hours of the night. Why suddenly was he as furtive as a thief?

Styles held his breath, watching his father-in-law through the slit in the door. After a long pause, Baynard crept forward again. He followed the wall in the darkness by trailing his hand along it. At the narrow stairwell leading upward to the house-servant's quarters on the third floor, Baynard paused again and checked across his shoulder carefully. Good God! he was on his way to one of the servant wenches. Styles was shocked and astonished. No wonder the old bastard was creeping around like a tomcat.

Styles waited until Baynard was almost to the head of the short staircase, then he opened the door far enough to slither through. He went on his toes along the carpeted corridor to the stairwell. He was in time to see Baynard go off the stairs into the narrow, unfinished third-floor corridor.

Styles followed but the steps creaked at each step he took. They were exaggeratedly loud in the late-night silence. It took him some moments to climb high enough that he could see along the third-floor hallway. It was an uncarpeted, shadowed place of many closed doors. It was empty. Baynard was gone.

Styles sank into the shadows on the stairs to wait. He stared at that darkened corridor trying to uncover its shameful secret. Old man Baynard! The respected citizen, the revered parent, the burdened husband so admired and pitied by those who knew him and his unhappy wife. The damned old hypocrite. Looking with contempt along his nose at men like Baxter Simon who openly admitted bedding down black wenches. Stealing in after dark into the bed of his own ebony concubine.

Time slipped away slowly, like the measured drip of water in a Chinese torture. Night sounds rose and abated, mice chattered and raced in the unceiled attic. Styles grew uncomfortable and cold but he did not fall asleep. He was not even sleepy. Rather, he'd never been wider awake in his life. The mendacious old bastard had played into his hands, at last.

He had no idea how long he waited. He knew only that he had not even yawned. His eyes burned and were dry, but they had not closed for an instant. At the near end of the corridor a door was opened stealthily. A small candle burned deep inside the room. The two people illumined in the doorway were so close that Styles retreated as hastily as safely possible into the deep shadows of the lower stairwell.

They were so engrossed in each other they did not hear him. Baynard looked down at Jeanne d'Arc for a long time, his face gentle. Then he reached out and cupped one of her full breasts in his hand and, holding it, drew her to him. She wore a striped cotton gown; her hair was caught in a tight ponytail at the nape of her neck. Baynard kissed her lingeringly. Somehow, there was more sadness than eroticism in his kiss. It was the sort of farewell one might witness at the gangplank of a steamer or in a railway station.

Styles watched them a moment longer and then he retreated cautiously down the steps. He was very calm. There was no element of surprise that Baynard's mistress was the lovely *os rouge*. The only astonishment Styles felt was at his own obtuseness. How blind and trusting he had been all these years! God alone knew how long this affair had been going on in this house. It was perfectly obvious that Baynard was the natural father of Jeanne d'Arc's child. Baxter Simon had recognized the truth instantly. *Scandal.* The only truly shocking aspect of the entire business was that he had not even suspected the truth long before this. He made no moral judgments now. He didn't care what Baynard did, except as that information could be used to his own profit. He smiled coldly, returning to his own bedroom. And I will use it against you, you pompous old lecher. . . .

His new name was Brother Alexander.

He had taken the name as his own along with his vows of poverty, chastity, obedience, and loyalty to the pope. There was never any sense of soul-stirring commitment in any of the ceremonies that inducted him into the new life at the seminary. He could view it only as an escape from the purgatory his life had become. Even his new name was a release from being known as Ferrell-Junior. Ferrell Baynard, Junior. He tried never to think of the name in connection with himself. He wanted to disassociate himself from the past, the old name, the old life, the old hurts. He tried to maintain silence, to follow every rule of the school to the letter, to get through one empty, unhurried day at a time. Sometimes he prayed he would find purpose in his life in this place; so far, nothing. He found greatest peace in the retreats—those hours and days of imposed silence when the society could not speak among themselves, even at mealtimes. He found security in silence.

The classroom work and the religious studies were most difficult and emotionally exhausting for him. He was the only novice who was forever tired. He charged this to his lack of commitment. He studied the faces of the other young men, who had abandoned the world for the labor and self-sacrifice of the society. There was contentment and even anticipation in these faces. They had come here to serve, not to atone. These people were where they wanted to be; they were satisfied; they were dedicated; they believed in what they were doing.

His worst moments were those alone in the darkness of his cubicle. He lay on the cot in the bare room. He could reach out and touch the rough thick walls on each side. In the deep shadows he remembered Lorna, even when he prayed he would not. His mind and his body needed her mind and her body or he was incomplete. The greatest self-denial in his new existence was the rejection of every natural instinct in his being, the abrogation of all earthly compulsions and ties. He saw her face in the darkness; he sensed her heated body in the night. He needed her. And then, in agony, he would see again the distress and hatred in her eyes—as he had seen them last. He had hurt her, he had almost destroyed her. He would never see her again. This night and all the lonely nights like it ahead were all there was for him in this place, on this earth. He lived among the godly, but he was damned.

He found some escape in the library because he had so much work to do. He was so far behind all the other novitiates. He had been only a casual student; nothing had prepared him for this seminary; the demands made upon him were overwhelming.

He sat crouched over his books at one of the bare, unadorned reading tables and smiled grimly. For the first time he felt true compassion for Morgan's working with the tutor back home. Poor Morgan! It was too much for Morgan. Poor Brother Alexander! It was too much for him too.

A tall, slender young man sat on the bench close to Ferrell. There were only a few others in the book-lined hall; there were many of these tables, built by the students from logs. The youth was extremely dark, with thick black hair, black brows that met over his nose, Latin in complexion, except for the strangely pale blue eyes. His lashes were long and upturned. He batted them as he gazed at Ferrell intently and gave him an odd, unyielding smile. "Brother Alexander," he said.

"Brother Luis."

"Do you paint your lips, Brother Alexander?"

"What?"

"They're so red. They're beautiful. But they are red."

"Just naturally healthy, I guess." Ferrell glanced around, deciding to move.

Brother Luis, still smiling that unflappable smile, laid his hand tentatively on the inside of Ferrell's leg above his knee. Ferrell felt the trembling of the heated fingers as the student primed his courage to slide his hand upward to Ferrell's crotch.

"Afraid you're wasting your time, Brother Luis," Ferrell said. "Unless you've got tits. I like girls."

Brother Luis stared at him a moment to see if he were joking. Seeing that he was not, the youth withdrew his hand and his smile. He spoke accusingly, "Then what are you doing here?"

"Studying for the priesthood."

"You're in the wrong place."

Ferrell smiled bleakly. "Is there a right place for me?"

"I don't know. But this is not it. Not for you—with your attitude. Why did you come here? What are you going to do when Father Theodore calls you into his study—for a *personal* conference?"

"What am I supposed to do?"

"You're *supposed* to respond when he puts his hand —up under your cassock. He will certainly expect you to."

Ferrell shook his head. "And if I don't?"

"Go ahead. Be smart and clever about it. I can see you think that I'm exaggerating—"

"No. It's too horrible to be anything but the truth."

"Horrible? What is the matter with you?"

Ferrell shrugged. "Beats me. And all the time I thought I was one of the boys."

Brother Luis laughed without a trace of mirth. "You'll see. He reaches up under your cassock, undoes your fly, and takes your—your cock—out to hold in his fist. He works on you the whole time you're in there. . . . A good-looker like you, he's going to want to go down on you. . . . He may want you to bugger him. . . . He really likes that. It makes him squeal and moan and he loves it. . . . In one way, you may be lucky. He likes to take it—you can pretend to like it. You sure as hell better pretend to like it. He's passive—not aggressive like me. He gets his joy from—taking it. . . . He may not expect you to take it."

"Oh, I was born lucky."

"Go ahead. Make your stupid jokes if you wish—"

"I assure you, I'm not joking. I've never cared about another man's religion, tastes, or sexual preference. If he likes old men with beards, young boys, or wild ducks, that's his affair, that's up to him. . . . I just never expected to have it forced on me—or to become an untouchable because of my needs."

The dark youth peered at him. "Maybe you're ragging me. Maybe you're rejecting me because I don't—appeal to you—even though I've looked at nobody since you got here. I'm sorry if I don't appeal to you." His mouth twisted. "But if you are telling the truth, I don't know why you came into this life. Did you plan to be a celibate, for Christ's sake?"

"For Christ's sake."

"That smart talk won't get you anywhere around here. No. It won't be appreciated, Brother Alexander. As you won't be. No. You're in the wrong place."

"You said that once."

"Be glad that I am talking to you now. You may look back on this evening as the good old days. . . . Once the word gets around about you, you may well find yourself isolated and ostracized. . . . an outsider. . . . Oh, you can get by—if you can stand being excluded. But you'll never belong. If you are not one of us, the word gets out about you—and you'll remain alienated—an outsider—no matter how long you're in the order. They'll all know what you are."

The youth gathered up his books and moved away to a table far across the dimly lighted room. Ferrell sat unmoving for a long time. He felt the rage of savage laughter boiling up inside him. He had asked for this. He had earned it, and now he'd gotten it—he'd vowed to spend the rest of his life in this order where they wouldn't want him because he was different from them. He shook his head. There was to be no easy escape for him, after all. There was no sanctuary. He had plunged headlong from purgatory into hell. . . .

CHAPTER 40

A CHILL DRIZZLE of rain blew in against the bedroom windows when Styles awoke at seven that morning. He had returned to bed from his long vigil on the stairway and slept soundly. He opened his eyes and glanced around, smiling and pleased with his prospects. Kathy was already up, dressed, and out of their room. Her adjacent dressing room was cluttered as she always left it every morning, the door standing ajar, her dresses bright on hangers beyond it. Styles lay back, luxuriating. He stretched, thinking backward and ahead, letting his thoughts wander, his sense of self-satisfaction underscored by the new and certain promise of triumph.

He shifted on the bed. Things were working out as he had always believed they should—to his advantage. He was a special person, born on the highest level of the landed gentry, possessing exceptional potential. And he was free of the weaknesses and vices that so often tripped or defeated inferior men. He had waited a long time, watching as this estate was ineptly and unwisely managed. He felt no stab of conscience at what he planned; sometimes cruelty was kindness in the long run. If he were cruel and unyielding in the present, it was in the future when his actions would be understood and vindicated. The fact was, he didn't give a damn what anyone thought—now or later.

Smiling imperiously, he got up and dressed, looking with clear, cold vision to the tasks immediately ahead. When he stepped out into the corridor, he was able to set his plan into motion with an incredible stroke of luck. He saw Miz Claire come alone from her solitary bedroom. He stood, with a fixed smile, awaiting her. She fluttered slightly under his gaze. Poor woman. No wonder she wandered around in a confused world of her own. It was easier on her than trying to share the existence Baynard had forced her into with his licentious behavior. He said solicitously, "Did you sleep well, Miz Claire?"

She gestured with her fingers like butterflies, simpering under the heat of his attention. "Oh, I've been up for hours, Styles. . . . I went up to the chapel."

"In this rain?"

"I feel better—when I pray. . . . I pray for all of us. For you. For Ferrell. And I don't mind the rain."

He shook his head in a thoughtful way. "This has been a particularly busy household last night and this morning."

"Oh?"

"Yes . . . oh, I hope Jeanne d'Arc is feeling better."

"Better?" Miz Claire paused at the head of the stairs. "Is she ill?"

"Oh, isn't she? I thought she was. . . . I heard Mr. Baynard up a little past midnight—"

"He's been very upset, unable to sleep, since Ferrell—"

"Yes. I thought maybe I could help calm him down. Talk to him. About Ferrell. But when I went out into the corridor, he was going up the stairs—toward the servants' quarters. So I knew something must be amiss. I followed to offer any assistance I could. He went into Jeanne d'Arc's room. He stayed so long I was worried—sure she was ill."

She gazed at him. Her face betrayed nothing. "She must have been," she said.

Baynard removed his soaked, muddy boots and rain slicker at the front door. He handed them to Thyestes. "Make me a hot toddy," he ordered. He leaned against the doorjamb a moment, feeling queasy. When Thyestes moved to help him, he waved him away. "I'm all right. Just a little bushed. I'll be in my study."

In his stocking feet he plodded slowly along the corridor. He felt old and tired, and colder than he had any right to be. His feet were like ice. Unable to sleep after he left Jeanne d'Arc around three this morning, he had prowled his bedroom for an hour as if it were a cage. Then he stood slump-shouldered at the window, staring into the empty dark. The morning star was rising. Another light—lanterns glittering in the stables—caught his eye. There was something going on down there that perhaps required his attention—a dam in foal, perhaps. He dressed hurriedly. As he left the house, pleased to have something to occupy his mind and his hands, the sky was darkening with thunderheads and thunder rumbled through the earth so it trembled under his feet. He carried his light oilcloth raincoat and strode downslope toward the horse corrals. Laus and three other slaves were huddled over a prostrate dam in the stables. "Foal got twisted around ass-backwards, masta," Laus said, looking up. "She squealing like a scairt pig. We come a-runnin'. Afeered me might lose them both."

The delivery had been rougher and far more prolonged even than the slaves had anticipated. Before it was over, and the foal delivered, Baynard was sagging against the uprights, breathless with exhaustion. He slogged through the rain and mud upslope to the house, feeling empty and sick at his stomach, but not hungry at all. In fact, the thought of food nauseated him. He wanted only to sag into his chair in his study, to rest, to get one full breath into his aching lungs.

When he opened the study door, Miz Claire heeled around from the desk where she had been standing, obviously for a long, tense time, awaiting him. Her face was pallid, her eyes wild. She waited only until he closed the door before she screeched at him. "It's got to stop, Mr. Baynard. Do you hear me? It's got to stop."

He sagged against the door, too tired to cross the room for the moment. "Lower your voice, Claire," he said as if speaking to a child. "Whatever it is you've got to say is between us."

"Is it? Or is it common knowledge? Does the whole community know and laugh behind my back? Well, I don't think what's going on is between us—not anymore. Oh, I've known about it—and I've put up with your—carrying on—with that black woman in your kitchen all these years —as long as you were discreet. . . . Well, you are no longer discreet—if you ever were. And it's got to stop. . . . I won't tolerate your shameful behavior another day. . . . Either that black kitchen slut leaves this house—or I do. . . . Is that clear?"

He drew strength from some inner reservoir and crossed slowly to his desk and leaned against it. He stared at Claire, but she was oddly fuzzy, just out of focus. He kept his voice deadly calm. "I hoped I'd never have to say this, Claire. But we better face it now. I don't feel you have any right to dictate what I do with my sex life."

"No right? I'm your wife."

"Are you, Claire? You're the mother of my children. You've been a good mother. You've kept a well-run home. I try to take nothing from you. But you haven't been my wife—in almost sixteen years."

"If you mean the filthy kind of sex that dogs have to have, you're right. But there's more to marriage. We're not children. Not lovers. And there are vows, Mr. Baynard. You made vows."

He laughed coldly. "Vows are made in the expectation that they *can* be kept. But human drives are older than vows, Claire. When it comes to a choice between vows and sanity—a man makes the only choice his inner compulsions will permit. A marriage is not a pretty picture spread out for the neighbors to approve as a whole. A marriage is a matter of minutes, and hours, and days, and weeks and months and years, piling up slowly, one on the other. You have never wanted sex with me. Not from the first. You hated it, even when you pretended the most to enjoy it. You *endured* it until you turned me from you. I had needs, Claire, that were part of my being—no matter how I tried to control them, repress them, suppress them, inhibit them. . . . I had them, Claire, whether they are shameful or normal, I had them. Needs that revolt you and that you can't even understand because you never felt the first twinge of them. . . . All right, if that's the rational order of this life, then I congratulate you, and I envy you . . . but I was not made that way. . . . I needed sex. . . . My God, I felt driven to it—not once a year—but twice a day. . . . I could not live with vows alone."

405

"Does it somehow please and uplift you to admit you are as low as an animal?"

"I tried to make you see. That's all. I should have known better."

"I am your wife. . . . Don't you owe me anything?"

"Strange, no matter what emptiness one is offered in return, the only important consideration is what one owes others—not himself—not what he must do to hang onto his sanity. . . . All right, Claire, what do I owe you that you wanted and that I did not provide you?"

"Respect. Decency. Fidelity."

"And from you—in exchange for that? What? Words are so damned easy to say, Claire. It's life that's hard to live—sweated, day-by-day life. Can you even understand that? What was I suppose to have? The empty life of the celibate? Well, I wasn't built that way. I'm sorry, abjectly sorry, but I have had needs and drives—almost as strong as the need for water and air—needs and drives that would disgust you if I enumerated them—"

"You disgust me."

"I'll spare you. But in return, I beg you, spare me your accusations. . . . You've done all to me that you can, Claire, unless you emasculate me totally. . . . You have turned into a religious fanatic—"

"Without my religion I'd have nothing, damn you!"

"I never gave a damn what you did—until you turned Ferrell—from the life here—to an existence in your church where everything he could have been will be wasted on an unnatural, abnormal existence. . . . I'll never forgive you that, Claire. . . . I think if you got out of here now—and concentrated on your own life—I would not interfere—as I pray to your God you'll stop interfering in mine."

He felt himself losing consciousness, but he did not faint, managed to keep from fainting. His hands shook and the backs of his knees quivered with the tremors of weakness. He was afraid he was going to vomit. He could feel his heart battering erratically against his rib cage.

Claire stood tense watching him. There was much more she was going to say. His foul defense of his behavior didn't even reach her. She heard the words, but didn't let them penetrate her mind or register on her consciousness. His evil was indefensible. But when he sagged suddenly into his chair, she hesitated, gripped by a paralyzing fear. She had never seen him look so strange. His head fell back against the rest. The way he opened his mouth, gasping for air, reminded her of a fish out of water she'd seen when she was a girl. It was too painful to watch, and she had wanted to run away. She wanted to run away now. His face was flushed and yet somehow it looked gray under its erubescent surface.

Claire shook her head, retreating. "I'll send for Dr. Townsend," she said, aware that he didn't even hear her. "Then I'll have to change my dress. . . . Yes, I'll go do that now. . . . I couldn't let the doctor see me like this. . . . I'll send Styles in—right away. . . ."

"Keep that—son of a bitch—away—from me," he said, but she was already out of the door, escaping this room. She didn't hear him.

Baynard had no idea how long Claire had been gone from his study before Styles came in and closed the door behind him. Perhaps it was only a moment or two—perhaps an hour. Nothing was clear; his mind was confused; he was disoriented and felt sick at his stomach. "Send Thyestes," he whispered. "Send for Jeanne d'Arc. . . ."

Styles evidently didn't hear him. Styles gave him a chilled smile, but gave no indication that he noticed anything amiss about his father-in-law. "Miz Claire said you wanted to see me."

"What?"

"Yes. I thought it might be a propitious time to discuss my plans for managing this plantation."

Baynard struggled to get up. He was too tired. He burned with pain across his upper back. His arms felt too weak to lift. "You son of a bitch." He rolled his head on the chair rest. "Get out."

"It's time for me to take over for you, Baynard."

"You can't—run this farm. . . . Takes a man . . . not a goddamn pretty—fag. . . ."

"We all reach a time, Baynard, when we are too old for the job we are trying to do. Our minds are no longer clear enough. We make baseless accusations against those who try to help. . . . The wise among us face the truth and admit it. . . . Others try to go on—and drag the whole operation down with them and their muddled-minded, outmoded management procedures. . . . I can't let you do that."

"I want Thyestes . . . where is Thyestes?"

"I left orders that you and I were not to be disturbed until the doctor arrived—"

"What doctor, you bastard?"

"We've sent for Dr. Townsend, Baynard. You're an ill man. That's why I must assume the responsibilities—"

"Get out . . . you son of a bitch . . . get out."

"This illness may be a blessing for all of us. You included. Your direction of this farm has been a long history of misguided effort, ineptitude, and mismanagement. You have clung to methods your own father would have discarded years ago—"

"Thyestes!" Baynard struggled to get up from the chair. Styles watched him with the detached interest with which he would have witnessed a beetle trying to right itself in a dung heap.

"You had better stay where you are, Baynard. Conserve yourself. It may be hours before the doctor gets here—I regret to say I had no idea it was an emergency when we sent a rider into Mt. Zion to fetch the doctor. . . . In the meantime, you can rest in your chair. I simply want your word that in the future you will not interfere with my management of this farm—"

"I'll kill you. . . ."

"If you agree. I'll write up a simple form, something like a power of attorney—"

"Never on this earth."

Styles shrugged. "I'll have the management anyway. It would simply make it easier, all around. You are incapacitated, Baynard. If I have to, I'll go into court to prove your ineptness, your mismanagement, your neglect."

Baynard nodded weakly, his hands shaking. "Yes . . . Court . . . let's go to court, you bastard."

"That's up to you. If you want Kathy to know how you've been bedding down a half-breed kitchen slut all these years—in neglect of your responsibilities and obligations on this farm—"

"You—" Baynard fought to push himself up. Styles seemed an eternal distance away, but his voice was abnormally loud, magnified many times as if in an echo chamber.

"If you persist—if you force me," Styles continued in that calm, conversational tone that vibrated like thunder in Baynard's ears, "I'll put that *os rouge* wench on the witness stand—"

"I want—Jahndark—"

"We'll force her to admit her bastard child—so aptly named Scandal—is yours. . . . Are these the elevating facts you want Kathy—and the world—to know about you? I don't want to do it, Baynard. But I will do it. For your own good."

With an incredible strength of will, Baynard lunged upward from his chair. His eyes were wide, his face contorted. His hands reached like peregrine talons for Styles' face.

Styles stood calmly before him, smiling in contempt. As Baynard grabbed for him, Styles retreated a step or two. Breathing raggedly, Baynard staggered, caught his balance, and lunged again toward that contumelious face.

Styles retreated quietly. As Baynard shook his head to clear it, Styles opened the corridor door. He spoke in a calm, warm voice, "I'm glad you agree, sir. We'll work it all out as you suggest."

Baynard leaped for him, growling. Styles stepped through the door and closed it behind him. Baynard struck hard against it. He slid helplessly along its rough facing, his nails clutching at the wood for support. He was dead as he slumped to the floor. He fell in such a way that his body blocked the door. They could not get in to him until a young house servant broke an outside window and dragged him away from it upon the rug.

CHAPTER 41

A MARROW-CHILLING wintry mist blew in across the family cemetery on a knoll above the house and the chapel. The light rain persisted during the graveside ceremonies and still enshrouded Blackoaks in the lowering blue-gray afternoon. The last melancholy mourner departed in a slowly moving carriage. The Baynards stood silently on the veranda as the last of the somber caravan descended the bleak lane beneath the rows of leafless pecan trees. The carriages appeared to dissolve into the pale lavender vapors that almost obliterated the ghostly trail beyond the huge monolithic posts at the gate.

In the family cemetery, slaves tossed mounds of fresh-turned earth over the remains of Ferrell Alexander Baynard. None in the family looked that way. Alone in her kitchen, Jeanne d'Arc stood at the window watching the dark knoll where the slaves buried her master—her lover —her life. Her eyes were bleak, filled with tears. She was afraid she was going to break down into uncontrollable sobbing. But she went on standing there, as if in this way she could delay his passing, somehow cling to him one more final moment.

She breathed deeply, painfully. He had reached back from the grave to aid her in the best way he had been able to devise. He had never mentioned freedom to her as long as he lived. She heard the word in relation to her for the first time last night when the lawyer had read Baynard's will to the family and a few of the older house slaves. One of its first stipulations was manumission for Jeanne d'Arc and her progeny, issue, heirs, lineage, and successors forever—in return for her selfless service and unceasing loyalty. Miz Claire had whispered it, but those around her heard her clearly—Jeanne d'Arc heard her. "Payment for papa's whore."

A second stipulation had granted Jeanne d'Arc $10,000 for her own support and that of any of her offspring, to assure that she live as a freed person in any place of her choosing. The family had congratulated her on her freedom, but none had mentioned the matter of money to her. She had not said anything because the very fact of her freedom was too new, too overwhelming. She had no clear thoughts, even now. The notion of living in New Orleans occurred to her. People of color made their homes in that metropolitan city, lived their own lives, accepted for what they were. The fearful thought of moving north, rearing Scandal as a white child clamored for her attention, but she was afraid to consider it in detail. There was too much danger; too much of the unknown. And so, she stood, un-moving, watching the slaves bury the only man she had ever loved, the man who had given her the gift of free-dom. She needed his counsel now more than ever. What should she do with her freedom? Where was she to go?

"Miz Jahndark?" Thyestes had limped into the dimly lighted kitchen. He waited until Jeanne d'Arc turned from the blue-misted window. "Masta Kenric—he in Masta Baynard's study—he ast to see you—right as soon as possible with you, Miz Jahndark, ma'am."

Jeanne d'Arc opened the study door, stepped through, and closed it behind her. A sharp thrust of pain plunged through her. She had not known it would be so agonizing to come into his room, knowing she would never see him in it again. She bit her underlip, afraid she might sob in protest. But she didn't cry. A flaring of rage at the sight of the man sitting at Baynard's desk burned out the pain and left only dregs of hatred. "You sent for me, Masta Styles?"

He glanced up from the papers spread before him. "I thought your decision—last night—was to go on working here."

"Yes, suh, Masta Styles."

He smiled in a jaundiced way. "Where's my coffee, Jahndark?"

"I'm sorry, suh. I'll get it now."

"Never mind. I'm sure your Master Baynard never had to remind you about the coffee?"

"No, suh."

"And the buns. You served hot iced buns—"

"Yes, suh."

"You might bring me buns with my coffee."

"I'm truly sorry, suh. Tomorrow, mayhap. We don't have any buns today. We so rushed—feeding so many people at the funeral and all."

"And you had no heart to make cinnamon buns this morning."

She said nothing.

"All right, Jahndark. You may bring my coffee."

"Got some nice sour-milk biscuits. Melt right in your mouth. With fresh-churned butter."

"All right." She turned to go. His voice stopped her. "We may as well understand each other, Jeanne d'Arc. I am master of Blackoaks now."

"I know, suh."

"You may as well also understand, Jeanne d'Arc, that I know—what you were to old man Baynard before he died."

She stood staring at the floor.

"I know that baby of yours is his child."

She nodded without looking up.

"You served him quite well, didn't you?"

"As best I knew, suh. He needed me. And I knew he needed me. And I was glad to be where he needed—when he needed."

"And it paid off handsomely, didn't it?"

"You mean I'm free, masta? Yes. I'm free. My daughter is free. I chose to stay here . . . for now." She tilted her head. "Is that all, suh? I'll get your coffee now."

"You may find, Jeanne d'Arc, that you may not be welcome here—perhaps that is why your master had you manumitted."

She nodded. "Then I leaves. When I must. When you

gives me the money he left me and my baby. Then I leaves."

He laughed. "Your being willed money, Jeanne d'Arc, and my being forced to pay it to you aren't really related. Free or not, you are a black woman in Alabama. You better think that over. You may want to stay where you are—as you are."

"Yes, suh. I'll think about it." She turned and left the room without looking at him again, but she was aware his insolent smile trailed her from the room like something malevolent. She walked toward the kitchen, hurrying, suddenly afraid. She felt hackles at the nape of her neck.

Ferrell-Junior came into the kitchen while she was heating coffee and sour-milk biscuits for the new master of Blackoaks. He walked up behind her and put his hands over her eyes. "I know who it is," she said. "It's that new priest—it's Brother Alexander."

He laughed and turned her, still in his arms. "Thyestes said you wanted to see me."

"I'm sorry, Masta Ferrell. I didn't know no other place where I could talk with you as I must. . . . Did that lawyer speak true last night—am I free?"

"As free as I am." He laughed. "Come to think of it, that's not as free as a butterfly. Yes, Jeanne d'Arc, you are free."

"And the part about the money? He meant that too?"

He frowned. "Are you having trouble, Jeanne d'Arc?"

"I'm scared, Masta Ferrell. Scared to ask for that money —though I know it's mine. He said—I better think first that I'm a black woman in Alabama. . . . That means he don't have to give me that money less'n he wants to. . . ."

He smiled. "It's all right, Jeanne d'Arc. I'll speak to Styles. Now. While you're here—if you need me—get word to me at the school."

"How I going to do that—I can't write a letter."

He laughed. "Soapy can. Morgan might even be able to hack one out for you. . . . Hunt would do it—if he didn't get tarred and feathered for it. . . . Kathy would do it—"

"She his wife—"

"You don't have to tell me anything in your letter, Jeanne d'Arc. I'm his son. I love you, too, Jeanne d'Arc. I'll know you need me—if I get a letter from you—even if the letter says hope you're well."

She laughed, sighing heavily. "You always was a caution, Masta Ferrell-Junior."

"You've just got to quit worrying. You've got a lot more friends than you have enemies. . . . And it doesn't matter anyway. No matter what—you've got me."

"God is good to me. Better maybe than I deserve."

"I don't know much about that. So far, He's out of my jurisdiction. . . ."

Ferrell rapped on the study door. After a moment, Styles spoke from within. "Come in." He frowned when Ferrell stepped inside and closed the door behind him. "Thought you had to get back to school immediately."

"I didn't want to leave without telling you how beautifully you delivered that eulogy for my father."

"Thank you."

"There wasn't a dry eye in the cemetery."

"He lived a useful, selfless life of achievement and accomplishment."

"Yes. He did. And you delineated it—with sincerity and emotion."

"I felt it—deeply."

"Yes. That's what is so fantastic. When I am convinced that you killed him."

First, Styles laughed, and then he stopped laughing. He gazed at Ferrell coldly. "Your humor is tasteless."

"I assure you I am not joking. From all I have heard—from my mother, from servants, the doctor—I am sure of it. You killed him, all right. I even know why."

"Do you?"

"You'd have killed anybody to get control of this farm."

Styles shrugged. "Well, I've got it now, haven't I? And I can tell you, you won't be welcome here if you persist in making slanderous charges against me. No one killed your father. Ask Dr. Townsend—"

"I did—"

"His report is clear enough. Your father died of massive

congestion—heart failure. No one laid a hand on him."

"Of course not. You—last of all. Don't misunderstand me. I have no proof that I could present in a court of law, no charges I'd ever make in public. There's nothing I can prove—except that you and I know you killed him. . . . I simply want you to understand that I do know that. As long as you run this estate well—and treat its people—black and white—fairly and honestly—as my father did, you won't hear from me. You'll rarely see me."

Styles laughed at him. "This sounds like a veiled threat."

"There's nothing veiled about it, Styles. I want it understood—out in the open between us. You're the master here. But you're not as free as you think you are. Nothing separates me from your throat but distance. Once that distance is removed—for cause, Styles—nothing will stop me. Life is not so sweet in the order that I would want to cling to it."

Styles stopped smiling. "You're not serious."

"I was never more serious. I'll kill you without thinking about it. Look at me, Styles. See the turned collar, the cassock, the symbol of the holy man. Well, I swear on all that's holy that I'll kill you. You killed my father. . . ."

"You talk crazy. How could I kill him? Why would I knowingly do anything—"

"I think you knew what you were doing, Styles. You were well aware—from your studies and your reading—of what pressures could do to my father's heart, his whole system. You knew that enough emotional pressure would kill him—as surely as a bullet."

"I won't even dignify such charges with a reply," Styles said, "except to inform you, there is *no* scientific evidence to date that tensions, or pressures, or emotional anxiety have any effect on the physical health of a man."

"You're right. About all these ills I didn't even mention. No accepted medical evidence. I didn't suggest there was. But there is research, study—there is proof among the enlightened scientists in Paris, London, and Munich. Ordinary people won't know of such advanced theories for maybe another fifty years. But we both know you're not ordinary, Styles. In education, in reading, in advanced technology, you're not ordinary at all. Are you? You know, Styles, about these theories of blood pressure and tension. Eh? You did know—and you did use that special knowledge. And we both know that you have proved it is true—over my father's dead body."

Styles merely watched him silently.

Ferrell said, "No one expects you to admit such a fantastic charge. No one would believe it today if you did."

Styles shrugged. "Well, thank God, you don't expect me to admit this. I'm sorry, *Father* Alexander, I find this whole conversation ludicrous—and pointless." He laughed. "Why don't you pray on it, *Father?*"

"If I had the same factual evidence that you had that driving an exhausted, hypertense man beyond his endurance can be fatal, I would pray, Styles. I'd get down on my knees right here."

Styles laughed. "There's no sense embarrassing us both."

"No. I'm not going to pray. I hope I've made my point in a much more practical manner, Styles—you'd never understand a prayer, but I think you understand a threat when you hear one."

"I'm becoming bored by this entire conversation. I'm sure you want to say good-bye to your mother and sister before you leave Blackoaks."

"We have one more little bit of business, Styles."

"Do we?"

"A matter of a bequest to Jeanne d'Arc."

Styles swore. "Did that bitch—"

"I'm sure you don't want to test the validity of my threat on your life at this early date, Styles. Shall we arrange payment to Jeanne d'Arc before I leave here?"

Styles laughed coldly. "If you can find the money in the bank—or anywhere else, I'll gladly pay her off—and ship her out of here. . . . I'm sure your poor betrayed mother would be glad to see her go."

"What you think you're telling me about Jeanne d'Arc and my father—it's not news to me, Styles, and won't add any luster to your crown with me. . . . I happen to know my father kept cash stored away in mother's chapel. Perhaps Thyestes knows the exact hiding place. If not, we should be able to find it without too much difficulty. It's a very small chapel."

Ferrell, Styles, and Thyestes walked up the knoll in the misting rain to the chapel. Thyestes carried a lantern. "I got no idea where Masta Baynard hid that money, Masta Ferrell, suh. No idea. He always made us stay outside. I knowed it was money he brung out. It was heavy. But I don't know where at he kept it."

The hiding place was simple enough to find. The altar appeared to be a solid piece, but it was not. The top and front slid away to reveal a metal storage box set in the wall.

"Any money in that storage box belongs to this farm," Styles said. "As manager of this estate—"

Ferrell's cold glance across his shoulder silenced Styles. Ferrell opened the storage box and removed the leather pouches from within it. There were three pouches, but only one had anything in it. He poured the gold coins out on the lectern. Light glittered on the polished metal. Thyestes stood holding the lantern high while they counted the coins. There was a little over 500 in gold eagles.

Styles laughed abruptly, savagely. "Are you going to pay the black slut? There's no money for her. I tried to tell you. The great Baynard. This is the result of his management. This is what he left. Too mighty to borrow any more money from Garrett Ware's bank. . . . What in hell did he expect to work with?"

Ferrell laughed coldly. "I don't know, Styles. Maybe he knew you as well as I do. Maybe he knew he was going to die. . . ."

CHAPTER 42

LUKE SCROGGINGS gazed across the president's desk in the First Bank of Mt. Zion. He said to Styles and Ferrell, "Good morning. Welcome, gentlemen." But he did not bother to smile. His gaze brushed across Styles and settled for a long breath on Ferrell, the black cassock, the gold cross on a chain about his neck, the turned white collar. A look of cold contempt chilled the freckled face.

Ferrell was shocked to find Scroggings in the office where he'd always visited stout old Leonard Forsythe with his father. Luke seemed unchanged since that first hot Saturday afternoon Ferrell had met him outside Lorna June Garrity's house. Luke had impressed him as an ugly, pugnacious-looking bulldog of a man. His impression had not changed. Luke had hated him that day—this was clear in his savage expression, illy concealed. This had not changed either.

Ferrell winced. Luke had instinctively despised him that long-ago Saturday when he had come between the red-haired bank clerk and Lorna Garrity. He had reason to hate him now. Scroggings' face paled so that his freckles stood in sharp relief on his cheeks.

"Where is old Mr. Forsythe?" Ferrell said.

"I'm afraid you'll have to transact any business you have with this bank with me, *Father*," Luke Scroggings said in that cold contempt. "Old Forsythe has retired."

"I'm afraid I neglected to tell Brother Alexander that you had been promoted here at the bank, Scroggings," Styles said along his nose.

Luke waved them into the leather chairs across his

desk. He watched Ferrell narrowly. "Yes. I run this bank now, *Father*," Scroggings said. "There's been a lot of changes here in Mt. Zion since you went off into the church, father. Reckon you didn't hear. Heard you had given over your life to God. Was real surprised. Both Mrs. Scroggings and me."

"How is—Mrs. Scroggings?" Ferrell said.

Luke smoothly ignored his question about Lorna. This told Ferrell clearer than any savage words that Luke would never willingly discuss her with him. He said, "Yes. We didn't think of you—as religious—or interested in the church in any way, father. . . . Well, life is full of surprises. . . . Old Mr. Leonard Forsythe had a stroke. Some months ago. Turned management of the whole bank over to me. Named me president. Yes, sir. There it is. Right on that nameplate. Luke Scroggings, President. Things change, father."

"How very interesting," Styles said in a dull tone of disinterest.

Scroggings went on smiling. "No, what happens here in this little ole town, in this bank may not be of much interest to you, Mr. Kenric, or you, Father. . . . On the other hand, changes—like me being made president of this bank—might vitally affect you—and your closest friends."

"In what way?" Styles inquired.

Scroggings shrugged. "At the present, perhaps in no way. On the other hand, one man might run a bank one way—another man might change the way that bank is run. And this could affect a lot of people—very fine old families."

Styles laughed coldly. "I have a feeling you are trying to tell us something, Mr. Scroggings."

Luke Scroggings smiled in a cold way and shrugged again. "Don't let me waste your valuable time, Mr. Kenric. I know since you are running Blackoaks, you got more to do than to listen to any talk about changes in a bank's operating procedures. In what way may I serve you gentlemen?"

Styles glanced at Ferrell. Ferrell said, "We're trying to find out what bank accounts my father may have left—

savings or checking. I know he's always had an account here. We'd like to know the present balance in the Blackoaks account."

Scroggings wrote something on a slip of paper. He glanced at Styles. "In the Blackoaks account?"

"Yes," Styles said. He sank back on the leather chair and carefully crossed his legs.

Luke summoned a clerk, gave him the slip of paper, and whispered something to him behind his hand. The clerk nodded and left the office. "While we are waiting, Father," Luke said. "Perhaps you might be interested in one change in bank policy. It may not affect you personally. On the other hand it may have considerable impact on the lives of very *dear* friends of yours, Father." Luke waited, then said in a mild tone, "Old Forsythe had a policy I disliked and which I changed immediately. When he collected on mortgages, he was often most lenient toward long-time plantation owners and farmers. Frankly, he *carried* them. This bank won't do that anymore."

Styles laughed at him. "Are you intimating, Scroggings, that you might foreclose on Blackoaks?"

Luke raised his hand, palm outward. "Not at all. Not as long as Blackoaks meets its notes with this bank—promptly. I'm not suggesting there is the slightest reason for concern where Blackoaks is involved—"

"Then why do you insist on this line of conversation, when I know I'm not interested," Styles said.

"I'm sorry, Mr. Kenric. I was thinking more about *Father* Ferrell here. He has such close and valued friends. Friends who belong to the very oldest families in the area, eh? Eh, Father? Mr. Gil Talmadge, for example. A very close friend of yours, eh, Father?"

Ferrell flushed. He nodded. "I've known Gil a long time. All my life."

"Yes. Of course you have. And Mr. Tetherow—young Mr. Link Tetherow. Good friends of yours before you—went into the church, eh, Father?"

"Of course I know Link. Very well."

"Of course you do, *Father*. And Mr. Walter-Roy Summerton?"

Ferrell felt his face burn—Link, Walter-Roy, Gil—the

men who had raped Lorna. Suppressed rage made Scroggings' voice quaver. Luke continued, voice low and deadly. "It would ordinarily violate ethics and bank policy to discuss such matters, but these dear friends of yours—among other old families around here, of course—have notes due and long overdue, which Old Forsythe carried —with their entire estates as collateral."

Styles shrugged. "You're right. You are being unethical —and this bank has always extended those notes. Mr. Forsythe will continue that policy."

Luke shook his head. "No. That's why I violated a policy of the bank in discussing the affairs of its depositors in talking with you and *Father* Ferrell. Mr. Forsythe ain't president of this here bank no more. I thought perhaps Father Ferrell might want to mention this to his close, dear friends. There ain't going to be no extentions on their mortgages. Not one day. That's just one of the changes around here, Father, since you been away. Of course, as notes come due, I'll write formal letters—and present notes of eviction. . . . I just know how close you fine old families are to one another . . . thought it might be easier on them—if the news come from you *gentlemen*." He made something slimy of the word. He looked up as the clerk placed a slip of paper before him on his desk. He glanced at the note for some moments, then looked up with a chilled smile. "Blackoaks has no outstanding notes or mortgages with this bank. I'm sure that will make you happy—and relieved, Father. There is a total of $3,000 in the Blackoaks checking account—on which Mr. Styles Kenric, Mrs. Kenric, Mrs. Claire Baynard—and you, Father—are authorized to draw drafts. Is this the information you gentlemen wished?"

They nodded, stood up, thanking him. He gazed at Ferrell with a twisted smile. It occurred to him that Styles Kenric had not mentioned a visit earlier in which he had transferred almost twenty thousand dollars from the Blackoaks account to his own personal account. He might have mentioned it, but it seemed somehow less than ethical. If Mr. Kenric had wanted the novitiate priest to know about his personal account, *he* would have introduced the subject. Luke got up and walked out of the

421

room and across the foyer of the bank with his guests. He held the front door opened while they went out. He even remembered, as an afterthought, to wish Father Ferrell every success in his new life in the service of God. "Paul was not always a saint, eh, Father? No . . . he was once despised as Saul of Taurus. Eh? Good-bye, *Father*."

Change set in at Blackoaks. Styles spoke caustically, if at all, holding himself aloof from the rest of the family. He locked himself in Baynard's small downstairs office, with his bottles of Baynard's whiskey, and his plans for the future of the big farm. He remained in a bitter, sarcastic mood that softened only after Ferrell departed to catch his train in Mt. Zion. Ferrell spoke dejectedly to Jeanne d'Arc. He could not believe that his father would leave her the sum of $10,000 in his will—along with her freedom—and then make no provisions for producing the cash. This simply was totally unlike the pattern of his father's existence. There was an answer, he told the *os rouge,* and he would find it. In the meantime, he remained as near to her as a brief note to him from her.

Styles knew how often Ferrell talked with Jeanne d'Arc, how long they sat speaking quietly. Tension crackled in the air between him and Ferrell though they remained unfailingly, deadly polite to each other. When Ferrell stepped up into the carriage beside Laus, Styles invited him to return soon. Styles spoke in an insolent, disdainful tone that certainly implied he hoped never to see Ferrell alive on this earth again.

Ferrell smiled across his shoulder and assured Styles that he would indeed be back. His voice assuredly carried a warning. Styles stood erect, unbending on the veranda, almost in a battle stance. Kathy felt a terrible sense of insecurity and disruption that she could not escape.

Styles followed her into the sun room from the veranda after Ferrell was gone. Kathy wanted to be alone, but for a change, Styles was in a talkative, almost exuberant mood. She tried to share his enthusiasm for their future, but she could not match his optimism, nor participate in his anticipated success in a world without her father's strength, or her brother's reassuring presence.

Styles paced before her chair, talking, looking ahead. They would be soon be traveling frequently, extensively. There would be trips to New Orleans, Atlanta, New York. They would tour Europe. There was so much he wanted her to see. They had been stagnating too long on this backwater plantation. He envisioned a restructured farm —fewer acres in corn, fewer in cotton, the planting and reaping more as exercise for the fancy-quality slaves they would breed than as a money crop. There were ways to great riches. He knew them and he would follow them unvaryingly.

He spoke with a self-assurance that chilled, rather than exalted her. He strode up and down the room, talking to her, talking aloud to himself, really free for the first time to indulge his ambitious projected programs for this estate with no one to oppose or obstruct him. His enthusiasm and excitement mounted. They would need financing, of course, though he confessed to her that they were far better situated financially than he had permitted Ferrell to discover or even to suspect. He laughed. Financing was no problem. What he could not borrow through the local bank at Mt. Zion, he could always get from Garrett Blanford Ware and his bank down in Florida. Thank God, unlike her father, he had been friendly with the Wares. He had courted their favor, ingratiated himself while Baynard was being practically boorish and insulting toward the banker. Oh, he could get the credit he needed, all right. Buying Fulani females would take great amounts of cash. But Ware would supply all he needed. He would write at once to Ware in Tallahassee. The banker would be flattered to advise him on the strongest negroid bloodlines, those most adaptable to labor, climate, and conditions of slavery. In a few years, Blackoaks would be recognized as the nonpareil supplier of quality and fancy blacks.

He spoke confidently and she wished she could share his confidence. She could not. Where he exuded self-assurance, she found only fear, and she wanted to press her hands over her ears to shut out the sound of his voice.

She watched him, troubled, as he paced. His voice vibrated with his inner self-assurance. His finely chiseled face was flushed, his eyes glittering with his enthusiasms. God! how she would have welcomed and responded to such ardor from him in their bed making love. But there he remained chilled and distant. She had never reached any of those peaks of happiness she had dreamed ahead to when she first met and fell in love with Styles. She supposed she never would; her marriage had been a long, slow lesson in living apart even when your bodies touched. She shivered again, unable to shake off that persistent sense of an unexplained, impending doom.

Styles was restless. The room, the house was not big enough to contain him and his plans for the future. His thoughts and ideas chased themselves in frenzied circles through his mind.

In contrast, she sat, barely hearing him, consumed by grief at her father's death, the sense of loss that had chilled her when Ferrell drove away, waving back at her as he went down that winter-bleak, leafless lane toward the gate and the trail beyond. She'd felt a wild urge to run after him, to call him back, to beg him to stay. What was to become of them without him? Where was the old security and strength and warmth that had informed and sustained the Baynard family? Her father dead. Her brother buried in the priesthood. Poor Morgan. Her mother indisposed in her bedroom again this morning. And she—listening to Styles' brilliant exposition of their life ahead and certain with cold shock that they were lost and had no future at all.

In the next weeks, this dread was compounded and deepened. Styles strode about, letting the slaves get used to him as the new master. He circulated about the place, swollen with the exalting sense of ownership and new authority. When he spoke and was obeyed, he smiled. When he was crossed, he ordered Bos to use the whip. They would see that things were different at Blackoaks; there was a new master. The sooner they learned to accept him, to move when he spoke to them, the better. This was his estate. His domain. The master of Blackoaks, after all. Kathy watched him, ill. In many ways he was like a young boy playing a game, removed from reality, from the real world.

They came to her with their complaints and their griefs. She listened with a mounting sense of helplessness. She promised to speak to Styles, even when she knew her speaking to him of plantation problems would only compound the evil. They begged her to write to Masta Ferrell. They pleaded with her to entreat the young master to come home to Blackoaks. Sometimes, in the eyes of the whipped slaves, she saw the threat of retaliation against Styles. But she couldn't even tell him this. She lived in a sense of confusion and distress. There was so much she had to do. These people were like children; they had to trust somebody; they had to believe in someone; they had to have faith in that person's strength and integrity. Oh, God, she thought, there's only me. It was an impossible task. She was too weak, too helpless against Styles. No one could stop him now, least of all, she. At last, he had what he wanted. It was as if the entire direction of his life had pointed him toward this moment when at last he became the master of Blackoaks.

Finally, she wrote to Ferrell. She explained that he had put the world behind him, that she had no right to pursue him with the woes of Blackoaks, and yet she could not believe his home meant so little to him that he could close his eyes to the despair of its people, the certain destruction that was ahead. She finished the letter, addressd it, handed it to Thyestes to send into Mt. Zion to be mailed. At that moment Styles stepped out of his office. She flushed guiltily, but he gave her only a glance and strode past her along the corridor.

She watched Styles go out of the French doors and across the veranda where Hunt Campbell spoke quietly, but with a desperate sense of frustration, of nouns and adjectives and adverbs and predicates to a confused Morgan and a drowsing Soapy.

The morning light filtered yellowly in elongated shafts across the carpeting from the tall windows. Sounds of the servants at their duties, the boys on the veranda, and distantly, the workers at the barns, scratched ineffectually at her consciousness. She was overwhelmed by a sepulchral sense of melancholy—a depression that rendered her empty stomached and shaken. She got up from the wing-back chair and walked out of the sun room, hurrying, almost with a feeling that she was escaping not only its oppressive quiet but as if she were somehow escaping Styles and all he meant in their future.

"Miss Kathy."

She hesitated, astonished to meet Hunt Campbell at the foot of the stairs. She paused, studying him. She almost smiled through her sense of depression. She'd decided months ago that he arranged these casual little accidental encounters. It had to be prearrangement. She was always meeting him unexpectedly on the stairs, in the upper corridor, the sun room. Suddenly there he was. To this moment it had been flattering, if totally unimportant. But all that belonged to a better time, a season of security and warmth—a long time ago when Ferrell was at home and her father was still alive—in a world lost.

"May I talk to you?" he said.

She looked up at him. He had such wide shoulders, such a look of manliness. Too bad he was a tutor, hiding behind his books, unwilling to fight. She needed a man on this place so terribly—but she needed a man, not Hunter Campbell. She shrugged and nodded her head toward Styles' small office. She even thought she chose it only as a miserable little gesture of defiance toward Styles—she was taking another man into Styles' sacrosanct domain.

She closed the door behind them and stood looking up at him. His face was flushed. He said awkwardly, "I appreciate getting to talk to you—alone like this, Miss Kathy. . . . I wanted to say that it's been—one of the great privileges of my life, knowing you—even from a distance."

Kathy laughed. He was so serious, so solemn and Boston proper. "How nice. But what prompts such a delightful confession?"

He smiled, realizing there was no way she could have followed the complex skein of his thoughts—his failure here, the death of her father, the sure knowledge that Styles was not going to continue a fruitless tutoring of Morgan, the desperate sense of loss that he would never see her again. "I'll probably be leaving. . . . There's not

426

much I can do—for Morgan. His father didn't care—as long as I tried. . . . I'm sure your husband won't feel that way."

Her heart seemed to slip its mooring. She had hardly known he was alive but she was stricken at the thought of his going away—too many people were going away, leaving her. She stopped smiling and shook her head. "No," she said. There was almost a tone of panic in her voice. "There is no need for you to go."

"There's nothing I can do here—for Morgan. Your husband has been aware of that for some time."

"I want you to stay—Morgan needs you."

"Thank you. But I'm afraid your husband doesn't agree. I'll have to go."

She shook her head again. "Please. Not now. You don't need to go—right away. . . . There's been enough—dying—enough going away. Our family is suddenly almost gone. . . . Why should you go now? . . . I don't want you to go."

Hunt shivered. He felt as if he'd been struck violently in the chest. He stared down at Kathy searching for some deeper meaning in her words. Her gaze fell away under his and her pale easter-lily complexion glowed warmly.

He winced. Her words were not coquettish. There was as much a cry for help in her quiet, taut voice as there could be without tears and wailing. She seemed still hardly aware of him as a person—as a man—but he belonged to Blackoaks, and she could not endure another loss, even an impersonal one, so soon. *Not yet. Don't go yet. I don't want you to go.*

My God, he thought, she needs help, and she is turning to me. My God, she *is* in trouble. She needs someone with strength and courage—and all she had available was this Harvard philosopher who declares physical violence beneath him. For the first time he admitted this was a cloak over his cowardice. Maybe in its way, this was the beginning of wisdom. If there were anyone for whom he could change his spots, it was Kathy Kenric. Something. He would have to do something. He did not know what it could be.

"No," he heard himself saying. "I won't go. If you don't want me to."

The small room was suddenly overheated, crowded. He was very close to her. He had only to reach out and draw her against him. He sweated. He stared down at her. Her head tilted, she looked up at him—as if she'd never seen him before.

His hand went against the small of her back. God! she was fragile! You might think she'd break if you touched her. She sagged against him. He waited. She offered no protest, did not pull away.

"Kathy," he whispered. "Oh, my God, Kathy."

Her eyes closed. He bent down and kissed her, lifting her slender body against his. She did not part her lips. Jesus. Married three years and she didn't even know how to kiss. There was so much he could teach her. She really did need him.

The soft fragrance of her assailed his nostrils, going through him. His head spun. He felt his staff growing rigid against her. God in heaven, such a hard-on. Just touching her, just kissing her closed lips, just inhaling the fragrance of her body. He'd never been hard like this before, not with Addie, naked in front of the fire, nor with Sefina, jungle wild and black and savage. Never. With his hand on the small of her back, he lifted Kathy a little more and her mons veneris settled against the rigidity of his rod. She quivered slightly, but she did not move away. He pressed her down upon him, in sweet agony.

"Oh, don't," she whispered. "We can't."

"We can. You need me, Kathy. . . . I know you need me."

"I'm a married woman," she whispered, frantic, breathless, lying upon him, resting against his solid fly, her toes barely touching the ground.

"You're starved. We can't lie to each other, Kathy—"

"I won't lie to you. . . . I don't want—another Styles."

"Me?" He was shocked, his tone revealed it.

"You're—as pretty as he is. Prettier. . . ."

"My God, you say that with such contempt—"

"Maybe I'll always hate pretty men—all the rest of my life—"

"I swear to you. . . . I'm not—like Styles."

Her head tilted back. She stared up at him, "What do you mean?"

"Trust me. I'm not. . . . I'm sorry for you. . . . Maybe you didn't know what he was when you married him—"

"What he was?"

"Wasted on him. But I'm nothing like him. Please, Kathy. Give me a chance—let me show you."

She writhed her taut little bottom against the rigidity of his staff. She laughed, pale. "You—are showing me—I never felt—anything like this—"

"God knows, Kathy, I get hard when you come near me—"

"Oh, how beautiful that sounds." She moved herself upon him, involuntarily.

"Let me show you—"

She struggled, trying to get free, but she seemed unable to thrust away from his hardness.

"You don't have to go on being starved," he whispered. "You've suffered enough. . . . It doesn't have to be like that. You need a man, Kathy—and I am a man."

She put her head back again. "So much a man!" She tried to laugh, but her hungers betrayed her. She lay her head on his chest a moment, holding herself close against the thunder of his heart, the strength of his arms, the clean man-scent of him. His hand closed on her breast. A tremor coursed through her, but for the moment she did not rebuke him or attempt to move away. She felt her eyes burn with helpless tears.

Her own heart pounded faster. For the first time in her life, Kathy dared to think what it might be like in the arms of a vital man, a strong man who really wanted her. His rigidity was something she had never encountered in all her life before. She could writhe upon it helplessly, but she could not force herself to pull away. She could almost believe she might yet glimpse real happiness somewhere in the future ahead of her. The promise of fulfillment and savage excitement and mindless pleasure made her tremble.

"Don't be afraid," he whispered. "Please don't be afraid."

"No . . . I won't be afraid."

Emboldened, Hunt slipped his hand into the open bodice of her dress, cupping her heated, bared breast in his palm. Her trembling increased, but she remained slumped passively in his arms, resting against the upright support of his rod. Her breathing was quick and labored, and he understood in the confusion that occluded his thinking processes that she wanted him to love her. She wanted him! Perhaps she had not, until this moment in his arms, but he knew in that instant that he could have her. He didn't know when, but he felt enthralled, uplifted, drunk with pleasure and the promise of every passionate dream fulfilled. "You're so lovely, Kathy. . . . My God, you're so lovely." He worked her faster and faster upon him.

"We must not."

"You know better. We've got to."

"Yes . . . Oh, I do know . . . I do know, Hunt . . . but you—mustn't rush me. You must—oh, God, you must give me time—I've never been faithless, never thought about being faithless. . . ."

"You can't be faithless to *him,* Kathy. . . . You must think about us now. You and me."

"Oh, I don't know." She laughed helplessly. Her hand reached up, gently stroked his cheek. "Hold me tighter, darling, down there. . . . Like that. . . . Oh, I promise you . . . Oh, yes . . . I promise you."

He parted her lips with his mouth, thrust his tongue between her teeth. She opened wide for him, submissive in a way that left him shaken. He felt shock too at the soft, heated fragrance of her mouth. She had never kissed like this before. And he knew he had never really kissed before either, never been overwhelmed with the need to *drink* the sweetness of her mouth. "Oh, God, Kathy . . . oh, God."

"Hold me, darling. Hold me. . . . Oh, you feel so strong—so hard—so good." Her eyes were wide open now. And she clung to him, but he saw the stark agony working deep in those shadowy eyes. . . . She was at the breaking point, torn between need and her life of fidelity and un-compromised values. She would come to him. Soon or late,

430

she would be his. He still didn't know when, but she would
need him, and she would come to him.

And he'd be there. . . .

CHAPTER 43

DECAY IN ITS WAY is a cancerous growth. As long as it is held in check, it spreads imperceptibly, but once it flares uncontrolled, it sweeps out rapidly in its destructiveness. It was like that at Blackoaks in the months after Baynard died, Ferrell returned to the seminary, and Styles succeeded the older man as master of Blackoaks. Only the most perceptive expert could possibly have pointed out the secret places where dry rot and neglect were taking their toll. But the deterioration showed itself in many ways. Old Thyestes answered the front door with his shoes unlaced, limping openly, taking his time. He openly drank from the liquor stock, was continually sneaking drinks against the pain in his feet. This was a small aberration, surely, but a significant one in the decadescent chateau: services fail as moral qualities decline. In the kitchen, though she remained in command of the cooks, bakers, and house servants, Jeanne d'Arc felt like an alien, barely tolerated by Styles—as if she might be forcibly removed at any moment. She might almost wish Ferrell had not willed her freedom; whatever he had intended for her, it was not the emptiness and insecurity in which she found herself. She hated and despised the new master of Blackoaks as fiercely as she had loved his predecessor. About Styles Kenric was an unwholesomeness that she didn't understand but which made the flesh crawl at the nape of her neck, and the chilled distaste in his face reminded her constantly that he owed her money, a great deal of money. . . .

In the fields, work slowed despite everything Bos Pilzer could do. He was still totally in command—he was too strong, too stubbornly Dutch ever to fail his job. But Pilzer's law was the law of the whip, and that law only, with all its restrictions. There was no longer a strong master above Pilzer, ruling the slaves distantly and dispassionately but with an iron will and with the final power of life and death. The slaves grumbled aloud when Pilzer herded them into the fields; they protested when he gave them orders. They stood against him until his whip laid open the face of their leader. They fell back then and went to work. But they still grumbled, and the black, ripped face reminded them constantly that Pilzer could whip them and there was no one to whom they could appeal. Pilzer was smart. He saw bad trouble brewing, but there was no one to whom he could express his warning, or from whom he could draw support. Styles Kenric didn't want to hear about troubles in the field. "Don't come crying to me, Pilzer. That's your job. When you can't handle it, let me know. I'll get someone who can."

Pilzer called the pretty man a son of a bitch, but prudently he waited until he was on his great horse and halfway across the plateau before he said it, snarling it. "You son of a bitch. You pretty son of a bitch. I hope they kill you in your bed some night. You son of a bitch. . . ."

The income from the distillery was a pleasant and distinct shock for Styles. He had no idea the old man had drawn such an income from the casks of whiskey that rolled down the trail each week for the train station at Mt. Zion. He was counting on that income to help him buy a couple of Fulani wenches when a fire almost totally destroyed the distillery. It would be a year before the slaves could get the still in operation again. . . .

Something that infuriated Styles more than the slackness of the slave work ethic was the whispers among them that sustained them and drove him into a fury. He would walk into the kitchen early in the morning and find the house servants crowding around the table and the whispers would assault him until he trembled, "When Masta Ferrell-

Junior come home, these triflin' niggers start steppin' lively then. . . . When Masta Ferrell-Junior come home, you gonna see. . . ."

Styles strode across the room. His face was livid. His voice shook with anger. "Shut up that talk. Ferrell is not coming back here. You understand that? He's never coming back. I'm the master here."

They stared at him, smiling. "Yes, suh, Masta Styles, suh."

But they looked at each other, suppressing giggles. They knew better said their stupid faces, their fatuous grinning. Masta Ferrell-Junior *was* coming home and Blackoaks would be a good, safe, and beautiful place to live again. They smiled at Styles and nodded. But they looked at each other and suppressed their giggling. No matter what Masta Styles say, they knew a great day was coming. Great day when they saw Masta Ferrell-Junior come a-striding up the lane under them pecan trees. Yes, Lord. . . .

"Goddamn you!" Styles shouted, trembling. "Get to work. Every goddamn one of you black apes."

Yes, masta. Yes, Lord. . . .

They knew they had found the one way to unsettle the cold and unapproachable Styles Kenric. It began as a late evening whisper and became a serenade, a black lamenting. The Negroes sank to their knees at the far slope of the plateau around the manor house. The keening sing-song sound in the glowering dusk was like a wind in the trees. Yes, Lord. Yes, Lord. That day coming. Yes, Lord. Yes, Lord. . . .

Styles would lunge up from his chair and rush out on the veranda. He would clutch up a gun, or a whip, and stand, legs apart, eyes wild, staring into the gathering dusk.

"Stop it!" Styles raged. "I'll have you whipped. All of you. Every damned black hide whipped. Laid bare—man, woman, or child. . . . Now get out of here, get out, get out."

Each night they would slowly retreat, drifting into the smoky darkness, dissolving into it, but the keening sound of their lamenting washed back up over him until long after dark. That great day coming. Yes, Lord. Yes, Lord. . . .

Styles had a dozen blacks whipped. He marched among them, choosing indiscriminately. He forced the black community to watch the lashings. When it was over, he stood gazing at them, his mouth twisted. "And we'll whip ten more tomorrow. Ten more everyday until it stops. Is that clear?"

Yes, masta. Yes, Lord. . . .

It even came to pass that he could laugh about the lamenting, and the cool way he had stopped it. He was master of Blackoaks. He was in command. He would show them how totally he was in command.

He summoned the family and the house slaves into the kitchen one morning at seven-thirty. He stood, waiting chilled and silently aloof until they all trooped into the room, black and white alike, silent and puzzled.

They glanced at each other, nervous and self-conscious, troubled. They thought about the public whippings. They remembered no such meeting of family and slaves as a single group ever before. Miz Claire, and the older slaves particularly, were perturbed and uncertain of the propriety of lumping the two castes together in this way. There should never be a breakdown between the whites and the blacks; this had proved fatal more than once before; the Bible said God separated the races, white and black. God wanted them separated.

When they were assembled, the servants pressed against the walls, some were openly trembling. Light from the morning fire in the huge bow-legged iron wood-burning stove reflected a warm chocolate glow on their sweated skins. The family and Hunter Campbell sat at the kitchen table. Miz Claire sat straight, her disapproval clearly indicated in the set tilt of her head. She waved a wispy kerchief soaked in spirits of camphor under her nose.

Styles was never more impeccably attired—silk scarf, wide-collared linen shirt opened at the throat, trousers with razor-sharp crease, and highly polished black boots. He drew his gaze across them without a flicker of a

435

smile. "I won't mince words with you. I am master of Blackoaks. Mr. Baynard wanted me to assume control in his place, and I am doing it to the best of my ability. . . . But I won't have my good efforts undermined by any of you—white or black."

He tilted his aristocratic head slightly and moved his gaze across their faces. Puzzled, and growing more troubled, they stirred, glanced at each other, and watched him in silence, waiting.

"I am master here, and master I intend to remain. I will be exactly as considerate of you as you permit me to be. But I shall also be as firm as you people force me to be. What happens to you—any of you—depends on your own conduct and your own willingness to cooperate with me—and to follow my orders. Changes are being made here at Blackoaks. But understand me well, the lasting changes are only those which I institute. I know what's best for this plantation, and I shall continue putting my plans into action."

Again he stared, chilled and unapproachable, at them. The blacks shivered, uncomfortable under his unrelenting gaze. Shiva sniffled audibly, but no one spoke.

"When I order a change in the old way of doing things around here—when I give an order—demand a punishment for some wrong committed against me, this plantation, or my property, I am the final arbiter. I am the highest court to which you can appeal. It will profit you nothing to write sniveling, whining notes of complaint to Ferrell Baynard—or Brother Alexander as he now chooses to call himself. Writing to Brother Alexander about what goes on here at Blackoaks will not only avail you nothing—it may cost you a great deal."

Now there was a slight response of agitation among his listeners. Kathy felt her face grow warm. Miz Claire fanned her sheer kerchief faster.

"Not only will I intercept any such letters going out from here, I shall severely punish the next person who writes such a letter of complaint to Brother Alexander. He is no longer in charge here. He never was. He is not now master of Blackoaks. He has made a wise selection for him—and embraced Catholicism. He is studying for

436

the priesthood. We do not want to, or need to, burden Brother Alexander with the daily routines of Blackoaks. He has by choice put all of this behind him. He serves a greater master. I won't have him harried by whines or petty complaints from malcontents or troublemakers among us here. Is that clear?"

He stared at each of them individually until the very intensity of his gaze elicited a nod of the head in acquiescence. Only Kathy stared straight back at him until he looked away, annoyed. His face paled slightly and he straightened his linen shirt up on his wide, square shoulders.

He took up a heavy baked-clay ashtray from the table beside him. On it were stacked at least half a dozen letters, sealed in envelopes. Kathy caught her breath, recognizing the letter she had written to Ferrell begging him to return. Each missive had been ripped across.

Styles walked across the room to the stove, disturbing a fat Maltese cat, which sprang out of his path yowling. He lit a slender piece of kindling and returned to the table with it as its fire flickered to a steady orange flame. "This is what happens to all such letters so far written. The precise same thing will happen to any other letters to Brother Alexander complaining of your life or treatment here at Blackoaks." He held the kindling, setting fire to the torn papers in the tray. The fire leapt up, brilliant in the gloomily lit room.

"Are you saying that we are your prisoners here?" Kathy asked in a scathing tone.

He smiled at her without the slightest trace of warmth. "We—each of us—make our own prisons, Miss Kathy. This can be a happy place—or it can be a hell. I suggest that all depends on what each of you makes of it."

"You can't refuse us the right to send out letters to whom and whenever we wish," she said.

"Can't I? If those letters serve this place no good purpose, I think I can. Anyhow, we shall see." He shrugged. "Now I have warned you. As plainly as I know how. I shall deal more severely with the next one who writes so piteously for help to Brother Alexander." He laughed, an abrasive sound. "Pray to your God instead—results will amount to the same."

He stood watching the flame die down in the ashtray. He waited and no one spoke. He appeared to relent slightly. He showed them a faint smile. "You are all free to write—to anyone, at anytime—if you write only letters which do not attack or condemn me and the decisions I make for the welfare of Blackoaks—which means the welfare of all of us. I am master. Whether Blackoaks fails or prospers depends entirely upon me. I cannot have my actions and decisions undermined by letters filled with lies and trumped-up charges against me. I have your best interests at heart. I know what's best for you. But I mean to run this place as I believe it must be operated."

Now, like a benevolent despot, he took up a small envelope and paper from the table. "Here is a letter I did not burn." He held the envelope for all to see. "As you can see, this letter is addressed to Brother Alexander at the seminary in Charleston. I'll tell you that this letter is from Jeanne d'Arc. It was written for her by Morgan. And I want to commend you, Morgan, for your penmanship—if not your spelling. This note says simply: 'Things are fine here, hope they are the same with you. Love, Jeanne d'Arc.' "

He waited another moment for all of them to absorb the brief, bland message. "I was so pleased with Jeanne d'Arc's letter when compared to the whimpering tones in these others that I copied it over for her and I will have it posted tomorrow from Mt. Zion. Any other such pleasant letters which will not embarrass me, nor burden Brother Alexander, are quite acceptable and I will permit them to be mailed. Is this clear?"

CHAPTER 44

FLORINE PILZER sagged dejectedly at the bare kitchen table and stared at her trembling hands. Bos's old Swiss clock struck the quarter-hour and then the half, and she remained unmoving. The remaining afternoon sunlight collected in a smeared pool of saffron on the floor and receded toward the shadowed wall. It was almost six, almost dark. She heard the great iron ringer being struck to summon in the fieldhands home to quarters for the night. Bos would soon be home with his ravenous appetite after a day in the fields, and with that unyielding Dutch temperament he would demand his hot meal on the table when he came in the door. She thought about this without emotion. She recalled the brutality Bos was capable of when roused. None of it moved her. She went on sitting slumped in the straight-back chair as if resigned to await doomsday, unmoving, unmoved. The room felt oppressively small, as did the fieldstone house, the farm, the world itself. Everything pressed in on her. She wanted to scream, to cry out in agonized protest. But she did not move at all.

She heard the heavy plod of Bos's huge gray horse, crossing the yard to the stables. After a few moments, she heard Bos at the barn, cursing, and then he came striding into the kitchen. The screen door squealed against its spring and slammed shut behind him. His swarthy, ruddy face was contorted with rage, and his voice shook with his anger.

"Where is he?" Bos said. He slapped a short crop against his booted leg.

439

Florine glanced up at him. At the fury contorting his face, she felt herself go weak—but only from old habit. She gripped the table, her knuckles gray. Had he heard at last—the truth about what went on in here while he was out in the fields? She wanted to sob in laughter at the irony if this were true. Now that Moab was gone, Bos would learn the truth. Now that she had lost Moab, she must pay for having loved him. Well, no matter what Bos did to her now, there was no payment worse than her losing Moab. And she had lost him.

She sank back in the chair and gazed apathetically up at her husband. She could not care what Bos did to her now. She'd had precious little to live for before. Now, with Moab gone, she had nothing. Less than nothing. She said in a tone of dull defiance, "Who, Bos?"

"The boy," Bos said. "The nigger Moab. The black bastard didn't do his chores. Hell—a fine mess if I got to start coming home to do chores after a day in the field with them apes."

"You do," she said.

"What?" He stared down at her and slapped the short whip against his boot. "What the hell? What you say?"

She exhaled heavily, did not look up. "They took our nigger." She spoke in that careful denigrating tone she'd learned to use in talking with Bos about all blacks, any black.

"Moab?" Bos shook his head, incredulous. "Who took him? By God, I won't have it. Who took Moab? We need him."

"Yes." She nodded dully. "We need him."

He smiled, almost grudgingly, thinking about Moab. "Only nigger I know except his brother Blade worth a tinker's damn."

"Yes."

"Well, speak up. Who took him? Tell me. I'll go get him."

She sighed, shaking her head. "You can't."

"The hell I can't. Don't tell me I can't. I work hard running this farm. Harder'n ever since the old man passed on. I need that nigger boy around the house here, taking care of things for me."

"Yes." She glanced up at him. "To do the things you can't do. The things you don't have time to do."

He nodded, pacing the room. "That's right. Aye, that's right. And that's why when we get us a good nigger that both of us need and trust, they can't come and take him away from us."

"They have taken him, Bos. Styles Kenric came. Himself. The snooty bastard came. Took Moab and his things from the tack room. He's moving Moab into the big house."

Bos cursed. "What'd he want to take Moab for? Moab ain't no fuckin' house slave."

Her fingers tightened on the bevel of the table. "Looks like he will be."

Bos swore, striding up and down. But his swearing was impotent. If Styles Kenric had taken their nigger, there was no way to get him back.

Bos sank into the unpainted kitchen chair across the table from Florine. The sunlight was only a shallow smudge at the edge of the wall. A smoky darkness settled, enveloping the room. They sat unspeaking for a long time, bereft, both of them, and helpless to fight for what they wanted. Bos didn't even notice she hadn't prepared his supper. When, after a long silence, she asked him finally and forlornly what he wanted to eat, he only shook his head and spoke in the kindliest tone he'd used with her since the third day of their honeymoon. "That's all right, hon. Anytime . . . I'm just not hungry." And so, in their grievous loss, they were brought closer together than they had ever been before. . . .

Bos stared at the scrubbed floor for a long time, musing. "Bet by God, Kenric's gettin' the nigger kid ready to stand stud."

"Who?"

"Moab."

"Moab." She shivered in the gray darkness. "Why, he's just a young boy."

Bos laughed. "No. Moab's sixteen—seventeen plantin's old by now. . . . He's ready as he's ever gonna be. He's built like a young stallion right now."

"Is he?" She strove to keep in her voice that inflection of

disdain, of disinterest. It was not easy. It was one of the most difficult things she'd ever done. Her throat felt constricted. She wanted to cry out in protest. Not Moab. They had no right. Moab was all she had. All she'd ever had.

Bos chuckled, nodding. "If you'd ever seen the nigger in the buck, you'd know he's built."

"Well, I never did."

He reached over and patted her chilled fingers with his rough, calloused hand. "I know that, hon. Just trying to joke a little. . . . I can tell you though. Way Moab's hung, he'll have the black bitches in heat all the time."

"Bos. Don't talk like that. I am a respectable woman, you know. Church going. Even if I am your wife. Don't appreciate your rough talk."

He laughed soothingly. "I thought you craved a little talk about sexing now and then, hon."

"Yes. But not about niggers. That ain't sexing. They animals."

"They're animals that have one hell of a lot of fun. When them black vixens see how our boy Moab is built, they'll want to get it poked in 'em every way they can. They takes it just any way that pleasures a man, you know. Why, they tell me black women go right down on a man's tool. Can you rightly imagine that." He was slightly breathless, considering it. "No white lady would do that—I reckon?" He peered across the table, watching her hopefully.

"Of course not. . . . I don't even want to talk about such a thing." But now that she'd started, she seemed irresistibly drawn back to Moab and his new chores at Blackoaks. "Though I will say he's a clean young black boy—"

"Sure he is. Them black wenches will be fighting to get holt of his tool." He squirmed on his chair and laid his heavy hand high upon the inside of her leg. She did not move away.

"He don't have no niggery smell," Florine said in a flat tone.

"Tha's right. He don't. Don't hardly have that niggery

442

stink at all. One thing I can't abide—niggery stink. Moab never had that stink."

"That's because you made him bathe every day, made him keep clean." She knotted her fist on the table. "We done all we could for that boy—and now they just come and taken him away."

Bos swore. "Bastids. It ain't right. Goddamn it, it just ain't right. We worked hard with that boy. . . . He was our nigger."

"Yes," she said. "Yes. He was our nigger."

Troubled, Kathy went tiredly up the wide staircase. It seemed to her she existed in a vacuum. Torn between her desire to feel again the manly hardness, strength, and honest desire of Hunt, and her life-long habit of fidelity, Kathy fell ill. Going to Hunt's arms was not as simple as crawling into his bed and out of it. When she went to Hunt, a whole part of her life would end—the years of devotion to Styles, whether he wanted her or not, whether he was worthy or not. Her life with him would be over, ended. It was nothing she could enter into casually, God knew. She carefully avoided Hunt, refused to meet his eyes—and lay sleepless all night dreaming of him, of that wondrous bulge pulsing at his thigh, at the way he trembled with need and longing for her. God knew she'd never known anything like this in her life. She tossed on her bed, with Styles deep asleep beside her but for the heated moment no longer a part of her world. Her body heated, liquid down there as it had never been, she thought about it. She would go to Hunt. How? When? Where?

She drew her tongue across her parched lips. Suppose —she went now? Suppose she slipped out of this bed in her fragile gown, went along the corridor to his room, to his bed? Perspiring, she nodded, breathless, her heart seeming to pulse, achingly, in the base of her throat. Yes, she must go to him. But it could not be a journey lightly undertaken. Once she went to Hunt, she could never come back to this room, to this bed, to this man, this marriage. Though she might return physically, she knew that the night she succumbed to her body's aching needs and crept out of here into Hunt's arms, her life with this man, in this room, was ended. Her eyes filled with tears that scalded her cheeks. Maybe even yet there was a chance for her and Styles, and so she delayed. She lay in the violet darkness, heated, sweated, anguished, and stared beseechingly at the dark ceiling. Oh, God, help me. Help me. . . .

Now, she mounted the stairs, aware that Hunt stood at its foot, his hand gripping the newel post, staring up after her. She knew he was there, but she did not look back. She went along the upper corridor, walking slowly, but admitting inside that she was running away. . . .

She opened the door to her mother's bedroom suite. She found obese, chocolate-colored Neva gently brushing Miz Claire's hair. The tireless Neva had fashioned Miz Claire a charming little lace cap ornamented in front with wide ruffles and loops of ribbon extending upward and forward, called a *fontange*. Nothing that might amuse Miz Claire, or please her vanity, was too much trouble for the aging body slave.

Neva glanced up and smiled the warm, loving smile that had been a reassuring bulwark in Kathy's life since her birth. Neva was like a stout symbol of integrity and strength of character. The big woman signaled with her finger across her lips for silence. Miz Claire had fallen asleep at last—perhaps for the first time all night. If the black woman were exhausted from her long ministrations, or anxious to escape her obligations, she did not reveal it.

Neva sat on the side of the bed with that ingrained patience that Kathy supposed developed over hundreds of years of oppressive slavery and inhumanity. Kathy nodded, blew the fat woman a kiss. She closed the door behind her carefully and walked down the hall to her own bedroom.

Shiva and two younger black girls were cleaning up Kathy's bedroom, making the bed. Shiva slouched from one task to another, whining about the increasing amount of work, the extra chores and responsibilities piled upon her slender shoulders, the tasks with which she was unfairly saddled. Kathy said, "Oh, shut up, Shiva, and get through in here."

Kathy crossed the bedroom and went into her dressing

room. She closed the door, leaving it slightly ajar, yet closed enough so that Shiva would understand she was not to follow her. A slight slit remained and she could hear the young slave girls whispering among themselves and Shiva's humming, unmusically and off-key. She went out the screen door of the dressing room to the small courtesy balcony.

Kathy stood at the railing, feeling somehow desolated and alone. Below in the garden, butterflies, humming-birds the size of a girl's thumb, bees, and bright moths vied over the fragile flowery terrain that was still traced with the emerald-blue tapestry of dew in the jasmine-scented morning. Remote sounds—a smitty's hammer against anvil, disembodied shouts, cries of blue jays and yellowhammers—floated up from the quarters and the hammock. These were sounds she heard daily, the world as she'd always known it, and yet she found no reassuring familiarity in it. About everything there seemed to hang an empty-bellied waiting—as if they all stood on the crumbling brink of their own graves.

This overpowering weight of depression didn't make sense. She tried to shake it from her thoughts and could not. She sank into the big wicker rocking chair that was older than she was. She had clung to it over Styles' objections because it held memories she couldn't bear to lose. Neva had held her in this chair, rocking her when she was a baby, a child fevered or unhappy or disappointed, a young girl in distress. How secure that world had seemed. How empty and lonely was this empty morning, hanging shroud-like over her.

Escape. Her mind kept making its way back to this one word. If only she could be free. This was all she could think. She wanted to run away and didn't know precisely what she was running from, except a threatening destiny. Certainly, nothing remained but dregs of her marriage to Styles. Yet, she had no real expectation of finding release from this bondage—she lived in that quiet desperation of how many other young Southern wives trapped in unre-warding marriages with men who didn't believe you touched a white woman except to create an heir. You certainly never did it with the anticipation of pleasure

445

given or received. This was her condign lot. She accepted it because she didn't know what else to do, didn't know how to escape. She curled in the chair, pressing into it, yawning helplessly. She couldn't run away—from Styles or from her vows. She shivered, growing heavy lidded with emotional fatigue. She could escape into sleep. This thought was all she remembered—sinking deeper and deeper into the worn chair, into the warm womb of the past. . . .

When she awoke again, the foreshortened shadows on the lawn showed her it was past noon. She'd been asleep for two or three hours. It was some moments before the drugging effects of her heavy slumber wore off. She became gradually aware of voices nearby—lowered, taut, and persistent. She could not immediately discover where they came from. She knew only that these disembodied voices had disturbed her sleep, finally waking her. She shook her head, trying to orient herself—the chair, the small, semicircular, white-plastered railing enclosing her balcony, the familiar garden below. Then, her mind clearing, she recognized Styles' voice. It came from behind her, from their bedroom beyond the small dressing alcove. Who was with him? Why were they whispering so tensely? She frowned, unable to recognize the other male voice.

She got up from the chair. Afterward, she realized she was no quieter than normal. She opened the screen door to the dressing room and it whimpered drily on its hinges. She walked past her row of frocks, dresses, gowns, and shoes. She reached out to open the dressing-room door to the bedroom when Styles' voice suddenly stopped her. "Strip down, Moab," she heard Styles saying. "I want to inspect you."

Kathy stood, not breathing, at the slitted door between the bedroom and the dressing closet. She stared, wide-eyed at Styles and the young Fulani boy standing at the foot of her bed. They were so engrossed in each other that they did not even hear her.

"Strip down," Styles ordered again. "I mean to make a thorough inspection. You understand?"

"Yas, suh, Masta Styles, suh. I understands, suh. You

446

wants to finger me—like you did Blade. . . . But why, masta?"

"Because I tell you, boy. Whatever I tell you, you do it, and you don't ask why. All you need to know is that I am the new master of Blackoaks—and you belong to me—to use as I like."

CHAPTER 45

KATHY STOOD unmoving, unable to move. The terrible moment of doom suddenly enshrouded her. She bit back cries of protest and leaned heavily against the doorjamb to keep from falling. There was no mistaking what was going on between her husband and that black boy in her own bedroom. The very atmosphere was sick-sweet with the unnatural, hothouse atmosphere of seduction. Even seeing it, she couldn't believe it. Styles had left no chance for doubt—he did not want her. She would have been stunned, heartbroken to discover Styles making love to one of her female friends. But her rage, her agony and repulsion were all stifled by the shock of seeing what Styles really was, what he really wanted, standing with a hard-on visible at the fly of his tight gray trousers, with his hands moving caressingly over that young black.

"Why you wants me stripped down, masta? Why, masta?" Suddenly the boy was weeping.

"Stop crying, Moab," Styles said in a gentle tone. "I'm not going to hurt you. . . . Now get your shirt and britches off. Stop wasting my time or I'll call Thyestes in and have you stripped."

Moab's whole body trembled. He tried to unbutton his shirt but his quivering fingers refused to function properly. He could not do it. He pulled at his shirt and then stood shaking, almost convulsed with fear and frustration.

"What's the matter with you, boy? Why are you scared?" The words were strong, but Styles' tone was questioning, soothing.

Moab's voice quavered with the terror that was unmanning him. "You fixin' to sell me, masta?"

"Sell you?" Styles frowned, astonished. "What are you talking about?"

"You gittin' ready to finger me, masta. . . . You checkin' to see if I —unmarked—if I brings you a good price when you sells me."

Styles stared at the boy. Then he laughed and his voice lowered, softening. "I'm not going to sell you, Moab. Not ever. You or Blade."

Moab burst into fresh tears of relief. "Ain't wantin' to be sold, masta. . . . I born a Blackoaks nigger. I wants to stay a Blackoaks slave . . . I swear, masta."

"Then you do what I tell you, Moab." Styles' voice was a caress.

"Yes, suh." The boy could hardly stand he was so nervous. His eyes were blurred with tears that spilled unchecked down his pallid cheeks and splashed on the backs of his trembling hands.

"Stop crying now, Moab." Styles spoke in a tone more gentle and seductive than he had ever used with Kathy. She dug her nails into the woodwork of the sill, watching through the cracked door. "I'm not going to sell you, Moab. . . . I've big plans for you . . . and Blade. . . . You're a fine boy, Moab, and I don't want anything bad ever to happen to you."

"Thank you, masta."

"You do what I ask you now."

"Yes, suh. All right, masta. I do it. I do what you tell me. I do anything so long as you don't sell me. . . ."

To assuage the boy's fears, Styles stepped closer and laid his hand gently on the boy's smooth, tawny face, stroking it and speaking so softly that Kathy could not make out the words. After a few moments of the whispering and petting, the boy quieted down and watched Styles with black eyes moist. Styles continued to whisper the soothing words, and under their hypnotic spell the boy stopped panting and remained quiet under Styles' hands. With his free hand, Styles calmly unbuttoned the boy's starched shirt. Moab shrugged out of it and let it fall to the floor.

"And now your pants, Moab . . . take them off," Styles urged in that cajoling tone. "We want to see what you're built like. . . . We're going to get you a girl of your own —a wench to pleasure you as often as you like—whenever you like. . . . Would that please you, Moab? She could never say no to you . . . she wouldn't dare. . . . She'd have to do whatever you told her . . . whatever you wanted. . . . Would you like that?"

The boy relaxed and his smile widened. Styles caressed Moab's throat, the nape of his neck and his shoulders, lightly. The boy jerked at the top button of his onasburg britches. His fly sprang open. He wore no belt. He released his trousers and they fell in a wad about his ankles and he stepped out of them.

In that second, Kathy saw, the whole tenor of the seduction changed. Moab was now at ease and Styles was driven by almost incapacitating compulsion. Moab stood calm, proud of his manliness, unselfconscious as a young panther in his nudity. Kathy saw Styles' labored breathing lift and drop his chest erratically. His face was flushed and his mouth parted. His eyes seemed to dilate and his hands shook.

Styles stood for one taut moment drinking in Moab's nakedness, the muscled perfection of that youthful bronzed body. Styles was like a man dying of thirst who delayed that first restorative taste of water. His eyes grazed across the boy's muscular chest, flat-planed belly, to the dark triangle of crisp hair at his mons pubis, to the thick, pendulent penis.

Styles let his hands slide over the boy's smooth chest, cupping his muscular breasts whereupon the boy brightened. "You think I built pretty good, masta?"

"You've a beautiful body, Moab. You're a beautiful young boy, Moab." Styles spoke in that compressed, seductive, almost breathless tone. "You'll be a beautiful man."

"I be bigger than Blade. I taller—almost—now."

Styles nodded, smiling, and resumed petting and caressing the boy. He stroked Moab's arms and armpits, and ran his hands over Moab's face and ears and through his hair, holding the boy's head for a long time in both hands —while Styles stood unmoving, his eyes closed.

Kathy watched the boy's penis grow slowly erect under Styles' caressing. Styles drew his hands along the boy's throat and down to his paps. He held these brown nipples for a long time, standing in front of the boy, breathing through parted lips.

After what seemed a mind-rending eternity to Kathy, Styles' hands left the boy's paps and ran down over his muscled belly. The boy's penis stood rigid now, painfully erect. The boy waited, entranced, fascinated, anticipating the next agonizingly delightful and arousing caress. His eyes closed like a sleepy baby's and then opened wide, displaying his ecstasy.

Kathy opened her mouth, willing herself to cry out. But it was like a nightmare in which one must scream aloud, but can work no sound at all up through one's constricted throat. She wanted to stop them but she could not speak or move. She could only stand as if in a trance, watching in fascinated revulsion. What would Styles do next to the naked black boy? Styles behaved with Moab as she had imagined a man might act with a girl he hoped to lure into bed. Styles was compelled by desire, mindless with need, but restrained, moving carefully even in an overwhelming passion so as not to frighten Moab.

"It's all right, Moab. It's all right . . . all right." Styles' modulated, seductive voice droned on, not making sense or attempting for intelligibility, only seeking to calm and arouse the boy. "We've got to know if you're a breeder. . . . You know what a breeder is, Moab?"

"Yas, suh. He de one mounts de wenches. He fills 'em with de cum and they drop a sucker come time."

"Yes. . . . Well, that's why I brought you up here, Moab. . . . I've got to test you—to see if you're a good breeder. . . . Do you see, Moab?"

"You got a gal you wants me to mount, masta?" The boy looked hopefully about the shadowed room.

"No. No . . . not now, Moab. We've got to be careful with you, Moab. . . . We can't have you mount just any female trash. . . . You're a Fulani. You are nobility among

451

all blacks, Moab. . . . We can't waste your seed. . . ."

"No, suh," Moab gasped.

"You do understand, Moab, what I must do?"

"Oh, yes, suh." Obviously, though, the boy had no idea what Styles was talking about. Moab realized only that his test was not to include a female. This depressed him slightly because Styles' petting and caressing had him painfully ready, the plum-colored glans thrusting from its foreskin like a turtle head.

"I'll check your balls," Styles said. He ran his hands down over Moab's belly which quivered in pleasurable reflex. Styles' hand brushed the boy's robust cock and slipped between his legs and fondled his gonads. "Sometimes a young boy has only one testicle," Styles said in that low, heated voice.

"No, suh . . . I got two balls. Two big 'uns," Moab said proudly. He bit his underlip, chewing on it in sweet agony as Styles' fingers probed and massaged his anus. His already pulsating member stiffened and quivered under added pressures of blood distention.

"Yes. Big testes . . . they're like gold," Styles whispered. "Pure gold, Moab. You'll be a strong breeder." His fingers went on massaging and probing at the quivering orifice between the cheeks of Moab's ass. The boy sweated in an agony of delight and his hips wavered involuntarily.

Styles laughed lightly and let his fist enclose the boy's engorged penis. "Let's get some of that white juice, Moab."

"Lawdy, Masta Styles, you keep on whipping my snake like that, it gonna be mighty easy to get that juice you wants."

Styles nodded. His fingers tightened and he slowly stroked the boy's penis until Moab's hips tightened and writhed in helpless reflex. "Do you like that, Moab?"

"Lawdy, masta. . . . law-dee. . . ."

The stroking motions increased in intensity and Styles gripped the pulsing penis tighter.

Trembling with horror and outrage at war inside her, Kathy saw that Styles was shaking visibly, like a young boy with his first lover.

She heard Styles mumble something unintelligible about

"fluid." His breathing quickened and he sank to his knees before Moab. Moab's eyes widened in disbelief at the sight of the white man on his knees before him. Moab was almost deranged with overwhelming passion. He could only stand, legs apart, as Styles caught him about the hips and pressed his face against his thighs. Styles gasped, "Viscosity."

"What, masta?"

"Viscosity, Moab." Styles mumbled frantically, his face pressed into the boy's crisp black pubic hairs. "I must test you . . . for viscosity. . . . Do you see, Moab? . . . Oh, my God, Moab, do you see? . . ."

"I see, masta," Moab whispered helplessly as the white man crammed the dark and distended penis between his lips, nursing furiously.

Styles clutched his arms tighter about Moab's hips, catching the cheeks of the boy's buttocks in his hands, working him back and forth in a mindless way. Suddenly, Moab could control himself no longer. His body quivered and his penis bucked erratically as he ejaculated. He slumped at the knees, barely able to stand under the intensity and impact of his ejaculation.

Shaking her head, half out of her mind at what she was witnessing, Kathy watched Styles embrace the boy passionately, holding him with all his strength while the boy drove his hips furiously, pistonlike, his back arching and slamming, the white semen exploding from him.

Kathy threw open the door between the bedroom and alcove, screaming.

Moab reacted, as he must have when trapped by Florine's raging jealous husband in a hundred nightmares on his tack-room cot. Moab broke free of Styles' locked arms, tearing himself free of the white man's frantic embrace. He looked around wildly, grabbed up his shirt and britches, and ran, naked, from the room.

CHAPTER 46

A HEAVY SILENCE enshrouded the bedroom after Moab raced naked from it and slammed the door behind him. Kathy stood immobile near the dressing alcove, its door thrown wide open at her back. Afternoon sunlight filtered through the tall windows in diminishing patterns upon the carpeting. Most of the room was veiled in blue shadow. Kathy was grateful for this obscuring gloom. She wished this room would deepen into total and lasting darkness because she never wanted to have to look into Styles' eyes again. She wanted to huddle, hidden in deepest shadow so that nobody could ever look into *her* eyes again either.

For some moments they held the rigid tableau. Styles remained slouched on his knees upon the floor, his face smeared with fluid, his eyes empty and disoriented.

The sunlit patches on the woven carpet evaporated and a sudden chilling winter rain blew in on sharp gusts of bitter wind. The room chilled abruptly. Kathy shuddered with cold, the agitation beginning in the pit of her stomach and radiating outward to her arms and hands. Her legs felt weak, unsubstantial. She was afraid she was going to fall. She was nauseated. She wanted to retch, to let the vomitus pour out of her until she was purged clean again. But she knew this would never happen. She would be covered with vile as long as she lived.

She tried to turn away so she would not have to see Styles crouched on his knees, his face stained with slime, splotched with drabbles of corruption. She could only remain anchored in fascinated horror, staring at the monstrous bulk of venality she once had loved and respected as a man. She swallowed back hot bile. How had she ever been so innocent—so ignorant—as to be deceived by this *exquisite* thing? How had she ever thought this pretty being a handsome man? She felt revolted. She despised him, and yet how could she ever put this ugliness out of her mind? How would she learn to live with what she knew about him? How could she purify herself? Anger and recrimination would not do it; they would be wasted on him and provide no release for her. There was no escape from this loathsome scene. She was obsessed by it. All her nightmares would replay this repugnant moment— her beautiful white husband on his knees sucking at that black boy—that black child! She could not wipe the depravity of it from her memory. She could never blot the hideous picture from her mind. She heaved, sick with revulsion.

The entire house remained brittlely silent. Sounds of the rain drumming against the panes, the wind in the magnolias and along the eaves, were exaggeratedly loud. She stood listlessly, hardly aware of anything around her. She dreaded the moment when sights and sounds and servants and routine would intrude upon her again. She longed to stay forever locked numbly where she was now, unmoving, unmoved, in the absolute still at the eye of the hurricane. There must be ahead that hour when she could pick up the threads of her life again, but for this chill time she could not endure even to contemplate it.

She watched Styles recover, retrieve his self-assurance, reorient himself to time and place. He got slowly to his feet. He removed an immaculately white handkerchief from an inner pocket. He shook it out and calmly wiped his face. He stood for another moment staring at the starchy blotches blemishing the linen. Then he refolded the cloth and replaced it in his pocket. He shifted his shirt up on his wide, slender shoulders, touched at his collar, straightened the ruffled cuffs at his wrists. He regained his composure before he deigned to glance along his patrician nose at Kathy. His mouth twisted in a sardonic smile. "When one spies, one had better be prepared to accept what one sees," he said.

"You queer bastard."

He winced, but only faintly. "I advise you to control yourself, your emotions and your language."

"Why should I? How am I supposed to behave, you pretty faggot? How does a wife accept the proof that her husband is a pervert—a corrupter of children?"

"I warn you, Kathy. I won't tolerate such irresponsible accusations."

"You won't *tolerate?*" She shook her head in helpless frustration. "You act as if I were to blame in this—this filth."

He shrugged. "If you had not hidden in there—"

Her laugh was as cold and bitter as the rain. "I didn't hide, Styles. I didn't have to hide. I walked through that room from the balcony. You were so—involved—with that black child's genitals you didn't know—or care—that I was in the world."

He walked to the mirror and glanced at himself, and then at her across his shoulder. "I'm sorry you're upset at what you think you saw—"

"Think I saw! I saw you on your *knees,* Styles—sucking —that black boy's—*cock.*"

"Keep your voice down."

"I'll scream if I like—"

"No." He took up military brushes and repaired the damage to his wavy hair. "If you had made your presence known, Kathy, none of this would have happened. If you had let me know you were there—"

"Why? Would that have mattered?"

"I think it would have mattered. Yes."

"Why? It was only your wife in there. I had to learn sooner or later, didn't I? I had to learn—what you are. What a contemptible, perverted hypocrite you are. I had to find out *why* you didn't want me—and broke my heart because you didn't want me—didn't I? I had to know that you didn't want me—or any *woman*—that you want only boys—black boys."

Styles shrugged. He turned and leaned against the dresser. "All right. I sucked him. It was not what you think. . . . Baxter Simon—the slave breeder—told me I had to test the—viscosity of—"

"Viscosity! Liar! You're a homosexual! Why haven't you the simple courage to admit it?"

"It takes more than simple courage in this world, my dear."

"Homosexual. Fag. Fairy. Queer."

His face blanched. "Stop that!"

"Homo! Homo! Homo! Being a homosexual is not nearly as rotten as your lying—your pretense."

He shook his head. His mouth pulled sourly. "This world is a place of lies. Don't you know that? Your own father—pretending to be a paragon of virtue."

"Leave my poor dead father out of this—"

"I'm trying only to tell you we all live on lies—because we have to."

"You do. I don't. . . . I won't live with you. I could never let you touch me again—even if you wanted to. . . . I want a divorce, Styles. Or I'll tell Ferrell—"

He straightened, taut. "You'll tell nobody."

"—tell Ferrell the truth about you. And get an annulment. In the church. Because you are a homosexual."

"Do you think I'd let you do a thing like that? Spread that in public? I'll kill you first, Kathy. I say that quite calmly and you'd better have reason enough left to take my warning. . . . If you speak that word outside this room, I will kill you."

Her laughter broke off in a sudden sob. "I wish you would kill me. It would be—easier—"

"Easier?"

"Oh, not for you. For me . . . for me. . . . Don't you think it would be easier for me to die than to go on living with you—knowing what you are?"

He stepped toward her menacingly. "Well, that's just what you *are* going to do, *Mrs. Kenric*. You are Mrs. Styles Kenric. And Mrs. Styles Kenric you will remain—until you die."

She stared up at him in cold defiance. She did not speak. He looked capable of calmly extinguishing the life from her, and capable of doing it if this were the only way to guard his ruinous secret. Exposed publicly as a homosexual, he could not exist in this land of modern-day chivalry where all white women were gentle, virtuous, and

457

untouchable ladies, and all men stalwart knights of strength and honor and virility. The women might be sluts and the men so perverted that they could not be trusted alone in a room with small boys, but these guilty secrets were carefully concealed and guarded behind façades of virtue and gallantry.

"All of us have our guilty secrets, Kathy," Styles said. "Some of those secrets must be kept hidden at all costs. . . . The very fabric of our lives would be ripped apart unless those secrets were closely guarded—"

"No matter how reprehensible."

"No matter how reprehensible. And in this I am no different. My reputation is as precious to me as your *sainted* father's was to him—"

"Don't mention my father in the same breath with your revolting crimes—"

"I suppose I am revolting to you, Kathy. . . . The doll bride and the playhouse marriage. . . . Well, you got what you wanted. . . . And finally, I've got what I want—this estate! And I'd have you committed to an insane asylum before I'd let you destroy what I have."

She gazed up at him, unmoved. He didn't offer her the options he supposed he did: the threat of murder, the death of imprisonment in a snake pit, or the slow agonizing death of living with him as his wife. She did not doubt what he said. His nostrils distended, his mouth set in a gray line, deeply indented with the contempt he felt for her. She remained unmoved, unfrightened, because she did not care. There was little choice for her in his threats, but he was too wrapped in self-involvement to see.

"Don't think I can't have you committed," he said. "Your brother Morgan. Poor retarded Morgan. Your mother. Incompetent. Confused. Vaporous. Depressed one moment and flighty the next. Your brother. Burying himself in a monastery. If you dared make slanderous and irresponsible charges against me, Kathy, I'd have no difficulty in having you committed. You have a history of mental instability in your family, Kathy, which would make my course very easy if I decided to have you—put away. . . . And I tell you this, calmly, that I will do it if you ever speak those words outside this room."

She went on watching him as if he were some specimen she'd never before encountered. He lifted his shoulders in a shrug that denigrated her and all her fears. "Maturity will show you, Kathy, how right I am. . . . As you grow mature—become aware of reality as opposed to pretty illusions—you'll see that few people could retain their respected positions in society without closely guarding some hidden secret. We're all tarred with the same stick. . . . Your sainted father—"

"Stop it, Styles—"

"—pretending to be a devoted husband, a model parent. For fifteen years he'd been bedding down that kitchen slut. I'm sorry to have to tell you this, Kathy, but you must learn—"

"You're not telling me anything I didn't already know, Styles. . . . Ferrell and I have known—for years. At first, I was shocked, distressed. But I saw—as Ferrell saw—that my father was a good man—a selfless man—with all the healthy appetites of a vigorous man—who was being robbed of his manhood by my mother in her illness. She couldn't help it. But he couldn't exist repressed and denied either. Maybe neither of them were to blame. They were what they were . . . as you are what you are. But my father gave his life for others—the kitchen slut, as you call her, was his only hope for releases that you wouldn't forgive—or even understand—because you don't have drives like that. . . . Don't think his poor little secret is the same as your hiding your perversion—your pretending to be a man—destroying me casually—while all the time you are a child-molesting monster who stands there now unable to see evil in anything he's done."

"Evil or not, Kathy, I mean to be master of Blackoaks. If that means concealing what you and I know about me —that's the way it will be."

She shook her head. "I won't live with you."

His smile made her shiver. Hackles quivered at the nape of her neck. "That's your choice, Kathy. . . . You'll live here—as my wife. Or you'll live in an insane asylum."

She brushed past him. She was free of him and his hold on her—she knew what he was now—and the truth freed her. She walked to his dresser and jerked open the

459

drawers. She threw his possessions upon the floor behind her, working furiously.

Styles caught her arms but she wrenched free so fiercely that he retreated, catching his balance. Her voice was low, deadly. "That's the last time you'll ever touch me," she said. "You've made your threats. They fail to frighten me. But I tell you this in return, if you ever touch me again, I will kill you."

He frowned, hesitating. "What am I expected to do?"

"I don't care what you do. But get out of here. Get out of my room. I loathe you, Styles. I tell you now. Never come in here again as long as I live. Threats of killing me, committing me—they don't move me. I am not afraid of you. You can keep your filthy secret one way—and one way only. You've tormented me long enough. No more. Now get out."

He stood some moments uncertainly. Kathy went on throwing his clothing from his dresser drawers. Then she went to the closet where his suits were hung and jerked them down and threw them on the floor behind her. At last his voice, modulated and reasonable, stopped her. "I'll call Thyestes and a couple of the houseboys. We'll move my things to your father's room."

She heeled around, laughter of contempt spewing across her lips. "That's perfect. You've taken my father's plantation. Why not take his bedroom? . . . I don't care what you do, where you go—just so you never come near me again as long as I live."

He smiled tautly and nodded, bowing slightly. "I accept the bargain, madam."

She glanced at him, disenchanted, repelled—but free of him. She laughed and returned to her dressing alcove. She threw a heavy cape over her shoulders, and pulling the hood about her head, she went out to the rocking chair on the gallery.

She stayed there curled up in the big chair until she heard Thyestes and the houseboys moving the last article of Styles' possessions from her bedroom. It was over. It was finished. She was chilled, her feet icy, but she felt exultant. She was freed of him. Whatever she did with life now, it belonged to her. To build or destroy, finally

460

it was her decision alone. She did not see how he could hurt her anymore.

She got up and went back through the dressing alcove to the bedroom. She was shivering with chill. She rang for Thyestes and told him to build a fire in her fireplace. She sat in a wingchair with the cape about her, a blanket across her legs, until he had the fire roaring. She moved nearer to its brilliant, lunging orange and blue and vermillion flames.

Thyestes said, "I best bring you a toddy—made from your papa's pridest whiskey."

"Yes, Thyestes. Bring me a bottle—of my father's *pridest* whiskey."

He smiled and limped from the room. The blazing fire soon dispelled the damp chill and lightened all the corners. She thought about Ferrell. He would get Jeanne d'Arc's brief note, and he would understand they needed him. He would come home to them, soon, hurrying, as he always had. She would tell him about Styles. The vile secret was too heinous to be borne alone. . . . And then, she stopped. Could she bring herself to tell Ferrell the whole execrable truth? Or had Ferrell guessed the truth long ago? She shivered and moved nearer the fire. He already hated Styles. What would he do when she told him what she had seen in this room today?

She closed her eyes tightly, trying to blot out the ugly scene.

Thyestes' voice released her from its horror. "Here you are, Miss Kathy. Nice hot mint water to make you a fine hot toddy." He set the bottle of whiskey on the table beside her chair.

Kathy took up the bottle and poured a couple of fingers of whiskey into a tumbler. She laughed. "You know, my father always said his whiskey was too good to be cut by ordinary water, Thyestes."

"Yes ma'am, Miss Kathy. But he mean that for gen'-mum."

"Don't worry, Thyestes. I can handle my whiskey as well as any gentlemen you know. I'm Ferrell Alexander Baynard's daughter."

"Yes'm, Miss Kathy." Thyestes retreated to the corridor door, limping. "We got Masta Styles situated right comfortable in the masta's bedroom, Miss Kathy."

"Yes. I was sure you would, Thyestes." Kathy took a long drink of her father's whiskey. She shivered involuntarily, afraid she was going to be unable to keep the hot liquid on her empty stomach.

She sagged back into the chair, staring into the flames, her eyes dry. Miz Claire came through the corridor door, which Thyestes held open for her. He closed it and Miz Claire crossed the room to Kathy. She laid her fragile hand on her daughter's forehead. "Are you all right, darling?"

"What are you doing in here? Are you well enough to be up?"

Miz Claire pulled a chair close beside Kathy's. The firelight leaped across her pale face. She smiled. "I am strong, Kathy. Stronger than anyone knows. I am a Seaton. A Henry. As you are. We have strength. . . . We bend like the reed, but we persist. You have that strength too, Kathy."

"Thank God." Kathy took another long drink of the hot toddy. She did not shudder this time, or feel the queasiness in her stomach.

"Yes. Thank God. . . . I couldn't help seeing, Kathy, that Styles has moved to papa's old bedroom."

"Yes. We thought it would be best."

"Oh, it will be. I've prayed you would be freed—of those bestial demands men make on us. . . . I felt as if God had interceded for me when Mr. Baynard moved out of my bedroom."

"Well, now God has interceded for me," Kathy said.

"It will be for the best, dear. Everything always works out for the best. Men are ugly. They don't realize—or they don't care—how base and vile they are."

Kathy poured herself another drink, sloshed in a soupçon of hot mint water.

Miz Claire patted her hand. "You'll be happy now. Now you won't be crying at night." Her mother shivered visibly. "Your sobs used to break my heart. But I knew there was nothing I could do . . . no one should intrude between a husband and his wife. . . . But I can tell you, your crying broke my heart."

"I won't be crying anymore."

"It will work itself out for the best. You'll see. We'll always have Blackoaks," her mother said. "No matter what happens, we'll be here. We're strong, and we'll persist. . . . And now that you're free of your fearful burden, you'll find your life will be brighter than ever."

"I'll drink to that," Kathy said. Her mother was right; she was free of her fearful burden, though it wasn't what her mother imagined at all.

Now she knew what Styles really was. She may have been incredibly naive and innocent not to have suspected before. Maybe stupid was a better word. But nothing in her sheltered existence had prepared her for what she saw happening between Styles and that black boy. The truth. She knew at last what Styles really was inside; there was no doubt about that. She understood at last why he had never wanted her, and what he really wanted.

She trembled, and took another long drink. She had prayed for a revelation of the truth about Styles. How could she have suspected the truth would be so devastating? She had felt as if she would go out of her mind. Seeing Styles with that naked boy broke her heart and destroyed her last illusions—and it had left her alone and sick and empty inside.

She straightened. She would recover. She would get well. It was as if she'd been ill with a debilitating and disabling sickness. But she would get well; she would recover; she would live again; she might even find happiness. At least, the break with Styles was total. Clean. Irreparable. Final. She would come back from this dark moment. She knew that in all her life ahead she could never suffer more deeply than she was suffering now. But time would help, time might heal. The filthy tableau would gradually fade and she could begin to think ahead. She closed her hand on the rough fabric of the chair arm, drawing strength from its rough familiarity. She had little to look forward to at this moment, but at least, and at last, her prayer was answered. She was free.

Had this been what she'd wanted? Long ago she'd

stopped praying for the miracle that would cement her hopeless marriage. She'd prayed recently—if at all—only to be free. Now she was free of him. Nothing he could do or say could ever touch her again. She could look at him with loathing, with disinterest. I am free, she thought. Nothing had changed except inside her, but there, at least, she was free.

Her spirits lifted at the thought of freedom and recovery and healing, and she smiled, exultant. She was still young; she still had Blackoaks no matter what Styles believed, and she was no longer enslaved by a blind, girlish adoration for Styles. She took a deep long drink of straight whiskey. Styles was a bad habit she had finally kicked. Styles still meant to rule Blackoaks with a heavy fist, but she no longer feared Styles, or his fist. She gazed out her tall window along the bare, stark winter rows of leafless pecan trees. Soon those limbs would be thick and green with foliage, bowed under the weight of its fruit. Soon—one day soon—Ferrell would come striding along up that lane and together they would reclaim Blackoaks. She laughed, thinking ahead, and leaned back in her chair. The warmth from the fireplace felt good and invigorating against her fevered skin. Ferrell would come. Blackoaks would be a happy, lovely place to live again. She didn't know when, but she was content in this unhappy moment to dream ahead, to live for that bright, great day, and until then, thank God, at last she was free.

Falls Church, Virginia, February 1975
Indian Rocks Beach, Florida, March 1976

This novel is the first in the trilogy under the encompassing title, *The Blackoaks Saga.*